Look what people are
D.B. Reyno
Vampires in America . . .

"D.B. Reynolds has outdone herself with this exhilarating story; and VINCENT is a worthy addition to Reynolds's always excellent Vampires in America series."
—*Fresh Fiction*

". . . this romance keeps readers shivering in anticipation with lots of suspense, excitement and passion."
—*Literary Addiction* on *Vincent*

"Terrific writing, strong characters and world building, excellent storylines all help make Vampires in America a must read. Aden is one of the best so far." A TOP BOOK OF THE YEAR!
—*On Top Down Under Book Reviews*

"In one of the most compelling vampire books I've read in a while, Reynolds blends an excellent mix of paranormal elements, suspense and combustible attraction."
—*Romantic Times Book Reviews* on *Lucas*

"Reynolds takes us on a roller coaster of emotions and delivers reading satisfaction. She can write rings around so many of today's authors. She develops her characters to the point where we live in their skin."
—*La Deetda Reads* on *Duncan*

"Remarkably fresh and stunningly beautiful! Sophia is as enchanting as she is dangerous!"
—*FreshFiction.com*

"Move over Raphael, there's a new Lord in town."
—*Bitten by Paranormal Romance* on *Jabril*

D.B. Reynolds's
Vampires in America
from ImaJinn Books

Deception

Vampires in America: The Vampire Wars
Book 9

by

D.B. Reynolds

ImaJinn Books

This is a work of fiction. Names, characters, places and incidents are either the products of the author's imagination or are used fictitiously. Any resemblance to actual persons (living or dead), events or locations is entirely coincidental.

IMAJINN

ImaJinn Books
PO BOX 300921
Memphis, TN 38130
Print ISBN: 978-1-61194-589-8

ImaJinn Books is an Imprint of BelleBooks, Inc.

Copyright © 2015 by Donna Beltz writing as D.B. Reynolds

Published in the United States of America.

ImaJinn Books was founded by Linda Kichline.

We at ImaJinn Books enjoy hearing from readers. Visit our websites
ImaJinnBooks.com
BelleBooks.com
BellBridgeBooks.com

10 9 8 7 6 5 4 3 2 1

Cover design: Debra Dixon
Interior design: Hank Smith
Photo/Art credits:
Man (manipulated) © Lumy010 | Dreamstime.com
Tropical scene (manipulated) © Cardiae | Dreamstime.com
Woman (manipulated) © Alexandr Vasilyev | Dreamstime.com

:Ldsf:01:

Dedication

This book is dedicated with love and gratitude to my mom,
who gave me the world when she taught me to read.

"All warfare is based on deception."

—*Sun Tzu, THE ART OF WAR*

Prologue

Malibu, California

THE LETTER ARRIVED by Federal Express, just one of many delivered to the gates of Raphael Enterprises on a cool spring afternoon. As with all such packages, it was left unopened until after sunset when the vampires woke for the night. It was then taken to the security headquarters beneath an eighteenth century French mansion set well back among the trees of Raphael's estate. That mansion had once been the home of his sister, Alexandra, but no longer.

The package was first turned over to a small team of highly trained vampires. It was x-rayed, and then examined for tampering. Vampires were hard to kill, especially one as powerful as Raphael, but his people took no risks with his safety, just as he took no risks with theirs.

Finally, after it was determined to be nothing more than it seemed, the package was carefully opened and the contents revealed—it was an envelope with Raphael's name on it, handwritten in an elaborate calligraphic style. The vampire tech examining it frowned, his nostrils flaring at the familiar scent. Blood. Raphael's name had been written in blood. The tech inhaled deeply and realized it was very likely that there was even more blood inside, that the letter itself had been scribed in the same ink.

His frown intensified, but he was old enough to remember when such things were customary among powerful vampires. He didn't like what such a letter might mean for his master, but he recognized its significance. Standing from his station, he picked up the envelope and walked down the hall to the office of Raphael's security chief, Juro. Finding the room empty, he placed the envelope on Juro's desk, along with a form noting the date, time, and method of its arrival, as well as the security precautions already taken.

And there it sat until Juro found it hours later, the letter that would change everything . . .

Chapter One

CYNTHIA LEIGHTON stood in the darkened room, unmoving, barely breathing, as she watched her lover slowly destroy another being, a vampire, in the next room. This was Raphael at his most cruel. He was often ruthless, relentless in his determination to get to the truth, to tear an individual's deepest secrets from his screaming throat. But he rarely toyed with his victims like this. He was rarely this cruel. It took a special kind of offense to bring that out in him. But the vampire who was currently the unwilling focus of Raphael's attention had brought it on himself. He'd killed Raphael's sister, and he'd done it without a second thought, because she'd become a nuisance, because she was of no more use to him.

Cyn bet he regretted it now, although, privately she was relieved Alexandra was dead. The bitch had deserved what she got. She'd betrayed Raphael over and over again, and, had she lived, she'd no doubt have figured out a way to do it again.

But despite all of that, Raphael had loved her, and her death had grieved him deeply. As far as Cyn was concerned, that alone was enough to earn the vampire in the next room a lifetime of suffering. Not that Raphael had consulted Cyn or anyone else about the justification for what he was doing. And no one had dared offer an opinion . . . although she was pretty sure his closest vamp advisors all agreed with his methods of interrogation. In fact, judging by their gleaming fangs and straining muscles, it looked to her as if Jared and Juro would have liked to join the mayhem. The two of them—Juro and Raphael's lieutenant, Jared—were in the interrogation room with him. Ostensibly it was to protect him against the prisoner, although Raphael hardly needed their protection. But one never knew. The prisoner's name was Damien, and his European masters were both old and powerful, some of them centuries older than Raphael, with knowledge of things long forgotten by most of the world. For all Raphael or his people knew, Damien might have some sort of vampiric time bomb hidden in his brain.

Cyn had no doubt that both Jared and Juro would willingly throw themselves on an exploding bomb, or an exploding prisoner, to save Raphael's life. But she also suspected they simply liked to watch the so-called interrogation up close and personal. Vamps were a bloodthirsty lot.

For all of Damien's obvious suffering, though, Cyn had to admit that Raphael had shown great restraint in deferring his personal revenge until after he'd extracted every bit of information the vamp had about his European masters and their plans for invading North America.

Damien Casimir. That was the vamp's full name, and he'd announced it with great pride and pomposity when Juro had first ushered him into the interrogation cell. He'd been so confident in his power, so certain that no one could best him and that he'd soon be on his way back to France.

What an idiot. Even Cyn, a human and therefore not sensitized to the strength of a vampire's power, knew that Raphael had let Damien win their initial test of wills back in Mexico City. And he'd done it to elicit just that sort of response from the French vamp. Raphael had wanted his prisoner to be arrogant and self-assured, wanted to see the shock in his eyes when Raphael broke him like a toothpick.

Cyn stepped up to the glass. There was no arrogance left in the creature who sat in the room beyond. He was exhausted and beaten, his skin glistening with bloody sweat. Dull eyes followed Raphael's tiniest move. He trembled when the vampire lord drew too close, an animal whine rising from a throat that had been ruined hours ago by his screams.

Cyn listened closely as Raphael repeated a question he'd already asked several times, a question he already knew the answer to and which served only one purpose at this point—and that was forcing the prisoner to sign his own death warrant.

"Tell me again," Raphael crooned in his deep, velvet voice. "Why did you murder Alexandra?"

Damien sobbed, his body shaking so hard he could barely force out the words between shredded lips. "She betrayed you, my lord," he whined. "She told me everything she knew."

Cyn shook her head. Did the fool think this would save him? That Raphael didn't already know the depth of his sister's perfidy? Reminding him of it would hardly earn his mercy.

"Ah," Raphael said, his lips drawn back in a friendly smile, toying with his prey. "So you killed her to avenge *me*, is that what you're saying?"

Damien appeared confused for a moment, as if actually considering what Raphael was saying. But then he blinked and his eyes filled with fear once more. "No, no," he stuttered. "I, please, my lord . . ." He sobbed openly, knowing that more pain would follow no matter what he said.

Raphael's expression went cold and still as he gazed down on his prisoner. He was unearthly beautiful in that instant, but it was a terrible, dangerous beauty. Tears filled Cyn's eyes as Raphael's gaze lit with the silver glow of his power, as his fangs emerged to press against his lower lip. She couldn't have said why she cried, whether it was because this ordeal was finally almost over, or because it had ever started in the first place. But she wanted her Raphael back. Wanted to pull him out of the dark place this interrogation had sucked him into, back into the warmth and light of her embrace.

Damien's eyes went wide a few seconds before he began to scream. Cyn knew it was Raphael's doing, just as she knew he didn't need to touch someone to inflict pain. A line of red stained the prisoner's tattered shirt, spreading outward over his torso until that was all she could see. And through it all he howled in terror, slamming himself into the corner as he tried desperately to get away. But there was no escape. In some part of his brain, Damien must have known that, but his agony was clearly too great to permit rational thought. Or perhaps it *was* rational to attempt the impossible when facing a vengeful vampire lord.

Raphael reached out, his teeth bared in a parody of a smile as he traced a line down the center of Damien's bloody chest. Cyn wanted to look away, but she couldn't do that to Raphael, couldn't reject even this terrible part of him. Damien's screams reached an inhuman pitch as his chest cracked open, as Raphael reached into the gory cavity and rooted around until his hand re-emerged with Damien's beating heart held between his fingers. Such a thing seemed impossible, that a heart could be torn from someone's chest and still beat long enough to taunt its owner, but not for a vampire like Raphael. Call it magic, call it impossible, but she'd seen Raphael do it before, and had heard stories of it happening to others.

Damien stared in horror at his bloody heart as his screams dwindled to muttered words that made little sense and bore more than a touch of madness.

But then Raphael seemed to grow bored with it. His gaze turned lazy a moment before the heart he was holding incinerated and fell into so much gray dust, quickly followed by Damien himself. But Raphael had turned away long before Damien became ash on the floor. Slapping his hands against one another to get rid of the dust, he yanked open the door and left the interrogation room.

Cyn was waiting when he came through the door. She would have hugged him then, but she knew him too well. He might not care what he did to himself in that room, but he wouldn't want to contaminate her with it.

She went up on her toes and touched only her lips to his, then handed him one of the warm, wet towels kept on hand for just that purpose, waiting as he wiped first his hands, and then his face, cleaning away ash and blood. He touched her cheek then, cupping it in his big hand, his eyes meeting hers for just a moment before Jared and Juro pushed out of the interrogation cell behind him.

They went directly to the warming bin with its supply of towels. Cyn could have grabbed towels for the two of them as well, but she still wasn't sure she liked Jared well enough to offer him the courtesy, and she wasn't petty enough to get one for Juro while ignoring Jared. So, she left them both to their own devices. Juro gave her a conspiratorial wink as he pulled two towels from the bin and handed one to Jared. Juro got along with Jared well enough and trusted his loyalty to Raphael, which was all that mattered to Juro. It was all that mattered to Cyn, too, but she was still working on getting past her initial dislike of the lieutenant. She'd get there eventually, though. For Raphael.

Across the room, Raphael tossed his bloody towel, hitting the trash basket in the corner. Cyn didn't wait. She stepped into his space and wrapped her arms around him. He stiffened for a moment, but then sighed and relaxed into her embrace, as if he'd been holding himself in abeyance, waiting for her to release him. Which wasn't far from the truth. His powerful arms surrounded her as she rose up on her toes, rubbing her cheek against his, sliding her lips along his jaw to his mouth, and then giving him a warm, lingering kiss. His body loosened further as their lips separated and he rested his forehead against hers. It was times like this that he needed her most, Cyn thought. When he needed her humanity, her warmth, to bring him back from the frozen wasteland of emotion where he sometimes ventured.

"Lubimaya," he murmured for her ears only.

"Love you," she whispered back to him.

They remained locked together until Juro and Jared finished cleaning off, but even then Raphael kept one arm around her, holding her close.

"So, this guy was nobody," Jared said, collapsing the info gained over the many hours of Damien's torture into a few succinct words. "A malcontent who thought he could get a foothold on this continent by killing Raphael before his bosses moved in for the takeover. And when that didn't pan out, his fallback was to seize Mexico from Enrique."

"He seemed very confident in his ability to take out Enrique," Juro commented.

"Not in a stand-up fight," Jared sneered. "He took one look at Enrique's court and figured the Mexican lord was ripe for a good backstabbing, figured none of his people liked him well enough to defend him. Fortunately for all of us, well, for all of us except Damien"—he amended, laughing—"Vincent got there first."

"Unfortunately, his European masters didn't trust him any more than he trusted them," Juro said darkly. "They endorsed his plan to test Raphael,

knowing full well he was likely to die in the attempt, which shows how little they valued him. But they gained either way. If he succeeded, Raphael was gone. If not, they got rid of a troublemaker."

"I would have loved to get my hands on that Violet chick who headed up the team facing off with Raphael in that dinky church," Jared muttered. "Damien believed her loyalty was his, but she didn't waste any time rushing back to Europe once the outcome was certain. I'd bet good money that she belongs to someone over there."

"We'll almost certainly see Violet again before this is over. And her master, too," Raphael agreed, his words putting an end to the conversation in the same moment that Juro's cell phone, which had been sitting on the table while he was in with Damien, rang a jarring note in the small room.

Juro stepped over and glanced at the caller ID, then took the call, giving nothing but monosyllabic responses to whoever was on the other end, even as he exchanged meaningful looks with Raphael who was probably hearing every word the caller said. So was Jared, for that matter. Which meant Cyn was the only person in the dark. Damn vampire hearing.

Juro disconnected. "Sire," he said to Raphael with a nod. "I'll get back to you as soon as I know something." He let himself out of the observation room without another word.

Jared caught the door before it closed, mumbling something about catching a shower before the shit hit the fan, then disappeared just as quickly.

Cyn ground her teeth, waiting until Jared was gone and they were alone. "What was that all about?" she demanded.

"A letter arrived today. Juro will check it out," Raphael said, steering her toward the exit.

"A letter. From the European vamps?" she asked, her heart fluttering at the idea that war might be imminent, even as part of her rejoiced that the waiting was over.

"It seems likely," Raphael confirmed, reaching around her to pull the door open.

"How do you know it's them?"

"In times past, important communications between vampires utilized an ink that left little doubt as to the letter's origin."

Cyn thought about that a moment, then wrinkled her nose in distaste. "It's written in blood, isn't it?

He nodded.

"Nifty," she muttered. "Well, let's get this party started then."

Chapter Two

RAPHAEL AND CYN made their way upstairs from the detention cells under the garage, taking the outside route across the estate to the main house, where they walked up more stairs to his office, and then traveled down via secured elevator to their private quarters. It was a lot of up and down, but it was all about maintaining their personal safety, as well as the security of the entire estate. There were only three vampires—Raphael, Juro, and Jared—who had access to every building and level, and that didn't include the quarters that Raphael shared with Cyn. He wanted her to feel completely secure and relaxed when she was home. Hell, it had taken him nearly a year to persuade her to consider his Malibu estate to *be* her home. She'd clung to her condo down the beach, as if waiting for him to tell her it was over, that what they had wasn't forever after all.

But that was never going to happen. He'd known the truth of it in his soul even before he admitted it to himself. He loved her more than he'd ever loved anyone, more than life itself. He was never giving her up.

If Raphael had been alone tonight, he would have gone straight to his office and opened the mystery letter. He assumed it was from someone in Europe, if only because he couldn't think of a single vampire in North America who would have used the old traditions that way. At least, not anymore. They were all dead. One of Aden's opponents had scribed her challenge to him in blood, but she, too, was dead, and not sending bloody letters to anyone anymore.

This letter was almost certainly the first move in the coming war with the Europeans, and Raphael was curious to discover what their opening volley would be. He wasn't curious enough to forego his lover's affection, however. Cyn wanted him to herself for a while. She needed to know that he was safe inside his own head, that he'd come back from the dark place he'd gone when he'd been interrogating Damien earlier.

And he was inclined to give Cyn whatever she wanted. He'd known from the moment they met that she would turn his world upside down, which was the main reason it had taken him so long to admit his feelings for her. He sometimes thought about those months he'd wasted running away, months that could have been spent with her in his life, teasing him as they worked in the evenings, reminding him of his own humanity with every touch of her hand, every kiss of her lips . . . making love to him with an unquenchable desire that made him want to chain her to his bed and never let her go.

She loved him with a furious passion and hated it when he descended into the cold place in his soul that was necessary to carry out the kind of interrogations he did. And the vengeance he'd sought against Damien had driven him even deeper into the darkness than usual. It was that vengeance which had seized him at the end, a primal wrath that had demanded its due for Alexandra's death. It hadn't mattered that Alexandra had betrayed him, that in her jealousy she'd nearly gotten Cyn killed, or even that he'd never forgiven her treachery. In that final moment with Damien, Alexandra had still been his Sasha, the baby sister he'd protected from the moment of her birth, the beautiful teenager who'd begged him to save her from a loveless marriage on the very day that a vicious attack had left them both vampires. But perhaps more than anything—and he knew it didn't speak well of him that this was true—his rage was rooted in the fact that Alexandra was *his*. And no one could ever be permitted to touch what was his.

"Come on, fang boy, let's hit the shower."

Cyn's voice jolted him out of his thoughts. "You're showering with me?" he half-teased. She had no reason to shower. She just didn't want to leave him alone with his thoughts.

"Of course," she said casually, pulling her stretchy top over her head and drawing his gaze to the swell of her lovely breasts above the champagne silk and lace of her bra.

He slipped his finger under one narrow strap, sliding it down her shoulder, letting the cup fall to bare a rosy nipple.

"What are you doing?" she asked breathlessly.

"I'm helping you undress," he murmured, rubbing his thumb back and forth over the sensitive nub, watching it stand up and beg for more.

"You should—" She gasped softly, her head rolling back, eyes closed, as he pinched the swollen peak in the way she liked, just hard enough to cause an erotic pain, enough to make it flush with sweet blood. Her fingers clenched in his T-shirt, digging into his skin.

Raphael wanted her. But then, he always wanted her. What he didn't want was her getting anywhere near the filth of that asshole Damien.

He kissed her softly, then whispered against her lips, "Strip, or I'll do it for you."

Cyn pulled back with a surprised laugh, but immediately began taking off her clothes, stopping only long enough to order him, "You, too."

Raphael grinned; his first real smile since he'd walked into that interrogation room, then tore off his clothes with the speed of his vampire nature.

He beat Cyn to the shower, stepping inside and turning on the hot water, letting it pour out of the multiple jets until the oversize enclosure was filled with steam. Cyn joined him a moment later, slipping directly into his embrace, skin against skin, until nothing separated them.

She then proceeded to wash every inch of him, as if understanding his need to erase the smallest lingering trace of Damien Casimir. She started with his hair, her strong fingers digging in and massaging his scalp, wrapping her arms around his neck and nibbling on his lips as the hot water sluiced the shampoo over their joined bodies. She moved on to the rest of him, squeezing shower gel all over his skin, then rubbing him down like a horse, using a purple net poufy thing that he'd never in a million years have used himself. But in Cyn's hands, it felt good. Better than good. It was the sweetest torment as she skimmed the scrub over his ass, her arm brushing his stiffening cock, her mouth tantalizing close as she knelt to do his legs and feet.

"Cyn," he hissed a warning, fisting his hand in her dark hair, forcing her to look up as she knelt before him.

She met his hot gaze, feigning innocence, but the wicked gleam in her eyes gave it away. She knew what she was doing to him.

"What is it, baby?" she crooned. "Does it hurt?" Without breaking eye contact, she folded gentle fingers around his cock and kissed the tip, letting him feel the barest touch of her tongue, before she began stroking him. Lightly at first, faster as her grip tightened and shifted to the base, and she took more of him into her mouth, sucking harder, her tongue swirling up one side and down the other, and all as she gazed up the length of his body, her green eyes filled with hunger.

Raphael growled wordlessly as he reached down and grabbed her by the arms, dragging her to her feet, pulling her close. Her eyes widened in surprise. He loved having her mouth on him, and she knew it. But tonight he needed more. He needed to be buried in the heat of her body, needed her legs around his hips and her breasts against his chest. And so he spun them both around until her back was against the wall, holding her there with the mass of his upper body, gripping her ass with both hands as he lifted her, spreading her legs around his waist. Cyn reacted instinctively, sliding her arms around his neck for balance, closing her eyes and moaning with pleasure when he dipped his cock into the slick heat between her thighs. He dug his fingers into her hips, forcing her to be still when she would have thrust forward to draw more of him inside her. Her eyes flashed open, and he gave her a lazy grin.

"Say, please." He heard the rough need in his own voice, and didn't know why he was playing with her. His body was screaming at him to take what she offered, what was his already, but some small part of him desperately needed to assert control, to prove that he was more than the monster in the dungeon.

"Please, Raphael," Cyn whispered, her fingers stroking the back of his neck, her eyes shining with naked desire, and something else. Understanding. Of all the beings Raphael had known in his long life, she alone understood all that he was, both good and bad, and accepted him, loved him, without reservation.

Crushing his lips against hers, he plunged his entire length deep into her body with a single, powerful thrust. Cyn gasped, then groaned as he pulled out and did it again, her lips soft against his neck, making hungry little noises that shivered over his skin as he moved faster and faster, slamming into her, going deep enough and hard enough that he was bloodying his own hands as he protected her from the hard tile.

Cyn cried out as her body squeezed down on his cock, her hips flexing against his almost frantically as she chased the pleasure of her orgasm. Raphael growled and fucked her harder, his fingers sinking into her ass to open her even wider, driving deep into her body, grinding against her with every thrust. Cyn kissed his neck, his shoulder, and then, without warning, sank her teeth into his flesh, hard enough to draw blood, deep enough that the pain made him howl.

His fangs split his gums. Holding her slender weight in one hand, his chest crushed against her breasts, he lifted his other hand and twisted his fingers in her hair, yanking her head to the side and baring the elegant length of her neck. Without any of his usual finesse, he sank his fangs into her swollen vein and drew deeply. Cyn screamed, bucking against him as the euphoric in his bite threw her over the edge, right into a powerful orgasm. Her hot pussy clenched around his cock as her fiery blood poured down his throat. He sucked harder, drawing more of her living warmth inside of him, feeling her arms surrounding him, her fingers caressing the back of his head, holding him close as her ardent cries filled the steamy enclosure.

Raphael blinked back to awareness, feeling almost as if he'd blacked out for a second or two. Except that vampires didn't black out, and he sure as hell never did. Abruptly aware of Cyn lying limp in his arms, her head on his shoulder, he retracted his fangs and licked the two small wounds he'd made. There was bruising on her neck. He'd been rougher than usual in his hunger for her blood, but then he had no doubt his shoulder bore the violence of her bite as well. He smiled at the thought, then kissed a line from her neck to her jaw and over to her mouth.

"*Lubimaya,*" he murmured.

"Give me a minute," she breathed. "I don't think I have any feeling below the waist."

Raphael grinned and thrust his hips lazily, sliding his cock slowly in and out of her still-trembling sex.

Cyn gave a soft moan. "Let me revise that," she said, the smile obvious in her voice. "It's only my legs which have no feeling."

Raphael's hand rested on the perfect curve of her ass as he withdrew his cock from the snug glove of her body. Reaching back, he unwound her legs from his hips, easing her down his body and holding her until he was certain she could stand on her own. She raised her face to his and they kissed, long and wet and slow, with lots of tongue.

Cyn sighed against his mouth. "Can we stay in tonight? Or like, forever?"

Raphael lifted her wet hair off her neck and trailed his fingers over her already-healing bruises. "Not tonight," he said regretfully. "We need to know what's in that letter."

"Maybe it's a wedding invitation."

Raphael laughed, knowing that was what she'd intended with her comment. "Then we'll need to know where they're registered."

It was Cyn's turn to laugh. "Look at you, Mr. Modern Guy, knowing what a registry is."

"There's no need to be insulting," he responded, slapping her ass.

Cyn smiled softly and rested her forehead against his shoulder. She raised her head and met his eyes. "Okay, let's go find out what the damn thing says."

JURO SHOWED UP in Raphael's office just a few minutes after they were settled, with Raphael in his big chair behind the desk, and Cyn pacing around the room restlessly. She couldn't help it, couldn't stand still. This was too big; it was what they'd all been waiting for. The doors opened, and she stared as Juro strode in, with Jared only a few steps behind him.

Cyn stopped pacing and glanced at the envelope in Juro's hand. Knowing it was from a powerful vampire, maybe more than one, she half-expected it to morph into something else. A shrieking, flying lizard maybe, one that would spit poison to blind them while it tore Raphael's heart out. Vamps were magic, after all. What was a little morphing between enemies?

She was letting her imagination, and her fear, run away with her. But she couldn't seem to stop it. Ever since Mexico, she'd had this lingering sense of doom, as if, despite all of their precautions, some insidious enemy was about to slip inside the barriers they'd erected and destroy every-thing that mattered to her. And the only thing, the only person, who mattered to her that much was Raphael. She'd never survive it if something happened to him. She wouldn't want to.

Her fears were an ache in her chest as she walked over to stand protectively next to him, inching over until her leg touched his. Seeming to sense her unease, Raphael ran his fingers along the back of her thigh before scooting closer to his desk and reaching for the envelope which Juro had placed there.

"Wait!" Cyn said, stopping him, "How do we know there isn't some-thing inside, something other than a letter, or in addition to the letter?"

Juro gave her an understanding look. "You're familiar with our secu-rity protocols, Cynthia," he said patiently. "It arrived via Federal Express, and the package was carefully examined before it was opened. When the separate letter envelope was discovered inside, it, too, was tested for all manner of threats, both physical and biological."

"What about magic?" she asked, feeling her cheeks flush with embarrassment.

"If it was magic," Raphael told her, his deep voice easy and unhur-ried, "I would know."

Cyn let out the breath she'd been holding. "Okay," she said reluc-tantly. What she wanted to do was toss the damn envelope in the indus-trial incinerator downstairs where they disposed of empty blood bags and, Cyn suspected, the occasional body. But she knew Raphael would never go along with that.

He gave her thigh another light caress, then reached for the letter once more.

It was a heavy linen envelope. The kind one rarely saw anymore, espe-cially in this day of electronic communication. Raphael's name was written on the front with lots of extra pen strokes and curlicues—the sort of writing that, these days, one found on wedding invitations and little else. The flap didn't have adhesive, but was closed with a wax seal.

"Pretentious fuckers, aren't they?" she muttered.

"They're very old," Raphael replied.

"So are you, but I don't see you sending people letters written in blood and secured with a fucking royal seal."

"The seal isn't royal, only personal."

"Raphael."

He smiled without taking his gaze off the letter. "Are you ready, my Cyn?"

"No, but go ahead."

Raphael slipped a finger beneath the flap and broke the wax, then turned the envelope upside down and let the letter fall to his desk. Cyn watched as Raphael used an elegant opener in the shape of a sword to flatten the letter to his desk.

She could see the writing. The reddish brown "ink" bled slightly into the heavy linen paper with every character, and she couldn't help but think that was appropriate, since it wasn't ink at all, according to the vampires, but blood. She wondered if they watered it down to make it easier to work with or if the vampire writing the letter simply ordered a minion to open a vein so he could use him as a living inkpot. She frowned at her own gruesome imaginings, then leaned forward to get a closer look at the text.

"French," she said.

"It is," Raphael confirmed. "Can you read it?"

"I spent two years in a French boarding school."

"But did you learn anything?" he murmured teasingly.

"Enough to know that it was written by someone a lot older than I am."

Raphael nodded. "The text is somewhat archaic."

"What does it say?"

"They want to meet under a flag of truce." Raphael's gaze lifted to meet Juro's, holding for a moment before dropping to the letter once more. "To discuss terms."

"Terms of what?" Cyn scoffed.

"They want us to accept their troublemakers, younger vamps who want more than the European lords are willing to give up," Jared suggested. "But I bet they didn't phrase it that way."

Cyn glanced at him, then back at Raphael who said, "The letter simply requests a meeting to discuss a reasonable accommodation, in order to avoid a war that none of us wants."

"That's it? Where's this meeting supposed to take place?"

Raphael seemed to be reading further, and then he said thoughtfully, "Hawaii."

Cyn stiffened in surprise. "I didn't know there were any vampires in Hawaii."

"A few, less than ten that we know of," Juro said slowly, as if he, too, was surprised by the request.

"But . . . who's their lord, then?" Cyn asked, confused.

"Strictly speaking, the islands would be mine," Raphael responded. He leaned back a little, his fingers steepled thoughtfully under his chin. "But the distance is great, and their true master is a vampire named Rhys Patterson. Most vampires don't like islands. But Patterson wanted his own territory and knew he wasn't strong enough to hold one, especially not against me. He's a strong master vampire, but will never be a lord. So he requested permission to journey to Hawaii and set up a colony of his own. He sailed to Oahu with a diplomatic delegation from the U.S. in the late 1800s."

Raphael had lowered his hands and was tapping one finger on the arm of his chair, a gesture of stress from a guy who rarely showed any outward signs, no matter how bad it got. Cyn wanted to comfort him, to sit on his lap and put her arms around him, but that wouldn't do. So instead, she moved closer under the guise of bending over the desk to study the vampire missive. Raphael immediately made room for her, pushing back a little and curling his arm around the back of her thighs, his touch comforting them both.

"He made vamps after he got there?" she asked.

"As Juro says, only a few," Raphael told her. "He's master enough to create his own children, but not strong enough to control too many of them. He's never sired a vampire more powerful than he is, at least none that he's permitted to live beyond the first night."

Cyn blinked at the casual, and brutal, revelation of that comment. "Does he come to the Council meetings?" she asked.

"He's not a member of the Council. He thrives in Hawaii by my goodwill. But I've never bothered with him. I did visit once, after air travel became feasible—I had my fill of sea travel on the journey here from Europe. It was an uneventful visit, but that was some years ago . . ." He looked up at Juro, silently asking if he remembered exactly the date.

"1968?" Juro suggested.

Raphael considered it, then nodded. "1968."

"And you haven't been back there since?" Cyn asked.

He shrugged. "No, but we talk on the phone a few times a year."

"Where in Hawaii do they want the meeting to take place, my lord?" Jared asked, returning to the matter at hand. It was a practical question, and one Cyn wished she'd thought of. It galled her to admit it, especially since it was Jared who'd pulled them back on track, but she was too emotionally involved in this situation and wasn't thinking straight.

Raphael didn't even glance at the letter. "Kauai, which is where Patterson lives."

"Are all of his people on one island?"

Raphael nodded. "As far as I know. He originally set up on Oahu, but he didn't think far enough ahead. He didn't claim enough territory to ensure privacy for him and his children, and the island got too crowded. By the time I visited in '68, he'd already relocated to Kauai and secured a big enough parcel of land to ensure he wouldn't have to move again."

"May I see the letter, Sire?" Jared asked.

Raphael handed it to him.

"You read French?" Cyn asked, concealing her surprise. She knew that Jared had been brought to this country as a slave, although, now that she thought about it, she wasn't exactly sure which country he'd been brought from. France had been very active in the slave trade, more active than the U.S., if truth be told. She'd have to ask Raphael later, because God knew she wasn't going to ask Jared about it.

Jared glanced up at her question and gave a single nod. "They're asking to meet on Kauai," he repeated, reading the letter. "But there's no mention of Patterson. You think he's still alive?"

Raphael shrugged. "He's sworn to me, but he's not my child. I'm not certain I'd feel his death at this distance."

Jared looked up with an unhappy expression. "You're going to go." He said it as a statement, as if Raphael's decision was a foregone conclusion.

Raphael nodded. "I see no other way . . ."

"Well, I do," Cyn protested. "Don't go!"

Juro gave Cyn a sympathetic glance, then bowed slightly in Raphael's direction. "You probably want to think on this, Sire, and the sun is near. We'll leave you to your rest."

Cyn choked back a scoffing breath as Jared offered a duplicate bow and followed Juro out of the office, closing the big doors behind him. She knew what Juro really meant to say. He was giving Raphael the privacy to argue with his crazy human lover over an outcome that wasn't going to change. Well, damn it, she sure as hell was going to try to change it.

Raphael took her hand and crossed over to the elevator, entered the security code to open the doors, and pulled her in after him. He didn't say anything until they were back downstairs in the privacy of their underground suite.

"Cyn," he began, but she put her fingers to his lips, stopping him.

"Do you remember Mexico, Raphael? I know you do, because it was only a few weeks ago, but you seem to have forgotten what happened there."

"What have I forgotten, my Cyn?" he asked gently.

He was humoring her, and she wanted to punch him. But she had to try anyway.

"It was a test, Raphael. They put ten master vampires up against you to see what would happen. If they'd managed to kill you, it would have been a bonus, but their real purpose was to test you, to gauge your strength. You should have killed Violet before she could report back to them."

"I should have," he agreed, with a short nod. "I don't think her death would have stopped what's coming, but it might have handicapped them somewhat."

Cyn still wanted to punch him, but now she wanted to scream in frustration, too. "Why are you doing this then? I know you've made up your mind to go, but why?"

Raphael tugged her against his broad chest, holding her with exquisite care with arms that could tear a man apart.

"If we fight this war, hundreds of vampires will die," he said.

"And if you go to this meeting in Hawaii, *you* could die."

He was silent a moment as if trying to figure out how to persuade her. Finally, he said, "How many humans live in the United States?"

Cyn frowned. "What? I don't know, something over 300 million."

"And in Canada?"

"Raphael—"

"Humor me. How many?"

She sighed. "Maybe thirty, forty million?"

"And Mexico?"

"What is this, a geography quiz?" she said, impatiently trying to pull away from him. "It was never my best subject." He didn't let her go, only looked at her expectantly. She rolled her eyes in disgust and said, "I'd guess that there are probably over a hundred million in Mexico, but I don't know how much over."

"So, in all of North America, can we agree on 450 million humans?"

Cyn shrugged, not caring what number he used as long as he got to the point. "More or less."

"By contrast, *lubimaya,* there are no more than 15,000 vampires on this continent. Answer one more question for me."

She thumped his chest. "Is there a point to all of this somewhere?"

He smiled. "There is. Tell me, if your president was asked to risk his life for a chance to save ten million human lives, would you expect him to do it?"

"Of course. It's his, or her, job. A leader must always be willing—Okay, fang boy, I see where you're going with this now. But, one, there aren't millions of vamps at risk—"

"Relatively speaking, with our smaller numbers, there is an equal percentage of vampires at risk in this war."

"—and two," Cyn continued, ignoring his reasoning, "you aren't their leader."

"But I am," he said, cupping her face in his strong hands. "I am, for better or worse, the most powerful vampire on this continent. With great power comes great responsibility, my Cyn. You know this. You would demand this of any other leader."

Cyn's eyes filled with hot tears. "But you're not any other leader, you're mine. My lover, my mate, my life. And I can't lose you, Raphael. I just can't."

"And you won't. Trust me." He rubbed his thumbs under her eyes, wiping away the tears that overflowed.

"Fine," she snapped, knowing nothing she said was going to change anything. "I trust you. But I'm also going with you."

"Of course you are. Because, my Cyn, if the shit hits the fan—"

"*When* the shit hits the fan."

"—I trust *you* to be there to turn the damn fan off."

THE NEXT NIGHT the four of them met again, but this time in the conference room where everyone could sit around the big table and discuss which airplane and which pilots, which house and which personnel. It was as if they were going on vacation instead of flying off to hand over Raphael's head on a platter.

Jared and Juro had shown up with all the relevant data already on their iPads. They hadn't needed to be told what Raphael's decision was. As soon as they'd seen the invitation the previous night, they'd known what he would do. In her heart of hearts, Cyn admitted to herself that she'd known, too. The difference was that she, at least, had tried to talk him out of it.

She didn't know why the other two hadn't. Maybe, she thought viciously, because they'd already done the same math as Raphael and they were willing to sacrifice his life to save their own. But the thought had no sooner formed than she knew it wasn't true. Not for Juro, anyway, and not for Jared, either, she admitted reluctantly. He might have been willing to go along with Raphael getting shot by a human assassin—assuming in his typical vampire arrogance that no human could outwit or outshoot vampire planning and reflexes—but she didn't honestly believe that even Jared would casually risk Raphael against a whole team of master vampires who wanted him dead.

No, the two of them were going along with what Raphael decided because he was their Sire and their lord, and the decision was his. There were no messy human emotions clogging up the works, just obedience.

"Should you bring another vampire lord with you?" she asked, interrupting their discussion of flight times and available housing.

Raphael swiveled his chair around to face her where she sat next to him.

"They didn't say in their fucking bloody letter who you'd be meeting with," she continued. "But we all know they'll send more than one vamp to negotiate with you. They're too scared to meet you one on one. And the vamps they send won't be a bunch of desk clerks. At least one of them, and probably more than one, will be a vampire lord, or at least powerful enough to be a lord. After all, the reason they're doing this is because they have too many powerful vampires and nowhere to put them. What better way to shuffle a few off the scene than to send them to confront you?"

"The letter specifies only that I may bring a security team of my own."

"Fuck the letter. Who says they get to dictate terms? You should take Lucas or Duncan," Cyn insisted stubbornly. "Either one of them would be happy to go with you. If it will make you feel better, you can say they're part of your security team."

"And if this is a ruse to pull Lucas or Duncan away from the continent along with me, so that the Europeans can attack? Who will defend their territories?"

"Well, who's going to defend yours? Maybe *that's* the plan. You're the one with the biggest territory, after all."

"Jared will hold the West in my absence. Lucas will assist him as necessary."

Cyn gave Jared a flat look, then, just to be obstinate, argued, "What if Lucas is under attack too?"

Raphael gave her an amused look and tugged her chair closer to his. "Then Aden will assist Lucas," he said patiently. "And Duncan will assist Aden, and Vincent will assist Anthony. We don't believe Mexico will come under threat, at least not immediately. We think they'll wait to see if Vincent will follow Enrique's lead or choose to ally with the rest of us. He's already allied himself with me privately, but they don't know that yet."

"So you've thought it all out."

"As much as it can be," Raphael agreed. "Juro will have my back in Hawaii, and so will you."

Cyn nodded, giving up the argument for now. But privately, her thoughts went in an entirely different direction. If she was going to have Raphael's back, if she was going to be anything other than window dressing, then she had some thinking to do. Cyn had proved more than once that she was someone to be reckoned with, but very few in the vampire community knew about those events beyond rumor. These foreign vamps certainly didn't. And even if they'd heard of her role in Lord Jabril's death, they'd have discounted it.

"Their mistake," she muttered to herself.

Raphael glanced over, but she only smiled and leaned back in her chair. The vamps had plans to make for the trip? Well, so did she. Back-ups for when *their* plans went to hell and *her* plans were all they had left.

Chapter Three

"HE'S LETTING YOU go with him?" Luci's brown eyes went wide with surprise.

They were sitting in the cramped office of Jessica's House, the teen runaway shelter that the two of them had founded years earlier.

Cyn gave her friend a skeptical look. "Really, Luci? You're asking *me* that?"

"I wanted to go with Juro and he totally shut me down. Wouldn't give an inch."

Cyn smiled. It still tickled her that Lucia and Juro were a couple.

"I know that look," Luci said, her lovely golden skin blushing pink as she pushed Cyn away. "Get over it, already."

"I can't. It's just so . . . cute!"

"Cute? Juro is not *cute*! He's 300 pounds of gorgeous muscle and sexy as hell, but he is *not* cute."

"Not Juro, you goofball, the two of you together. Look! I have tears in my eyes, I love it so much."

Luci narrowed her eyes in irritation. "How much longer is this bullshit going to last?"

"At least a month, maybe longer."

"Well, don't expect any phone calls, then."

"Aw, come on, Luce. I put up with your comments about Raphael."

"I hated Raphael. He broke your heart!"

"Yeah, but he made up for it."

"Eventually."

"See! Right there. You held out for at least a month, waiting for him to crash and burn after we got back together. So I get a month of cute."

"Whatever. Why'd you want to get together today? I know it wasn't just to tell me how cute I am."

"Not just you," Cyn cackled. "It's you and—"

"I get it," Luci snapped. "Moving on."

"You're no fun. Okay. You have family in Hawaii, right?"

Luci blinked at the unexpected turn of subject. "Lots, why? Juro told me he and Raphael had already made arrangements—"

"Raphael has *his* arrangements. These are *mine.*"

Luci studied her a moment. "What's up, Cyn?"

"I don't know how much Juro has told you—"

"Just the Cliff Notes version. We're not in *share everything* mode yet, especially not when it comes to his work. He's told me that Raphael was invited to a peace negotiation with the Europeans, and that they've picked Hawaii as a neutral location, or at least as neutral as vampires ever get."

"Did he tell you it's probably a setup and that Raphael's walking right into it?"

Luci gave her a doubtful look. "Nooo, he didn't mention that. Are you sure? Because I can't see Juro letting Raphael—"

"Like Juro has a choice. You know how those guys are. It's all *yes, Sire,* and *right away, Sire.* They'll give an opinion if Raphael asks, but they won't argue."

"I'm sure you make up for any lack in the argument department."

Cyn smiled. "I try. My point is, I have a really bad feeling about this so-called negotiation. I want to be ready if everything goes to hell."

Luci frowned slowly, then said, "All right. What do you need?"

"Housing and transportation, something that won't be tracked back to Raphael or to me. There's a chance they'd know about you. It's slim, but—"

"So, we'll go with the cousins on my mother's side. These are *her* cousins, not mine. Which means they're another step away from me, and have totally different names. Which island?"

"The meeting's on Kauai, so I'm looking for a place we can hole up, if we have to. No more than a day or two, just in case they make a move against Raphael and he's too injured—" She drew a deep breath, unable to think too deeply about what it would take to knock Raphael that far out of the equation.

Luci's hand covered hers on the office's cheap desk. "That won't happen, Cyn, because you won't let it."

"Raphael said he trusted me," Cyn confided in a hoarse whisper. "He said if the shit hit the fan, I could handle it. But what if I can't, Luci? What if I'm too late?"

"Come on, Raphael's a smart guy. He knows what he's getting into and he knows you. Besides, for all your talk of *yes, Sire, no Sire,* I don't be-lieve Juro would let Raphael walk into a no-win situation."

Cyn nodded, drawing in a deep breath through her nose. "You're right. Okay. So, any of those cousins live on Kauai?"

"Only about a dozen. I wasn't kidding, Cyn. My people are every-where in the islands."

"It needs to be an empty house. I don't want to put anyone in danger, and I can't have anyone gossiping down at the grocery story about weird vampire habits."

"Well, one of my mom's cousins has a big house in Princeville. The lot's nothing to speak of, but it's on a golf course, so that makes up for the small amount of property. And her husband's job just sent them to Europe for a year, so it's empty."

"Any kids?"

"They both live in New York. And with the parents gone, there's no reason for them to visit. She and my mom are close, so I know her pretty well. I could give her a call."

"That sounds perfect, Luce, thanks. And find out if the place has a security patrol, too. She needs to let them know someone might be using the house."

"I'll take care of it. You mentioned transportation?"

"I'm probably overthinking this, but I thought it might be useful to have the name of a reliable private air service, just inter-island stuff. You know Raphael has his own plane, but if we can't get to it, or if we need something more discreet, it would be nice to have a fallback that would get us off the island."

"That's easy. My cousin Brandon runs an air charter. He does helicopters and small planes. Even better, he's an honorary cousin, so there's no way to track him back to me. He's my actual cousin's best friend who moved into their house when his military parents got transferred overseas. He was a big football player at the local high school, and looking at a full-ride athletic scholarship to college. He'd have lost that if he went with them."

"Any chance you can make some calls before we leave tomorrow night?"

"Absolutely. And once you're over there, I can activate the Shinn network for whatever you need."

Cyn was already on her feet and heading for the hallway when Luci's chair scraped the floor behind her. "Um, Cyn . . ."

Something about her tone of voice made Cyn stop and spin back around. "What is it, Luce?"

"Well, you know Juro and I . . ."

Cyn gave her a puzzled look. "Yeah, I know."

"Well, yeah, but he bought a house in Malibu."

"I know that, too. The one right next to Raphael's estate. He said . . ." Her eyes opened wide as realization struck and a huge smile crossed her face. "*That's* why he bought it. You guys are shacking up, aren't you?"

"You have such a way with words, Cynthia. Juro's worried about me being all the way over here with nothing but a houseful of kids, especially since that creep used this place to draw your attention and infiltrate Raphael's security."

"Yeah, but he didn't succeed. I mean, Juro knew all along—"

"That's not the point. He tried, and Juro was after me about living here even before that. And now with this war, it's made him even more worried. But I couldn't leave my kids with no one to take care of them. He understood . . . no that's not right, he *didn't* understand. Total tunnel vision. The only thing he cared about was my safety and everything else could go to hell. But then, I got a phone call."

Cyn frowned. "Someone threatened you?"

"No, no, not like that. Have you heard of Halley-Willow.org?"

Cyn responded immediately. "Big online presence, aimed at runaway kids. They also run a bunch of shelters, mostly in the Southwest."

Luci beamed. "See, I knew you paid attention. You're right, and they approached me a couple of weeks ago. They want to bring Jessica's House under their umbrella and me along with it."

Cyn blinked in surprise. "But Jessica's House is your baby. You've put so much into it."

"We *both* have. We did this together."

"I wrote a few checks. You're the one who lived with the little monsters day in and day out."

Luci smiled. "Bullshit. You were always there when I needed you, when one of the kids needed you. This baby belongs to both of us. Which means this is a decision for both of us."

Cyn shrugged. "What do you want to do?"

"Haley-Willow wants me to help with outreach, fund-raising and stuff, but also to help set up new shelters in underserved communities. I want to do that, Cyn. Jessica's is great, but I can do so much more with a larger organization."

"Then do it."

"That easy?"

"For me, it is."

"That's what Juro said you'd say."

"He's a smart guy. In addition to being cute, that is."

"You can leave now," Luci said and started pushing Cyn out the door.

"Does this mean you guys *are* going to be shacking up on the beach?" Cyn persisted, talking over her shoulder. "You'll be living right next door to me! We can have breakfast together, trade sex notes while the guys sleep."

"Oh, my God, you did not just say that. Out."

They were at the front door by then. Luci pushed open the screen door to the porch and a big black guy jumped to his feet. A big, heavily armed black guy who happened to be Cyn's human bodyguard, Robbie Shields.

"Getting thrown out of the place again, Cyn? I can't take you anywhere."

"Hey, Rob," Luci greeted him.

"Where's the gang, Luce?" he asked. "There can't be kids in there, it's too quiet."

"Termites," Luci explained.

Robbie's face lost all expression. "You fed the kids to the termites? Geez, isn't that kind of—"

"Very funny," she said dryly. "The house is being tented in the morning, and there's going to be some remodeling work done after that. The kids have been moved to a temporary—"

"We should go inside," Robbie said in a voice that was too calm and too quiet. Cyn followed his gaze to the street where a muscular SUV was cruising past way too slowly. It was undistinguished—black with tinted windows and, unsurprisingly, no license plate.

"Someone you know, Luce?" she asked, even as she hustled Luci in front of her and back into the house, with Robbie right behind. He closed the door and crossed to the big picture window that looked out over the street. The drapes were open, but sheers kept anyone from seeing too much.

Robbie stood to one side, his hand on his weapon, which he hadn't drawn yet.

Cyn made sure Luci was out of any line of fire, then moved quietly into the living room, taking up a position at the opposite side of the window.

"You should stay back there with Luci," Robbie said, giving her a dark look.

Cyn didn't dignify the comment with anything but a dismissive snort.

"I think they're gone," she said, but waited until Robbie agreed with her enough that he took his hand away from the Beretta on his hip. His eyes searched the now-empty street for several minutes more, before he finally turned away and walked over to the kitchen where Luci was sitting at the table, expression alert but not cowed.

"You get a lot of this sort of thing, Luci?" Robbie asked, leaning against the open doorway.

"Once in a while. I have some younger gang members who'd rather hang around here than go to jail. That doesn't make their leaders happy."

"See, Rob, it wasn't me this time. They were after Luci."

"Gee, thanks, Cyn," Luci said. "Don't sound so happy about that."

Cyn hugged her friend. "It's not you, it's Raphael. He freaks every time someone tries to kill me."

"Imagine that."

"You know, of course, that Juro's going to do some freaking out of his own when he hears about this."

Luci stared at her. "So we don't tell him about it. It's not that big a deal, Cyn. They're just trying to scare me away. They've never done anything."

"Way too late to think about not telling Juro. Raphael keeps pretty close tabs on me. Anything that shoots the adrenaline up, he knows about. And what Raphael knows, Juro knows, especially if it pertains to the security situation. Get used to it. Your days of blissful singlehood are over."

"Damn, damn, damn. I need to call him," Luci muttered, losing her cool in a way that made Cyn laugh, if only because it was so unusual.

"Come on," she said, pulling her friend toward the front door. "You might as well come home with us and save Juro the trip over. They're tenting the house in the morning anyway."

"Cyn's right," Robbie said. "Vamps don't do things halfway, and the big guy cares about you."

"What have I gotten myself into?" Luci muttered.

"Do you love him?"

Luci looked up and met her eyes for a long time before answering almost miserably, "Yeah, I do. He says he loves me, too."

"Love's a risk, Luce. No one believes that more than I do. But I know Juro, and if he says he loves you, I think that's a risk worth taking. He's a great guy and also quite adorable now that he's in love."

"Who's adorable?" Robbie interrupted, looking up from where he'd been texting someone on his phone.

"No one," Luci said firmly, stepping in front of Cyn to face Rob. "I'll go with you."

"Good," Cyn said. "And, Robbie, I need to talk to you about Hawaii. We can talk on the way."

He sighed. "Yeah, I had a feeling you were going to say that."

CYN SAT ON Raphael's chair in their private quarters and yanked off her boots, kicking them aside as she walked barefoot to the closet. Her jacket went on a hanger, but the rest of her clothes were stripped off and shoved in the dirty-clothes hamper.

She was heading for the bathroom to get ready for bed, but turned back when her cell phone dinged an incoming message. She pulled up the text, expecting an update from Luci, but found something entirely different instead, something totally unexpected. Nick Katsaros was texting her. Talk about a blast from the past. She and Nick had been . . . well, "lovers" was too strong a word. They'd been fuck buddies. Nick traveled a lot on business, and whenever he'd been in town, the two of them had hooked up. He was dangerously handsome, lots of fun, and loyal in his own way. But she hadn't heard from him in more than two years. Not since she and Raphael had gotten together for good.

She opened the text, reading it with a frown. It said only that he needed her help on something. No details. Probably some investigative work he wanted done, she thought. But whatever it was, this wasn't a good time. She'd contact him after they got back from Hawaii. Maybe. Raphael wouldn't be too thrilled to have her dealing with Nick again. So maybe she'd just refer him to someone else instead. It wasn't as if L.A. was short on private investigators.

Turning the phone's ringer off for now, she tossed it on the table. Continuing her original path to the bathroom, she washed and brushed, then flipped off the lights and slipped naked into bed with Raphael, cuddling up to his long, muscled form. He lay on his back as always, one arm over his chest, the other at his side. She smiled, because she knew the arm at his side was for her. Putting her head on his shoulder, she slung her arm over his belly and bent her leg over his thigh. She sighed with pleasure, relaxing completely in a way she did with no one else, nowhere else.

When Raphael eventually woke with the sunset, his arm would come around her. It was always the first thing he did upon waking. Even before his eyes opened, he was hugging her to his chest. And if she wasn't there, he looked for her. He wasn't happy when that happened, and he wasn't shy about letting her know it. But then, Raphael wasn't shy about anything.

Cyn closed her eyes and breathed deeply, inhaling the unique scent of Raphael, listening to his heart thumping in his chest, soothing her, easing her into a deep sleep.

It seemed she'd just closed her eyes when Raphael's arm fell heavily on her back, holding her tightly as he rolled her beneath him.

"I don't think they were looking for me." She yawned, blinking her eyes open to gaze up at him. Their link was close enough that he'd have been aware of what had happened at Luci's place. The spike in her stress level would have made sure of it.

"I know," he said, his midnight voice a caress of sound. "But a bullet doesn't have to be aimed at you to kill you."

She grinned up at him. "Well, it sort of does. I mean—"

"Shut up, Cynthia," he muttered. Covering her mouth with his, he teased his tongue along the seam of her lips until she opened for him, then it slid in to twist invitingly around her tongue in a long, luxurious kiss.

Cyn wrapped her arms over his shoulders and pulled him closer. She loved kissing Raphael, loved the way he treated every kiss as a seduction even though he didn't need to seduce her any longer. She was already his.

"I missed you today, my Cyn," he whispered, nibbling kisses along her cheek, outlining the curve of her ear with his tongue and then down to her neck.

Cyn's body responded eagerly. She'd gone wet the moment he started kissing her, her breasts swelling against the hard planes of his chest, her nipples stiffening into hungry peaks. He stroked a warm hand over her ribs, fingers curling around her hip before sliding down to grip her thigh and bend her leg, opening her further as he fondled her pussy. She moaned softly, thrusting against his hand as he shaped her outer lips, spreading them gently, teasing her with his fingers while his thumb found her engorged clit. But he gave her no release. His thumb rubbed over and around her the sensitive nub, barely touching it, then circling to tease it again.

"Raphael," she whispered hungrily. She could feel his cock lying hot and heavy against her thigh. She reached down and took him in her hand, squeezing and releasing as her fingers moved up and down the hard shaft.

Raphael growled, and Cyn bared her teeth in an answering demand, stroking him until his black eyes sparked silver beneath half-lowered lids and fangs filled his predator's smile.

With no warning, he grabbed her wrist and slid his cock out from between her fingers with a flex of his hips. Then grabbing her other wrist, too, he forced her arms up over her head where he trapped both of her hands in one of his. With the other, he reached between their bodies and guided his cock to the opening of her sex, rubbing the tip in the wetness between her thighs as she spread her legs wide and thrust her hips upward.

"Be still," he ordered softly.

"I don't want to be still," she said defiantly, and bucked harder, hooking her leg around his hips and pulling herself up on his cock, or trying to.

Raphael laughed as he evaded her efforts, then crushed her to the mattress, letting her feel the full weight of his big body.

She gave a wordless cry of frustration when she was unable to move, but his grin only grew wider.

"I love fucking you, my Cyn," he murmured. "Your pussy is always so wet for me, so hungry."

Cyn sucked in a breath. His words, spoken in a deep rumbling voice as his cock stroked lazily up and down between her pussy lips, gliding in the cream of her arousal, sent shivers racing over her skin from head to toe.

She stopped fighting against his hold and whispered, "I *always* want you. It never stops. You walk into a room and I want you. I lie next to you every day and wait for you to wake up so I can make love to you all over again."

Raphael's eyes fired pure silver as he plunged deep into her body with a single forceful thrust. Cyn cried out, reveling in sensation as her body stretched to accommodate the width and length of his cock, as her pussy flooded with desire. He fucked her vigorously, hips flexing, driving his cock deep into her pussy, then pulling out and doing it all over again.

Cyn tugged at her hands, wanting to hold him, to stroke her fingers over the elegant muscles of his shoulders, to scrape her nails through the thick brush of his black hair. There wasn't an inch of him that wasn't beautiful, not an inch that she didn't love.

But Raphael was in a dominant mood this evening and didn't release her. Fucking her steadily, he bent his head to her neck, shoving against the curve of her jaw in demand until she surrendered, twisting her head to one side in offering. Her skin pulled in a taut line as his tongue rasped against her vein, his lips closing over the swell of it and sucking softly. Her heart, already racing with excitement, doubled its speed, pounding so hard against her ribs that she knew Raphael would feel it, would know how much she wanted his bite, wanted the touch of his fangs, slicing first into her skin and then her vein, wanted that moment of weakness when her blood began to drain into his throat, and then the incredible rush of pleasure, the thrilling heat of climax when the euphoric in his bite raced through her system.

She cried out when he scraped his fangs along her skin, the pain an erotic pleasure that had her rippling beneath him, every nerve in her body sensitized to his touch, his smell, the sound of his voice dancing over her skin as he whispered in Russian of all the things he would do her, all the carnal pleasures he would give her.

Cyn whispered only one word, "Yes."

With a hungry snarl, Raphael buried his fangs in her neck, sucking hard as the euphoric hit Cyn's bloodstream. He held her to the bed when she bucked against him, when the orgasm screamed through her body like a bolt of electricity; firing her nerves and contracting her muscles, making her pussy tighten down on his cock like a vise. He groaned with his fangs still buried in her vein, the sound humming through her body like a tuning fork. Her sex was trembling around him, caressing his length, squeezing and relaxing, pleasuring him, urging him to climax.

Raphael lifted his head, sliding his fangs from her vein with a hissed curse, as he pounded into her, every thrust of his shaft now a million different pleasures as the tiny nerves and muscles of her sheath clutched at him, demanding his release. Finally, she felt the hot rush of his orgasm and she was jolted into a fresh climax of her own until she lay limp and sated in his arms.

Raphael's thrusts slowed to a sensuous glide of his cock through the mingled wetness between her thighs. He freed her hands at last, and she wrapped her arms around him, holding him close, feeling their hearts beating in rhythm.

He licked her neck, sealing the wound, then kissing it gently before pulling her into his arms and rolling to his back, taking her with him so that she lay bonelessly over his chest.

They were quiet for a long moment, and then he said, "Tell me what happened today."

"Luci thinks it was gangs. It's happened before. Robbie agrees."

"Well, if Robbie agrees . . ."

"Don't be snarky. Besides, there's no reason for someone to come after me right now. If I died, you'd probably cancel your trip to Hawaii and they want you there."

"Why would I cancel the trip?"

She could hear the teasing humor in his voice, which was the only thing that saved him. She still punched him in the belly, though, just to make a point. He grunted in reaction—she was strong and she never held back with him—but then hugged her tight with a laugh.

"You're probably right," he agreed.

"Of course I am. By the way, you know that house Juro bought next door? Did you know that he wants Luci to move in there with him?"

He shrugged, rolling the perfectly formed muscle of his chest beneath her cheek. "There was no other reason for him to buy the house, so I'm not surprised. Is there a problem?"

"Not for me. I'm thrilled. Luci was living pretty much twenty-four seven at Jessica's House, which apparently concerned Juro even more than it did me. But now there's a larger organization that wants to pull the house under their umbrella. That frees Luci to pursue a real life again."

"I'm sure Lucia thought she already was."

"Maybe," Cyn said slowly, then, "I'd love to be a fly on the wall when Juro gets hold of Luci this evening, though. I've never seen him freak out before."

Raphael laughed. "Is that what I do? Freak out?"

"Oh, hell, yes. It was the first thing Robbie and I thought of when it happened."

"Good."

Cyn jolted when Raphael smacked her ass, and she rolled her eyes.

"Are we still leaving tomorrow night?"

"No, we'll go tonight."

Cyn lifted herself on an elbow to study his face. "You think they have a spy in your household?"

"Not in the household itself, but on the estate. I have no proof, but it's likely. It's what I would do in these circumstances."

"So, while they're expecting you tomorrow night, you'll arrive tonight."

"Exactly. Can you be ready in an hour?"

"Less."

"Take the hour, and I'll take it with you. Anything could happen in Hawaii. I'll take whatever time I have with you."

Cyn's stomach clenched with foreboding. He was right. Anything could happen. And she would damn well be ready for it.

THE LIMO PULLED to a smooth stop next to the gleaming Boeing jet. This was the largest of Raphael's private aircraft and could easily hold Raphael and all of his security people, both vampire and human. The original plan had called for an advance team to fly over tonight, with Raphael and his immediate staff taking the smaller jet tomorrow. But with the change of plans, they were all traveling tonight and that meant the largest aircraft had to be used.

Raphael swung the limo door open and climbed out, then offered a hand to Cyn. She didn't need the assist, but she took it anyway, because it was Raphael. Almost immediately, Juro pulled him away to consult with Jared, which left Cyn free to stroll over to the side of the hangar where Luci stood watching the proceedings with a worried look on her face.

"Hey, Luce," Cyn called as she drew closer.

Luci's attention shifted from a certain huge, Japanese vampire to Cyn. "Hey."

Cyn smiled and reached out to smooth away the frown lines between her friend's perfectly shaped eyebrows. "Don't frown," she scolded halfheartedly. "Gives you wrinkles."

Luci drew a breath, her chest visibly rising and falling in the noisy hangar. "How do you do it, Cyn?"

Cyn gave her a puzzled look. "Do what?"

"Send him off, not knowing if he'll come back."

Cyn sobered at once. "I always believe he'll come back. I can't think any other way."

"But you're a fighter. You can be there to make sure he's safe."

"There are no certainties. There's only my belief in Raphael."

Luci's troubled gaze shifted back to Juro. "And what if he falls?"

"Then I fall with him."

"Fall with . . ." Luci repeated, giving Cyn a stricken look. "Don't you dare, Cynthia Leighton."

"And that's the belief part. As long as we're together, we'll come back. Both of us."

"Fuck. Do I need to learn how to shoot a gun?"

Cyn gave her friend an uncharacteristic hug. "War isn't only about weapons, Luce. Someone has to keep the home fires burning and that's never going to be me. So it's up to you to be here when all of us get back. When *he* gets back," she added, jerking her head in Juro's direction. "He looks big and tough, but he needs someone to hold him, too."

"I know," Luci agreed softly, then drew another breath and straightened her shoulders. "Okay. I can do that. But you come back to me, Cyn. And bring those big bloodsuckers with you."

"Will do," Cyn said absently as Raphael called her name. She looked over to see him holding out a hand. He was ready to board. "Gotta go, but tell me quick, did you get hold of your family?"

"The cousins and aunties are all on board. I'll email the file to you."

"Thanks, Luci."

Luci nodded, then grabbed Cyn in a tight hug and released her, saying, "I gotta go kiss my vampire good-bye."

Cyn strolled over to her own impatient vampire, walking right into his arms.

"Are you ready, my Cyn?"

She nodded. "Let's go kick some European ass."

Chapter Four

THE FLIGHT WAS long, but the time zones were favorable, and so they arrived in Kauai with hours of darkness to spare. There was no welcoming committee since Raphael hadn't told anyone they were flying in a day ahead of schedule. If there really was a spy on Raphael's staff, he'd hopefully been foiled by the closely guarded decision to leave early.

Getting everyone from the Kauai airport to the estate where they'd be staying took several vehicles, which wasn't exactly low profile. But Cyn hoped that their middle of the night arrival, combined with the private hangar where they'd debarked, would provide some concealment. Either way, the best they could hope for was a few hours of breathing space, enough to get them secured in their temporary home before they had to deal with the enemy.

Because peace negotiations or not, the European vamps were the enemy. If they were here to negotiate peace, it was only as a pretext for talking long enough to suss out Raphael's strength, to decide if they could eliminate him right here, right now, before moving on to the continent.

Cyn sat close to Raphael in the limo as they traveled to the Kauai house, her hand gripping his too tightly. He never said a word, but she knew he was worried, too. Not for himself. Raphael never worried for his own safety; it was part of his arrogance, part of what made him who he was. But he hated the thought of Cyn being in danger along with him, hated the risk to his people. And that was what made him such a great leader, one who earned the love and loyalty of his people rather than simply demanding it as his due.

"What's this place we're staying at?" she asked him as they drove down dark roads, surrounded by lush vegetation and a steady, light rain. Kauai earned its nickname as the Garden Isle, but all that greenery came with a lot of rainfall.

"Outwardly, it's a vacation home owned by the president of one of Raphael Enterprises' subsidiary companies. Legally, it's the subsidiary company itself that owns it. It's a sizeable estate, used mostly as a goodwill benefit to significant clients. There's a full staff during those visits, although obviously, they won't be there during our stay."

"Is the subsidiary run by vampires?"

"In the background. The public face is human, as are most of the visitors to this house."

Cyn frowned. "Will the house be safe for you guys then?"

Raphael nodded once. "There are vampires on the board of directors. Accommodation has been made for their unique needs. Discreetly, of course."

"Who's going to be making the beds if there's no staff while we're here?"

Raphael laughed. "The bigger question was who was going to provide food for the humans in our company. Most of my daylight security guards are former military and fully capable of cooking for themselves, but Irina was kind enough to send one of her cooks to supervise," he said, referring to his vampire housekeeper who also happened to be Robbie's mate. "The cook she sent is a male, at my request. This assignment is not without risk."

"Hey, real live girl here," Cyn protested.

Raphael freed his hand, pulling her close to his side instead. "I'm very aware of that. But you, my Cyn, are a true warrior."

"Aw, you say the sweetest things."

Raphael smiled absently, his attention drawn out the window as they turned down what seemed to be a driveway. It was hard to see in the dark; at least, it was hard for her. Raphael's vampire eyes saw as clearly as if it was daylight. He didn't need much more than the reflected light of their several vehicles, even though the vampire drivers were navigating with only the parking lights, the full beams actually being too bright for their eyes.

Cyn couldn't tell where they were going until a tiny light speared through the jungle, growing brighter the closer they got to their destination. By the time the building itself came into view, the light had resolved into the turquoise glow of a large swimming pool. She saw the vamp driver of their limo slip on a pair of sunglasses, then saw Juro, who was sitting in the front passenger seat, do the same just as the driver of the lead SUV turned on his high beams and bathed the front of the place in light.

It was a big house, but she'd expected that. Life with Raphael never involved a two-room cabin. Three stories tall, the whole back half of the ground floor was built into the hillside behind it. This was no doubt where the vampire-compatible quarters were located, since a basement was mostly out of the question. There were the usual—for the islands—lanais on every floor and off almost every room. Cyn didn't know the acreage, but she couldn't see any other lights through the surrounding jungle. She'd scope it out better during the day tomorrow, when she and

Robbie would be taking one of the SUVs for a drive, mapping their location and learning the neighborhood. She also wanted to locate Luci's cousin's place. She wouldn't be entering that address into the GPS. In fact, she'd make sure all of her wanderings were deleted from the nav system's history before they left the vehicle. This giant house seemed nice, but if things went south, as everyone seemed to believe they would, she wanted an escape route and she wanted it secret. It was all part of the backup plan.

"I hope they have Wi-Fi in there," she muttered as they pulled to a stop, thinking about the info Luci was going to email her. Info that she'd need for tomorrow's recon.

"I'm sure they do," Raphael commented as Juro stepped out of the limo and pulled their door open.

A wave of warm, humid air swept into the limo, bringing with it the overwhelming scent of jungle and wet soil. Cyn drew the scent into her lungs. She'd been to Hawaii many times over the years. It wasn't really that close to L.A., but it always seemed like it was. High school graduation gifts included trips to Hawaii with friends, people got married in Hawaii, post-divorce flings were in Hawaii. Bottom line, she'd been here a lot. She preferred the California coast, but Hawaii definitely had its charms.

Raphael's security people were spreading out, making certain there were no surprises. Normally, they'd have done that before he arrived, but the change of plans had nixed their usual routine. Humans might have found a nighttime arrival to be a complication, but not the vamps. They had enhanced hearing to go along with their super night vision and could easily detect anyone lurking on the perimeter by heartbeat alone. Hell, some of the vamp guards would be able to hear an intruder's thoughts. There'd be no sneaking up on this house.

But then, Raphael wasn't worried about anyone sneaking up on him. Cyn knew that the danger here wouldn't be hiding in the bushes. It would meet him face-to-face with a smile.

God, she hated this!

The inside lights suddenly flicked on, then just as suddenly dimmed. That was another indicator of a vampire residence, dimmer switches on all the lights. There were enough humans in their party, though, that some lights were necessary. In fact, the human half of Raphael's security contingent would be finding their beds almost immediately, so they could grab some sleep before they took up their duties with the sunrise.

"Are you hungry, my Cyn?"

She shook her head. "Irina took care of me and Robbie before we left L.A. She kept us company while we ate, and packed us some sandwiches in case we get hungry before we're stocked up here. She likes her Robbie well fed."

She smiled then, and leaned against Raphael, wrapping her arms around his waist and looking up at him. "What about you, fang boy? Are you hungry?"

Raphael's black eyes gleamed through sinfully long eyelashes as he gazed down at her with blatant desire. "Always."

"We should find our bedroom."

"The secure quarters are in the back," he said and, taking her hand, followed the rest of the vampire contingent past a gleaming gourmet kitchen to an open vault door that was camouflaged as a bookshelf.

"A bookcase door?" Cyn commented. "That's awfully *Young Frankenstein* of you."

"The door has an entry code to prevent unauthorized access, but most of the clients who use this house are human, so the façade was necessary. *Young Frankenstein?*" he added, puzzled.

Cyn stared. "You've never seen that movie? I can't believe I didn't know that already. As soon as we get back to L.A., you and I are having a movie date. I'll bring the popcorn."

"And you'll eat all of it too."

She stuck her tongue out as he pulled her down a narrow hallway that was lined with heavy doors, each with a keypad on the outside.

"How does that work?" she asked. "Who knows all of these codes?"

"There's a master code, but they're individually programmable by the occupant, like the safe in a hotel room."

"Cool."

They reached the end of the hallway and a door that was wider than the rest. Raphael tapped in a code and the door popped open.

"Is this one programmable, too?"

"Yes. Though it takes a slightly longer code sequence."

"Can I pick the code?"

"We'll discuss it."

Cyn gasped in joking disbelief. "You don't trust me to choose a good code?"

"I don't trust your sense of humor."

She pushed the door closed and shoved him back toward the big bed, but only because he let her. If Raphael didn't want to move, she could push all night and he'd just stand there and look bored.

On this occasion, though, he fell back onto the mattress and took her with him, promptly rolling on top of her. Cyn draped her arms around his neck, her fingers playing in his short hair. He had beautiful hair, coal black and thick, though he always wore it short in a typical businessman's style, longer on top and razor cut in the back. Put Raphael in one of his elegant suits, and he'd be right at home in the highest echelons of Wall Street.

He stretched out on top of her, still fully clothed, wearing 501 denims, a black, short-sleeved T-shirt, and a well-worn pair of Frye engineer boots. There was nothing Wall Street about him tonight.

"I like the clothes," she said stroking a hand over his firm pecs beneath the T-shirt, "but you're wearing too many of them."

Raphael lowered his head and gave her a long, slow kiss, his tongue curling around hers, his sensuous lips moving over hers in a warm caress. The kiss went on so long that they were both panting for air when they finally broke apart. Raphael's black eyes were filled with silver as he touched his mouth to hers again, this time to lick away the blood on her lip from his fangs.

"You can choose the code, *lubimaya*," he told her, smiling.

Cyn gave him a narrow look. "That was too easy. What's up, fang boy?"

Raphael sighed, shaking his head at her favorite term of endearment. She knew he privately loved it, though, or he'd have asked her to stop using it by now.

"I have a meeting," he told her.

"I kinda figured," she said dryly. "How long 'til sunrise?"

"Regrettably, not long enough. I'll be back in time to sleep with you."

"I'll leave the door open so you won't have to figure out the code."

"That would be wise. You don't want to make it necessary for me to tear the door off."

"I'm not afraid of you."

"No," he agreed. "You never were. That's one of the reasons I love you."

"You'll have to tell me the rest of those."

"The rest of what?"

"The reasons you love me."

He smiled and kissed her softly. "If we have time. It's a very long list."

"You're just saying that so I'll let you go to your meeting."

He laughed and levered himself up and off of her to stand next to the bed. "I'll be back as soon as I can."

She jumped up and grabbed two fistfuls of his T-shirt, pulling him in for a quick, hard kiss. "I'll be here."

Cyn watched from the open doorway as Raphael started down the long hallway. Juro emerged from the room next to theirs, so that the two of them ended up walking together, their broad shoulders nearly brushing the walls on either side. She waited until they'd passed through the vault door masquerading as a bookshelf and were out of sight. Then she quickly read the instructions for coding in the lock, entered a series of numbers that she hoped were random enough, texted the numbers to Raphael, then closed the door.

Pulling out her laptop, she settled on the bed. The house's Wi-Fi came up, and she entered the access code, which had been included on the same information sheet as the instructions for the door lock. Going directly to her in-box, she found the email from Luci. It included several names and phone numbers for her various relatives, not just on Kauai, but on the other islands as well. Luci really did have a shitload of cousins over here. The Kauai house was at the top of the list with the address and a picture, plus her cousin's number in Europe just in case. Next on the list was the honorary cousin Brandon who owned an air charter business. Cyn would give him a call in the morning, just to touch bases, so he'd know who she was if she needed him in a hurry. The rest of the list was a variety of cousins and services, including a restaurant or two which Cyn would have checked out if this has been a vacation. But since it wasn't, she skipped over those.

Her priority for tomorrow had to be the Kauai house owned by Luci's cousin. If everything went to hell, she and Raphael and the others would need a place the European vamps wouldn't know about. She and Robbie would need to check out the house, make sure it suited their purpose, and then make it as vampire-friendly as they could on short notice.

She was still going down Luci's list when someone knocked, or pounded, on the closed door. Looking up with a guilty start, she shut her laptop, then jumped off the bed and entered the lock code with jerky punches of her finger. The door popped open to reveal her vampire bodyguard, Elke, standing just outside and looking mightily miffed.

"What the fuck, Cyn? It's a lot easier to be your bodyguard if I can see your skinny body."

"Get over it," Cyn scoffed, pretending her heart wasn't racing. And what was that all about? She had nothing to feel guilty about. She was only doing what Raphael had asked her to do.

"I was just setting the door code," she told Elke, pulling the door all the way open and gesturing her inside. "Which one's yours?" she asked, nodding at the line of identical doors along both sides of the hallway, trying to deflect Elke's ire.

"Second door on the left, next to Juro. You'll be happy to know that Jared's right here," she added, nodding at the first door on the right.

"Stop it. I'm trying to get along with him these days. Where are the human guards quartering? I want to talk to Robbie."

"Yeah, but does he want to talk to you? That usually ends badly for him."

"You're exaggerating. Do you know where he is or not?"

"Of course I do. What are you planning?"

"Nothing. What makes you think—"

Elke stepped further into the room and pushed the heavy door shut again. "Cyn. I know *you*. We're in an unfamiliar location and Raphael's getting ready to meet a bunch of vampires who, by any criteria, are the enemy. And you, my friend, are not the trusting sort. You assume, as we all do, that this will not end with a friendly meeting of the minds. But while our lord and master, he whom we all love and admire, assumes he can power his way out of just about anything, you always plan for the worst. So, tell me. What are you planning?"

Cyn stared at Elke, her lips flattened in irritation. Was she really that obvious?

"Don't worry. You're only that obvious to people who know and love you. And there aren't very many of us, so you're safe. Now tell me."

Cyn blew out an irritated breath, but the truth was that if her plan went into effect, she'd need Elke with her.

"Okay, you're right. I don't trust anything about this situation, so I made a few inquiries. Robbie and I are going to check some stuff out tomorrow and maybe the next day, while the sun is up. I also have a contact who runs a flight service, and I'll be checking in with him about transit times between the islands."

"Does Robbie know about it yet?"

"No, but I know he'll agree with me when he hears what I have in mind."

"I never thought I'd say this, but I think you're right. What can I do?"

Cyn gave her a genuine smile. "I'll know more by tomorrow night. What time's Raphael's meeting with the Eurotrash gang?"

"We don't know yet, since he wasn't supposed to arrive until tomorrow night. It won't be until two nights from now, though, because even his enemies won't expect him to go from the airport directly into a meeting. Especially not these enemies. They're mostly old, and I mean *old*. But more importantly, they're old *school*, which means they're not all that thrilled with modern conveniences like airplanes. They'll expect Raphael to be similarly afflicted, and while they'd love to pull him into a meeting when he's off his game, they'll assume he would never agree to it."

"That might work in our favor when things go south," Cyn said thoughtfully.

"You mean *if* things go south."

"Not really. I've got a bad feeling about this."

"I wish you hadn't said that."

"I wish I wasn't feeling that."

Elke sighed. "Come on, let's go find Rob."

"Thanks, Elke."

"Yeah, yeah. Just make sure my ashes find their way back to Malibu when it's all over."

RAPHAEL SHOVED the camouflage bookshelf aside and started down the hidden corridor toward the room he was sharing with Cyn. Behind him, Juro secured the vault door for the day. It was very nearly sunrise. His human security staff had taken over, and most of his vampires had already retired to their rooms. Raphael could feel Cyn's presence in their private quarters and was eager to get to her before the sun rose. The meeting with his staff had taken longer than expected and had involved a brief reconnaissance outside the estate's grounds.

Juro was of the firm belief that the European vamps were very nearby. Kauai was the home base of Rhys Patterson, the master vampire who controlled what there was of vampire life on the islands, and Juro was convinced that the Europeans had somehow persuaded Rhys to help them. Why else arrange their meeting on this island? Oahu was easier to get to with more direct flights and a larger human population. It would have made more sense to hold the meeting there. The question remained as to whether Rhys's cooperation was voluntary or not. It was very possible the Europeans were coercing his assistance, threatening his people or him personally. But, either way, it seemed likely that the Europeans were using one of his places as their home base.

Raphael had decided to do a recon of Rhys's primary residence, which was only a few miles away. It was one of the reasons Raphael had originally chosen to build in this location. There were exceptions, but vampires generally tended to live in groups, or at least build their homes in the same neighborhood. Safety in numbers was a lesson hard-learned over the centuries, and it was one that few vampires ever forgot.

Juro had objected violently when Raphael announced he would lead the recon himself. Juro had even raised the specter of Cyn's reaction if she found out about it, as if that would dissuade Raphael from going. He respected his mate's opinion and, frankly, loved her displays of aggressive protectiveness toward him. But he wasn't going to cower behind walls like some fragile flower. He was a vampire lord and a damn powerful one. His people needed to be reminded of that sometimes.

As it turned out, Rhys's nearby estate had been empty. Which was odd in itself. It hadn't confirmed Juro's theory that the Hawaiian master had been co-opted, but it certainly hadn't disproved it. Rhys had at least two other homes on this island; the Europeans could be staying at one of those. But it was curious that there wasn't at least a minimal security force at the estate they'd checked out tonight. It made Raphael fear for Rhys's safety and that of all his people.

"They expect us to arrive tomorrow night," Raphael said, stopping outside his door. "But not until later. First thing after sunset, I want a recon of all of Rhys's other properties, and I want someone with each of the recon patrols who's strong enough to tell me how many vampires are on the property, if any."

"And you, Sire?" Juro asked cautiously.

Raphael grinned. "I will lead one of the recons again, but this time I'll take Cyn along to protect me."

Juro grinned, knowing Cyn well enough to assume there'd be an argument about Raphael's safety before they ever got out the door. Raphael figured he wasn't wrong about that. On the other hand . . .

"Would you like to wager on the outcome?" Raphael asked his security chief.

Juro chuckled deep in his chest. "No thank you, Sire. But I hope these walls are sufficiently soundproofed."

Raphael laughed, then said, "Sunrise is near, and I have a mate to bid good night. We'll meet one hour after sunset in the kitchen. Sleep well."

And with that, he quickly punched in the door code which Cyn had texted him earlier and entered.

Cyn was sitting on the bed, one long, bare leg dangling over the side, sticking out of the rose-colored silk robe she was wearing. Her laptop was open in front of her and she looked up when he came in.

"How was your meeting?" she asked, closing her laptop and sliding it into her backpack.

Raphael eyed her cautiously, wondering if she already knew he'd gone exploring earlier. "Productive," he said with intentional vagueness. "Did you stay in?"

She slid off the bed and he saw that she was wearing nothing under the robe, her full breasts swaying beneath the silky fabric. "I did some computer work, then Elke and I went to find Robbie. Just, you know, getting the lay of the land, finding out where everyone's sleeping, grabbing some food—for Robbie and me, that is. Elke had already eaten."

Raphael slipped an arm around her waist as soon as she was close enough, pulling her roughly against his body and loosening the tie on her robe until it fell open. Time was very short. Sunrise was nearly upon them and while he was stronger than most and could resist the sun's demands for a brief time, there wasn't time for a lot of foreplay. Not if he was going to taste his Cyn before sunrise.

Cyn responded readily, draping her arms over his shoulders and giving a little shimmying motion against him. Raphael bit back a growl and stroked his hand down the curve of her back to palm her ass, pressing her hips even closer, letting her feel his arousal.

She raised herself onto her toes and kissed him, no tongue, only a gentle caress of her soft lips, breaking away with a quick flick of her tongue over his mouth. She kept kissing him, moving down his jaw to his neck, her fingers working as she moved, pulling his T-shirt out of his pants, popping the buttons on his 501s one at a time. It was his habit to go commando unless he was wearing a suit, and tonight was no exception. Cyn looked up, meeting his gaze with a satisfied smile when she slipped her hand into his fly and surrounded him with her elegant fingers.

She kept her eyes on his as she began to stroke him and it was everything Raphael could do not to pick her up and throw her onto the bed. But his Cyn was in an odd mood tonight. She wasn't a natural submissive, but she could play one convincingly when she wanted to. And he loved it when she did.

He groaned when she dropped to her knees and took him in her mouth. Christ, she had a hot mouth. A talented one, too. She closed her lips over him and sucked hard, drawing him deep inside, her tongue a swirling caress around his shaft, licking him up and down like her favorite stick candy. He put a hand behind her head and, unable to help himself, thrust his hips forward. His cock slipped down her throat, and she moaned softly, the sound vibrating around his hard length, nearly tipping him over into orgasm. But he wasn't finished with her yet. He began to move slowly, sliding his cock in and out, fucking her sweet mouth, watching himself move in and out between her lips as she gazed up at him, her eyes filled with desire.

When he couldn't stand it anymore, when he thought he would burst out of his skin if he didn't relieve the pressure, he tightened his grip on her hair and began moving faster. Cyn slipped a hand between her spread thighs and began stroking herself as he watched, her fingers moving rapidly in the creamy wetness of her pussy, until she cried out, triggering his own powerful release.

She gazed up at him as he climaxed, swallowing and swallowing, catching every drop. And then she licked him, cleaning him off like a good little slave, until with a final long, sucking glide out of her mouth, she kissed the tip of his cock and sat back on her heels, her eyes never having left his.

Raphael stared down at her as her smile grew. It totally ruined the slave persona, but it was a hundred percent Cyn. She looked like the cat who'd licked the bowl of cream clean. He matched her grin, then put his hands under her arms and picked her up, throwing her onto the big bed. Quickly shedding the rest of his clothes, he followed her down, rolling them both beneath the covers.

Cyn draped herself on top of him, propping her chin on her hands so she could look him in the face as she reached into his hair and pulled out a fern leaf.

"Good recon tonight, fang boy?" she asked with a wicked gleam in her green eyes.

Raphael frowned. She'd known all along that he'd gone out with his teams tonight. And she'd given him a blow job anyway, playing the sweet submissive.

She winked at him when she saw the realization cross his face. But before he could say anything, the sun stole his awareness, leaving him with two thoughts—first, he wasn't going to be able to chastise her for whatever it was she and Robbie had planned for the day, and second, he really *was* going to have to take her with him when he went out on recon tomorrow night.

Chapter Five

CYN KNELT ON the bed and rested her hand on Raphael's chest, waiting until she'd felt five full heartbeats before lifting her hand away. Leaning over, she kissed his lips and brushed the rare errant lock of hair from his forehead.

"I'll be back, fang boy. And I'll be careful."

She was never sure how much Raphael was aware of during a given day. She knew that any strong emotion from her, especially fear, definitely brought him into her consciousness. But beyond that, it wasn't clear how often he actually stayed with her. She supposed it depended on how determined he was, the way he'd been early in their relationship when he'd felt himself falling in love with her and had tried to break it off. Except that, while he hadn't wanted to commit to her, he hadn't wanted her to commit to anyone else either. So, he'd lurked in her subconscious, sending her such incredibly erotic dreams that she hadn't known what was real and what wasn't. Dreams that had made her ache when she'd wake to find herself alone.

But that was long ago, and on this particular day, she suspected Raphael would be staying close in her mind for entirely different reasons. First, because just being on this island was an exercise in uncertainty and danger for them. They knew, or at least strongly suspected, that the European vamps were already here. This meeting was their idea, and they'd have wanted to get set up before Raphael ever arrived, seeking the advantage of familiar ground. And then there was the fact that the Europeans couldn't be trusted and pretty much everything they said was suspect.

She also knew that Raphael would be watching her today because he'd realized, at the last minute this morning, that she'd played him, that she'd known all along he'd taken precisely the sort of risk last night in wandering around the island with his vamp buddies that he'd have been furious with her for doing. Which meant, he had no grounds to argue with her over what she and Robbie would be doing today. That didn't mean he was going to let it slide. He'd be watching her to the best of his considerable abilities, even if his body was trapped here in the vault. But she didn't actually mind it. Not today. There was a sort of comfort in knowing that if she and Robbie totally screwed the pooch, if the Europeans had daylight spies of their own, then Raphael and his vampires would know where to find her and Rob, hopefully still intact. Because as much as she enjoyed taking risks, pushing the envelope, she didn't have a death wish. Not even close. No matter what some people thought.

She coded the door locked behind her, sealing Raphael inside. Then did the same for the bookshelf door thingy. On a whim, she paused long enough to examine some of the titles on the bookshelf and found they were very real—cookbooks and general books on food and wine. Probably for the non-vampire clients who used the house. She walked over and pulled open the fridge. It was filled with real food too, for the human security staff, and for her. For the vamps, there was a smaller kitchen off the secret hallway with a huge stainless steel sub-zero refrigerator that was stocked with bagged blood.

"You looking for breakfast?"

Cyn spun around with a smile for Robbie. He was a very big guy, around six foot two and all muscle beneath his smooth, dark skin. He was also a former Army Ranger who was mated to Raphael's vampire housekeeper, Irina. Cyn and Robbie had been through some heavy shit together not so long ago. He was more than her bodyguard; he was her friend, and she trusted him more than almost anyone else when it came to fighting by her side.

"I'm not hungry enough for breakfast," she told him. "I might just grab a yogurt. You?"

"I already ate with the security guys earlier, a big breakfast. I'm good for a couple of hours at least."

Cyn shook her head with a smile. Robbie had a huge appetite to go with his huge physique, and since he was mated to a vampire, he was never going to have to worry about middle-aged spread. He had the metabolism of a much younger man, and he was just as active, which meant he could eat as much as he wanted.

"Let's go," she told him, grabbing her backpack. "We'll make the grocery store our first stop. You can pick up some sandwiches for later."

Robbie fell in with her as they headed for the front door. "The grocery store? The guys did a big shopping last night."

"I know. But I want to be sure no one's following us before we get down to business, and we'll need some supplies."

"And what is our business?"

Cyn stopped on the stairs outside the front door, eyeing the SUVs all lined up and parked facing forward for a quick escape. She heard the door thud shut behind her, then the rattle of the door handle as Robbie made sure it was locked. One of the human security guys materialized, nodding when he recognized Cyn. She nodded in reply as he blended back into the jungle, then hit the button on the remote Elke had given her. The SUV nearest the front door flashed its lights, and she walked over to it.

"As I said last night," she told Robbie as she opened the door and slid behind the wheel, "Luci's mother's cousin has a house nearby that I want to check out. And then I think we're flying to Honolulu."

The big vehicle dipped as Robbie settled into the passenger seat. "Why the hell are we going there?"

"I want to check out travel times, locally here in Kauai, but especially in Honolulu. That airport's a zoo and I want to know how long it will take us to land, get a car, and get on the road."

"Does Raphael know about this?"

Cyn gave him a smug smile. "Trust me, Raphael won't mind."

"Uh huh. You should let me drive," he said, in a complete non sequitur.

"Why?" she demanded.

"Because I'm a better driver."

"You are not."

"Yeah, I am, babe. Especially if it comes to evasive maneuvers."

"It's not going to come to that. We're just two tourists seeing the islands."

"Two well-armed tourists. And how are we going to get our guns on a plane?"

"It's a private charter, another one of Luci's cousins. He knows what to expect. And I'm driving."

"Give me the address then, and I'll program it into the nav. Otherwise, you'll kill us trying to do both."

She handed over the hard copy of Luci's email, pointing out the local address, which she'd circled.

"Don't let me forget to erase the history when we're finished today," she said starting down the long driveway.

"Will do," Rob said absently, his big fingers tapping the information into the nav system as Cyn pulled onto the main road and turned in the direction of the local grocery.

THE SUN WAS still in the eastern sky when Cyn finally pulled into the driveway of Luci's mother's cousin's daughter's house. Or something like that.

"Not exactly a grand estate," Robbie observed.

"Not a hovel either," Cyn said. "Houses in this neighborhood go for over a million."

"Huh. You have a key?"

"I know where to find it."

"Please tell me it's not under a flower pot."

Cyn smiled as she climbed out of the SUV and walked down the side of the house, with Robbie a close shadow. He took his bodyguarding seriously. Raphael had almost killed him the last time she'd been injured. It hadn't been Robbie's fault, but Raphael hadn't cared. It had been on Robbie's watch and that was enough.

Going around the back of the house, she dug into a pile of decorative rocks near the big outdoor grill and found what she was looking for. It looked like all of the other grey rocks, but it was one of those phony ones with a key compartment. She slid it open and held the key up for Robbie to see.

He took it from her as they circled back to the front of the house. He inserted the key in the door and pushed it open, one hand on the 9mm Beretta at his hip and the other making sure she stayed behind him as the door swung open on silent hinges.

The house had that empty feeling that told them no one was home and hadn't been for a while. The air was musty and damp, despite the air conditioning that clicked on as they walked through to the kitchen. The temperature on the AC was set just low enough to combat the pervasive, and potentially damaging, humidity and heat, but not low enough for human comfort. Cyn didn't care about that right now. Her only concern was checking out the bedrooms and other living quarters and doing whatever was necessary to make them safe as an emergency refuge for vampires.

Robbie was already through the kitchen and opening the door to the garage. "The garage is empty," he was saying. "I'll pull the SUV inside."

Cyn tossed him the keys, then did a quick walk-through of the ground floor. The house was much nicer than it appeared from the street. The interior was open and airy with what she thought of as typical Hawaiian décor—lots of light colors and bright floral patterns. There was a big patio that looked out on a golf green, with plenty of trees providing cover between the green and the house itself.

Robbie came back inside and they headed upstairs together. There were four bedrooms, including a roomy master suite. A broad, wraparound lanai was accessible from each bedroom through big sliding glass doors. That was a problem, but it was one she'd anticipated. Some of the supplies they'd picked up at the grocery would deal with that.

"We'll have to cover those doors," she said, stating the obvious. Robbie was mated to a vampire, he understood the situation as well as she did.

"Maybe we should have bought some sleeping bags. Vamps are going to have to double up, and there aren't enough beds," Robbie observed. And he was right. There was only one bed in each of the four bedrooms. Raphael would naturally have a room to himself, which meant the others—including Juro and all of Raphael's vamp guards—would have to squeeze into the other three. It helped that once the vamps were out for the day, they were truly out. There was no getting up to take a quick pee, no rolling around or snoring. At least not in Cyn's experience, which was only with Raphael. For all she knew, some vamps snored like crazy.

"We humans can bunk downstairs," Robbie continued.

"We shouldn't be here any longer than a day," Cyn added. "Everyone can suffer through one fucking day."

"Agreed. I'll go find some blankets and towels to use on the windows. There should be plenty of beach towels, if nothing else."

"We can use sheets, too, if they're dark enough. We'll overlap if we have to."

"I hope Luci's people don't mind us sticking holes in their linens."

"I'll buy them all new ones."

Robbie started for the stairs. "Don't get into trouble while I'm gone."

"You're going to be right downstairs," Cyn snapped.

"Exactly."

Cyn snorted dismissively and began opening boxes of pushpins and unwrapping rolls of duct tape. Good old duct tape.

Robbie was back in minutes, dumping a double armload of blankets, sheets and towels on the big king-sized bed in the master suite.

"It'll go faster if we work together," she said and started pulling pieces out of the pile. "We'll go room to room."

Robbie took the linens from her. "I'll hold, you stick."

It took longer than Cyn expected, but a little over an hour later, they had every window upstairs covered, even the ones in the bathrooms and at the end of the hallway. They couldn't do anything about the light coming up the open stairwell, but that shouldn't be an issue. Even covering the windows in the baths and hallway was overkill. If the vamps were cutting it so close that the sun was already up, they'd have much bigger problems than a little light leakage. Hell, if that was the case, they might all end up daylighting in the garage.

"You know," she said slowly. "We should cover that little window in the garage. Just in case."

Robbie met her gaze thoughtfully. "Good thought. We can do it on the way out. When are we supposed to meet your pilot?"

Cyn checked her watch. "His name's Brandon, and he's waiting for my call. I'm supposed to give him an hour's notice. If I call when we're leaving here, it should time out. The airport's about an hour's drive, but I have no idea what traffic's like. That's one of the things I need to know."

"What about at the other end?"

"I've arranged a rental car in Honolulu. Another of Luci's cousins has an empty rental on Diamond Head, so I'm having Brandon fly us into Honolulu International. I Google-mapped the house and it should be a short trip from the airport, but again, I don't know what traffic's like. Also, we won't be doing the whole blackout treatment, since I don't know if we'll ever use the house. But I want sufficient supplies on-site so we can make it vampire-ready on short notice, just in case."

"Why are you looking at Honolulu at all? What's happening here, Cyn?"

Cyn gave him a troubled look. "I don't want to sound paranoid or anything, but I don't trust these European vamps. I know what you're going to say," she added hurriedly, holding up a hand. "That Raphael doesn't trust them either, that he's going in with his eyes open. But the difference is that while he'd *like* to tell them to go fuck themselves, he can't. He has to meet them, which is the same as saying he has to walk into a trap if that's what they're planning, and I'm really afraid it is. I think Acuña was nothing but a dress rehearsal for this meeting, and I intend to be prepared for the real thing."

"Okay, so that explains having this house as a temporary bolt-hole, but what's with Honolulu?"

"What if we wanted, or needed, to get off this island in a hurry? To get away from whatever trap the Europeans have planned? They'll expect Raphael to go for his own plane at the main airport. But having Brandon fly us out instead would be the last thing they'll expect. And Honolulu's a big city, easy to lose yourself in."

"You're kind of overthinking this, babe."

"Maybe. But it won't cost us much to be prepared."

Robbie shrugged. "You got me there. So . . . can we at least grab lunch in Honolulu?"

Chapter Six

MUCH LATER THAT night, Cyn was following Raphael through the jungle—did Hawaii qualify as a jungle? What made a jungle anyway?

"I can hear you thinking, *lubimaya.*"

"All I can hear is you *walking,*" Elke muttered from behind her.

Raphael stopped beneath the broad leaf of a palm tree . . . or maybe it was a giant fern. Whatever it was, it sheltered them from the persistent rain that had started falling just after sunset and never let up.

Wanting to protect Raphael's night sight, she flicked off the small Maglite flashlight that only she needed and tried to remember why she'd wanted to come along on this little excursion.

Raphael smiled down at her, clearly amused by her predicament. "You *are* typically stealthier than this. You seem preoccupied."

Cyn considered telling him that her preoccupation mostly had to do with the overabundance of Hawaiian flora, but decided against it. Let him think she'd been doing important stuff all day, which she had, and that it was weighing on her mind, which it wasn't. She was satisfied with what she and Robbie had accomplished.

"I'll try to be quieter. Is it much farther?"

Raphael tapped the Bluetooth bud in his ear, his eyes going distant as he listened. They had three teams checking out different properties tonight, so the call could be from one of the others, or it could be someone from Raphael's own recon group of five who were spread out around him, not including himself or Cyn and Elke.

Raphael tapped the bud again to disconnect, then said, "The forward scout has reached the perimeter. He'll hold there until we join him. No more than a hundred yards."

Cyn struggled not to sigh. A hundred more yards of wet jungle. She much preferred her own recon, which only involved checking out expensive houses. "Ready when you are," she said cheerfully.

Raphael took her hand. "Stay behind me and step where I step. It will go easier for you."

"And quieter," Elke hissed falling into line behind her.

"No more talking," Raphael ordered. He gripped Cyn's hand tighter and picked up the pace until finally they broke through a final line of trees and stopped abruptly.

The house was right in front of them, across a wide swath of neatly trimmed lawn that was probably emerald green in daylight. There were no lights on outside, not even a porch or patio light to break up the shadows. But inside was another story. Dim light bled through tightly covered windows on both levels of the two-story house. She could see movement behind the translucent panels downstairs, while the upstairs windows were covered with imperfect blackout shades that showed thin lines of light around the edges. It sure looked like vampires were in residence.

Raphael's scout materialized next to him, moving so quietly that Cyn hadn't even noticed him until he was there. Elke nudged Cyn, giving her a meaningful look when she glanced over, as if to say *that's how it's supposed to be done.* Cyn just shrugged. She'd never be able to move the way the vamps did; it was pointless to pretend otherwise.

"Definitely vampires, my lord," the scout said, his voice barely discernible. "They have perimeter security, but only close in to the house. They, too, are vampires, though I recognize none of them."

Raphael nodded and got that not-really-there look on his face that told her he was examining the house for himself, using his far superior senses. He crouched down slowly, taking her with him. On his other side, the scout mirrored his movement, staring at the house as if trying to see what his master was seeing.

They stayed that way for a few minutes until, between one blink and the next, Raphael was back with them. He didn't say anything, simply jerked his head at the scout, indicating the trail behind them, which Cyn took to mean he wanted them to go back to their vehicle. More trekking through wet jungle. *Fantastic.*

Raphael stood, pulling Cyn to her feet, then turning her around the way they'd come. He lifted his chin at Elke who went first, then Cyn and Raphael followed. Cyn figured there were probably a couple of his vampires forming a rearguard. Raphael might be their lord and master and über-powerful, but Juro would flay these guards alive if anything happened to his Sire.

They no sooner reached their vehicles—which fortunately were four-wheel drive, because they'd been concealed down a narrow track that was little more than an animal trail and Cyn had no desire to walk back to the house because their rides got stuck in the mud—when Raphael received another call. But this one had him jolting into action.

"In the truck now," he snapped, opening the door and propelling Cyn inside.

"What is it?" she asked, no longer caring about the rain or the mud.

The SUV's powerful engine roared to a start. The driver slammed it into gear, wheels spinning as he maneuvered it onto the trail and reversed at high speed toward the main road.

"Raphael?" Cyn asked.

"We assumed our hosts would be watching the airport tonight, alert to our arrival, so we arranged a decoy of sorts, an arrival scenario for anyone watching."

"But they'd know it wasn't you getting off the plane, wouldn't they?"

"Not necessarily. They wouldn't expect me to broadcast my presence, so they'd have to go by physical description alone. The jet tonight pulled into the hangar on arrival, just as we did last night, which has the benefit of concealing disembarking passengers from casual view. Three vehicles then departed the hangar and headed this way. That phone call was from the leader of the team driving those vehicles. They picked up a tail right outside the airport."

"But that probably means they fell for the decoy and don't know you're already here. That's good, isn't it?"

"Indeed."

"So why are we racing back?"

"One of our SUVs hung back and confronted the followers, letting the other SUV and the limo go ahead. They'll assume I'm in the limo, which means I have to be at the house when the watchers finally arrive."

"Why lead them to the house at all? Let our guys take them out."

Raphael gave her that smile which meant the violent side of her personality was showing again.

"It was meant to be a welcoming committee, my Cyn. An emissary from the master of these islands."

"Yeah, right. They were snooping, plain and simple."

"They were curious," he acknowledged. "But I can't *take them out* for trying to meet our plane."

Cyn pursed her lips and shrugged, letting her body language say that she didn't know why not. "I'm assuming Juro will be at the house, too."

"Try keeping him away," Raphael said dryly as they made a fishtailing turn onto the long driveway that led to the house.

The two other recon teams were on their tail by then and followed them into the multiple-car garage. For once, Cyn was glad it was raining, since it would wash away most of their tire tracks in case anyone bothered to look. The garage doors were rolled down by remote as soon as the vehicles were clear. A door led from the garage to the main kitchen, and, from there, it was only a few steps to the private hallway behind the bookshelf.

Raphael hustled Cyn directly to their room and entered the door code in a blur of vampire speed. He opened the door only enough for them to slip through, then closed it behind them.

"Is there a dress code for this meeting?" Cyn asked only half-facetiously, as she hurried toward the closet. If these guys were as old school as Elke had told her, maybe they expected Raphael's mate to dress formally. She'd brought a dress and heeled sandals, thinking there might be something like a formal dinner, so she was more or less prepared.

"Cyn."

It was only her name, but the way Raphael said it, and the look in his eyes when she turned to study him, told her there was more bad news coming.

"I don't want you with me."

She frowned. "With you where?"

"Tonight, tomorrow. I don't want them to know you're here, or even what you look like."

"But they already know what I look like. I was in Mexico, I fought Violet with you."

"But Violet was the only survivor of the night," he pointed out. "The rest haven't seen you in person, and none of them know you're here. And I want to keep it that way."

"Why? Don't you trust—?"

Raphael grabbed her by the shoulders, giving her a small shake. "Don't say it. I trust you with my life. I trust you more than any other, including my own children."

"Then why?" Cyn cursed the tears pressing against the back of her eyes, but her feelings were wounded and she needed to know what he was thinking.

Raphael gentled his hold on her. "Two reasons. The first is that I don't want you hurt. These vampires would have no qualms about using you against me. It's why I didn't defend you in Mexico, so they wouldn't see how much you mean to me."

Cyn nodded. "But I want to stand *with* you, Raphael, not behind you."

"Which brings me to my second reason. If they don't know about you, they can't guard against you. If something goes wrong, you're my secret weapon."

Cyn pounded a fist against his broad chest. He was right, but she hated it. "That's so unfair," she whispered.

"I know. And I know it goes against every instinct of yours to stay back and wait. But I'm asking you to do that for me."

She closed her eyes, fighting the fear and sadness lapping against the back of her brain, threatening to overwhelm her thoughts. Raphael put his arms around her and pulled her close, his lips against her hair. "I love you, my Cyn."

She nodded against his chest. "I know. And I'll do what you want on one condition."

She felt his mouth curve into a smile. "What's that?"

"You promise me, Raphael, that you'll stay alive, that you'll come back to me."

"I will do everything in my power to come back to you, *lubimaya*. Always."

"Okay." She stepped out of his arms, then backed away to sit on the bed. And there she remained, watching as Raphael stripped away his dirty and wet clothes, then washed his face and ran a towel over his wet hair. He changed into a pair of slacks and a dress shirt, no tie, the shirt open at the collar. She liked him better in his 501s and T-shirt, but Raphael looked good in everything, and this was the Hawaiian version of his Master of the Universe uniform. When he met the others—the ones who'd orchestrated this meeting and were the real threat to all of them—he'd go for the full suit and tie, no matter the tropical weather or location. But tonight was casual, since he'd supposedly just arrived on a long flight from L.A.

When he finished dressing, he came over to the bed and pulled her to her feet, then tugged her head back by her hair, and gave her a long, wet kiss.

"I won't be long. This is a courtesy call, nothing more."

"Am I supposed to wait in here?"

Raphael grinned. "Am I a fool?" he asked rhetorically. "Come on. I don't want them to see you, but I definitely want *you* to see *them*. Walking over to the door, he entered the code, and it popped open. Turning back, he gave her a wink, then opened the door wide to reveal Juro's brother, Ken'ichi, waiting down the hall from them beside an open door.

Cyn gave him a surprised smile. Ken'ichi hadn't flown over with them last night, which had puzzled her at the time, since Juro and his brother were an almost constant presence at Raphael's side. But now she realized he'd arrived with the second plane tonight, which had clearly been the plan all along. Still, why was he standing there waiting for her now? Were they supposed to keep each other company? Play canasta or watch movies to keep her mind off the fact that Raphael was meeting the bad guys only yards away from her? She liked Ken'ichi well enough, but he wasn't exactly a chatty guy.

Raphael had his hand low on her back and was urging her forward. "You flew in on the decoy plane?" she asked, knowing the answer but needing to make conversation.

Ken'ichi nodded silently, only his eyes offering a warm greeting.

She and Raphael drew even with the open door where Ken'ichi was standing, and Cyn glanced inside. She hadn't been in any of the rooms except the one she and Raphael shared, so she was curious.

"Oh!" she said, staring at racks and rows of equipment and monitors, one of which was showing a couple of Raphael's guards greeting their guests at this very moment.

"A surveillance system!" she said delightedly.

"A security control center," Raphael corrected.

"Does it have sound?"

"It wouldn't be much use otherwise."

"Cool." Spinning, she rose up on her toes and kissed Raphael on the lips. "Be good, fang boy. I'll be watching."

Raphael rolled his eyes, something she was sure he'd never done before he met her, then he patted her on the ass and headed for the concealed doorway. Their unexpected visitors meant the door was closed, so he had to enter the code before pushing it open. Cyn watched him disappear into the kitchen, then leaned back and watched Juro join him in there on the video monitor. The two of them then went from camera to camera until they showed up in the main living room where their guests waited.

Slipping into the security room, Cyn pulled one of the smaller chairs over to the main monitor, leaving the more comfortable chair for her companion, who, being Juro's identical twin in every sense, needed the extra space and support. She reached over and turned up the volume.

"Lord Raphael," their guests said in unison when Raphael walked into the room. There were three of them. Two appeared to be of Hawaiian origin, with black hair and dark eyes, medium height and stocky, but not fat, builds. They were dressed in nearly identical outfits—light-colored linen pants and Hawaiian style shirts, but in solid pastel colors, rather than wild floral prints. They also appeared to be roughly the same age, late thirties, but appearance meant little on a vampire. Raphael would know the moment he walked into the room how old they really were, and how powerful. There was no way for Cyn to judge those things on the monitor, or even if they'd been standing right in front of her. She could distinguish vampire versus human, but that was it.

The third emissary didn't look like he'd normally hang out with the other two. No more than early twenties in appearance, he was wearing black jeans and a black, button-down shirt with the sleeves rolled halfway up his forearms. His dark brown hair was gelled into spikes, his ears and eyebrows were both pierced, the ears more than once, and he wore black-rimmed glasses. That last made Cyn blink in surprise. She'd never seen a vamp wearing glasses before and wondered if he did it solely for effect. Going for the geek look, maybe.

"Do you think those are real glasses?" she asked.

Ken'ichi seemed to consider it, then said, "Yes, you can see the distortion in the lenses. They're prescription."

Cyn glanced over with a smile. It was a night for surprises, it seemed. That was the most she'd ever heard him say at once.

"Have you ever seen a vampire wear glasses before?" she asked, pushing her luck.

He frowned, thinking, then shook his head.

"Maybe he's not a vampire. Can you tell that from here?"

He shook his head. Cyn drew breath to ask another question, but Raphael and the others were speaking and she didn't want to miss it.

"Welcome to Hawaii, Lord Raphael." That was one of the two older guys, the one in the peach-colored shirt.

"And you are?" Juro asked, none too friendly.

"Forgive me, my lord. I am Kale and this—" he said, indicating the baby blue-shirted vampire at his side. "—is Jonathan."

Raphael gave the geeky guy a pointed look.

"Donovan Willis, Lord Raphael. I'm Rhys Patterson's security specialist. Master Patterson didn't know what your setup here was and sent me to offer my services."

Next to Cyn, Ken'ichi snorted in disdain.

"I know, right?" she said agreeably. "What does this guy think, that we're just going to let him waltz in here and bug our system?"

On screen, Juro's expression reflected her assessment, but Raphael seemed almost amused. "My people are quite skilled, Mr. Willis, but thank you for offering."

"Are you certain, my lord? There are specific aspects of the network—"

"Let it go, boy," Kale snapped. "Apologies, my lord. He is human."

"Well, that answers one question," Cyn muttered. Kale's snide comment about the human Donovan Willis brought to mind Raphael's earlier caution. He was right about their dismissive attitude increasing her danger, but, under the right circumstances, she could make that attitude work for her.

But Kale, or Mr. Peach as Cyn was mentally referring to him, wasn't finished yet. "I bring greetings from Master Patterson, and from his guests."

"Where *is* Master Patterson?" Raphael inquired mildly.

"He remains with our European visitors tonight, my lord. Their journey here was long and trying."

"It is some distance," Raphael agreed, without bringing up the unpleasant subject of precisely when they'd made that long and trying journey. Especially since it would probably force Mr. Peach to lie. Although it might have been fun to watch him try.

"Master Patterson is honored to serve as mediator in this dispute, Lord Raphael," Jonathan (aka Mr. Blue) chimed in. "He looks forward to what will surely be an amicable resolution."

"As do we all."

"Is there anything else?" Juro asked abruptly. "Lord Raphael, too, has had a long journey."

"Of course. Forgive us, my lord," Mr. Peach said immediately. "If you've no objections, Master Patterson would like to begin the negotiations tomorrow evening at his personal residence." He held out what looked like an oversized business card to Raphael, but Juro intercepted him, taking the proffered card himself.

Mr. Peach seemed startled by Juro's quick movement, or maybe his size, which was easily twice that of Mr. Peach. Either way, he gave Juro an uneasy look, then fidgeted with the shirt pocket which had held the business card, as if wondering if he should have brought more, before finally addressing Raphael again. "The card bears the location for the meeting, my lord. May I tell Master Patterson you'll accept?"

Raphael didn't say anything for a long moment, long enough that Peach and Blue were both looking distinctly uncomfortable, while the geek Donovan Willis only seemed amused. *Interesting.*

"We'll be there," Raphael said finally, a small smile seeming to play over his mouth, although it was hard to see details on the security footage.

"Excellent, my lord," Peach said.

If he hadn't been a vampire, Cyn would have sworn Peach was sweating with worry, which was odd considering his only purpose tonight was to be part of a glorified welcoming committee. Minus the lei. But the source of that worry—apart from Raphael's general bad-assedness, of course—became evident with his next words.

"Uh, that is, forgive me, Lord Raphael, but . . ."

Raphael didn't make it easy on the guy. He just watched, and waited for him to stutter it out.

"The, ah, terms of the negotiation stipulate that the parties to the, er, negotiation, may bring only one attendant each to the meeting itself."

Raphael tilted his head at the stuttering vamp, which literally made Peach take a half step back before he caught himself and stood still.

"Those were the terms," Raphael said.

What he didn't do, Cyn noted, was agree. But Peach had clearly used up the last shreds of his courage and wasn't up to pushing Raphael for a more specific commitment.

"Thank you, my lord, and once again welcome to the Islands," he blurted out, then gave an aborted little bow and hurried toward the front door, with Blue shuffling in his wake.

Donovan Willis, on the other hand, watched the two vampires with obvious dislike before he started to follow them out. At the last minute, he turned and gave Raphael a searching look, and Cyn would have sworn there was something he wanted to say. But, then, he gave a little shake of his head and with seeming reluctance, followed in the wake of his erstwhile companions.

Cyn waited until the front door closed, until the front security camera showed their visitors piling into a town car and driving away, and then she pushed her chair back and headed for the vault door. Before she reached it, however, the concealed door swung open and Raphael was there. She went right into his arms, feeling as if he'd been in danger, even though none of those three had represented any real threat. At least, not that she could tell.

"You're not really—" Cyn started to protest, but Raphael eased her back into the hallway and waited until Juro closed the vault door before pulling them all into the crowded security control room.

"They were lying about Patterson, my lord," Juro rumbled in his deep voice. "Are they such fools to think they can lie to you?"

"They were lying," Raphael agreed. "Although their motivations are more difficult to discern. It is possible that they were not fully briefed. I know Patterson's people, however, and neither of those two were his."

"Could they be new?" Cyn asked.

"They were not," Raphael said plainly.

"So they're allied with the Europeans, and assumed you wouldn't know the difference as long as they looked the part. That doesn't spell good things for your friend Patterson."

"No, it does not. Although I don't think he's dead yet. They'll need him to at least make an appearance tomorrow night."

"What about the geek?" Cyn asked. "The human," she clarified, at Raphael's quizzical look. "He didn't like Peach and Blue all that much."

"Peach and Blue?" Raphael asked in obvious amusement.

"Those shirts were so new, they probably still had the tags on them. And they dressed more like twins than you guys," she added, gesturing at Juro and his brother who stood side by side against the wall, all but filling the small room with just the two of them. Add in Raphael, who wasn't exactly a small guy, and there was definitely an abundance of vampire per square foot.

"The geek, as you call him," Juro commented, "did *not* have fond feelings for his companions, but he very much *did* want to get his hands on our security system."

"That was odd," Cyn said. "He didn't actually think we'd let him, did he?"

"For all that he wanted that access, I don't believe it was his real purpose in coming here tonight. It would be interesting to know more about Mr. Willis."

"I'll do some digging," Cyn offered, wanting to contribute more than just hunching over security monitors in a small room and touring expensive houses.

"The house we had under surveillance earlier, before we had to rush back here, is almost certainly one of theirs," Raphael said, changing the subject. "I detected ten vampires, two of whom were lords, and the others most likely masters, including the two on guard duty."

"They could only bring so many of their people with them, so they probably brought only master or above. They didn't bring a full security contingent, because most fighters are not master vampires. So the masters they brought are doing double duty," Juro commented, then pulled the card Peach had given him out of his pocket. "The address matches the house you were at earlier, Sire. Although the location my team reconnoitered also contained at least one lord and several other vampires of considerable strength. The power signature was substantial. They could have ten such houses on the island," he added somberly. "We have no idea of their numbers."

"What about our man at the airport?" Raphael asked.

"He saw a private jet arrive five days ago. It pulled directly into a hangar, but he was able to see that only six passengers deplaned. They were all vampires, but he's not sensitive enough to determine their power levels. Judging by their body language and that of the others around them, however, he hazarded a guess that two were, if not lords, then at least powerful masters. Per my instructions, he didn't follow them from the airport, but remained on watch. There have been no arrivals that he's seen since then, but he's only one man, and he's only been stationed there for a week. It's entirely possible that our enemies have been staffing up for some time now."

Cyn shuffled closer to Raphael, sliding her hand into his as her stomach roiled with fear. Juro was right. The bad guys had learned from Mexico. They'd bring more firepower this time. More and stronger vampires. Maybe a lot more.

Raphael squeezed Cyn's fingers and sighed. "What would you have me do, Juro? Should I go home, refuse to meet with them?"

Juro frowned, conflict written all over his face. Clearly, the part of him that was fiercely loyal to Raphael wanted his Sire to do just that. Go home and let the fight come to them on their own territory. But the security chief in him, the part that looked at every situation and weighed the pros and cons, knew they had to stay. The entire continent was at risk, not only the West, and they needed to know more about this enemy, about his strengths and weaknesses. Right now, they didn't even know for sure which of the European lords were behind the invasion. The letter they'd sent hadn't been signed by any individual vampire lord. Raphael had made his knowledge of, and opposition to, their agenda for expansion very clear. And the blood ink alone had been enough for him to take the invitation seriously.

"No, my lord," Juro said finally agreed reluctantly. "I believe we must at least meet with them." He opened his mouth to say more, but Raphael raised a hand to stop him.

"You'll accompany me into the meeting tomorrow night, of course. We'll take a full security escort as far as they'll let us, then leave them stationed close by in case we need them."

"Cynthia—" Juro started, but Raphael cut him off.

"Will remain here," Raphael said, turning a soft gaze in her direction. "We're in agreement on that."

Juro met Cyn's gaze, his eyebrows raised in question. She nodded. She still wasn't happy about it, but she understood. It made sense to have a backup that the enemy didn't know about.

Raphael tugged Cyn closer to his side and told Juro, "If you would, call Jared and brief him on these latest events. And tomorrow night, have the team ready to leave one hour after sunset."

"Sire," Juro acknowledged.

Raphael nodded at Juro and Ken'ichi, then pulled Cyn down the hall to their room.

Once inside, Cyn left Raphael to enter the lock code and crossed over to the closet. Before tonight, she'd been half-convinced that Raphael had asked her to be his "backup plan" simply as a way to keep her occupied and out of the way. And she still thought his concern over her safety played a role in his decision. But there was more to it than that. His need for a fallback was real and she needed to get her ass in gear.

She ran down her mental checklist. First up had been the need to secure safe housing. She had two safe houses secured and more or less vampire-ready, one here on Kauai and the other in Diamond Head on Oahu. So, check that off the list. Next, escape from the island. Check. Luci's cousin had assured her he'd be available twenty-four hours a day for the next week, if necessary.

Next on her list was a getaway plan, and she'd realized, when she'd been tramping through the jungle with Raphael tonight, that she didn't know the surrounding area very well. What if they had to skirt a road block? Or if they needed a roundabout way to the airport? Or simply a way off this property other than that long, vulnerable and too obvious driveway?

She and Robbie needed to acquire an untraceable vehicle with a good GPS system and do some exploring. When they were finished, they'd store the vehicle off-site, preferably somewhere within walking distance in case they had to escape through the jungle.

Her head was filled with all of these details as she sat down to unlace the combat boots she'd worn for their trek through the jungle. Tossing the boots aside, she pulled her tank top over her head and had just stood to unzip her pants when a pair of big warm hands reached out to cup her breasts, thumbs strumming her nipples roughly through the lace of her bra.

"Come to bed, *lubimaya*," Raphael murmured, grazing his fingers over her ribs and down, sliding into the waistband of her jeans as he framed her hips, and then delving lower to dip into the silk of her matching panties.

Cyn turned in his arms, reaching up to pull him down for a kiss that was warm and luscious and full of desire.

"You're wearing too many clothes," she whispered against his lips.

Raphael seemed more interested in *her* clothes, shoving her jeans and panties down and filling his hands with the twin globes of her butt, squeezing and releasing as he lifted her up until the hard ridge of his erection fit neatly in the cleft between her thighs.

Cyn moaned softly and flexed her hips against the bulge behind his zipper, then realized unhappily that she was naked, her pants around one ankle, while Raphael still stood fully dressed. Bucking against his hold, she regained her feet and tackled the buttons on his shirt, yanking it out of his pants with one hand while she worked the buttons with the other. Clearly deciding it was taking too long, Raphael ripped the shirt open, sending buttons flying.

Laughing wildly, Cyn shoved his shirt off his shoulders, then leaned in to taste the perfectly smooth skin of his chest, licking her way from one nipple to the other, pausing only long enough to close her teeth over each of the hard, little nubs, biting hard enough that Raphael hissed with pleasure as he finally released the buttons and zipper on his pants.

Letting them fall to the floor, he picked Cyn up bodily and, stepping out of the crumpled pile of clothing, strode the short distance to the bed. He didn't throw her as he sometimes did, but laid her on the too-soft mattress and followed her down, quickly covering her, letting her feel the full weight of his body, the firm curves and planes of muscle, the long length of his legs and the narrow span of his hips as he slipped between her thighs and spread her legs wide around him.

He bent to kiss her, fingers tangling in her hair, forcing her head back as his mouth moved from her lips to the smooth line of her neck, sucking the skin over her jugular hard enough to sting, hard enough that she'd have a high school hickey there in the morning. Hard enough that her vein plumped, eager for the touch of his fangs. But he didn't bite, soothing the sting with the caress of his tongue instead, even as his grip on her hair eased and he cupped her head gently, his thumbs smoothing over her cheekbones.

Cyn met his black-eyed gaze when he bent to kiss her again and what she saw there thickened her throat with emotion. His kiss was tender and full of feeling as one hand glided over her shoulder and down her back to pull her close, until there wasn't an inch of space between them when he slipped his hard, hot cock inside her.

Overwhelmed with emotion, with the sensation of Raphael touching every inch of her, Cyn closed her eyes and held on to him, smoothing the lean muscles of his back, the firm swell of his ass, and back up again to hold him as tightly as she could, wishing they could forget the rest of the world, the threats of the vampires from the Europe, the thousands of vampires back home who were waiting for Raphael to protect them, to make their world safe. They didn't care what it cost him, didn't care about the other vampires that might die, about the fact that Raphael risked his life over and over again so they could live their lives without worry.

Raphael's hips thrust slowly, his cock sliding in and out of her, gliding easily in the cream of her arousal, her sheath caressing and releasing him as he made love to her.

Cyn frowned as something clicked in her brain. Her eyes flashed open, her legs crossed over the curve of Raphael's ass, and she shoved at his chest until he was forced to look down at her.

"What are you doing?" she demanded.

Raphael gave her a quizzical look, but didn't say anything.

Cyn's eyes narrowed. "Don't you do this, Raphael. Don't you dare."

"Do what?" he asked, his face carefully blank. Too blank. And Cyn knew she was right. He wasn't fucking her, wasn't even making love to her. No, he was saying *good-bye* because he didn't expect to survive tomorrow night.

Well. Fuck. That.

Cyn let her legs fall to either side of his hips, then bucked hard, rolling them over until she was on top, straddling him, staring down at him, almost too furious to talk. Almost.

"You do *not* get to say good-bye to me like this. You do not get to say good-bye at all. You *promised* me you would come back, and that does not mean I get your ashes in a fucking box, do you hear me? No one gets to kill you but me, and I swear, Raphael, I will stake you myself if you let them kill you."

One corner of his sensuous mouth curved up in amusement at the illogical threat, and she growled, actually *growled* at him. Which only made him smile harder.

"Perhaps I simply wanted to take comfort in the sweet and silky flesh of my mate before going into battle."

Cyn gave him a doubtful look, but she smiled. "In that case, you have the wrong woman."

Raphael wrapped both arms around her and rolled them again, putting him once more on top. "I have exactly the woman I want, *lubimaya*. There is no other."

She stared at him a moment longer, trying to see the truth in his star-flecked gaze. "I love you," she told him solemnly. "I won't survive without you. I don't *want* to."

Raphael's expression turned fierce in an instant. "Don't say that," he snarled.

"Why not?" Cyn demanded. "It's true. If something happened to you, I—"

"You will live your life."

Cyn gave him a smug smile. "Sauce for the goose, fang boy. Guess we'll both have to survive, huh?"

Raphael's only answer was to begin moving again, sinking deep into her pussy with every stroke, then pulling out almost completely, teasing her for a beat, and plunging all the way into her once more.

Cyn wrapped her legs around his hips, ankles crossed over his ass, her arms around his back, hands wide to hold him close as their mouths met in a kiss that was so much more than tongues and teeth. It was a profession of love, of desire, a promise not only to survive but to protect.

Raphael's fangs punched out of his gums, ripping Cyn's lips as their kiss changed, turning hot and passionate as Raphael's thrusts became harder, faster, his hips slamming into her, powerful muscles bunching and releasing. Cyn felt the rough brush of his tongue as he lapped up the blood from her torn lips, felt his groan hum down her throat when she bit him back. He lifted his head with a snarl, his eyes wild and gleaming silver in the dim light, his fangs filling his mouth as he bent to her neck. His breath was hot against her skin for a brief moment, and then he was biting her. Sharp points sliced into her skin, her vein giving way as he began sucking, taking long, smooth draws of her blood. The euphoric in his bite raced into Cyn's system, soaring along her nerves, sending her into an instant climax that bowed her back. She cried out, her head thrown back, her legs scissoring around his narrow hips as her sheath clenched around his cock, rippling over his hard length, caressing him, urging him to join her.

Raphael lifted his head, fangs easing out of her vein, his tongue rasping over the puncture wounds without thought as his hips hammered between Cyn's legs, his groin grinding against her with every thrust. His cock swelled as Cyn's pussy squeezed and released, until finally his orgasm spilled forth in a searing wave of pleasure and their voices joined in ecstasy.

Cyn lay in Raphael's arms, wrapped in the heat of his climax. He tensed to move, to take his weight off her, but she held on for a moment longer, relishing the pounding of his heart against her breasts, the warmth of his breath on her neck as he struggled to regain his control. A control she'd made him lose. She stroked a soothing hand down his back, comforted by this proof that she wasn't the only one shattered by their lovemaking.

Without warning, he gathered her in his arms and rolled to his back. The cool air flowed over her heated skin and she shivered. Raphael yanked the blankets up over both of them, holding her until she was warm again.

"The sun is rising, my Cyn," he murmured, touching his lips to the top of her head.

"I'll be here when you wake up."

"But you have plans for the day," he said dryly, correctly interpreting her words.

"More backup stuff. Robbie will be with me, though. We're being extra careful."

He sighed, a long gusting breath that sounded more exhausted that she'd ever heard from him.

Her chest tightened in unaccustomed fear. "Raphael?" She propped up on an elbow to look down at him, but he was already gone. Resting her cheek on his chest, she waited for the steady, slow thud of his heart, for the deep expansion of his lungs. She blew out a relieved breath of her own when the expected signs of life came right on schedule. Sitting up, she studied his face, brushing his short hair back with her fingers.

Everything was fine. Normal. For now.

But tonight, he'd be meeting the enemy, and that was another matter. She knew she wasn't the only one worried, but she did seem to be the only one who thought they should simply say *fuck it* and go home. The problem was that, while they all believed the Euro vamps were going to try something underhanded, they just as clearly believed that Raphael was powerful enough to defeat or at least derail whatever it was. Raphael was a power like the world had never seen before. It was almost unimaginable that anyone could defeat him. Almost.

Unfortunately, Cyn could imagine it all too easily.

CYN OPENED the door of the SUV and slid to the ground, hanging on when her tired legs threatened to give way. Part of the problem was the flimsy sandals she wore. The kind of trekking she and Robbie had done today demanded better shoes. She'd considered that when she'd left Raphael's bed earlier, but her primary concern had been to blend in with the other tourists, and combat boots just didn't do the trick. Not in Kauai's muggy heat. But now, her entire body was sticky with sweat, her bare legs were scratched, and she just knew there were bits of greenery sticking to her clothes and hair. She only hoped the souvenirs of her tramping through the jungle were limited to the plant variety.

Sighing wearily, she stepped away from the vehicle and slammed the door, hearing it beep behind her when Robbie keyed the remote. He came up next to her as they started for the stairs to the house.

"We're ready here, Cyn. You've done all you can."

"I hope so. God, I hope so."

"Whatever happens, you'll handle it. You always do."

Cyn stopped in the middle of the kitchen and looked up at the big Army Ranger who was more than a bodyguard to her. "Thanks, Robbie. That means a lot to me."

"Don't go all mushy on me. I'll lose my badass cred if I cry." He reached out a big hand and ruffled her hair, coming away with something green.

Cyn eyed it doubtfully. It looked like plant matter, but . . .

"It's a leaf." He laughed and turned her in the direction of the book-shelf door. "Go sleep with your honey. I'm going to do the same, minus the honey, but I'll be here. If you need me, call my cell."

Cyn nodded, then punched in the entry code and opened the vault door just enough to slip inside. The hallway beyond was perfectly quiet. Every door was closed, the security control center running silently, moni-tors flickering with images. There was a regular guard room elsewhere in the house where Raphael's daylight security kept watch. It was the only control center that regular, i.e., human, visitors to the house ever used, and even then, they remained unaware of the full extent of the surveil-lance network hardwired into the house.

Cyn leaned her forehead on the cool door as she entered the code to the room she shared with Raphael, again opening it only enough for her to slip through before securing it behind her.

Raphael slept just as she'd left him, lying on his back, sheet pulled up to his waist, his face serenely beautiful in the dim light. All she wanted to do was crawl into bed next to him, but she had to shower first. She stripped off her clothes as she walked to the bathroom, leaving them on the floor or the chair, wherever they fell. The shower was tepid at first, but it felt refreshingly cool. Thinking of possible insect riders, she waited until it ran hot, then washed thoroughly and shampooed her hair.

She toweled dry and slid under the sheet next to Raphael, pulling up a light blanket to cover them both in the cool room. She checked the time. Three hours more or less until sunset.

THE SUN WAS still low on the horizon when Raphael woke. His first sensation was of Cyn lying next him, soft and warm and still deeply asleep. Slipping his arm around her, he pulled her against his side. She murmured wordlessly, one limp arm falling over his belly, her head on his shoulder. But she didn't wake. He could feel her exhaustion. She'd been out again earlier today, making plans. He didn't know exactly what she'd done. He didn't want to know. He only knew he trusted her.

His vampires were waking up, their minds clicking to life around him like a series of light bulbs, some brighter, some not. Juro first, the brightest of them all, then his twin Ken'ichi, only seconds behind and very nearly as bright. And then the others. Most of them would go with him to meet the Europeans, even though it was likely that no one but Juro would be permitted to enter the house. The European lords would want a witness for whatever they had planned, someone to carry the story back to Malibu after they defeated Raphael, in hopes of discouraging Raphael's people and weakening his territory's defense. But Raphael knew his people better than they did. Whatever happened to him, the West would not fall.

Cyn stirred next to him, the first signs of her wakening. She would be furious if she knew the depth of his certainty about the outcome of this meeting. He wouldn't walk out of that house tonight. As far as he was concerned, the only question was how the Europeans would manage to contain him. He knew the extent of his power, and he knew most of the old country vampires. None of them had been able to control him back in the day, when he'd been young and inexperienced, and they sure as hell couldn't do it now. But they thought they could. He was missing something. The only question was what.

Cyn woke finally, and his arms tightened around her.

"Are we leaving?" she asked, her voice slumberous and sexy. His cock hardened in response, but he ignored it regretfully. They didn't have time for such things tonight, as enjoyable as it would be.

"I'm afraid not," he said, knowing that she meant departing the island and going home, not simply leaving the bed or the house.

She sat up, pushing her hair back when it tumbled into her face, her breasts swaying tantalizingly close. She was the most sensuous woman he'd ever known . . . and the fiercest fighter. Oh, certainly, he had met others who were stronger, more skilled with one weapon or another, masters of various martial arts. But he'd never known anyone with a stronger will than his Cyn. If she believed in her cause, if she believed in *you*, she never gave up.

"Can we at least shower together?" she asked, knowing the time constraints as well as he did.

Raphael wrapped his arms around her and leapt from the bed, taking her with him and eliciting a startled yelp. He smiled, pleased that he still had the power to surprise her.

"We'll shower, but you must avoid the temptation to molest me," he told her sternly.

Cyn gave a girlish laugh and settled her arms around his neck. "No promises, fang boy. No promises."

RAPHAEL STUDIED himself in the mirror, smiling when Cyn came up behind him, her deceptively slender fingers smoothing over the shoulders of his suit jacket as she circled around to stand in front of him and straighten his tie.

"I know you're being super Raphael and all, but isn't it awfully hot for a suit and tie?"

"It is, but my counterparts will be dressed very formally, even more formally than this. And, as much as I would rather not bother, first impressions matter when conducting negotiations."

Her green eyes were solemn when she gazed up at him. "You really think they're going to negotiate?"

Raphael considered lying, but things were too critical and she needed the truth. Besides, he'd promised over a year ago, when he'd almost lost her, that he wouldn't keep things from her anymore.

"No," he admitted, "I expect them to demand our surrender. They will begin by offering incentives in return for our cooperation— power-sharing, perhaps, albeit with the territories broken up and the authority of the current lords severely limited. When that doesn't work— and it won't—they will resort to threats. At which point, I will thank them graciously for their invitation, return here long enough to gather you and the others, and immediately leave the island."

"You really think that's how it will go?"

"I think that's the most optimistic scenario."

She sighed. "That's what I thought." She patted his chest. "Okay, that's as pretty as you're going to get, which"—she went up on her toes to kiss him—"is awfully damn pretty."

Raphael looped an arm around her waist, holding her close. "Kiss me good-bye," he said against her lips.

Cyn twisted her arms around his neck, pressing her soft breasts against him as she deepened their kiss, her tongue dashing between his teeth, curling around the fangs that emerged in eager response. A growl slid up Raphael's throat as he cupped the back of her head, holding her in place as he sank deep into the sweet warmth of her mouth, tasting her blood when she scraped her tongue over the pointed tip of a fang. He gathered these sensations—the softness of her lips on his, the hard pearls of her nipples crushed against his chest, and, more than anything, the exquisite honey of her blood—storing them away against the possibility that it might be far longer than he'd ever anticipated before he held her in his arms again.

CYN STOOD BACK as Raphael and the others left. She didn't go to the door. If their enemy was watching the house, they didn't want anyone to see or recognize her. Especially since there was still the possibility that they might try to kidnap and use her against Raphael. Besides, she and Raphael had said their good-byes before they ever made it as far as the living room. There was nothing else to say.

That didn't stop her from racing to the security room in the vault to watch as Raphael climbed into the limo with Juro. Ken'ichi was staying at the house with her, as was Elke, but Raphael was taking the rest of his vamp guards, a full dozen of his best warriors, along with him. One of them was driving the limo, while Juro sat in the passenger seat up front, and Raphael sat in the back alone. It made her heart ache that she wasn't there with him, but there were good reasons for that. Just as there was a good reason why Juro sat up front instead of joining Raphael in the back. Apparently, it was all about propriety when it came to these old vamps, and Raphael was simply playing the game, to lull them into complacency if nothing else.

The rest of the guards piled into two other SUVs, leaving a single vehicle at the house for Cyn or the human guards, all of whom had stayed behind. Normally, those guards would be winding down their day, having dinner, kicking back, going to sleep early in order to be ready for the beginning of their sunrise shift. But not tonight. No one was kicking back tonight. They were gearing up to fight, and packing to leave at the same time. No one knew exactly what this night would bring, least of all Cyn. But they all hoped they'd be going home at the end of it.

As soon as Raphael was gone, Cyn would be doing her own packing and preparing. Clothes she could live without, or buy whatever she needed, but weapons were another matter. She'd checked into Hawaii's gun laws before leaving L.A. With legal residence and enough time, one could obtain a permit and purchase just about anything short of a submachine gun. But while she could probably finesse the residence, time was something she wouldn't have if everything went to shit. So, she'd brought her own arsenal. The duffle bag stored in the closet she shared with Raphael was full of blatantly illegal, but very necessary equipment. It contained mostly guns, but a couple of knives, too, and ammo, ninety percent of which was what Cyn called her vampire killer rounds. There was also a ballistic vest, custom made, since she was difficult to fit and admittedly a pain in the ass about wearing a vest. She'd asked Robbie to bring his gear, as well, although she doubted it had been necessary to ask. Even if he hadn't been the excellent bodyguard he was, his years in the Army had left him with habits that were difficult to break. Good habits in Cyn's view. She was sure not everyone would agree with her on that, but fuck 'em.

She watched until not even the red glow of the taillights could be seen, and then she went back to their room to prepare. And yeah, sure, she hoped for the best, but in her experience, hope was a fragile shield. She went to prepare for the worst.

Chapter Seven

RAPHAEL NODDED to the head of his vampire guard detachment, telling him without words to be prepared. They'd discussed what might come of this evening, considered every possible outcome they could imagine. His guard knew what to do.

Predictably, his vampire hosts had forbidden Raphael's guards from approaching the house. They were stopped a good hundred yards down the road, before the turnoff to the short driveway. Even his driver had to step out and join the others.

Only Juro was allowed to continue all the way with him, which was nothing more than they'd expected. As he stepped out of the limo, Raphael scanned the residence. There were ten vampires present, three of them lords. Not a surprise there, either. They wouldn't want to face him with anything less.

He and Juro climbed the stairs. A single master vampire stood just inside the open front door, eyeing Raphael with blatant dislike.

"Godard," Raphael said coolly, acknowledging the other vamp. "I'm assuming your presence means Mathilde is inside. Are you still her attack dog, or has she finally made good on her promises, and elevated you to her bed?"

Godard's eyes flashed red with rage, before he seemed to remember whom he was facing. Either that, or he simply remembered that his mistress, the Lady Mathilde, was not forgiving of minions who disobeyed her.

"Raphael," Godard sneered. "My lady is looking forward to renewing your acquaintance after so long."

"Is she?" Raphael asked, more curious than he would ever admit to a worm like Godard. The vampire actually had been more than Mathilde's attack dog all those years ago, before Raphael left Europe. Godard had been her torturer, a job that he'd embraced with far too much enthusiasm.

Mathilde's presence here in Hawaii wasn't a surprise, however. She was a powerful vampire, and certainly ambitious enough to want more than what Europe had to offer her. That she'd brought Godard . . . that was more troubling. Although it was entirely possible the sadistic vampire had finally gotten as close to Mathilde as he'd always desired.

Armed with knowledge of at least one of the lords he was going to meet, Raphael strode warily forward. This was the residence he and Cyn had reconnoitered two nights ago, and nothing much had changed. The difference tonight was that Raphael was inside, close enough to weigh the combined power of those gathered here and measure it against his own. The power signature in the house came up wanting, which he found both reassuring and not.

If necessary, he could stand alone against every vampire here, either individually or all at once. But they had to know that. And what about all those vampires that Juro had detected at the other house nearby. Where were *they*? Why bring them to the island, if the European lords weren't going to use them to stand against Raphael?

He exchanged a knowing glance with Juro, who was powerful enough in his own right to have calculated the strength gathered, and smart enough to have caught the same troubling concern.

Permitting himself no more than that one glance, however, Raphael kept his face carefully expressionless—what Cyn called his master of the universe face—as he followed the vampire who'd met them at the door and who was now escorting them down the hall to the room where he could *feel* the three vampire lords waiting for him. He recognized Mathilde now, as one of those. But he caught the taste of another familiar mind, and knew that Rhys Patterson, the master of the Hawaiian Islands, was waiting there also. Raphael felt a moment's relief that Patterson was still alive; he'd feared the worst after meeting the welcome delegation the other night. But at the same time, the Hawaiian's presence worried him. Had Patterson conspired with the Europeans, after all? Or were they using him?

Godard slid open a pair of teak pocket doors, then stood back, inviting Raphael to enter first. Juro snorted in disdain and stepped in front of the other vampire, not so subtly brushing against him as he passed and knocking the much smaller vamp back a few paces. Juro paused, blocking Raphael from entering as he scanned the room and its occupants, his head turning slowly from side to side.

Raphael waited patiently, although he already suspected the identities of all three lords inside the room. The *taste* of their minds had grown stronger with every step he'd taken toward the house. It had been a long time since he'd left Europe, but not so long that he would have forgotten any of the old lords, the ones who'd refused to make room for him despite his obvious superiority in power. The same ones who had now brought the vampires of two continents to the brink of war because of their persistent refusal to acknowledge the growing powers among them.

In front of him, Juro's massive shoulders lifted in a deep breath, then slowly exhaled as he turned and bowed to Raphael. "Sire," he said simply, his eyes saying everything he couldn't, or wouldn't, say in front of their audience. Juro hated this. He saw its necessity, but he hated it.

Raphael gave his security chief a half smile, resting a hand on his shoulder briefly as he walked by.

They waited for him in a line, standing there dressed in their finery like something out of a costume drama on American public television. Mathilde was the strongest of the three. She ruled a significant territory in the south of France that included Nice, and was one of those most opposed to sharing. She also happened to be the Sire of the recently departed Damien, the vampire who, only a few days ago, had been a guest in Raphael's interrogation chamber. Raphael had been somewhat surprised at learning of Damien's parentage, since if it were up to Mathilde, young vampires who tested out as too powerful would be destroyed soon after their awakening. She liked her young males good-looking and just strong enough to serve her purposes without being threatening. She'd liked Raphael once upon a time, until she'd discovered the depths of his power. And then she'd turned her eyes elsewhere. They had a history, he and Mathilde. And he wasn't at all surprised to find her at the helm of this invasion.

But Mathilde alone wasn't a match for Raphael, and she knew it. It was why she'd sent Damien and his child Violet to confront Raphael instead of doing it herself. And the reason she didn't stand alone against him now.

The two who stood with her tonight were Berkhard of Munich and Hubert of Lyon. Significant powers in their own right, although one step below Mathilde. But even with the two males by her side, Mathilde couldn't defeat Raphael, which made him wonder, yet again, why she'd insisted on this meeting.

"Raphael." It was Mathilde who spoke first, her voice the childlike chirp of a much younger girl, though she'd been a married woman in her late twenties by the time she'd been taken and turned by her now-dead Sire. She stood there in a pale blue satin period gown that his dead sister Alexandra would have appreciated. Raphael half-expected her to lift her skirts and curtsey like the aristocratic lady she'd once been.

He glanced at Berkhard and Hubert, in their black formalwear, waiting for them to voice their own greetings. But they'd clearly designated the speaking part of the evening to Mathilde, as neither of the males offered anything more than a dip of the head in acknowledgment, standing as silent as if they were mute.

Raphael's gaze then traveled beyond the greeting line to Rhys Patterson who stood several steps behind the three lords. He was dressed much like Raphael, although without the tie. Rhys had been in the Islands so long, he probably no longer owned a tie. His stare was fixed on Raphael, as though he would have liked to say something, or was trying to communicate some silent message. But whatever it was, Raphael wasn't receiving it. Raphael permitted no reaction to show in his expression or body language, but inwardly he was dismayed at this evidence that Rhys was not a willing participant. He remembered the two unfamiliar vampires who'd shown up as the Hawaiian lord's emissaries. Had Mathilde and her crew harmed Rhys's people, or threatened to do so?

Raphael turned a flat stare on Mathilde, meeting her pale blue eyes. "Mathilde," he acknowledged. "Berkhard, Hubert," he added, glancing at each of the others in turn.

"You're looking well, Raphael," Mathilde said pleasantly, as if they were old friends greeting each other.

His mouth barely moved in an amused smile. "Are we pretending to like each other now, Mathilde? What do you want?"

She *tsk*ed loudly. "Your time in the New World has coarsened you," she chided him. "Can we not conduct ourselves as befit our stations?"

Raphael's smile grew slightly. "Our stations, Mathilde? I was born the son of a Muscovite peasant. I believe my behavior is well in keeping with my *station*."

Her mouth pursed with distaste. "Very well." She stepped forward and offered a handshake, although it was more in the way of a fine lady offering her hand to be kissed by someone unworthy of the honor.

He took the half-step necessary to bring him close enough, then took her fragile fingers in his own much larger hand . . . and several things happened at once.

Across the room, Rhys Patterson's mind suddenly blared a warning. Raphael had time only to blast a warning of his own before an invisible force snapped into place with a sound like thunder, and metal bands circled his wrists, metal so cold it burned, searing his flesh and marking his bones.

Juro roared his fury as Raphael slammed to his knees, shaking his head as he struggled to pull his thoughts together. He reached for his power but for the first time in nearly 500 years, it wasn't there. Or rather, it was, but he couldn't reach it. It was as if some great weight was pressing down on him and it was all he could do simply to remember who he was and what he was doing there.

But then Raphael hadn't lived all those centuries without learning a few things. He didn't have his power, but he still had his intellect. Forcing himself to ignore the fear trying to choke the life from him—fear not for himself, but for his people, for Juro . . . for Cyn—he evaluated the situation using everything he knew, everything he'd learned, and what he found both terrified and infuriated him.

His people had known there were more vampires on the island than could be accounted for, but they hadn't come close to guessing the real numbers. Violet had warned the Europeans after Mexico. She'd given them proof that ten wasn't enough. But they hadn't doubled or even tripled that number. They'd brought ten times that number, more than Raphael could accurately guess. Mathilde and the others must have been shielding like crazy to protect so many from his discovery. There were more than a hundred master vampires arrayed against him somewhere, their minds working in tandem, and every one of them was focused solely on containing Raphael.

He'd been arrogant and a fool. Cyn was right. He should have killed Violet when he'd had the chance, before she could run home to share information with Mathilde. But his pride had made him use her; a message sent to her handlers that they could not defeat him, that they should drop their ill-considered plans for expansion into North America. He hadn't once considered that they would take it as a challenge. That instead of acknowledging his superior strength and backing off as powerful vampires had done for centuries, they'd joined forces and set themselves to overcoming his advantage. They must have been planning this for months. It would have taken at least that long to gather together so many master vampires. And how had the locals not noticed? Hawaii was a relatively insular place. You couldn't drop a hundred vampires into one community and hope no one would notice. How were they being fed?

He'd been wrong about Mexico. So wrong in his arrogance. Mexico wasn't some grand gesture on Mathilde's part. She'd been planning this incursion long before Mexico. She'd no doubt learned something from that confrontation, but it was entirely possible that entire fiasco had been played out simply to fool him into complacency, into believing they were still feeling him out and coming up short.

"Stop him, Raphael, or I'll kill him."

Mathilde's childish voice brought Raphael up short, dragging him back into the room where Juro was standing over him protectively, tossing aside vampire after vampire as they tried to force him back. Mathilde and her fellow conspirators had retreated to the sidelines, of course. Risking nothing of themselves, content to stand by and watch as their own children were damaged or destroyed in the face of Juro's rage.

"Juro," Raphael said.

His security chief threw a final vampire across the room, then paused, breathing heavily, but with emotion, not physical strain. Juro could have tossed full-grown men around for hours without raising a sweat.

"Sire," he said, his voice filled with grief.

Raphael found he could look up easily enough and meet Juro's eyes. "You know what to do," he said.

He could see the denial in Juro's tormented gaze, the desire to refuse. But the big vampire was too loyal, too disciplined. He knew what had to be done, and what dice had to be rolled.

Juro's eyes closed as he drew a resigned breath through his nose, releasing it in a long exhale before his eyes opened again and he nodded. "Yes, Sire."

Raphael smiled. "Trust, Juro. And take care of my people."

Juro nodded again.

"That's a good boy," Mathilde chittered almost gleefully, as if she'd already won.

Raphael hated her in that moment, not so much for himself, but for Juro, for her inability to recognize the loyalty and discipline it took for the big vampire to remain obedient to a Sire who was quite literally kneeling before him, helpless. To trust that this was not the end. Because it wasn't. That silly chit Mathilde might think so, but Raphael knew better. She had won the round, no doubt of that. But this was war, and there were many battles yet to be fought.

"Raphael will remain with us," Mathilde said, and Raphael realized she was speaking to Juro who was regarding her with undisguised hatred. "But you and all of his vampires and guards will return to Los Angeles, or wherever else you're from," she added dismissively, as if L.A. were some two-cow town in the American Wild West. "We are permitting this as a show of good faith."

Raphael doubted that was true. It was more likely that they'd run out of strong vampires and couldn't hold his powerful children and him at the same time.

"You may go back to Raphael's estate and defend your territory. We seek only a fair fight."

It was everything Raphael could do not to scoff in her face. If they'd wanted a fair fight, they'd have been willing to face the territory's proper lord, rather than disable him with trickery. Because it wasn't only the hundred vampires holding him down, it was the metal cuffs wrapped around his wrists like bands of cold fire. They were ancient and reeked of magic, and just as the hundred masters were crushing his vampiric power, the bracelets were stealing his will, sapping his tremendous physical strength.

"You will depart these islands before sunrise, or your Sire dies."

Raphael could feel Juro's torment. They'd succeeded in containing his power, but not the link with his children. Which meant . . . Cyn. She'd know something was terribly wrong by now. Her heart would be demanding that she race over here to save him, but she was smarter than that. He was counting on it. He focused briefly on the image of her in his head, the intellect behind her beautiful, green eyes, the wicked smile on her lush lips . . . her loyal heart and brave soul.

I love you, my Cyn. He didn't know if she heard him or not. But they'd been separated before and he'd found a way to reach her. He would do it again. It wouldn't be easy; it might take him a day or two to break through the hold they had on him. But he would do it. He wouldn't leave her alone. He wouldn't leave *her*. Not like this.

"Juro," he said again, drawing his loyal security chief's attention. "You know what to do," he repeated firmly.

Juro's expression turned grim and he nodded. "Yes, Sire. I will take care of it."

"Thank you." He could tell Juro wanted to say more, but anything they said at this point would give too much away. So they exchanged a silent farewell, then with a final hate-filled glare for Mathilde and her posse, the big Japanese vampire spun on his heel and strode from the room.

Leaving Raphael alone with his captors.

"Forgive me, Lord Raphael." Rhys's voice was low and raspy as if he hadn't used it in a while. "They have all of my children." The master vampire's emotions were roiling with regret and fear, all genuine enough. But he was staring at Raphael intently, as if willing him to understand something he wasn't saying.

Raphael gazed back at him, giving away nothing of his thoughts. There would be time to puzzle out what Rhys was trying to tell him, but for now. . . . "I understand, Rhys. Are your people safe at least? Was anyone harmed?"

Rhys hung his head as if ashamed, or maybe in despair for his failure in communicating whatever his hidden message had been. When he looked up, his eyes were pink with unshed tears. "As far as I know, they are well, and true to their rightful lord."

Raphael permitted himself a smile then, as much for Rhys's benefit as to goad his captors.

"Their rightful lord." Mathilde's ridiculous voice interrupted their exchange. "Neither of you knows the meaning of it," she insisted stridently. "We are your betters in every way. *We* are your rightful lords and will soon rule all of you as is our due."

Raphael shifted his gaze to the ancient female, letting his expression say what he thought of her and her yards of blue satin. "This is a blatant violation of the flag of truce, Mathilde," he said calmly. He knew she wouldn't care. That much was obvious. But he wanted it stated for the record, so to speak, so that later on, she couldn't claim that he hadn't warned her. "By the laws of our people, this action is a declaration of war."

She bristled at what she no doubt considered lecturing on his part. "I know our laws as well as you, Raphael. But your people will surrender quickly enough if your life is at stake."

"You think so?" Raphael asked, letting his amusement show.

Mathilde stared, then gathered what passed for her courage into a sneer. "I so look forward to meeting your female, Raphael. The stories I've heard . . ." She shook her head. "Ridiculous to think that a single human could actually accomplish all that they attribute to her. But then, it's part and parcel of the legend, isn't it?" She raked her glance over his kneeling form. "The great Raphael. I am not impressed."

Raphael permitted a vicious grin to crease his face as he remembered the last vampire who had said that to him, and where that vampire was now. He responded to Mathilde as he had to Damien. "You will be."

Chapter Eight

CYN PACED THE living room, unable to sit still. She'd started out in the security control room, but once Raphael's motorcade had disappeared, there'd been nothing to see. And even though she knew logically that the convoy's return would show up on the security screen, she couldn't stay trapped in that little room any longer.

Robbie had appeared a few minutes after Raphael left. He'd walked right over to Cyn and pulled her into a big hug, something no one else would have dared. "It'll be okay, sweetheart. You'll see."

Cyn hugged him back, but couldn't agree with his assessment. She had a feeling they'd be hiking through the jungle before the evening was over, and there was only one reason that would happen. Because everything had gone to hell and it hadn't even bothered with the handbasket.

Feeling ready to leap out of her skin, she was on her way back to the security room when she felt it, a hammer blow of power that had her grabbing the doorway, convinced the earth itself was shaking beneath her feet. One minute Raphael was in her mind as always, and the next, he disappeared. Gone. A terrifying heartbeat later, he came back, but he was weaker, so weak she barely recognized his essence as the powerful vampire she knew him to be. She spun, racing back to the living room where Robbie stood by one of the windows as if on guard.

"Gear up, Rob," she said tightly. "We're going live."

He stared at her. "Cyn? What happened?" Robbie had no direct link to Raphael. He wouldn't have felt any of what she'd experienced.

"I don't know yet, but it's bad." She didn't waste any more words, knew that Robbie wouldn't wait for any. The bookshelf door was standing open, and she slipped through the opening, racing down the hall to the room she shared with Raphael. Elke popped out of the control room.

"Cyn?" Elke's voice was tight with worry, as close to panicked as Cyn had ever heard it.

"Did you feel it?" she asked Elke as she punched in the code to their room.

"What was that? Is Raphael—"

Cyn spun around with a vicious expression. Was Raphael dead? That's what Elke wanted to know, what she'd been afraid to ask. "He's your Sire, Elke," she snarled. "You know the answer to that."

Elke nodded, rotating her shoulders, shaking her hands and arms as if casting off her alarm. "You're right, I'm sorry. What are you doing?"

"Arrangements have been made—"

"What arrangements? I don't know about any—"

"No one knows. Raphael wanted it that way. Robbie and I have been working during the day, setting things up. But the time has come. Be ready to move."

Ken'ichi appeared behind Elke. "Juro—" he said, his already deep voice a low rumble of tension, his forehead creased with worry. Cyn had to force herself not to stare. It was more emotion than she'd ever seen on his usually impassive face.

"My brother is *furious* . . . and terrified."

All of the breath left Cyn's lungs. What would it take to terrify Juro? Gripping the door edge so hard that it hurt, she looked within herself, checking for the spark that was Raphael. Her hold on the door was the only thing that kept her standing when she found it, found him. Still frighteningly weak, but there.

At that moment, the radio squawked in the control room and Ken'ichi sped back down the hall in a burst of vampire speed. Cyn followed in his wake, arriving at the open door just in time to see Ken'ichi pull on a headset, then tap furiously on the keyboard.

"What is it?" Cyn demanded.

"Gone," he muttered.

"Gone?" Cyn heard the panic in her own voice as she asked the question.

"The signal," Ken'ichi clarified. "I can't . . ." He stiffened abruptly. "Juro," he whispered.

Cyn wanted to grab his massive shoulders and shake him, tell him enough with the terse bullshit. It was time to use his fucking words.

"Talk to me," she said with forced patience.

Ken'ichi raised his eyes to meet hers. He looked so much like Juro.

"Juro was raging, his anger a storm in my mind, and then like a switch being thrown, he was gone. And now . . ." He turned back to the keyboard and started working furiously again. "Our comms are down. I can't reach the security detail."

"That's it," Cyn snapped and spun back toward the hallway. "Robbie!" she called. "We're going out there. Elke, you're with us. Ken—"

"Bad idea, Cyn," Robbie cautioned, walking toward her. "Raphael wanted you out of sight for a reason. All that prep we did could go to shit if you go out there."

"I can't just sit—"

"And what if that's what they're waiting for? What's the best leverage they could have against Raphael, huh? I'll tell you. It's you."

"But they've got—"

"You don't *know* what's happening out there. The comms are down, Cyn. That's all you know so far."

"I *felt* it happen. Something awful—" Her words were cut off by a high-pitched squawk that had everyone covering their ears. Voices came next, one voice above the others, trying to reach Ken'ichi.

"Base, go ahead," Ken'ichi said.

"We're at the house," the same voice said, and Cyn recognized it as belonging to the head of Raphael's security detail. She heard shouting and then, "We've found Juro, he's . . . yes, sir." More yelling and then . . .

"Cynthia?" It was Juro's voice, tight with tension and as grave as she'd ever heard him.

Cyn pushed into the room as Ken'ichi put the comms on speaker.

"What happened?" she demanded. "Where's Raphael?"

"We're on our way back," he said, which didn't answer her question.

"Is Raphael—"

"We'll be there in three minutes, Cyn," Juro said gently.

Cyn blinked in surprise, quickly followed by fear. Juro never called her "Cyn." Everyone else did, even Raphael. But Juro didn't.

Her lungs constricted with terror. She reached out blindly, her hand falling on Ken'ichi's thick shoulder. "He's not dead," she whispered, the words barely audible.

"He's not."

She looked up in surprise as Ken'ichi's bass voice agreed with her.

"You would know," he said, meeting her gaze solemnly. "We all would."

Cyn swallowed hard, then nodded. Movement on the screen drew her attention to the trail of vehicles racing toward the house, spitting gravel all the way. She jumped to her feet too fast, nearly tripping over the chair in her urgency to get out there to meet them.

The front door opened before she got to it. Juro stood there, his face pink with tears as he stared at her.

Cyn jerked to a stop. "Juro?"

"They took him," he said simply. "I fought, but . . . he ordered me to stop."

"Raphael?"

He stepped further into the house, closing the door behind him. "He made me promise, Cynthia. He knew—"

"He knew they'd try something like this," she said, suddenly deflated. "He knew they might take him."

Juro nodded. "He gave me orders. If it happened, when it happened." He'd crossed the room while they spoke, standing right next to her now. His black eyes were wells of sorrow, his face wet with bloody tears.

"They've demanded we leave the island, or—"

"I'm not going anywhere without Raphael," she snarled. "And someone better damned well tell me what the fuck is happening. Who has him? And how?"

"Mathilde—" Juro paused, gathering his breath when Cyn threw her hands up in disgust. "She's one of the vampires who was there tonight," he explained. "There were others, but she seemed to be in charge. She rules a territory in Southern France. She's very old, Cynthia. Much older than Raphael, and very dangerous."

"Is she stronger than he is?" Cyn asked in confusion. "How could she have—?"

"Because she was not alone. She had not only the two who stood with her but so many others. A hundred or more, all working—"

"More than a hundred?" The knowledge was like a boulder crashing into her chest, crushing her heart, her hope.

"A hundred or a thousand, they can still be killed," Robbie growled behind her.

Cyn spun around to see him standing in the doorway.

"We're ready for them, babe," he told her. "Don't forget that."

She stared at him, fighting tears. Tears wouldn't do any good. She clenched her jaw until it hurt, then swallowed her tears and nodded.

"You don't need to kill all of them," Ken'ichi said quietly, coming up next to Robbie.

"What do you mean?" Cyn asked.

"My brother is right," Juro agreed. "These are master vampires, not lords, but like all vampires, they will be more accustomed to working alone rather than as a single force. Some will be stronger than others, but you would only need to destroy one or two, to disrupt the flow between them and create a weak spot for Raphael to break through."

A tentative smile creased Cyn's face. "A weak spot. I can do that."

"Cynthia," Juro said heavily. "I would give you that chance, but. . . . We have to leave. Raphael's life—"

Cyn opened her mouth to snap at him, to insist once again that she wasn't going anywhere without Raphael, but something in Juro's face made her stop. His gaze was steady on hers, but his eyes suddenly shifted to the right, in the direction of the room she shared with Raphael.

Cyn frowned, then her eyes widened in understanding and she shouted, "Fuck you, Juro!" and stormed away, her hand slapping the heavy door angrily as she shoved it open.

"Cynthia," Juro called after her, and followed down the hall through the open doorway, pushing it closed behind him.

Cyn spun around, staring questioningly at Juro. He held up a finger, telling her to wait as he seemed to listen to something she couldn't hear.

"All right," he said suddenly. "Ken'ichi's jamming electronics for now. He can't leave it too long without raising suspicions, so we have to talk fast."

"You think there's a spy in the house? One of the guards?" Cyn asked, remembering Raphael's suspicion that there might be a spy on his Malibu estate.

"None of our people, no. I believe they bugged the house before we got here."

"Are we safe in here?"

"I suspect that they can't hear us as long as we're in the vault. Patterson didn't know about these rooms and wouldn't have had the password to the door even if he did. But I'd rather err on the side of caution."

Cyn nodded. "Okay, so what happened?" she asked, trying for calm.

"It was a trap—"

"I know that much, but—"

"—which Raphael expected," Juro continued through her interruption. "But we didn't expect this. I was standing right next to him. I saw everything, but I still don't understand. Mathilde shook Raphael's hand and . . . the next thing I knew, he was on his knees, as if he no longer had strength to stand. She must have used magic against him, or some kind of mind trick. I've never seen . . . Raphael," he said in disbelief, his expression bereft, like a child who'd discovered for the first time that his parent wasn't infallible.

Cyn was just about to nudge him to continue, when Juro visibly gathered his wits and said, "She stole his physical strength somehow, drained him for a critical moment. It was enough for them to contain his power."

"Them. Who's them?"

"All those master vampires she had backing her up. I've never felt so many minds in one place, and all focused on the same goal. Someone must be binding them, Mathilde maybe, or maybe the three of them together—"

"Where are they?" Cyn demanded, cutting off his babbling. Juro wasn't normally as taciturn as his twin, but he didn't chatter either. Cyn knew what she'd felt. It was like standing next to a huge crater the moment a meteor hit. How much worse must it have been for Juro, standing so close to Raphael when it happened. "Will they be together? I mean, all in one place? The same place where Raphael—"

"Not the same place. They've already abandoned that house. That's why the comms went dead, why they knocked me out. I wasn't out long, but by the time I woke, they were gone and they took Raphael with them."

"Fuck," Cyn swore, but she didn't dwell. There was no time for such indulgences. They had to move now and they had to move fast.

"They've ordered us to leave the island, to leave Hawaii altogether, or they'll kill him."

Cyn stared. "Kill him?"

"They won't do it," he said wearily, rubbing his forehead. "Raphael's death would be felt by every vampire on the continent. Challengers would come from all over to fight for the territory. Mathilde doesn't want that, or she'd have killed Raphael outright instead of capturing him. She may be strong, but she wouldn't be able to rely on her allied lords in this. Challengers can pull power from their supporters, but they must still meet one on one in battle. And there would be battles. Jared or I, or any number of others loyal to Raphael, are strong enough to seize the territory, and our enemies know that.

"What she wants is to waltz into Malibu and issue a challenge to Raphael personally. And when he doesn't respond to her challenge, because she's made sure he can't, she'll declare herself the winner by forfeit."

"But you won't stand back and let that happen."

Juro shook his head. "Lucas won't either, nor will Duncan. But Raphael's territory holds thousands of vampires. Mathilde may plan on seizing power and then draining Raphael's vampires dry in order to defeat anyone who challenges her takeover."

"But power also goes the other way, doesn't it? Raphael's vampires suck power *away* from him far more than they help him out."

"It may seem that way, but Raphael can draw from them whenever he wants. He doesn't take advantage of it, but in a war he certainly would. And they would give willingly. He is much beloved."

Juro's posture changed, taking on that blank mien that meant he was listening to some vampire or other in his head. Probably his brother.

"Our time is short. I'm sorry, Cynthia, but I have to go back to Malibu. Even if Mathilde and her ilk had not demanded it, Raphael commanded me before we ever left Los Angeles. They will attack soon, thinking us weak and unprepared. We are not, but Jared will need my support to stand against them. Mathilde alone he could hold off, but if they join forces again . . ."

"I understand. You and the others—"

"You must leave with me," he said gently. "They want all of us—"

"Juro," she said flatly. "I am not leaving this island without him. They don't know I'm here. They don't know about Robbie, or, for that matter, Elke either. We will stay, and we will free Raphael. And then we'll kill every last one of them."

Juro's mouth tightened into a flat line as he stared down at her. "My Sire chose well, Cynthia. You are his match. But for all your courage, you will need more than Elke. She is a fierce fighter, and loyal to both you and Raphael, but as vampires go, her power is not enough."

"I'm not going to fight this battle on their terms. I can't match them when it comes to your kind of power, so I'll do it my way. They won't expect it, and I'm going to use that against them."

Juro nodded. "A smart strategy, but in the end you may need power. Our kind of power."

Cyn shrugged. "You said it yourself, you need to get back home. Besides, they'll be watching for you, especially, to leave the island."

"But not my brother."

Cyn frowned. "What do you mean?"

"Ken'ichi has always preferred to stand back, but his strength is a match for my own."

Cyn's eyes widened. Juro and his twin were identical in appearance, but she'd learned enough over the last couple of years to know that appearance meant little when it came to vampires. Ken'ichi was always so much in the background, in the shadow of his brother, that Cyn had assumed his power was less. But maybe it was only his ambition that was less, or maybe he simply preferred life in the shadows.

"But won't they make sure both of you leave?" she asked.

"Some shuffling on my part and a nudge in the right direction, and Mathilde's spy will see what he expects to see. We are identical, after all."

Cyn nodded. "Done. We'll slip out the back while you all make a fuss of leaving out front." She started to turn away, details storming through her head as she thought of all the things she needed to do in the next ten minutes.

"Cynthia," Juro said quietly, drawing her attention back to him. "Bring Raphael home. We'll hold the territory for him. But bring him home."

"Count on it," Cyn said. Some people might have hugged at this point, but Cyn wasn't a hugger, and the only person she'd ever seen Juro hug was Luci. So, she met his eyes with what she hoped was confidence and determination and gave a short nod.

Juro did the same, then, without a word, he turned and left the room, closing the door behind him.

Cyn immediately pulled out her cell and dialed Robbie. "Juro thinks we're bugged," she said when he answered. She didn't have to say anything else; the former Army Ranger knew more than she did about covert operations. "Elke's with us," she told him. "So's Ken'ichi. We're leaving through the back in five minutes."

Chapter Nine

CYN TORE THROUGH the room she'd shared with Raphael, her brain going a thousand miles a minute, trying to remember everything she needed, all of the plans they'd made . . . anything that would prevent her from thinking about Raphael and what he was going through, what they might be doing to him. She'd seen the kind of pain he could inflict on others. She wanted to believe that she'd know if he was in pain, if that bitch Mathilde was torturing him, but she couldn't say that for sure. Not with the link between them as weakened as it was now. Not with Raphael's tendency to protect her.

She jammed a few toiletries into a zippered canvas tote, hissing irritably when she sliced her hand on the scissors already in there. It seemed stupid to be worrying about her favorite shampoo and soap at a time like this, but she knew from experience that such conveniences would matter as the days dragged on. There was no telling how long it would take to get to Raphael, or how much longer to figure out a way to free him once they found him. She and her team would be four against who knew how many? Not only the hundred or more master vampires who were tag-teaming Raphael to keep him prisoner, but whatever security Mathilde had brought along on top of them. And then there were the logistics to consider. Moving Raphael in daylight would be problematic. It would do no good to free him only to let the sunlight injure, or even kill, him instead. And if they decided to stage their rescue at night? What if he'd been tortured, what if he was injured or starved, and unable to move under his own power?

She had so many questions, and none of them would have answers until they found Raphael. Hell, he'd already been moved from the house where the meeting had been held. The meeting that wasn't a meeting at all, but an ambush. Chances were good that he was still on Kauai for now. It would be risky to try to move him tonight. Juro had told Cyn that Mathilde would have spies at the airport, but the vampire bitch had to know, or at least suspect, that Raphael had spies there, too. And what about the vampires' power circle, the hundred or so master vamps? Were they here on Kauai? They'd have to be moved, too. And all before sunrise. Could the hundred already be on another island? Was it possible for

Mathilde to link their minds into a single unit over such a long distance? She'd have to ask Juro before he took off.

Cyn wanted to ignore the blood dripping from her hand. It was a shallow cut and would clot soon enough. But this was the tropics. A small wound could become a serious infection. So she fished one of those big Band-Aids out of her tote, and slapped it on, then zipped the tote and threw it into the duffle already packed on her bed—their bed. She'd left the door open and when she heard Juro's deep voice, she strode down the hall to the kitchen where he was giving orders for everyone's imminent departure. Standing in the doorway to the private vault, she caught his attention with a jerk of her head, then retreated back to her room. Her and Raphael's room, she corrected mentally.

"They'll move him off-island, won't they?" she asked.

Juro turned from closing the door and gave her a reluctant nod. "Not tonight, but sooner rather than later."

"He could end up anywhere," she whispered, feeling despair threatening to drown her.

"Not anywhere, Cynthia," Juro replied, putting a hand on her arm.

She sucked in a deep breath. She had to focus. "You're right. A hundred vampires can't hide just anywhere. And they can't be moved that easily, either. They also have to eat, don't they? Maybe even more than usual with the energy they're expending."

"Mathilde will have planned for that. This was not something she came up with on the fly."

She almost punched him then. Like she needed something more to get depressed about. But he was right. She knew he was right. Damn him.

"You're right," she said grimly. "But still, a hundred vampires or more. You don't move that many vamps in a two-seater Cessna, and even vampire planes file flight plans."

Juro nodded his agreement. "We can help with that. Once we're back in L.A., Raphael's contacts are extensive."

"Right. We need a way to stay in touch. Burner phones would be best."

Juro grunted dismissively. "I'm not security chief for nothing. I've given Ken'ichi a box of burners along with a list of numbers you can reach us at. Your phones are numbered one through twenty-five. Ours are twenty-six through fifty. We'll use a fresh one each day. If we need more than that—"

"We won't," Cyn insisted. "We can't."

Juro looked as if he wanted to disagree, but instead he nodded grimly. "You'll check in daily."

"Yes, boss."

"I'm serious, Cynthia."

Cyn met his solemn gaze with one of her own. "Me, too, big guy. We'll stay in touch. But right now, we have to disappear."

"Just remember. I know you like to work alone, but you're not alone in this."

Cyn looked up at him and smiled. "I know. I've got my team, but even more than that . . . I've got Raphael."

Juro gave her a half-smile, then pulled the door open and disappeared down the hall. Cyn went back to the bed and pulled on her shoulder holster, then checked the load on her favorite Glock 17—nothing but vamp killer rounds for this mission—snugged the 9mm in place, then tucked an identical weapon into her waistband at the small of her back. The black cotton jacket she shrugged on was going to be too hot, but she could hardly walk around in nothing but a T-shirt and harness with her guns on full display. Black jeans were tucked into the top of her combat boots, and she was as ready as she could be for a trek through the jungle. She and Robbie had secreted a car nearby—a mid-size, four-door import, typical tourist rental.

She zipped her duffle and slung it over her shoulder, and was turning for the door when she caught sight of the leather jacket that Raphael had flung over the back of a chair when they'd arrived. He'd commented on the suffocating heat, and they'd laughed, because usually it was the cold that irritated him. Cyn had teased him about being impossible to please. Tears filled her eyes now as she remembered how he'd locked the door and shown her just how easily *she* could please him, how they'd pleased each other until they were both quite literally drained. The tears spilled out, wetting her cheeks, as she admitted to herself at least that she was genuinely afraid for the first time in her life. She'd fought battles before. Hell, she'd survived a gun fight with the Russian mafia and faced down that asshole Jabril who would happily have raped her to death then drained her blood as she lay dying.

But she'd never loved anyone the way she loved Raphael. If she lost him . . .

She swallowed hard, scrubbing the tears from her face. She couldn't think that way. She *would* get him back. Raphael was counting on her. He'd practically warned her that this very thing would happen. Grabbing his leather jacket, she shoved it into the duffle, then rushed around adding a change of clothes for him. Once he was rescued, he'd need them. She zipped everything into the duffle and hitched the bag securely over her shoulder. A final look around assured her there was nothing in this room that they couldn't live without. She had Raphael's iPad in her duffle along with her laptop. Everything else was replaceable. With a silent nod of encouragement for herself, she left the rest behind and set off to rescue the love of her life.

RAPHAEL KEPT his eyes closed behind the blindfold, kept his muscles relaxed beneath the powerful hold of the enchanted manacles they'd bound him with. Magic. He was a practical person, believing in his own strength above everything else. All that he'd accomplished, all that he'd built, was the product of his own power and intellect, his hard work and determination. But one couldn't be a vampire without believing in magic. Science could possibly explain the vampire symbiote, with its massive healing powers, but it couldn't account for Raphael's ability to stop a vampire's heart with a thought from a thousand miles away. Or to break every bone in an enemy's body simply by wishing it. There was magic in the world. It had simply faded from human awareness until it only *seemed* to be nonexistent.

But Mathilde was so much older than he was, hundreds of years older. Enough that she might have been around when magic was waning but still active in the world, when such devices as the manacles currently sapping his strength still littered the earth, buried in caves and ruins.

He swallowed a sigh of equal parts resignation at his predicament and disgust that he hadn't anticipated it. Under other circumstances, he might have feared for his life. But Mathilde and the others didn't want him dead, at least not yet. There was no doubt in his mind that they planned to kill him before the end. But not until after they'd conquered North America. And they seemed quite confident that they would succeed to that end. They hadn't even bothered to guard their conversations around him. Rather the opposite, in fact. They'd taken gloating pleasure in letting him know just how easily the continent was going to fall to them.

Their confidence was badly misplaced, but he wasn't going to be the one to tell them that. In fact, he wasn't going to tell them anything. They'd tried to engage him at the beginning, taunting him, making up lies about Juro and the others as they evacuated back to California, about the state of affairs among his people in Malibu. Did they think he was head blind? That, because they'd bound his body and smothered his power, he'd lost that most basic of connections between a vampire lord and his people?

Maybe one of them should have tested their magic handcuffs before slapping them on him. He knew exactly what was happening in his territory and with his people. He couldn't communicate with them as he normally would, but he still knew whose heart was beating and whose was not, who remained bound to him and who did not.

One of Mathilde's lesser vampires—physically strong, but not a significant power—put a hand under his elbow and jerked him to his feet. It took an effort of will, but Raphael kept himself limp and unresisting as he was hustled out of the house into the muggy heat of the Hawaiian night, and eventually into a vehicle. They kept him blindfolded, but he still had ears, still had his sense of smell. He knew there were multiple vehicles, that there were more people than just him and his guard who were leaving. Doors slammed, footsteps shuffled, and vampires called to each other. This was his second move of the night. They'd evacuated the house where he'd met Mathilde within minutes of his capture, and now they were moving again, probably anticipating a possible rescue attempt by Juro and the others.

He could have told them that wasn't going to happen, that they were wasting their time since Juro had strict orders to return to California and join with Jared in defending the territory until Raphael could make good his escape and protect it himself. But then, he wasn't inclined to make their lives any easier. Let them scurry about and waste time and effort with their hundred-plus vampires all focused hour after hour, night after night, just to hold him in place.

He reached tentatively for Cyn with his mind, but could only skim her awareness. It was like struggling through the fog to reach her. He could *hear* her, not her voice but her heartbeat, her existence in the world. She would be looking for him. Juro and the others would be going back to California, but he knew Cyn would stay. It was frustrating not to be able to touch her, not to hold her the way he'd done in the past when they'd been separated. More than any of the others, he needed his Cyn. Her absence was a grinding ache in his chest, digging deeper with every hour.

He settled back into the leather seat of the limousine where they'd put him, reminding himself to be patient, to bide his time. His captors would soon grow bored and complacent in their task, and every time one of the hundred's diligence weakened, Raphael's power would grow.

And besides, his Cyn was coming for him. Dear Mathilde was about to learn just how lethal one human female could be.

CYN SLOGGED through the wet jungle, her clothes soaked through to her skin. At least half of the moisture weighing her down had to be sweat. It was so fucking hot and muggy out here. Whose idea had it been to hold this little confab in Hawaii anyway? Couldn't they have picked somewhere cooler? What about Alaska? It was nice this time of year. Well, except for the mosquitoes. And the sixteen hours of daylight. Not exactly an ideal vampire vacation spot.

Ahead of her, Robbie cursed succinctly as it suddenly started raining again. Although, really, what harm could a little more water do? He was leading their merry band because he and Cyn were the only two who knew where the car was hidden, and he'd refused to let Cyn go first. Elke was directly behind Cyn, with Ken'ichi taking up the rear guard. They'd slipped out of the house from the back, as Juro and others departed very noisily from the front. And now her three bodyguards surrounded her, never letting her take the lead, never letting her bring up the rear, as if she needed protection more than any of them. It bugged Cyn to be treated like the weak link, or, even worse, like someone who deserved to live more than the others. But she didn't protest, because they were just doing their jobs, and they meant well. Besides, when push came to shove, it wouldn't matter. They'd all fight side by side.

She caught a big, green leaf before it hit her in the face. Fern? Palm? She still had no idea what it was and still didn't care. A glance down at the navigation app on her cell phone told her they were nearly there. *There* being the unpaved road where she and Robbie had parked their getaway vehicle. She only hoped the rental car was up to the task. Maybe they should have gotten—

A flash of warmth washed over her, bringing a scent, a touch. Raphael. She stumbled and nearly went down, before grabbing a thick branch of something and holding on, unable to move. She heard his voice call her name, but it was far away, like a whisper in a cathedral, echoing off the walls, impossible to pin down.

"Cyn?" Robbie's voice jarred her back to the present, back to the wet jungle and their desperate escape. "You okay, babe?"

Cyn closed her eyes, shutting out Robbie and everything else as she reached for Raphael, struggling to hold on to the fragile thread that was his awareness. She wanted to scream his name, but forced herself to be still and quiet instead. Her anger and frustration wouldn't do him any good. Focusing as hard as she could, she sent him her love and told him she was coming. And that he better be waiting when she got there.

"Cyn?" Robbie said again, his voice careful and filled with worry.

Her throat was thick with emotion, but she managed to whisper, "I'm okay."

Robbie studied her for a minute. "Raphael?"

Cyn smiled ruefully. She forgot sometimes that Robbie was mated to a vampire, that he'd been with his Irina much longer than she'd been with Raphael, and probably understood the mate bond better than she did.

"Yeah." She accepted the hand he offered, holding onto him for a moment until her head stopped spinning. "He's still . . . far away," she said, struggling to describe what it had felt like. "But the connection is already stronger than it was."

"Lord Raphael is far more powerful than I think even Mathilde understands," Ken'ichi said quietly, drawing her attention to the fact that both he and Elke were crouched under the leaves nearby, their eyes glowing as they scanned the jungle around them.

"She's judging him on what he was two hundred years ago," Cyn said in sudden understanding.

Ken'ichi nodded. "And what little she learned from the encounter with Violet. But she will not be expecting the mate bond you share with him, and she will be hard-pressed to suppress such a significant connection."

"Good," Cyn snapped. "I look forward to showing her just what we can do together." She stepped away from Robbie, patting his arm in reassurance. "I'm okay. We need to get going."

He studied her carefully in the moonlight, then nodded. "All right. I'll take lead."

"Of course you will," she muttered good-naturedly, and barely managed to duck under the branch he intentionally let go of in retaliation.

They made good time after that, slogging the last mile or so to the spot where she and Robbie had concealed the rental car. Although not before Cyn doubted her navigation more than once. It had seemed like such a straight shot in the daylight, and much shorter, too. But then, that's why she'd programmed the damn location into her phone's GPS in the first place. One piece of jungle looked just like all the rest to her.

Robbie pulled off the palm fronds and other greenery that they'd piled on top of their escape vehicle, then circled the small car as if expecting to find booby traps.

"You don't think they'd actually put on bomb on it, do you?" she asked him doubtfully. She figured if someone had discovered the rental and wanted to be sure no one could use it, they'd just slash the tires. That's what she would have done. But there was no reason for their enemies to be even looking for it.

"Not really," Robbie agreed. "I'm more concerned with mud than bombs."

Cyn eyed the wet ground, thinking they'd never get out of here if the car got mired in mud. This wasn't much of a road. If they'd been in the hills near Malibu, she'd have called it a fire road—a functional lane for utility vehicles, but not meant for regular travel. Plus the car they'd rented was a mid-sized sedan and not exactly equipped for off-road trekking. On the other hand, it was so dinky that, with their vampire strength, Ken'ichi and Elke could probably lift it right up and set it back on the road if it got stuck.

Apparently satisfied with what he found, Robbie popped the locks and slid behind the steering wheel, then maneuvered the vehicle onto the narrow path and waited for the rest of them to pile in. And pile in is what they did. Generally speaking, Cyn hated it when the guys sat in front, with the women relegated to the backseat like second-class citizens. She was six feet tall and her legs were longer than most men's. If anyone needed the extra legroom up front, it was usually her. In this case, however, Ken'ichi and Robbie were not only taller, but they each outweighed her by more than a hundred pounds. The only place they'd *fit* in the vehicle was up front, and even then, they had to push the seats back almost to their limits. Elke, on the other hand, could kick ass just as well as the two males, but at only five feet, five inches she had no problem with the seating arrangement. She smirked when Cyn had to shift sideways in order to fit into the stupid backseat.

"We look like a clown car," Cyn muttered. "I should have gotten something bigger."

"We'll drive the other tomorrow," Robbie said easily. "This is good enough for tonight, and it was easier to conceal."

"Easy for you to say," she added under her breath, earning another grin from Elke who, being a vampire, heard the comment.

"How far is this place we're going?" Elke asked, pretending to look like she wasn't enjoying Cyn's predicament.

"Just over three miles," Robbie provided. He'd been moving at a steady pace up the narrow road and was already slowing for the turn onto the main highway behind the estate where they'd spent the last two nights. Just thinking about her last hours with Raphael made Cyn's heart clench painfully.

"The house is smaller," she said, desperate to think about something else. "But Robbie and I fixed up all the bedrooms, covered the windows and stuff. And since it's just us, it should be big enough."

Elke gave an exaggerated shrug. "Hey, I don't need much room."

"Midget," Cyn murmured.

"Freak," Elke muttered back. Cyn felt her mouth curl into a half smile and immediately felt guilty. She shouldn't be smiling, shouldn't be enjoying any of this. They weren't playing hooky, ducking out on some boring meeting. They were racing to save Raphael's life.

As they made the final turn onto the street where the safe house was, Robbie tapped the remote for the garage door. It was open by the time they hit the driveway, and he pulled right into the open garage, closing the door behind them as soon as the car was fully inside.

"This house belongs to Lucia's family?" Ken'ichi asked.

Cyn startled at the familiar tone of his voice when referring to Luci, then realized she shouldn't have been surprised. Juro was his twin brother, after all. He'd probably known before Cyn did that Luci and Juro were moving in together.

"Yes," she said, answering his question as they all piled out of the too-small car. "But on her mom's side and a couple of branches removed, so even if the European vamps know about Luci's connection to us, which is stretching it, they shouldn't be able to ID this place. Assuming they're looking at all. With any luck, they'll fall for Juro's deception and think we've all flown back home."

Ken'ichi nodded silently, then turned to Robbie and said, "We need to disconnect that light."

Robbie glanced up at the light on the garage door opener and said, "I'll take care of it today."

Cyn went ahead, pulling out the key that she'd kept from their previous visit, opening the door between the garage and the house. She walked into the dark kitchen, immediately going over and dropping the blinds.

"Elke, you should check out the sleeping arrangements and make sure they're safe for you guys. Sunrise isn't that far away. Robbie and I will arrange a watch schedule, sleeping in turns through the day so that one of us is always awake. I think we're safe, but it's better to be careful."

She circled around the rest of the ground floor, checking shutters and curtains, and dropping the shades. It was dark out for now, and by morning, Elke and Ken'ichi would be upstairs where the windows were all covered, but she was worried about more than just the looming sunrise. She didn't want anyone looking in and noticing the house was occupied, and then getting curious about who was visiting. Better that they simply assume it was a vacation rental and leave it at that.

"Everything's good up here," Elke said, coming down the stairs. "We should discuss what our next steps are."

Cyn nodded. "Agreed." She glanced around the big living room with its comfortable furniture. "Let's sit here. It's probably best for the guys."

"Yeah, no wicker," Elke commented with a smirk.

Cyn managed a weak smile. "How long before sunrise?" she asked, glancing at the windows, looking for any sign of daylight around the edges of the blinds.

"About an hour. Enough time to decide on a plan for later tonight."

Cyn waited until everyone was settled, then drew a breath. "I've been thinking about this, and I'm pretty sure they'll move Raphael again as soon as they can." She didn't mention her earlier contact with him, not knowing whether it was a one-shot deal, or whether he'd reach out to her again with more information. Right now, the only thing she knew for sure was that Raphael was alive, but they'd all known that already, especially Elke and Ken'ichi. If Raphael died, every vampire in the western territory—and that was thousands of vampires, including the two in this room—would know instantly. Hell, Raphael's death would probably be felt by every vampire in North America, no matter how strong or weak they were. He was just that powerful.

But then, if Raphael died, there wouldn't be a hole deep enough for Mathilde to hide in. Lucas would hunt her down and stake her for the sun, and Cyn would be right there, holding the hammer.

"Mathilde and her gang must have another hideout set up, either on this island or another," Cyn said, forcing herself to stop thinking about what would happen if Raphael died, and focus instead on keeping him alive. "It has to be someplace not associated with Rhys Patterson, because that would be too easy for Raphael's allies to locate. Juro said there were a hundred or more vampires working together to bind Raphael. Let's call it an even hundred, for simplicity's sake. I don't know exactly how that works, but I'm guessing it's something like a power circle with someone, presumably Mathilde, tying them all together. Am I right?"

"I don't know that anything like this has ever been done," Ken'ichi said thoughtfully. "Mathilde has clearly brought them together, but Juro believes, and I agree, that her plan is to travel to Malibu where she'll issue a personal challenge to Raphael, knowing that he can't respond. This means she can't be the focal point of the power circle. More likely, she has several of the more powerful master vampires at her disposal and they're the ones binding the others together."

Cyn flattened her lips in thought. "Would they all have to be in one place?"

Ken'ichi and Elke exchanged a thoughtful glance before Elke spoke. "We think so. It has to be taking a hell of a lot of energy just to keep that circle cohesive. Why waste energy trying to do it at a distance?" She looked at Ken'ichi for confirmation, and he nodded his agreement.

"Okay. Let's say I'm right about them moving Raphael," Cyn continued. "Is it possible the hundred or whatever vamps are already at the new location? Even if it's on another island?"

Elke looked to Ken'ichi to answer Cyn's question. Juro had said that Ken'ichi's power was equal to his own. Elke's reaction told Cyn that his greater power meant he also understood questions about vampiric power better than Elke did.

Ken'ichi seemed to mull over the question, then spoke slowly. "I have never met Mathilde or her allies, and have no firsthand knowledge of their individual strengths. But the fact that they required subterfuge to subdue Raphael is very telling. The three of them could be working in concert to maintain the integrity of the group over a distance, but only in the short term. A day or two at most."

Cyn considered this a moment. "The odds are, then, that they're going to be moving Raphael to wherever she's hiding her hundred vamps. It must have taken months just to get that many of them here in the first place. Relocating them quickly would be a major headache. And, frankly, for all she's a bitch, I don't think Mathilde is that stupid. I think the circle is somewhere she considers more secure and that they'll move Raphael there sooner rather than later."

"Makes sense," Robbie agreed. "They've demanded Juro and the others leave, but they can't believe we won't be sending a team to investigate. And the first thing any such team would do is tear apart any property owned by Rhys Patterson."

"Our first job then is to figure out where they've gone. Because while I'd like to believe we'll catch them before they leave Kauai, I don't think we will. I think they'll leave this island as soon as the sun sets tonight, if they haven't already. So where do we start?"

"Normally, I'd say short-term rentals," Robbie commented. "But this is Hawaii. Vacation rentals are as common as palm trees."

They were all silent a moment, then Elke snapped her fingers and said, "Food."

Cyn frowned a moment before understanding clicked in. "Blood. You're right. That's a lot of vampires needing to be fed. Even if Mathilde was inclined to fly blood in from Europe, it would be nearly impossible to keep enough on hand to feed them for more than a day or two. That's a lot of flights, which are expensive and easy to track. My guess is she's either letting them feed on the streets, or she's robbing blood banks. So that's where we'll start. We check police blotters, official records, anything we can tap into, looking for unusual crime waves that indicate a vampire presence."

"That's a big search, Cyn," Robbie commented.

"I know, but we can at least eliminate Kauai. I really don't think she'll stay here."

"It's still a lot of ground to cover. The bigger islands have lots of different police jurisdictions, and we don't know if they're centralized, or even computerized."

"But the vampires will have to stick close to a big city, won't they? If all those vamps start feeding somewhere with a small population, it's going to be noticed. So we stick with the bigger centers for now. They're more likely to be computerized anyway. You also have to figure that at least a few of the vampires involved might get over-excited and rip out a throat or drain someone dry. Something like that is more likely to show up in a local news story and probably end up on the Internet."

"It's a place to start," Robbie agreed.

"I'll take a run at it this morning," Cyn continued, "but I'm not exactly a hacker. If the info's as accessible as we hope, I shouldn't have a problem. But if I don't turn up anything, I'll reach out to some people I trust. I'm also going to check with Luci's charter pilot cousin and see if he knows anyone in local law enforcement. Again, that kind of crime might create a buzz. Hopefully I'll have some leads for us to follow later tonight."

"I think we should check out the two houses that we know Mathilde spent time in," Elke suggested. "I think you're probably right, and she's gone, but some of Patterson's people might be around. Juro briefed me and Ken'ichi while you were getting ready, and he felt pretty strongly that Patterson was an unwilling accomplice. If that's true, Mathilde was probably holding his people hostage. Now that she has what she came for, Patterson's vamps might be loose and willing to talk."

"And if Mathilde's left a guard force?" Robbie asked.

"Then we'll observe for a while and report back."

Cyn nodded. "We should communicate by cell until this is over. We still don't know how or when they hacked into the house security. I don't want to take a chance that our comms are compromised as well. Juro gave me a bunch of burner phones before he left, but I want to save those to communicate with Malibu. Robbie and I bought some when we were stocking this place, so we'll use those. They're in a black duffle bag in the kitchen, so help yourself. Just make a note of which phone you take."

Cyn stood, stretching sore muscles, both exhausted and wired at the same time. She needed caffeine. There was a coffeemaker in the kitchen and coffee had been among the groceries she and Robbie picked up the other day. She started for the kitchen as Elke and Ken'ichi moved toward the stairs. The sky was still dark outside, but Cyn knew sunrise had to be near.

Robbie was leaning back on the sofa, scrubbing his face with both hands. He jumped to his feet when she stopped next to him. "I'll take first—" he started to say, but Cyn cut him off.

"No," she said. "You've been up almost nonstop for two days. Besides I'm expecting some calls, and I won't be able to sleep anyway." She walked over and grabbed a prepaid phone from the duffle sitting on the island in the kitchen.

"The mates' club's been activated, huh?" Robbie asked, nodding at the phone in her hand. "You guys have a secret code word or something?"

"Not yet. But we might come up with one after this." Her personal cell phone rang. She checked the caller ID and wasn't surprised at the identity of her first caller.

"Hey," she said answering her cell. "Let me call you right back." She hung up, then turned to address Robbie as she turned on the prepaid phone. "It's okay," she told him. "It's Murphy. You can go to bed, and I'll wake you in a few hours."

"Say 'hi' to Murphy for me," Robbie said, then gave her a silent salute and headed up the stairs, taking them two at a time. Cyn collapsed onto a big overstuffed chair, coffee forgotten for now as she punched in Colin Murphy's number and hit *call*.

He answered on the first ring. "Leighton."

"And hello to you, too," she said, greeting her counterpart from Canada. Colin Murphy was mated to Sophia, the only female vampire lord in North America.

Cyn didn't have to explain the unexpected number she'd called in on. Murphy would have expected that after she'd said she'd call him back. They'd actually discussed just this sort of thing among the various members of the mates' club, what with a vampire war looming on the horizon.

"How're you doing, Leighton?" Murphy's voice was softer than the cynical tone he usually took with her. She and Colin had been through hell and back together. They covered up their affection with snarky banter, but they liked each other, and in a different life might even have been more than friends. Colin was an experienced warrior, a former Navy SEAL. And right now, he'd understand, better than any of the other mates would, her frustration at not being able to *do* anything, at not having anyone to shoot.

"Not great," she admitted briefly, but she didn't elaborate. If they started discussing feelings and how she *really* was doing, she'd end up blubbering into her nonexistent coffee instead of figuring out how to rescue Raphael.

"Gotcha," Colin said, and she knew he understood. "So what do you need?"

"Nothing yet. We're still trying to determine exactly where Raphael's being held, then we'll figure out how to get to him."

"Where are you? Juro gave us the official line that he'd evacuated everyone from the island, but I bet Sophia a thousand bucks that you'd still be there."

"Tell her to pay up, but keep it to yourselves. I don't want Mathilde to get wind of our whereabouts before we're ready to make our move."

"Who's us? Is Rob there with you?"

"Of course. He says 'hi' by the way. Elke and Ken'ichi are here, too."

A moment of silence and then Colin said, "Who the fuck is Ken'ichi?"

"Juro's twin brother," Cyn told him, surprised that he didn't know.

"Shit, really? I wasn't sure that guy *had* a name. I've never even heard him talk. In fact, I kinda figured he was all muscle, no brain."

"Wrong on all counts. He talks just fine and, believe me, his brain is fully functional. He just doesn't like people all that much."

"But he likes *you*?"

"What can I say? I'm loveable." This was closer to their usual level of snark, and Cyn found it oddly reassuring.

"If you say so. Now tell me what I can do to help. I can't leave Sophia, but—"

"You absolutely can't leave Sophia right now. They think they've neutralized Raphael, so they'll hit the continent next. We expect Mathilde to hit Raphael's territory directly, but she had a couple of powerful allies with her that night. She wants the West, so it's doubtful she'll want them with her to muddy up the water on her challenge there. The fact that they're here means they've probably set their sights on other—"

"Cyn," he interrupted quietly. "About Raphael—"

"I'm getting him back," she said firmly.

"If anyone can do it, you can."

Cyn found herself dissecting that last sentence, wondering if it was Murphy's way of saying he didn't really think Raphael could be rescued. She didn't believe that for a minute. She would rescue him. She almost said something, but then realized exhaustion might be clouding her thoughts, because Murphy would never have suggested such a thing. He didn't believe in giving up any more than she did.

"What I really need is a cop," she said wearily.

"A cop? What the hell for?"

"Access to police reports mostly, but also gossip. Cops talk to each other. I want to know if there's anything weird going on locally."

"You're looking for a spike in vamp activity."

"Exactly. You know, I keep telling people there's a brain underneath all those muscles of yours," she teased automatically.

"Nice," he responded, then flowed right back to business. "I don't know any cops personally, but I have a buddy on Oahu. A Navy brat who grew up there. He left the teams about the same time I did, and went back home to raise a family. I can give him a call. He might know someone who knows someone."

Cyn thought about it. "How much does he know about vamps?"

"He knows I'm all but married to one, and he knows what I do for her."

"Okay, give him this number. I appreciate this, Murphy."

"Hey, that's what the club's for, right?"

"It is now. Although originally, I was thinking more along the lines of three-martini lunches and shopping trips."

"I'm guessing that was before I joined."

"You don't like martinis?"

"You're funny. I like martinis just fine."

"So you can stay in the bar and watch over the bags while the rest of us keep shopping."

"Yeah, because I don't get enough of that with Sophia."

Cyn laughed, then said softly, "Thanks, Murphy."

"Anytime, Leighton. I'll be in touch."

He hung up, and Cyn had no sooner disconnected the call on her end, than her personal cell phone rang again. A quick glance at the screen told her it was the FBI's turn to check in.

"Kathryn," she greeted, then went into the same routine as she had with Murphy, saying she'd call right back and then redialing on the pre-paid phone.

"Cyn. I'm sorry," Kathryn said the minute they reconnected.

"Thanks. Lucas must be going nuts, yeah?" Lucas was the vampire lord who ruled the Plains territory, and Kathryn's mate. Raphael was Lucas's Sire, and of all Raphael's vampire children, he and Lucas had a unique connection. Cyn didn't know if it was because Lucas had been Raphael's first, or if it was because Lucas had only been a teenager when he and Raphael had first met. He'd been a street thief whom Raphael had plucked from the gutter to be his human servant years before he made him a vampire. The first time Cyn met Lucas was when Raphael had narrowly avoided an assassination attempt. Lucas had made a special trip, flying hundreds of miles just to see for himself that Raphael was alive and well.

Kathryn made a dismissive noise. "I threatened to shoot him if he got on a plane without talking to you first," she said, sounding like she was only half-joking.

"Bullets don't really hurt them, you know," Cyn responded.

"They do if it's a big enough bullet."

Cyn choked a laugh. "I know it's Lucas and all, but you don't really want to kill him, right?"

"Sometimes it's a toss-up, but so far, the answer's no. I only threatened to shoot his leg this time."

"I'm surprised that stopped him."

"Okay, so maybe I actually said both legs. I needed him to cool down and *think* instead of rushing off on a rescue mission that you already had in hand."

"What if I don't?" Cyn asked hollowly.

"Come on, Cyn. I have faith in you, and so does Lucas."

Cyn wished privately that she could be as confident as they were about her chances. But she didn't say that out loud.

"Official word is that Juro came home with the whole team, including you," Kathryn told her. "But I didn't believe it for one minute."

"That's what Murphy said, too. Let's hope the bitch doesn't know me as well as you guys do."

"The bitch you're referring to is Mathilde?"

"One and the same. Does Lucas know her?"

"Yeah. He says Raphael has a history with her, and that history is one of the reasons Raphael left Europe when he did."

"A woman scorned?" Cyn said, hating the bitch more with every new detail she discovered about her.

"Lucas didn't give me any details. You can ask him when he calls later, which will probably be one minute after our sunset."

"Consider me warned. Give him this phone number, would you? It's a pre-pay."

"Smart move." There was a moment of silence. "How can I help, Cyn? There must be something I can contribute besides witty repartee."

It was funny, Cyn thought. Her reasons for organizing the mates' club in the first place had been exactly what she'd told Murphy. It was supposed to be about martinis and shopping, something entertaining to do while the big bad vamps held their various meets. But it had become so much more. Mostly because the mates had turned out to be such a diverse and capable group of women . . . and man, she added, thinking of Murphy.

"I'm in research mode," she told Kathryn, coming back to their conversation. "So far, we're looking at local sources—official police reports, police blotter columns in local newspapers, and any unexplained happenings covered in reliable articles. With an emphasis on reliable."

"You're looking for unexplained vampire activity," Kathryn guessed, just as Murphy had. "I can help with that. A lot of times rogue vamp attacks get lumped in with serials, and end up in VICAP," she said, referring to the FBI's national database for violent criminal activity. "I'll run a search and see what turns up. I'm guessing you're still looking at all of the islands?"

"I'm ruling out Kauai for now. Nothing else makes sense. I'll go back to it if nothing else pans out, but I'm trying to narrow down my search."

"I'll do the VICAP run this morning and get back to you either way."

"Thanks, Kathryn. That'll be a huge help."

"It's the least I can do. Well, that and chaining Lucas to the bed so he doesn't show up on your doorstep."

"You poor thing."

Kathryn laughed out loud. "Yeah. He can be a pain in my ass, but he is awfully pretty."

"I'll talk to you later?" Cyn said, anxious to get off the phone. She knew others would be calling and she appreciated their support. But she needed to get that part of it out of the way, so she could focus on the problem.

"I'll call as soon as I hear back."

"Great, talk to you later, then." She disconnected the burner phone, and headed for the kitchen with coffee on her mind. She was reaching for the coffee filters when her cell phone rang again. She crossed back to the table to get her phone, and lifted her finger to accept the call just as her brain processed the ring tone and recognized it as an incoming text rather than a voice call.

Frowning a little, she pulled up her messages and saw that there were actually two. The first was from . . . Nick again? It was the same cryptic message as before, that he had an issue he needed her help with. But this time he'd added an insistent *Call me!!!* She guessed the three exclamation marks were meant to convey urgency. Unfortunately for Nick, she had only one urgent issue right now, and it wasn't his.

Moving on to the next message, she found an incoming number that she didn't recognize. Apparently this was her morning for mysterious messages, because this one consisted of a link and a single line of text.

I thought you'd find this interesting.

Cyn stared. The attached link was from one of those utility sites that shortened overlong links. Very handy, but the result gave away nothing of where the link would take her. Normally, she'd have deleted a message like this without a second thought.

But these weren't normal times.

Still, it couldn't hurt to take some minimal precautions. She forwarded the message from her personal phone to the burner, then clicked the link. It opened on what looked like a marginal Internet website that targeted paranormal news stories. There were the usual tales of alien sightings, but those were consigned to the margins, running in a left-hand column that was filled with stories of the bizarre, like two-headed snakes and six-legged lambs.

Going by the blood-dripping fangs which featured prominently on their headline banner, however, vampires were the website's number one interest. So, it was no surprise that their main story today—and a quick scan told her it was true of most days—featured reports of vampire sightings or rumors. And not the sparkly, fictional kind of vampire either.

These were real-life sightings, often including photographs, of some of the most powerful vampires in North America. Cyn scanned the image archives quickly and found several claiming to show Raphael, but when she checked them out, the only thing they showed was the top or back of his head in the middle of his security team. She was shocked to see herself visible in one of the photos, but only from the back, which was a relief. She noted in passing that her hair looked great, but she also thought that the photo must be an older one, probably from right after that clusterfuck up near Seattle, when she'd been still recovering from her wounds. Because she looked way too thin.

There was no reason for her mysterious sender to call her attention to old pictures of her and Raphael, however. Far more interesting was the story dominating the current headline, the one detailing a sudden increase in the Honolulu area of dead bodies with their throats ripped out. The reporter also claimed to have inside knowledge about an increase in assaults where the victim survived but was left with some serious neck wounds and a sharp reduction in blood volume. In other words, survivors of vampire attacks.

Cyn hadn't even known there were vampires in Hawaii at all until this trip, so she didn't know the common practice on the Islands. But in North America generally, vampires didn't leave dead bodies lying about, and they didn't leave "victims" either. Most blood donors were volunteers with no desire to complain to the cops or anyone else about their interactions with vampires. Exceptions happened, of course, but in those cases, the offending vampire was dealt with quickly and often fatally by either the vampire lord himself or one of his enforcers. She had to think the same policy held true in Hawaii, or Raphael would have done something about it before this.

Which meant, if the reports on this Internet site could be believed, Honolulu was experiencing a vampire crime wave, which was precisely what she'd been looking for.

For a moment, Cyn felt like one of those anemic, vampire-bitten victims herself. Her heart was pounding, but the blood seemed to be rushing everywhere but her head. With her vision graying, she leaned forward, head between her knees, the phone falling from her suddenly nerveless fingers. She must have passed out for a few minutes. Because the next thing she knew, Robbie's heavy footsteps were pounding down the stairs and he was calling her name.

"Cyn?" He went down on one knee in front of her. "What is it?"

There was fear in his voice, and she knew he thought something had happened to Raphael, something powerful enough that she'd felt it through their link. Robbie feared for Raphael, but it was more than that.

His wife, Irina, was one of Raphael's vampires. If the worst befell Raphael, it would hit Irina hard, maybe even kill her. At best, she would end up beholden to a new vampire lord, and there was no guarantee who that would be.

Cyn couldn't lift her head right away, not without passing out, but she reached out and blindly squeezed Robbie's thick forearm. "It's not Raphael," she managed to whisper. She searched for the burner phone, which had slid down two steps, gripping it with clammy fingers when Robbie handed it to her. She held it up for him to see the display, which was still showing the Honolulu news story.

Robbie read it silently. "Okay, so someone did our work for us. But what's up with you, babe?"

She raised her head enough to say, "I saw the story and knew we were right, and I just—"

"You went girly on me and fainted?" he teased, but rotated his arm beneath her fingers and squeezed her hand tightly.

"I didn't faint," she insisted, hearing the shakiness in her own voice. "I think I'm just hungry. I can't remember the last time I ate." She sat up slowly. "Fuck, I hate that feeling. Makes me want to puke."

"Here."

She looked up to see him holding out a bottle of water.

"Where'd you get that? You always carry a spare?" she asked skeptically, but took the proffered bottle and drank it down. "Is that a Ranger thing?"

"That's a 'we're-in-Hawaii' thing. It's fucking hot here, easy to get dehydrated. You feeling better?"

Cyn nodded. "Why are you awake?"

"Couldn't sleep. I thought I'd take the first shift for you, or at least keep you company."

"We're a pair, aren't we? The bad guys'll come through the door, and we'll be so tired, we won't be able to lift our guns."

"Hey, Army Ranger here. I'm never too tired to lift my gun."

"Whatever. You feel like breakfast?"

"You offering to cook?"

"I can make scrambled eggs and toast."

"*French* toast?"

"Ordinary toaster toast. You want anything else, you're on your own."

Robbie stood and held out a hand. He pulled her to her feet and held onto her until they were both sure she wasn't going to fall over, then turned her toward the kitchen.

"I can't remember," he said conversationally, "did we buy bacon?"

Cyn nodded. "You insisted. And if you want it, you cook it. Scrambled eggs are about as complicated as I get."

"No wonder you're so skinny. You don't cook anything."

"I mostly eat out. And I'm not skinny, asshole."

"Touchy. You must be feeling better."

"That fucking website had a picture of my ass."

"We should hack their site for that alone. Cover their pages with hearts and flowers."

"Good idea. I'll get someone on it as soon as we get Raphael back home."

They were both silent for a long moment, Cyn's comment serving to remind them of exactly what had freaked her out in the first place.

"You think the site is trustworthy?" Robbie asked, moving to the fridge and pulling out their breakfast ingredients.

Cyn leaned against the counter, another bottle of water in her hand. She took a long drink before responding. "Trustworthy? Probably not. But that doesn't mean there's no truth to their story. Someone sure thinks there is. Enough to send me the link anyway."

Robbie frowned. "Yeah, but who? And why help us out?"

"It could be one of Rhys Patterson's people. According to Juro, Patterson only cooperated with Mathilde because she threatened him. But he's been ruling these islands on his own for a long time. Not even Raphael really knows how many vamps he has, or who they are. If Mathilde missed someone, that vamp could be fighting back by directing us to information we can use."

"Or it could be someone from Mathilde's camp, sending us on a wild goose chase in order to divert our attention from wherever they're really hiding."

"But that assumes Mathilde knows we're here, and we don't think she does," Cyn protested.

"Whoever sent you that message doesn't have to know that you're here. For all they know, you're sitting in Malibu biting your nails."

"Maybe."

"Tell you what, Cyn. Instead of driving ourselves crazy with *what if*, why don't you finish the eggs, and I'll scan the local legit news sources and see what they have."

Robbie pulled her laptop over from where it was sitting on the counter and started typing. "What'd Murphy have to say?" he asked without looking up.

Robbie had been with her and Murphy the day she almost died. He'd held her guts in with his hands, while Murphy had raced her back to the compound where Raphael was just waking up. A shared experience like that created a bond one never forgot.

Cyn started cracking eggs. "Murphy has a SEAL buddy on Oahu. He told me to expect a call. I'm hoping the buddy will know a friendly cop who can help us track down these stories, since you gung-ho types all tend to hang around together."

"When's he going to call?"

"Soon as Murphy gets hold of him, I guess. Hopefully soon."

Robbie continued to work on her laptop, his thick fingers hitting the keyboard hard enough to make her wince.

"Here we go," he announced suddenly.

"What've you got?" Cyn asked. She set aside the bowl of raw eggs, then walked around to look over his shoulder. "*Honolulu Star-Advertiser*," she read. "Is that a major paper?"

"Biggest circulation in the state, or so they claim."

"And?"

"They don't have the assaults, and they don't describe quite the bloody massacre the vampire groupie site made it out to be, but they do have three dead bodies, all with the same wounds, and all within the last two weeks."

"Three bodies isn't much," she commented, still reading over his shoulder.

"Not in L.A. But I'm not sure about Honolulu. And taken with the other reports, it's a strong possibility for Mathilde's new hideaway."

Cyn stepped back. "I'd sure like to know who sent me that link in the first place. It stinks of a trap."

"Did they leave a callback number?"

"The number was blocked, but I can always try texting them back and see what happens."

"So, do it. Just straight out ask who they are."

Cyn walked around the counter and into the living room where she'd left the burner phone when she'd had her episode that absolutely was *not* a fainting spell. Picking up the phone, she quickly typed, "Who the fuck is this?" Then thought better of it, and changed it to simply, *Who are you?*

The reply came before she'd even gotten back to the kitchen. Robbie looked up at the message chime, his eyes meeting hers in question. She nodded, then came up next to him so they could both read the text. It said simply, *An ally. We should meet.*

"Oh fuck, no," Robbie said immediately. "No meets, Cyn. We don't have any idea who this clown is."

"There's only one sure way to find out," she countered reasonably. "We agree to a meet."

"Bullshit. Ask him for some bona fides, see what he says."

Cyn shrugged, then typed, *You know me. But who are YOU?* She capped the last word for emphasis.

She set down the phone, then turned on the heat under the pan and poured the eggs into it. When her phone dinged, she was fluffing eggs, so Robbie picked it up and read it out loud. "Donovan Willis. I work for Rhys Patterson."

Cyn frowned. *Donovan Willis.* "I know that name," she said absently. If he worked for Patterson, he had to be local, someone she'd met or heard of in the last few days. But she hadn't met that many people. In fact, other than Luci's pilot cousin, she hadn't met anyone at all. Raphael had seen to that. But . . .

"Donovan Willis!" she repeated in sudden recognition. "He showed up the second day we were at the house, as part of that welcome committee. I was in the control room, watching the video feed with Ken'ichi. There were two vamps trying to pass for local in matching Hawaiian shirts, and then there was Willis—human, spiked hair and piercings. He wanted . . ." She thought back to what she'd heard of Willis's conversation with Raphael.

"He offered to *fix* the house's high-speed Internet, said he could make it faster or some other bullshit. We all figured it for an obvious ploy to plant a bug in our system, and Raphael declined. Politely."

"What about the two vamps? Did they seem cozy with Willis?"

"Cozy? Is that one of those Spec Op code words we civilians don't understand?"

"You're just jealous they don't take girls."

Cyn snorted. That was kind of true, though she'd never admit it. "*Cozy* isn't the word I'd use to describe those guys. In fact, I'm pretty sure I haven't used that word since I was about six. But, in point of fact, Willis and the vamps didn't seem to be playing as a team. When he thought they weren't looking, Willis's feelings about the other two were pretty obvious, and they definitely weren't full of admiration."

Cyn dished out the eggs, and added toast to each plate. The kitchen was quiet for a few minutes as toast was slathered with jam and eggs were consumed. Cyn surprised herself by eating nearly as much as Robbie. Apparently, she'd been hungrier than she thought.

Robbie got up and poured coffee for both of them. Cyn nodded her thanks then pushed away her plate and said, "Okay, let's go with the idea that Patterson wasn't a willing accomplice to the kidnapping. Where does that leave us?"

"It leaves us with Willis, a human who worked for Patterson, offering his services."

"Could be worth investigating."

"How does he know you're still on the island?"

"Maybe he doesn't. L.A.'s only a six-hour flight from here."

Robbie frowned. "I don't know. He asked for a meeting, not a phone call. That tells me he knows you're here."

Cyn glanced down at the burner phone in her hand, and felt the light bulb go on over her head. "My cell phone," she said, giving Rob a *duh* look. "He originally texted my cell phone, and he's a hacker. A security specialist from what he told Raphael. How hard would it be for a guy like that to trace my phone's location? Even if I'm not using it, it's turned on and we both know what that means. Maybe he can't narrow it down to a specific location, but he sure as hell can tell I'm still on Kauai."

"Shit. We need to turn off all our personal phones and pull the batteries. Nothing but burners from here out."

Cyn gave him a distraught look. "But what if Raphael—"

"Babe," he said patiently. "We both know Raphael doesn't need a phone to contact you."

"I know you're right," she said, drawing a deep breath. "But I can't do it. I need to leave that connection open, just in case."

"I get it. Let's just hope Mathilde's people aren't as sharp as Willis when it comes to cell phones."

"Let's hope Willis isn't already working for Mathilde."

"Good point. We should meet him, though."

Cyn looked at him in surprise. "Why the change of heart?"

Robbie frowned. "If he's on the up and up, he can help us. If he's not, we need to know that, too. Because it'll mean Mathilde knows about you."

"We should probably set the meet for daylight, then. So that none of Mathilde's allies, at least none of the most dangerous ones, can be lurking about."

"I'm not sure that's a good idea," he disagreed. "We can't leave the vamps unguarded."

"You could stay here while I—"

Robbie's laugh was a bark of disbelief. "There is no way in hell I'm letting you meet this guy alone. We'll wait until after dark, and take Ken'ichi and Elke with us. Message him back. Set the meet for ninety minutes after sunset, somewhere close."

"Who died and made you boss?"

"When it comes to shit like this? Uncle Sam. Hooah."

"Whatever," Cyn muttered.

"You stay here 'til sunset, then bring the vamps with you to the meet. I'll head over early and see if anyone other than Willis shows up. You remember what he looked like? Anything I can recognize him by?"

"Dark brown hair gelled into spikes. Piercings in both brows and ears, black framed glasses."

"Height? Weight?"

"I only saw him on video," she said thoughtfully. "He was next to Raphael, though, so, five foot, ten, slender but fit, maybe 160 pounds."

"Right. Have him meet you at the McDonald's next to the grocery store we went to yesterday. I'm assuming he knows what you look like, even though he didn't see you at the house. Regardless, make sure he understands that we know what *he* looks like. There's a picnic area on the south side of the drive-thru. It won't be as crowded as the restaurant or play areas, especially after dark."

Cyn's thumbs were flying as she messaged Willis, breaking Robbie's instructions into two separate texts to make it easier to follow.

Willis's response was instantaneous. Three words. *I'll be there.*

She looked up and met Robbie's dark brown eyes. "We're on." She had to force herself to remain calm, to keep her hands steady and her voice cool. This was the first really good lead they'd had, an inside man in the enemy's camp. She tamped down her excitement by reminding herself that Willis might not be inside Mathilde's camp anymore, if he ever had been. The fact that he was willing to help Cyn argued against it, but he still probably knew more than she did about what was going on.

Robbie was watching her closely, seeming to understand her internal battle. What he'd said about Uncle Sam training him for situations just like this was true. Robbie had seen real war, had made life-and-death decisions on three different battlefields. Vampires were a bloody lot, and Cyn had fought her share of skirmishes since taking up with Raphael, but she knew her experience didn't come close to Robbie's. Which was probably why she was practically jumping out of her skin with what she hoped was well-concealed excitement, while he was standing there doing a fair imitation of the iceman.

"I'll take the rental car," he told her. "It's less conspicuous. You call the rental company and have them bring something bigger. Ken'ichi and I need some leg room. And I want something with power."

"You should try the backseat," she grumbled.

"Yeah, no thanks." He walked over and grabbed a couple of burner phones from the duffle. "Take down these numbers."

Cyn dutifully entered the numbers on her own burner, then looked up at Robbie. "You've got ammo? Everything else you'll need?"

"I got two spare mags, and, hey, I'm going to be at McDonald's. I'm probably better off there than in this house with two bloodsuckers and a woman who barely eats food."

"I just made eggs!"

"Babe, that's an appetizer."

"Fine, go off to McDonald's and pollute yourself with fast food."

"You're dying to go *with* me, aren't you?"

"*Dying* is such a strong word."

"Want me to get you a burger and fries? I could bring it back—"

"No, no. I'll get something later. Hell, Willis is a computer geek. Maybe we can bond over junk food."

"I'll lock up. You should try to sleep—you're going to need it."

"I'm not much of a guard if I'm sound asleep."

"So grab a pillow and some blankets and sleep at the top of the stairs. That love seat thing on the landing looks pretty comfortable. Not for me, but you might fit. Or sleep down here."

"Maybe," she said, though privately she was thinking *no way*. The only thing that even tempted her to sleep was the memory of how Raphael had used her dreams to contact her before, when she'd been in Texas with that asshole Jabril. Granted, those dreams had been pretty much nothing but sex, but that didn't mean he couldn't do other things, too. Her heart ached, an actual physical pain, when she thought about Raphael, about what he might be going through, about how much she needed to believe that nothing and no one could keep them apart.

She clenched her jaw so hard that it hurt, swallowing the emotion threatening to swamp her. She wasn't going to let Mathilde win. The bitch thought she was so clever, thought she had Raphael, and that no one and nothing could touch her. Well, good luck with that. Because Raphael belonged to Cyn, and *no one* was going to take him away from her.

"Now that's the Cyn I know and love," Robbie commented with a half-smile, as he eyed the determined expression on her face. "And that's the Cyn I need for this op."

Cyn gave him a surprised look, then laughed ruefully. "I'm just trying not to collapse into a soggy lump like a wussy girl."

"Go ahead and lump it for a few minutes—after I'm gone, please—and get it out of your system. Then forget about it and come out fighting."

"Thanks, Robbie," she said sincerely.

"Hey, we've been through the fire together, babe."

"And come out the other side," she added. "And we'll do it this time, too. Don't worry."

"Not worried. And now I'm leaving before I'm the one who turns into a wussy girl."

"I'll get an SUV over here from the rental place as soon as you leave. You stay in touch."

"Yes, ma'am. And I'll see you there later."

Cyn headed upstairs, watching through the window as Robbie

backed the sedan out of the garage. She heard the rumble of the door closing beneath her, then immediately went downstairs to check the garage, and all other doors and windows. She made a quick call to a different car rental company and arranged for an appropriate SUV to be dropped off in two hours, then she grabbed a pillow and stretched out on the love seat within sight of the stairs. Although, *stretched out* wasn't entirely accurate—the small couch was at least a foot shorter than she was—but she didn't figure she'd sleep that much anyway.

SHE JERKED AWAKE at sound of a cell phone right next to her ear. She'd placed two of the prepaid phones next to her before going to sleep so she wouldn't miss any calls. The ringing phone was one of the ones Juro had given her, and a quick check of the time told her who her caller was going to be. It was still daylight on the west coast, but the sun had set in the east, and the vampires were awake.

She touched the call screen. "Duncan," she said quietly, sliding off the too-short love seat to sit on the heavily carpeted floor.

"Cynthia," came his familiar, reassuring voice with its slight Southern drawl.

She'd known this call would come. Juro would have started notifying the others as soon as he was in the air last night. After all, Raphael's abduction was very likely the first blow in the coming war, and the other vampire lords needed to know, to prepare. Not so long ago, the very opposite would have been true. Raphael's people would have gone to any lengths to keep his abduction a secret. But the North American vampires were an alliance now, and they'd all agreed that the enemy's most likely first strike would target Raphael. Now that Mathilde had succeeded in that—at least in the short term—Juro would have warned the others that a broader attack might be imminent.

"Duncan," she repeated, once again fighting tears that thickened her throat and made speech almost impossible. She was becoming a real gusher of emotions lately. If she didn't get Raphael back soon, he wouldn't recognize the human waterworks she'd become.

"I won't ask how you're doing, Cynthia. I know." Duncan said, the obvious affection in his voice doing nothing to bring her emotions under control. Duncan had been Raphael's lieutenant for over a century. He'd left just the previous year when he'd fought for and won his own territory. Cyn and Duncan hadn't trusted each other initially, but they'd eventually grown close, and she still missed his daily presence, since he'd moved all the way across the country to Washington, D.C.

"Juro told us about your plans," he said, probably to fill the silence created by her current inability to speak. "How can we help?"

Cyn leaned her head back against the love seat and closed her eyes. He wasn't going to try and talk her out of rescuing Raphael. But then, he wouldn't. Duncan knew her too well to think he could talk her out of anything, especially when it came to Raphael's safety. Besides, he loved Raphael as much as she did. He might be sounding like his usual unflappable self, but she knew he was fighting the urge to hop on a plane and join her in Hawaii himself.

"We're still gathering info at this point," she told him. "But don't worry, if we need anything I'll call. How are *you* doing, Duncan? And no bullshit."

"Suffice it to say the last twenty-four hours have been stressful," he admitted, which was the equivalent of a primal scream from anyone else. The continued presence of his drawl alone was an indicator of his stress levels to anyone who knew him well. The more upset Duncan got, the more his drawl became evident. "They don't need me here, Cynthia," he said, his voice subdued and his words rushed, as if he didn't want anyone there to catch what he was saying. "Miguel can—"

"Duncan," she interrupted him, bemused to find herself taking the logical position in the present conversation. "You can't leave your territory right now. And even if you could, Anthony needs your support. We don't know where the next attack will come."

"Fucking Anthony," he said viciously. More evidence of his emotional state. Duncan rarely lost his cool and even more rarely cursed. "Raphael should have replaced him long before this."

"Yeah, that Raphael's a real slacker," she agreed, affecting a drawl of her own. "'course, there *have* been a few other demands on his time lately."

Duncan sighed. "You're right, I know. But if there is *anything* I can do to help—"

"I'll call. But Robbie's here with me, and Elke and Ken'ichi. And I think we're better off with a small team, going guerilla style."

"Guerilla, huh?" She heard the smile in his voice.

"It suits me, don't you think?"

"Amazingly well. But, Cynthia, whatever you need, even if it's no more than a friendly voice on the phone, you must promise you'll call."

"I'll call," she repeated patiently. "Should I expect to hear from Lucas next?" she asked.

"I'm only surprised I got to you first," Duncan told her. "Last I spoke to him, the boy had his jet fueled and ready to go."

"You have to stop him, Duncan."

"I believe I've convinced him to stay where he is for now. But should something change . . . he can get to you faster than I can, Cynthia."

"I don't think we need Lucas's idea of help right now."

"He can be subtle when necessary."

"I'll take your word for that, but—" She broke off as her phone indicated another incoming call. "Speak of the devil," she told Duncan. "It's Lucas."

Duncan sighed loudly. "I do wish we weren't all so far away."

Her phone beeped again. "Shit, I have to take this, Duncan. I have to talk to Lucas, or he'll convince himself I'm dead and show up here before the night is over. You know he will."

"You're right. Take care, Cynthia, and remember—"

"Anything I need, I know. And, Duncan, I'll bring him back. I promise. Give my love to Emma." She caught Lucas's call just before it went to voicemail. "Lucas," she answered.

"Cynthia darling," Lucas greeted her, his voice the very opposite of Duncan's drawl, in that energy sparkled from every syllable. "We're geared up and ready to go. Give us a target and we're there."

"Lucas," she chided him. "I know you and Raphael talked about this. Juro and Jared need you right where you are."

"Fuck them," he said with a sudden viciousness that matched Duncan's earlier outburst. "Nobody said anything about Raphael being captured by that bitch Mathilde."

"You know Mathilde? You've met her?" she asked urgently, thinking she should have asked Duncan that, too. The more information she had, the better. Lucas had been with Raphael in Europe, so he was more likely to have met the bitch.

"I met her, but I was still human at the time and well beneath her notice, so I don't know much about her," he admitted, and Cyn felt despair hovering like a thick gray fog. "Raphael spent some time in her court, just a few months. They never got along well, but they almost came to blows right before we left for good. I'm not sure what the argument was about, but Raphael was as pissed as I've ever seen him, and we left the next day."

The fog of despair seemed to creep closer, but then she remembered the main reason she'd taken his call. "Don't come here, Lucas. Mathilde thinks all of Raphael's people have left the islands, and I want her to keep thinking that. If she doesn't know we're here, she won't bother to guard against us."

"Darling. I do love smart women."

"You love *all* women."

"Alas, no longer. I am a one-woman vampire now."

"Kathryn just walked into the room, didn't she?" Cyn asked, feeling her mood lighten despite their desperate situation. She heard a low-pitched female voice in the background a moment before Lucas came back.

"My beautiful Katie sends her regards and says to tell you that her VICAP search turned up nothing useful, but she'll keep looking."

"Tell her thanks, and I'll call if I have more to go on."

"Know this, Cynthia," Lucas said in a rare moment of seriousness. "There are very few beings who truly matter to me in this world. I will do *anything* for Raphael. Anything."

"I'll bring him back," she vowed yet again, making the same promise to Lucas as she had to Duncan and to Juro before that.

Because the truth of it was, she was either going to save Raphael . . . or die trying.

"You stay safe, Lucas. You and Kathryn both. I'll be in touch," Cyn said. She disconnected the call, but didn't get up right away, taking a few minutes to rein in the emotions the two calls had stirred up, to build a wall of steel and then stick all of her emotions behind it. She needed that detachment, in order to function on the level necessary to see what needed to be done and then to follow through and do it. She knew her strengths and weaknesses. She had a talent for weeding through the reams of data that came in on a case and finding the few bits that mattered. She excelled in tactical thinking and was single-minded, some said obsessive, in pursuit of her goal. But she sure as hell wasn't fearless. There was no such thing. There was only the ability to keep going despite the fear, and she could do that. Unfortunately, her biggest fear in this case was not for herself, but for Raphael. And that was so tangled up in her love for him that it was far more difficult to shove behind the wall.

Sighing, she dragged her blanket and pillow down onto the floor, hoping to catch another hour or two of sleep before sundown. She'd never be able to relax in the bedroom, knowing the vamps were unprotected, but, at least on the floor, she could stretch out.

She'd just begun to drift off, however, when the doorbell rang. The unexpected sound brought her up onto her knees in an instant, Glock in her hand and pointed toward the stairs, before she remembered the damn SUV she'd arranged for the rental company to deliver.

Heart pounding with the adrenaline rush, she headed downstairs. With the Glock still held ready and low at her side, she opened the door just enough to check out the very earnest-looking young man standing there with a clipboard. Cyn smiled, trying to look like your average, friendly tourist, but judging by the flare of alarm in the kid's eyes, she figured she failed miserably. She understood his reaction even better when she reached behind the door to put her gun down and caught her reflection in the mirror hanging above the table there. She looked like an ax murderer. No wonder the kid's hands were shaking.

She dug her wallet out of her backpack before following him to the Suburban sitting in the driveway. Using one of her several fake IDs, she managed to calm the kid enough to finish the paperwork. She'd just initialed and signed the last form when his buddy pulled up with his ride back. She gave the kid a smile and a hundred dollar tip, trying to make up for his earlier fright, then headed back into the dark and silent house. She briefly contemplated giving sleep another try, but then surrendered to reality and turned for the kitchen instead.

She was going to need coffee. Lots and lots of coffee.

"WHAT DID DUNCAN have to say?" Those were the first words out of Elke's mouth when she strolled into the kitchen several hours later.

Cyn looked up from where she'd been hunched over her laptop for hours, poring over crime reports from the last few weeks. She didn't bother to ask how Elke knew Duncan had called. Elke had known Duncan much longer than Cyn had. They'd worked together almost daily for decades.

"Duncan and Lucas both called, and both offered to fly out. I told them to stay put for now."

"Lucas will be more difficult to rein in if this continues much longer," Ken'ichi commented quietly, joining the conversation as he came into the kitchen. His thoughts mirrored Cyn's almost exactly, and she found herself constantly having to reevaluate her assessment of him. He'd remained in Juro's shadow for so long that she was still adjusting to this new version—the one that talked.

Cyn covered her confusion by taking a sip from what felt like her hundredth cup of coffee for the day. It didn't even taste good anymore. She put the cup down with a grimace, and brought both vamps up to date.

"Lucas isn't our problem tonight. I received *this* text message today." She handed her cell phone across the bar to Ken'ichi who placed it on the counter between him and Elke where they could both read it. Cursing softly, Elke scrolled until they'd read the entire conversation, then she looked up with an accusing glare.

"You agreed to meet him."

Cyn nodded. "Robbie and I discussed it, and decided it was worth a try as long as we were smart about it. It's always possible Mathilde sent him, but that doesn't add up. If she knew I was still here, she wouldn't waste time with a computer geek. She'd either send a full hit squad, or she'd ignore me altogether.

"But Willis says he worked for Rhys Patterson, and the last we heard, Patterson was only with Mathilde under duress. So Willis might just be trying to help out his boss."

"So, he thinks we can help *him,*" Elke said dryly. "But what's in it for us?"

"That's what I want to know, and I'm willing to meet him to find out."

"You and Rob have already set this up?" Ken'ichi asked, meeting her eyes solemnly.

Cyn nodded. "Tonight, at the local McDonald's. Robbie's already there. He's been keeping watch, just in case Willis tries to sneak in an ally or three. The deal was that he would come alone."

"What time are we meeting him?" Elke asked.

"The meet is ninety minutes after sunset, but I told Robbie we'd get there early."

"How are we supposed to get there if Rob took the clown car?" Elke asked. "I mean Ken'ichi and I can run it, but you—"

"I had a different rental place deliver another vehicle."

Elke stood. "I hope you got a real one this time."

Cyn smiled. "I took care of it. You guys ready to rock and roll?"

"I am ready to depart," Ken'ichi agreed, pushing away from the counter.

Elke rolled her eyes at him, then looked at Cyn. "What he meant to say was, 'Hell, yeah, let's go fuck up a geek!'"

THE MCDONALD'S was busy when they pulled into the parking lot. With summer still weeks away, darkness came early, and rush hour was in full swing. But as Robbie had predicted, the picnic area was all but deserted. In fact, there was only one person sitting outside, and that was Donovan Willis. Cyn recognized him from his brief visit to the house. In fact, he looked exactly the same, right down to the clothes he was wearing, which made her think he might be in hiding, just like they were.

He was sitting at a table several rows back, but facing the parking lot, a laptop computer open in front of him as he pretended to work. Cyn could tell he was only pretending, because even in the short time that she'd been observing him, his eyes had been fixed far more often on the cars coming and going than on his computer screen.

Cyn picked up her burner phone and hit Robbie's number.

"Yo," he answered. "Nice wheels."

"Elke thinks so. Anything we need to know?"

"Not that I've seen. Our boy showed up five minutes before you did.

Guess he doesn't trust us either."

"I find myself reassured by that. How do you want to play this?"

"I'll make first contact. If everything's secure, I'll stand up and turned toward your position. Then you come ahead with the others."

"Sounds good."

"Don't approach alone, Cyn. Let Ken'ichi and Elke do their job."

"No argument. I have only one goal here, and that's to get to Raphael. I can't do that if I'm captured or dead."

"No one's going to get to you. Not on my watch."

"I know. We'll wait for your signal."

She disconnected and set the phone aside, not bothering to tell the others what Robbie had said. They were vampires. They'd probably been able to hear him better than she had.

"There he goes," Elke said softly.

Robbie came out of the darkness surrounding the picnic area, moving steadily but not rushing, clearly trying to avoid spooking Willis. Cyn wasn't sure it worked. Willis jerked to his feet, nearly falling over when his knees caught on the picnic table bench, barely managing to catch himself enough to plop gracelessly down on his ass.

Never taking his eyes off Robbie, he pushed his glasses up on his nose in what was plainly a habitual gesture. He said something that Cyn couldn't catch, and she wished they'd had enough time to pick up some communications gear. She put that on her mental to-do list. They needed the kind of Bluetooth comm devices that all of Raphael's security people used. If she'd thought about it, or if they'd had more time, she'd have grabbed a few as they'd snuck out the back door of the big house. But it shouldn't be too difficult to find something equivalent, even here in paradise.

She focused back on Robbie who was saying something to Willis. He leaned forward and, reaching out with one big hand, slapped the other man's laptop lid down, keeping his hand on the device, fingers splayed, as he spoke intently. Willis leaned away, his posture stiff, hands raised in front of him, mouth moving as he responded quickly to whatever Robbie had said.

Robbie eyed the other man briefly, then spun toward the parking lot. His gaze went directly to the dark corner where Cyn and the others sat waiting, and he gave a barely perceptible nod.

"Looks like it's a go," Cyn announced, careful to let none of the anxiety she was feeling reflect in her voice. Her concern wasn't for herself. It wasn't even for Robbie or the others. What she worried about, what had fear skittering along her nerves like a swarm of biting ants, was the possibility of failure. The chance that she'd make the wrong move at the wrong time, and Raphael would pay for her mistake. She could accept her own death, but not Raphael's.

"I will go first," Ken'ichi informed her. He wasn't asking her approval, or soliciting her compliance. This was her bodyguard telling her how it was going to be.

"Elke will follow," he continued, "and then you. You will remain within our cover until we know it is safe."

"Robbie okayed it. He must think—"

"Rob is an excellent bodyguard, but he is, nonetheless, human. There are more reliable methods to verify Willis's intent."

"Don't hurt him," Cyn cautioned. "If he's on the up and up, we'll need his cooperation, if not his trust."

"I'm aware. Are you ready, Elke?"

Elke nodded once, all business, just like Ken'ichi. She opened her door and came around the front of the SUV to stand just to the rear of Cyn's door. Once she was in position, Ken'ichi exited the vehicle, which apparently was the signal Elke was waiting for. She reached for Cyn's door handle, but Cyn beat her to it, opening the door from the inside, stepping over the running board as her feet hit the parking lot and she straightened. The two vehicle doors slammed shut with virtually simultaneous *thunks* of sound, and then they were moving.

Cyn caught the moment Willis saw them coming. His eyes fixed on Ken'ichi first, widening in shock, and it occurred to Cyn that Willis probably thought Ken'ichi was Juro. The twins were truly identical in appearance. It was only after you got to know them that they were easily distinguished from one another.

But Willis didn't know any of that. He saw what he probably thought was Juro bearing down on him, when he'd believed that Juro and the others had all gone back to L.A.

He rose slowly to his feet, looking like he was getting ready to bolt.

Cyn stepped out of Ken'ichi's shadow, ignoring his growled warning as she pasted a smile on her face and held out her hand in greeting. She knew it was against the rules, but she didn't want Willis to disappear before they had a chance to speak.

"Mr. Willis?" she said unnecessarily, still offering her hand. "I'm Cynthia Leighton." She spoke quietly, lest anyone eavesdrop. She had faith in both Robbie and Ken'ichi, but their group wasn't exactly inconspicuous in a McDonald's picnic area. The breach could be something as inadvertent as a busy mom catching sight of them and passing it on as casual gossip, and the next person doing the same until it wound its way somehow to Mathilde's ear.

Willis ignored her hand at first. He was too busy scrutinizing her, from the clothes she wore to the shoulder harness peeking out from beneath her jacket, to a careful scan of her face.

Finally, he stretched a hand across the scarred table, with its layers of thick paint, and said, "Call me Donovan."

Cyn shook his hand. "And I'm Cyn. May I join you?"

He smiled at that, a nervous half grin that crooked the right side of his mouth. "That's why we're here, isn't it?"

Cyn swung a long leg over the bench and sat down, shooting a smile at Robbie who remained close to Donovan, his 9mm Beretta drawn and held down by his thigh, out of sight to passersby, but clearly visible to Donovan. Robbie obviously didn't trust the computer tech yet. But then, that's what made him so good at his job.

"This is Rob," she said, "but you probably know that. Behind me are Elke and Ken'ichi."

"Ken'ichi," Willis repeated, mostly to himself, as he stared at Ken'ichi. "He looks just like—"

"He does," Cyn agreed. "But he's not." She didn't explain why the two Japanese vampires looked so much alike. That was none of Willis's business.

"So why are we here, Donovan?" she asked directly.

Willis's hands trembled ever so slightly as he raised them to rest on the table to either side of his laptop, his eyes downcast, as if gathering himself for whatever came next. Finally, he looked up and said, "Because we've both lost someone we love."

Cyn met his gaze steadily. "I haven't lost *anyone* yet. And I don't intend to."

Donovan shook his head impatiently. "I didn't mean . . . no one's dead, at least not that I know of. And I think I'd know."

"You're human," Ken'ichi said, stating the obvious. "So who is your mate?"

Cyn blinked at the question that seemed to come from nowhere, then she realized . . . Donovan claimed he'd know if someone had died. And the only way he could know that was if he was mated, just as Cyn would know if something happened to Raphael. So who *was* Donovan's mate?

Donovan swallowed hard, staring first at Ken'ichi, then at Cyn, his eyes blinking rapidly as if fighting back tears. "Rhys," he said finally, speaking in a near whisper. "Rhys Patterson."

Cyn eyed him closely. They'd assumed Patterson was being forced to help Mathilde. Donovan's words seemed to confirm it. Careful to keep such speculation from coloring her words, she said only, "I thought Rhys Patterson was master of these islands."

Donovan nodded. "He is."

"And the two of you are mated."

"We are," he said almost defiantly.

"Relax," Cyn told him. "I don't care who Patterson loves. All I care about is whether he holds faith with his sworn lord. And that's Raphael, not some interloper from France."

"Rhys did not betray Lord Raphael."

"You'll pardon my skepticism."

"I know what it looks like, but you don't know everything. Mathilde has Rhys's people. She took them without any warning, before he even knew she was here. Rhys isn't a lord. He's not like Raphael or the others who can tell the moment a foreign power crosses their border. He didn't know Mathilde was even in Hawaii until she showed up at our house, and by then it was too late."

"How's she holding the others? I mean they're vampires. If enough of them get together—"

"They're starving. She gives them just enough blood to keep them alive, but no more."

"How do you know? I mean, no offense, but you're human."

"So are you," he snapped, but Cyn only shrugged.

"You said it," she told him. "Raphael is far more powerful than Rhys. Our minds are always touching."

"You're right. Rhys isn't that powerful. But I'm connected enough to Rhys that I can feel his pain, not only for himself, but for the others. They're his children and they're suffering terribly."

Cyn didn't know if any of this was true, but she was convinced that Donovan believed it. She was also convinced that he loved Rhys Patterson.

"So where's Rhys now?"

"He's with that crazy cunt Mathilde. I don't know exactly where anymore, because she moved everyone. I only know she keeps Rhys close."

"Why isn't she worried about what you're doing, left all alone? Doesn't she know about you and Rhys?"

"Mathilde doesn't have a mate and is very dismissive of those who do, claiming it weakens them, makes them more like their prey. She doesn't even have a regular lover that I can tell. Her vamps go out hunting and bring home a selection of donors, like a dessert platter. Mathilde makes her pick, takes a bite, fucks them if she finds them appealing, and then she forgets about them."

"Are they killing people?" Cyn asked, leaning forward intently.

"Mathilde's people aren't. But I can't speak to the others."

"Others?"

"You must know about them," he said, looking up and giving Ken'ichi a confused look. "Mathilde flew in a whole army of master vampires. They're the ones blocking Raphael. Soon after they arrived, Rhys was furious because they were leaving their human victims, or donors if you want to call them that, injured and close to death. He said Mathilde's people were shitting all over his home, and leaving him to clean up their mess. Then a couple of people were killed, and he nearly lost it."

Cyn exchanged a look with Robbie. If Donovan was right, then those news reports he'd given them might lead to wherever Raphael was being held. Unless . . .

"Do you know where they've moved to? Where they're holding Raphael now?" she asked urgently.

But Donovan shook his head. "They're all gone. Even Rhys. That's why I contacted you. She promised Rhys that she'd release him and our people once Raphael was secured. But when I went back there this morning . . . everyone was gone. And Rhys hasn't contacted me."

"Where were you when they disappeared?"

"I was trying to find the house where she's holding our people. We thought, that is, Rhys and I thought that if I could get to his vampires, and if they all worked together, then maybe he could break away. He was sure he knew where Mathilde had stashed them, but . . . he was wrong. And when I went back to tell him, he was gone, too."

"Is that the house where Raphael met Mathilde?"

He shook his head. "No, she only used that place for the meet. She was staying at the house Rhys and I live in. She moved Raphael there that first night, right after he was captured. But I went back last night, and it's completely empty."

"What was Rhys's plan? I mean, if you'd been successful in freeing his vamps? What about Raphael?"

"I don't know," Donovan said without looking at her. But then he raised his head with a glare and snarled vehemently, "And I don't care! The great Lord Raphael. Even Rhys talked about him like he was a god, the big bad made flesh. So he can save himself. I only care about Rhys."

Cyn shrugged. "So why call me?"

"Because whether I like it or not, Rhys's best chance of surviving this fuckup is if Raphael breaks loose. And I know your reputation. You're going after Raphael, and I can help make that happen."

"How'd you know I was on the island?" she asked, still very suspicious.

"I tracked your cell phone."

"You hacked my phone?"

"Like it was even a challenge," he said dismissively. "I told you, I've heard about you. I wasn't sure you'd originally come over with Raphael, but I knew if you weren't here already, that you would be soon."

Cyn digested all of that. At least Willis was being honest. He admitted that he didn't give a fuck about Raphael, that he was only hitchhiking on her investigation to save Rhys. But as long as he could help out, she didn't care what his motivations were. If he was telling the truth about that much . . .

"Ken'ichi?" she said, locking her gaze on Willis.

"Cynthia."

"Is he telling the truth?"

Willis's eyes widened in realization. He didn't know Ken'ichi, but with her question, Cyn had just informed him that the big vampire was more than muscle, that he was also powerful enough to know when a human was lying. Cyn waited for Willis to panic, maybe even to try running—although he'd never have succeeded—but while his throat moved in a nervous swallow, he stared right back at her and waited for the verdict.

"He tells the truth," Ken'ichi said, his deep voice dark with dislike. "He truly doesn't give a fuck about my lord Raphael. Who is also my Sire, human."

Cyn bared her teeth in a grin as Willis shot a nervous glance over her shoulder. She didn't have to turn and look to know that Ken'ichi was giving Willis his menacing best.

"All right," she said, drawing Willis's attention back to herself. "So, I understand why you'd want *our* help, I just don't understand why *we'd* want *yours*. I'm not exactly working alone here," she said, lifting her chin in a half circle to indicate Robbie and the two vamps. "Why do I need you?"

"Because I know the Islands, and I know Mathilde. She's been strutting around here for weeks, making demands like some kind of queen, treating the rest of us like dirt. I know how she thinks. And I have skills," he added with more than a touch of arrogance. "Skills that, all due respect to your team here, I doubt they can duplicate. I can crack any database, any computer. And if you find Mathilde, I have a back door into every system she owns, from her personal cell phone to the comm units her security is using."

"I'll grant your hacking skills could be useful," Cyn admitted, although she wasn't about to tell him that she'd been bemoaning the absence of those same skills just a few hours earlier. "But why would Mathilde have included you in any of her planning?"

"Who said she included me? I wasn't even a blip on her radar. Which is exactly why I overheard as much as I did. She had to include Rhys, because he was the only one who knows the Islands. Not to mention, his participation was necessary to fool Raphael. But here's the thing—Rhys brought me with him to most of the meetings, and I paid attention."

"And Mathilde didn't notice that?"

"No more than she'd notice a dog sitting at Rhys's feet."

Cyn tapped her fingers on the table absently, trying to find a hole in his story, a reason why she shouldn't accept his help. She came up with nothing.

"Okay," she said abruptly. "We have a house we're using for now. We'll move as the investigation demands, but for now, it's convenient. We'll head back there and decide where we go next. You have a car?"

IT TURNED OUT that Willis did have a car, and after a bit of shuffling between the three vehicles and the two-car garage, it was agreed that Willis's car should definitely be out of sight. It might be as he said, that Mathilde barely knew he was alive, but there was no need to tempt fate. As for the other garage bay, they decided the clown car looked more like the typical tourist rental, so that was left in the driveway and the Suburban was parked in the second bay, dwarfing the hacker's tiny two-seater.

Cyn had already pushed her way into the kitchen, figuring the big parking debate didn't require her input. She had only one thing on her mind, and that was to sleep, and if she was really lucky, maybe to dream of Raphael. She grabbed a bottle of water, and started for her bedroom, but found herself sinking onto the stairs, too tired to keep going, or even to pull off her jacket. She wondered if Raphael would reach her in her dreams if she slept right here.

Without warning, Robbie's big hands lifted her bodily to her feet. "Go upstairs, Cyn. If anything happens, I'll wake you up."

Cyn stared at him blearily. "Will you carry me?"

Robbie grinned. "No, but you can lean on me so we don't lose you before we get there."

When they reached the room she was calling her own, Cyn patted Robbie's thick chest in thanks, then closed the door as he walked away. Stripping off her clothes one piece at a time, she left them wherever they dropped. The only exception was her shoulder harness and the 9mm Glock that was holstered there. The harness she draped over a chair close to the bed, the Glock went on the table close to her pillow. Her backup weapon was still in her duffle. She hadn't worn it to meet Willis, because she had plenty of firepower in her team without it, but from here on out, she'd have both weapons on her person whenever they went out.

Dropping onto the too-firm mattress in nothing but her underwear and a stretchy tank top, Cyn contemplated taking a shower, but couldn't generate the willpower to do anything except pull back the covers and crawl beneath them. The sheets were cool and clean-smelling, and her body ached with relief at finally being prone. She called up the image of Raphael as she'd last seen him, as he'd kissed her good-bye before going off to meet Mathilde. And she wondered what he was doing right now, what he was going through. It was nighttime. No matter what else they were doing to him, he'd be awake and aware. Were they torturing him? Was he wondering why she hadn't found him yet?

Her gaze fell on Raphael's leather jacket, the one she'd grabbed on her way out the door, the one he hadn't worn because he'd wanted to dress properly for the negotiations with Mathilde. The bitch.

Cyn stretched out an arm and snagged it from the chair, then burrowed back into the pillows, hugging it to her chest. She felt the first warm trail of liquid along her cheek as a tear leaked out and soaked into the pillow. And then she slept.

THE MATTRESS next to her dipped as if someone knelt on the bed, the covers shifting as he pulled them back and slipped in behind her. She recognized the scent of him, knew the strength of his presence as he reached out a powerful arm and dragged her across the crisp sheets, snuggling her into the curve of his big body.

Cyn whimpered softly, weaving her fingers with his over her abdomen, trapping his arms in place before he could disappear.

"Sleep, *lubimaya*," he murmured.

"I can't sleep. I have to find you," she complained, hearing the fretful quality of her own words. She sounded like an overtired child.

"I'm here. I'll always be right here," he said, pressing a hand to her heart.

"No!" she almost shouted, shoving his hand away. "Don't say shit like that. I don't want you in my fucking heart like a memory. I want you in my arms where I can touch you, where I can drive you crazy."

His lips moved against her hair with his smile, and she rolled over, burying her face against his chest. "Are you really here, or am I dreaming?"

What a stupid question to ask, she thought. If the whole thing was a dream, her dreaming mind wouldn't know that. Duh.

"Never mind," she muttered, then caved and asked the question that had haunted her every waking moment since he'd been taken. "Are you okay? Are they . . . hurting you?"

Raphael's arms tightened around her. "They are not powerful enough to hurt me," he said. "It is all they can do to hold me. And even that control frays with every passing hour or I would not be with you now."

Cyn listened to every word, every syllable of his reassurances, straining to hear the tiniest hint of deception, anything that would tell her he was saying what she needed to hear instead of the truth. But she found nothing. Raphael was an accomplished liar, but not with her, not anymore. She believed he really was okay . . . for now.

"Where are you?" she whispered, almost afraid to ask the question, afraid that he would disappear the moment she left the realm of feelings and crossed into the real world of strategy and rescues.

"I don't know," he admitted, regret and even embarrassment plain in his thoughts. "It was night when we left the house, but daylight before the plane departed."

"Plane," Cyn repeated urgently. "You were on a plane . . . Raphael?"

He was gone. Not gone as in real life, not a gradual slipping away, but just . . . gone. And she wanted to scream. Had she done that with her stupid questions? Would he have stayed longer if she'd just shut up and kissed him? Kissed him. She never even got to kiss him.

Cyn woke to the intense light of sunset streaming through the uncovered window, and tears streaming from her eyes. She curled into a ball hugging Raphael's jacket to herself, holding the memory of him close as she let the tears come. *Get it all out now*, she thought. Get rid of all this useless emotion, then get up, take a fucking shower, and get ready to kick some ass.

Chapter Ten

"THEY'VE MOVED him to another island."

Everyone looked up at Cyn's announcement, as she strode into the kitchen a short time later, after a quick shower and change of clothes. She went directly to the coffeemaker and poured a cup of java, added sugar, then turned around, mug in hand, still stirring.

Ken'ichi was the first to respond. "Raphael contacted you?" When Cyn confirmed his assumption with a nod, his expression became fiercely smug, as if he'd known all along that no one could hold his Sire down for long.

Elke and Robbie were both grinning, but Willis only seemed confused.

"Come on, dude," Robbie said impatiently. "You're mated to a reasonably powerful vamp. You guys must mind-speak on some level, right?"

"Well, yeah, but . . . are you saying he talked to you while you slept? While *he* slept? During the day?"

Cyn shrugged. "Yeah."

Willis just stared at her, apparently speechless. And Cyn was reminded that what she took for granted as part of life with Raphael was really quite extraordinary, even among vampires.

"Okay," she said, suddenly uncomfortable. "We have confirmation that he's off the island, but we still don't know where. Our best leads so far are the reports of vampire-like murders from Honolulu. I'm going to call Murphy again, and see if he's made any progress with his buddy from Oahu. It would be really helpful to have a cop on our team."

"You don't need a cop. I can get into HPD's system any time I want," Willis said, clearly eager to prove his worth.

"That's great, and that's why we need you. But cops talk, and not everything they say makes it to the official record. I'd like to tap into that, too."

Willis nodded in reluctant agreement. Hackers tended to believe everything could be found somewhere online.

"Either way," Cyn continued efficiently, "we're leaving this house and probably not coming back. That means the window covers come down, along with any other evidence that screams *vampire*. I'll have Luci arrange for a housecleaning service to come in and take care of the rest."

She chugged the last of her coffee, then rinsed the mug and put it in the dishwasher as the others all pushed back chairs and stools.

"Robbie, you've met the pilot, Brandon. Call him, please, and arrange a flight for later tonight. As soon as he thinks it can be done. And I'll go call Murphy."

She started out of the kitchen, stopping only to meet Ken'ichi's dark eyes with a confident smile. "We'll find him. And then we'll take care of the rest of them."

Ken'ichi gave her a rare grin, as exultant as it was predatory. "They die, Cynthia. Every one of them."

"They sure as hell do."

THE PHONE RANG only once, before Colin Murphy answered with a short "Leighton."

"Am I the only person you never say hello to, Murphy?" Cyn asked dryly.

"No, that's pretty much my standard greeting method. Unless I don't know who's calling, then it's, 'What the hell do you want?' So, count yourself lucky."

"Luck is good, but a contact in the local police force would be better. Did you talk to your SEAL buddy yet?"

"I did, and I have a name for you. The cop's name is Mal Turner, and he's a detective with HPD, that's Honolulu Police Department. If you need a different jurisdiction—"

"No, that's perfect. What do I tell him?"

"My buddy's name is Doug Burgess. Doug's called Turner, so he's expecting to hear from you."

"That's great. Thanks, Murphy. How's the northern front?"

"Quiet for now, but we're all getting ready for the worst. We're trying to anticipate strategy, but that's difficult to do with so little information."

"And so much territory to cover," Cyn said, referring to Sophia's territory, which was all of Canada.

"Raj and Aden have really stepped up on that front. Lucas, too, although with Raphael missing, he's pretty focused on helping Juro and Jared in the West."

"Raphael saw this coming."

"Seems like. We'd be in much worse shape without the alliance."

Cyn wanted to feel good about that, and she did. She was proud of what Raphael had accomplished in pulling the eight vampire lords of

North America into a single working alliance. But it was difficult to feel good about Raphael's accomplishments as long as he remained Mathilde's prisoner.

"Mathilde and the others are going to be sorry they ever left Europe."

"How's it going there, Leighton?"

"They've moved him off this island. We know that for a fact. And we have a solid lead on where he might be. Your cop friend is going to come in very handy in narrowing that down."

"So you're optimistic."

"I don't do optimistic. Not when it comes to the people I care about. I just get the job done, and I do it with a vengeance when someone fucks with Raphael."

"Uh huh. Now that we've got that out of the way, how are you really feeling? The no bullshit version."

Cyn sank to the bed with a sigh. "I'm scared to death."

"Everyone's scared going into stuff like this, that's—"

"No, Murphy. I'm not scared for myself. I'm afraid I'll do something stupid and Raphael will pay the price."

"Fuck that. I'd trust you with my life, Leighton. Your instincts are as good as any operative I know, and I know some of the best."

Cyn smiled wryly. "Thanks, Murphy. Even if it's not true, it's nice to hear."

"Damn it, Cyn. I meant every fucking word."

"Okay."

"Rob's still with you, right?"

"Every step of the way. He won't let me out of his sight."

"There you go. If a warrior like Rob follows you, you're doing something right."

"Okay," she repeated.

Murphy swore softly. "Call Mal Turner, Cyn. And if you can't get him, you can call my buddy Doug. I'm texting you their personal cell numbers, and I've also included Turner's HPD number, just in case. But I warned Doug that you'd probably be calling at night, given the circumstances."

Cyn looked down as her phone dinged an incoming message. "Got it," she told Murphy.

"All right. I've got to go. It's later here and the meetings are back to back, trying to get everyone ready."

"I understand. Good luck, and I'll talk to you when we get back to L.A."

"Call anytime, Leighton. Especially if it's good news."

"Same goes. 'Bye, Murphy."

Cyn disconnected, then opened a fresh burner phone and dialed Mal Turner's personal cell. She steeled herself, not knowing what to expect. She'd never been anything but a street cop, and she hadn't lasted that long in the LAPD. But she'd known a few detectives. They were generally overworked and didn't appreciate having to play nice for someone's friend or relative. They all did it, because their network of contacts was critical, but they didn't like it.

The phone rang five times and she was about to hang up when a harsh voice growled, "Turner."

Cyn didn't waste time on niceties. "This is Cynthia Leighton. Doug Burgess gave me your number."

"Yes, he did. What's this about?"

"Burgess didn't say anything?"

"I wouldn't ask if he did, sweetheart."

Cyn grimaced at the endearment, but let it pass. "I'm looking for a killer who I think is operating in your jurisdiction."

"Yeah? Funny thing. That's kind of what *I* do. So tell me why I need you to do my job."

"Because this killer's a vampire, Detective Turner. And I know a hell of a lot more about vampires than you do."

She waited. The silence went on for several minutes, but she knew he was still there. She could hear a game of some sort playing in the background, then Turner cursed, and the noise cut off.

"Who the fuck are you?" he demanded.

"I told you. My name is Cynthia Leighton. As for the rest, we should meet, because this isn't the sort of thing you discuss on the phone."

"How do I know you're not full of shit?"

"Check me out. You have my name. I'll give you whatever other info you need. I'm former LAPD and now a licensed private investigator in the state of California. You'll probably find other stories out there, too. Some of them are even true. But most importantly, detective, I'm the person who can help you kill whoever's ripping out throats on the streets of Honolulu."

"You mean capture, don't you, sweetheart? You said 'kill.'"

"Yeah. First lesson when it comes to murderous vampires, *darling*. If you catch 'em, you kill 'em."

Turner gave a surprised laugh that sounded like stones rolling around in his chest.

"I like you, Leighton. When can we meet?"

"I'll be in Honolulu later tonight, so anytime tomorrow day or night."

"So, you're not a vamp yourself, then?"

"I'm not."

"All right. Let's keep this out of the office. This a good number for you?"

"It's a burner, but it's good for another day."

"The mystery deepens. Okay. I'll text you a location. We meet there at 8:30 tomorrow night. Don't be late."

"I'll be there."

"And, Leighton?"

"Yeah?"

"I will be checking you out, so if there's anything you want to say—"

"Nothing *to* say, Turner. See you tomorrow night."

Cyn disconnected, then stood to gather the few things she'd unpacked, including Raphael's jacket. Her phone pinged, and she paused to read an incoming message from Mal Turner. He'd provided the name and location of a bar, but since she knew nothing of Honolulu, the information told her very little. She'd make a point of checking out the bar with Robbie during the day tomorrow. Friend of a friend or not, she never went blind into an unknown place to meet an unknown person.

Robbie stuck his head through the open doorway as she was pulling the zipper closed on her duffle.

"You about ready?" he asked. "Brandon's prepping the plane now. He says given our drive time, we can take off as soon as we get there."

She hefted the duffle, which Robbie immediately took from her. "Save your strength, babe. Did Murphy get a cop for you?"

"Yeah. Guy named Mal Turner. I called and he sounds interested in what we have to say. Reluctant at first, but no surprise there. As soon as I mentioned vampire kills, though, he changed his tune. We're meeting him tomorrow night."

"Evening's good. I feel better with Ken'ichi and Elke at our backs. I trust we're not meeting him at the station. Vamps and cops don't mix."

"We're meeting at a bar. You and I can scope it out tomorrow afternoon."

"Sounds good."

Robbie headed downstairs while Cyn did a final check of the upstairs bedrooms, to be sure the various sheets and towels had been pulled off the windows. Downstairs, all of the used linens had gone into a huge pile in the laundry room. Cyn made a mental note to text Luci about getting a housekeeping service in for everything else.

Elke was waiting when she finished her survey of the ground floor, and they joined the others in the garage to find Robbie and Ken'ichi already climbing into the front seat of the Suburban, with Willis a smaller shadow in the front seat of his own car. She'd almost forgotten about Willis. She wasn't even sure she still needed him, to be honest. But it couldn't hurt to have a hacker on hand, and his knowledge of the Islands and his connection to Patterson could still prove useful before this was over.

But that didn't mean she trusted him. He wasn't going to Honolulu with them. They were going to park him at a very nice hotel not far from Lihue airport in Kauai. Cyn had made the reservation using one of her own aliases and credit cards. He'd be safer there, and he'd be available if she needed him, but he wouldn't know any more than she wanted him to about where the rest of them were or what they were doing. Willis claimed to be on their side, and Ken'ichi's vampire truth-sense confirmed his intentions. But his interests didn't exactly coincide with theirs. If it came to a choice between Patterson and Raphael, there was no doubt in her mind as to which one he'd choose.

"Does this mean you and I are taking the clown car?" Elke demanded, drawing Cyn's attention with a broad gesture at the men in the Suburban.

Cyn sighed. *Really? Did she need to waste time on this?*

"You can go with the guys," she told Elke. "I'll be right behind you in the sedan."

"Like that's going to happen," Elke grumped. "Fine. I'll go with *you*, but I'm driving."

"Whatever you'd like," Cyn said easily, hiding her smile. She'd known Elke would never agree to leave her alone, even if it meant riding a whole thirty miles in the smaller car.

As their small caravan of three drove away, Cyn glanced back, not sorry to be leaving Kauai behind. For all the island's beauty, she would forever associate it with the recent, devastating events. For her next sunny beach vacation, she was thinking she'd stick with Malibu.

HONOLULU INTERNATIONAL Airport was predictably much more hectic than Kauai's Lihue had been. One of the busiest airports in the world, it processed roughly ten times the passengers. Cousin Brandon seemed to know not only the airport, but most of its controller personnel, chatting freely as they prepared for descent. No one asked him who his passengers were. They were just one more private charter. This was Brandon's business, after all.

Once on the ground, Brandon had an ancient VW that he kept in the hangar for running around Honolulu, and he gave Robbie and Elke a lift to the rental car location. Cyn had reserved two SUVs this time to avoiding bickering. Robbie and Elke had been chosen to pick up the vehicles, because Ken'ichi's size made him way too memorable, and none of them were going to let Cyn drive anywhere alone, not even around the airport.

Brandon was more than happy to remain on retainer for future flights. Cyn didn't think they be doing anymore inter-island travel, but one never knew. And as for how they'd get back to the mainland after Raphael was back with them . . . she hadn't thought that far ahead. There were too many factors to consider, too many still in play, to make that decision yet.

Once they were all loaded and on the road to their latest temporary home, which was near Diamond Head, Cyn felt oddly energized. She'd slept a bit on the plane, but that wasn't it. It was Raphael. He was close. She'd felt something different the minute they landed, and she was now confident that they'd made the right decision in coming to this island.

"He's here," she said softly. She and Robbie were in one SUV, with the two vampires in the second vehicle directly ahead of them.

Robbie gave her a sideways look. "Cyn?"

"Raphael," she said, not sure he'd heard her. "He's closer here. I can feel him."

Some people might have scoffed and figured she was letting wishful thinking run away with her, but not Robbie. He knew the kind of connection a mate bond forged.

"That means we're one step closer, babe," he said instead. "It won't be long now."

She gave a firm nod, mostly for herself since Robbie was focused on the road. "You're right. I want those police reports from Turner. And if he won't give them to me, I'll get Willis to make himself useful. I need to know where those vamp-looking deaths occurred."

"You think the same vampires will strike again? That's risky. Cops will be looking for them, now that they've left a few bodies lying around."

"Normally, I'd agree with you, but these are Mathilde's vamps. If they follow their mistress's lead, they probably consider themselves above human law. And they can't know the area that well, either. They'll go back to what's familiar."

"You may be right, but what then? Are you thinking to follow them to wherever they're staying? Vamps can be pretty wily. It's difficult to track them."

"I'm not going to track them. I'm going to find one, seduce him away from his buddies, then make him tell me what he knows."

Robbie laughed. "Yeah, right."

"You don't think I can?"

"Babe, you can seduce just about anything male. But how are you going to get him to talk to you?"

Cyn was silent for a long time, staring out at the black silhouette of Diamond Head growing larger and larger in front of them. She almost didn't say anything, because while she knew Elke and Ken'ichi would be on board with what she had planned, she wasn't sure how Robbie would feel about it. He'd fought wars. He'd had buddies who'd been captured and tortured by the enemy—sometimes for information and sometimes just because their god went by a different name.

But in the end, she respected him too much to lie to him, and it wouldn't be fair to include him in something without full disclosure.

"I'm going to ask him politely," she said quietly. "And if that doesn't work, then I'm going to do whatever it takes to make the bastard tell me everything he knows."

When he didn't respond, she looked over at him in the glow of the dash lights. "I understand if you can't be a part of this, Robbie. I'd like to say that it's because I've been around Raphael too long, and he's numbed me to the moral realities. But the truth is . . . this isn't on him. It's on me. I'm selfish. I want him back. Not for the hundreds or thousands of vampire lives he can save, although I've considered them, too. But mostly, I'm doing it for me. Because *I* need him back."

Robbie nodded slowly. "Thanks for being up front with me. But since my Irina is one of those vampires whose lives we'll probably be saving, I'm all in. Whatever you need me to do."

Cyn closed her eyes against a barrage of emotion. She could admit to herself now that she'd dreaded telling him what she had planned, that she'd hated the idea that Robbie might think less of her for what she was going to do. It wouldn't have stopped her, but it would have hurt her to know.

The somber mood was shattered by the stilted voice of the GPS telling them that their turn was coming up in half a mile. The next several minutes were busy as the two SUVs wound through the darkened streets, until they pulled into the driveway of their latest, and hopefully last, temporary home.

Cyn found the key where the property management company had left it for her. They'd been very clear to her on the phone that this was an exclusive property, and that leaving a key under the proverbial flower pot was *most* unusual. But apparently Lucia's cousin had made a call, and that was that. This was *his* house, after all. If he wanted to lend it to a bunch of shadowy night dwellers who couldn't be bothered to follow procedure, it was up to him.

"We're in luck with this house," Cyn told the others once they'd disarmed the alarms and done a quick safety recon of the house. "The bedrooms upstairs all have blackout shades. If I didn't know better, I'd wonder if vampires didn't live here already. Robbie and I stashed enough supplies to take care of any other windows that need covering, but we'll deal with that tomorrow."

It didn't take long to settle down after that, which was a good thing, since sunrise was far too close for comfort. This house was much bigger than the one on Kauai, and as the property management agent had indicated, it was in a much more exclusive neighborhood. The house sat right on the water, and had a view that went on forever. The common areas—the dining and living rooms and the kitchen—had floor-to-ceiling windows that slid open for the most part, bringing the outside in, which was a common Hawaiian building style. The six bedrooms, by contrast, all had modest windows which faced east, which probably explained those blackout shades. Vampires weren't the only ones who didn't care to rise with the sun. Cyn herself had been a confirmed night owl, even before meeting Raphael.

With Ken'ichi and Elke tucked into their respective bedrooms—no need to share, given the number of rooms available—Cyn and Robbie gravitated toward the kitchen with its spectacular view.

"You ever notice how unique every coastline is?" Cyn asked, staring out at the endless expanse of Pacific Ocean beyond the windows. "I mean, Malibu is across the same ocean, but you'd never know it by looking at this view."

Robbie gave her a look that either questioned her sanity or wondered where the hell she was going with this. Or both.

"The differences are mostly geologic," he said practically. "Hawaii is comprised of volcanic islands, while Malibu sits on the edge of a major tectonic plate."

Cyn slanted him a skeptical look. "Thank you, Mr. Wizard."

He shrugged cheerfully.

"I need coffee," she muttered. "And I need to change the password on the house Wi-Fi. We can change it back before we leave, but I don't want anyone else having access as long as we're here."

"You need *sleep,* not coffee. We both do."

"We have to check out the bar where we're meeting Turner."

"Later. We can do that this afternoon. Sleep first."

"We can take turns watching—"

"This house has a top-of-the-line security set-up. I'll add a few enhancements of my own, and take the downstairs bedroom. No one's going to get inside without me knowing about it."

She dragged herself to her feet. "Sleep," she agreed. But as she climbed the stairs, she wasn't thinking about sleep. She was thinking about Raphael, and wondering if he'd reach out to her in her dreams again. If now that they were physically closer, it might be easier for him. Maybe he could tell her more about where he was.

Stretching out under the covers of the king-sized bed in her room, she shoved the pillows around under her head, trying to get comfortable, trying to stop a zillion thoughts from zipping around in her brain— everything from what Juro had told her, to nightmare images of Raphael, half-starved because they weren't feeding him enough, locked in the dark, growing weaker by the hour. And layered on top of that was knowledge of the far-too-few facts she had to go on. She couldn't plan ahead for her battles. She didn't know enough. It would all depend on where Raphael was being held, how many guards there were—how many vamps and how many humans. And how was he being constrained. She knew that initially Raphael had been drained somehow of his physical power, some kind of magic, Juro had told her. But did Cyn believe that was possible? More likely it was simply a burst of power from Mathilde herself, something unexpected enough that it had succeeded in knocking Raphael down for the few seconds it had taken her gang of a hundred to contain him with their combined vampire strength. It was probably something they'd practiced over and over in anticipation of that one moment. And who knew? Maybe Raphael was even imprisoned in a vault of some kind, not unlike the ones Raphael and his vamps all slept in. There was just so much she didn't know. . . .

She sat up, abruptly wanting to slap herself on the head like one of those cartoon characters. She didn't know, but Raphael did.

Leaning over, she grabbed his jacket from where she'd shoved it into the top of her duffle and hugged it close, breathing in his scent. Leaning back with it in her arms, she pulled a blanket up to her shoulders, closed her eyes, and thought of Raphael. Not the way he might be now, but the way he'd always been. His grin when he teased her—so rare when they'd first met, but appearing more with every month they were together; the silver fire in his black eyes when he made love to her, when his fangs sank into her neck as she shuddered in climax; his sheer male beauty, so warm when he was relaxed, and so icily cold in his master-of-the-universe mode. She smiled.

And slowly, she drifted to sleep.

SOMETHING BRUSHED over her forehead and she rubbed it away, snuggling deeper into the jacket. Raphael's scent surrounded her, so much stronger in her dreams, warmer too. She frowned in her sleep, and felt the familiar touch of his fingers as he smoothed away the wrinkles the frown created on her forehead.

"Raphael," she breathed, terrified that he'd disappear if she spoke too loudly.

"*Lubimaya.*" His voice was the same as always, the same deep, midnight velvet sound. Wasn't it? Did he seem different? Was he weaker already? Or was she simply imposing her own fears, finding changes that weren't there?

His arms tightened around her, as if sensing her concerns. "I am stronger than they know, my Cyn."

She nodded, wrapping her arms over his where they held her, gripping tightly as if she could somehow keep him with her even when she woke up.

"You want to know what everyone—" she started to ask, but he interrupted.

"I want only to know that you are safe and whole in my absence."

She patted his crossed arms. "You know me. I'm just fine."

"You're not, but that will have to wait until I return."

Her heart clenched. He had so much confidence in her. She spoke quickly to cover her own insecurities.

"I talked to Juro. He said Lucas—"

"I know what Lucas will do. My time is short, *lubimaya.* You must watch and tell Lucas what you see. He will know what to do with it."

Cyn started to ask what he meant, when suddenly she was somewhere else, some *when* else, and seeing the world through Raphael's eyes . . .

France, 1819

RAPHAEL WAITED impatiently for Mathilde to make an appearance. She was habitually late. It was a pretense on her part, a way of demonstrating that she was more important than whoever was waiting on her, that her time was far more valuable. It was irritating as sin and one more reason why he would never agree to serve her.

He'd come to this part of France looking for a home, just the latest stop in his search for a territory of his own. But what he found was more of what he'd found throughout Europe—too many older vampire lords, all well-defended and grasping for power. He could have challenged any one of them and triumphed, but, frankly, Europe was broken into so many small holdings that he would have to fight challenge after challenge in order to create a territory worthy of his power and ambition.

Ironically, it was Mathilde's offer two nights ago that had made his decision for him. He was going to America and taking his few people with him. He expected the journey to be hellish and long, but these days, the trip was made routinely enough that he had no doubts they would survive the crossing.

And once there, the opportunities would be limitless. By all accounts, the continent was vast, wide open and, most importantly, empty of vampires.

But first, he had to deal with Mathilde. Assuming she arrived for their appointment before the sun rose on a new day.

"Raphael."

He spun at the sound of her voice, his gaze taking in her carefully cultivated appearance. She was an attractive woman, not beautiful, but sensuous and sure of herself, which was appealing in its own way. Unless one knew the manipulative mind constantly working behind that deceptive appeal. Mathilde did nothing without an ulterior motive, and her motives were always self-serving.

"Mathilde," he responded, intentionally omitting any title or honorific. She wasn't the only one who could play games.

Her delicate jaw flexed in irritation, but her expression never varied as she glided gracefully into the room and presented her hand to be kissed.

Raphael did so, but only because it was the human custom. He would have as willingly kissed the hand of a pretty flower vendor on the street. He took Mathilde's proffered fingers, touching them to his lips in the briefest of gestures.

Mathilde settled into her favorite seat, which was an oversized chair set alone at the front of the parlor, with other less elaborate chairs clustered around it.

Raphael pushed aside the smaller chairs, disrupting their careful placement in order to shove an abbreviated sofa into position instead. The chairs were far too fragile for him to sit on with any comfort, which Mathilde knew quite well. She frowned her disapproval of his impromptu rearrangement, but still offered no word of censure. She wanted something from him, and was willing to tolerate some minor insubordination to get it.

"So, Raphael," she purred. "Have you considered my offer?"

He didn't answer her directly. Instead, he posed a question of his own. "Have you heard anything of America, Mathilde?"

Her lips pursed in distaste. "Uncivilized place. Farmers and believers. Neither of whom I choose to associate with."

"Hardworking men and women creating something from nothing, Mathilde. A vast continent of possibility."

She shrugged minutely. "If you say so. Hardly a place for vampires, or anyone of breeding."

Raphael almost laughed in her face. Mathilde may have come from breeding, he didn't really know. But he certainly hadn't. In his former life, he'd been one of those farmers she so disdained.

"What does any of this have to do with me?" she snapped, before realization altered her expression into one of disbelief. "You can't seriously be thinking of going there?"

"I am not only thinking of it. I am determined to do so. We will make our way—"

"I have offered you a place at my right hand! I would make you my lieutenant, and you would leave me for that place instead?"

Raphael lifted one shoulder dismissively. "I want territory, Mathilde. I make no secret of it. And there is none to be had here."

"You don't need territory if you stand at my side. Is that not power enough?"

"You don't want to put your power at my back, Mathilde. You want my power at yours, and we both know it. I have no interest in being anyone's number two."

"Your arrogance astounds me. I rule hundreds of vampires, most of whom are my own children and owe me their very lives. What do you have? Not a single child of your own . . ."

Mathilde's words trailed off as a door in the back of the room whispered open and Lucas entered, making his way discreetly to Raphael's side, where he crouched, waiting to deliver whatever message had brought him to this room.

But Raphael wasn't looking at Lucas; he kept his attention on Mathilde. He saw the desire in her gaze as she watched Lucas, the avarice. For all her disdain of the human species, Mathilde's lovers were all young, male, and *human*. What was it the French called it? *Nostalgie de la boue*. Nostalgia for the mud. Just as Mathilde liked to prove her superiority by making others wait, so she preferred lovers who were socially inferior, lovers she could dominate and control.

And she wanted Lucas. She'd wanted him from the moment she'd first laid eyes on him, even going so far as to ask Raphael if she could "borrow" him on more than one occasion, as if the young man whom he'd rescued off the streets of London was a possession to be passed around and loaned out among friends. Or enemies.

But Raphael was never going to let that happen. Lucas was his to protect in ways Mathilde would never understand.

"Wait for me outside, Lucas," he ordered.

Lucas was no fool. He'd sensed the tension the moment he entered the room. He glanced at Raphael briefly, a silent offer of support if Raphael needed it. But then, that was Lucas. Raphael was faced off against a vampire nearly as powerful and far more wily than he was, and Lucas was prepared to stand with him, even if he was human and vulnerable.

Raphael touched his shoulder in reassurance. "I will be there directly."

Lucas nodded, then stood and left the room as silently as he'd entered, without even once acknowledging Mathilde's presence.

"Your slave needs to learn some manners, Raphael." Her expression turned calculating, and Raphael readied himself for whatever she was about to do next. "Perhaps I can help you with that. You know that I would prefer that you remain at my side, but if you are set on going, I will grant you leave. Lucas will have to remain, as payment for the protection I've given you over the course of your stay here. But you needn't worry for his well-being. I will take him for my own, and he will be well cared for."

Raphael laughed. He actually laughed. He couldn't help it. This shrew of a female thought she could claim Lucas as her due? As if Raphael *owed* her something for the months he'd wasted in her court? As if he'd *benefitted* in even the smallest way from her presence, when the truth was that she'd gained far more from their association than he had.

His laughter trailed off. "Lucas will never be yours. As for your permission to leave . . . I neither need nor desire it. We are vampires. If you believe you can stop me"—he stood to his full height and looked down on her—"then do so. If not, I bid you farewell. And I doubt our paths will ever cross again."

Raphael spun on his heel and headed for the door. Behind him, he heard the rustle of satin skirts as Mathilde rose to her feet.

"You do not turn your back on me!" she hissed. "I rule this territory and you will show me the respect due your proper lord."

Raphael looked back as he reached for the door. "This territory is yours," he agreed. "But I will never be, and neither will Lucas." He lifted the latch and stepped out into the hallway, closing the door behind him as Mathilde issued a wordless shriek of fury, accompanied by the sound of something breaking.

Lucas's eyes were wide when they met his. "Are we leaving tonight, my lord?"

Raphael nodded. "As soon as possible. The new world awaits us."

Honolulu, Hawaii, present day

CYN'S EYES FLASHED open to a darkened room and a moment of disorientation. She reached automatically for Raphael, but he was gone.

He'd never been there. Her brain knew that, but her heart took longer to come to grips with it.

She sighed and sat up, forcing herself to recall every detail of the dream Raphael had sent her. Or, more accurately, the dream within a dream. A check of her watch told her there were still two hours until local sunset. But back home, the vampires would be stirring already, and Lucas, whose territory spanned two time zones, was either one or two hours ahead of Malibu, depending on his location. But either way, he would have woken long ago.

She'd already discarded the old disposable phone she'd been using on Kauai, smashing it to bits and tossing the remains into several different airport trash bins, both here in Honolulu and at Lihue on Kauai. She pulled out the fresh one she'd used to call Detective Turner instead, aware that the number would register as "unknown" on Lucas's private cell. Under the circumstances, however, she also knew that he would answer the call.

"Donlon."

It took her a moment to recognize the stern voice that answered. She'd never seen the business side of Lucas, not even the warrior, although Raphael had told her that Lucas was a bloody force of nature on the battlefield. But the Lucas she'd always gotten was the charming playboy. No longer, apparently.

"Cyn here," she said, matching his serious tone. And she must have done it a little too well, because Lucas's next words were far from playful.

"Cyn? Did something happen, is Raphael—"

"Relax. Raphael is fine as far as I know. And anyway, you'd know as well as I would if he wasn't."

"Right, right. I know that. Things have been a little . . . intense around here."

Cyn didn't know if she was about to make things better or worse for Lucas, so she went right to the point. "I have a message for you. From Raphael."

"A message. I'm guessing this wasn't a phone call."

"Not hardly. More of a dream. He says you'll know what to do with it, or more specifically, I think, what to do with what it tells you about Mathilde. I can send you an email if—"

"No. Tell me. I want the emotion of the story, not just the words."

"Okay, here goes . . ." And Cyn proceeded to recount as closely as she could recall the story of Raphael and Lucas's last encounter with Mathilde.

Lucas listened, never interrupting, never asking a question.

When she finished, there was a moment of silence, and then he said,

"So Mathilde wanted me for her boy toy. I've got to be honest with you, Cyn. I'm sort of weirded out by that. I mean, she's like my great-grand-mother or something. I think I need a hug." He turned away from the phone and raised his voice to call out, "Katie, darlin', do you have a moment?"

Cyn *tsk*ed in exasperation. Leave it to Lucas. "I'm pretty sure that wasn't the point of Raphael's message, Lucas."

"Relax. A warm hug never hurt anyone. But I get it, and he's right. I do know what to do with it."

Cyn waited for him to share. When he didn't offer, she contemplated asking him about it, but decided she had enough on her plate without worrying about what was on Lucas's.

"Okay. If you've got this, then I need to get going. Say 'hi' to Kathryn for me, and . . . take care, Lucas. Of Kathryn, too."

"Always. You, too, Cyn."

Cyn disconnected. She could hear someone moving around down-stairs, presumably Robbie, since it was too early for the vamps to be awake. But also because the scent of brewing coffee had begun to drift up the stairs. The idea of coffee was enough to get her up and moving, but there was still one more call she had to make. Going to her duffle, she dug out the box of phones Juro had left with her and pulled out the one with the label, "#1."

Turning it on, she dialed the only number in its contact list and waited. Juro answered before it could ring twice.

"Is this your idea of daily updates?"

He sounded so disgruntled, and so unlike his usual, unflappable self, that she smiled. "Did I promise daily updates? I don't remember that." She spoke slowly as if she really was trying to remember.

"Cynthia."

"I didn't see the point in calling before I had anything to report."

"Other than the fact that you were safe and well, you mean."

"I figured you'd know that, what with you and Ken'ichi both being strong vamps, and also having that twin thing going for you."

"That twin thing," he repeated.

"Admit it. You already know what's going on, or you'd be a lot more pissed than you are. So, who'd you talk to?"

"Just about everyone, including Colin Murphy."

"Murphy? That's a surprise."

"We're coordinating our defenses with Sophia."

"Did Murphy update you on the situation here?"

"Only to say that he'd given you the name of a police detective in Honolulu, which I found interesting. Other than that, he didn't know where you were."

Cyn could have told Juro that his current lover and about-to-be housemate had a pretty damn good idea of where she was since it had been Luci's relatives who'd provided all of their housing. But if Luci didn't choose to share, that was her business.

"We're following a promising trail," she told him. "We haven't found him yet, but we're close. More importantly, I know that Raphael is safe."

"Raphael has contacted you?"

"In a manner of speaking." She didn't go into any detail, knowing that Juro would understand. "How's everything there? Any moves by the bitch queen yet?"

"Nothing overt. We're trying to determine her likely strategy. With so many of her master vampires tied up in the effort to lock Raphael down, I can't see her launching a frontal attack. She simply doesn't have the fighting strength."

"What if she shows up in Malibu and issues a challenge, like you said she would? Is there a formality to that? Does Raphael have a certain number of days to respond before he forfeits?"

"Three nights. If she follows the old laws—which I'm certain she will—Raphael has three nights to meet her challenge. But as Raphael's lieutenant, Jared also has the right to accept the challenge on his behalf."

"Can Jared defeat her? I know he's strong, but . . . Mathilde's a very old vampire lord, and she clearly isn't afraid to cheat to get what she wants, which seems to be Raphael's territory."

"Jared will be gratified by your concern," he commented dryly.

Cyn didn't have any comeback for that. Her main worry *had* been for Raphael's territory, although she honestly didn't want anything bad to happen to Jared either. He simply wasn't her first priority.

"*Can* Jared hold her off?"

"Maybe, maybe not. But Lucas certainly can."

"Lucas?"

"If Mathilde tries to claim the territory by default, Lucas will challenge her and claim the territory for himself."

Cyn didn't tell Juro about the dream Raphael had sent her, since it had been intended for Lucas. But it was now obvious that Raphael had anticipated the need for Lucas to step up to challenge Mathilde. Lucas must have gained some useful insight on how to deal with Mathilde from the details of that last encounter.

"But what about Lucas's territory? Won't that be in jeopardy?" she asked.

"Aden will assist as necessary. Sophia has offered, but I suspect she and Colin will be busy fighting their own battles, while Aden can easily merge the defenses of both his and Lucas's territories behind his leadership."

Cyn slumped down onto the bed, discouraged all over again. She'd been so optimistic before she'd called Juro. For the first time since this whole clusterfuck began, she'd begun to think they were finally on the path that would lead to Raphael's rescue, and that it was only a matter of time. But now . . . everything was so much more complicated than what she'd believed. Even after she rescued Raphael—and she would rescue him—he might have no territory to go back home to, or he'd have to go home and claim it all over again with maybe hundreds of his own vampires having died for nothing. What was the number he'd compared the likely vampire casualties to? Ten million humans?

She was suddenly furious. Furious that seemingly everyone had known Raphael would be attacked and they'd all simply taken it in stride as part of their strategy. And just as furious at herself for going along with it. Raphael had warned her point-blank about the danger. He'd come right out and told her that she needed to prepare for when disaster struck. Maybe instead of applauding her own cleverness while she'd been working with Lucia and Robbie to set that disaster plan in place, she should have been trying to talk Raphael out of meeting Mathilde at all. Maybe if she'd done that, she wouldn't now find herself working half-blind, fighting for every crumb of information, piecing together a trail to follow to get him back.

But more than anything else, she was furious that Raphael had to suffer even one day of imprisonment, or that all of those vampires might have to die, just so that bitch Mathilde wouldn't have to share power with her own vampire children.

"How long do I have to get Raphael back to Malibu in order to stop her?" she asked Juro tightly.

"We can't be certain of—"

"How long, Juro?"

"Mathilde will wait until Raphael is weakened sufficiently to—"

"Weakened how?"

"Starvation," he said bluntly. "She won't be feeding him."

Cyn felt like she'd been punched in the stomach. "Nothing? But he doesn't need much blood," she whispered.

"No," Juro said gently, "but he does need something. Tonight's the fourth night she's had him. Between the lack of nutrition and the pressure of all those minds constraining him, he'll be weakened enough by now that Mathilde's master vampires will be capable of holding him without her. And she'll head straight for Malibu."

"You mean—"

"I think she'll knock on our gates tomorrow night."

"But you said you can put her off for three nights once she gets there."

"And we won't exactly welcome her with open arms either. Given the circumstances of her attack on Raphael, we will be well within our rights to assume a hostile intent and defend our lord's estate. We'll eliminate as many of her warriors as we can when she first approaches, weakening her even *before* she has a chance to press her claim. Once she manages to voice the challenge, however, hostilities will cease and the waiting period will begin."

"And then?"

"Between Jared and me, and then Lucas stepping in to dispute her right to the territory, we can push it from three days to four, maybe even five. But after that, Lucas will have no choice but to fight her."

"So to be safe, after tonight, I have four days, or more accurately, nights, to get Raphael home."

"What are you planning, Cynthia?"

"The less you know, the better, big guy. But know this, when Mathilde finally gets around to making good on her demands, she's going to get the surprise of her life."

"What will you do?"

"Whatever I have to."

Chapter Eleven

"JURO SAYS WE HAVE four nights to get him back to Malibu before things get truly bloody."

Robbie gave her a worried look. "Including tonight?"

Cyn shook her head. "No. The countdown apparently starts when Mathilde knocks on the gate in Malibu. Juro's expecting her to show up tomorrow night, so that's night one. But *our* planning has to include enough time for Raphael to fly back home." She set down her cup of coffee and wandered over to the open sliding glass door, feeling the warm breeze off the Pacific and trying to picture what was going on all those miles away in Malibu.

Robbie came up and stood next to her, arms crossed over his substantial chest, the skull of his Army Ranger tattoo gleaming on a bulging bicep. "All right. Look what we've done already. We've gone dark so deep and so fast that they never even knew we were here, much less that we still are. We've already figured out the general area where they're hiding Raphael, and by this time tomorrow, we'll know even more. We're close now, Cyn."

She managed a forced smile that probably didn't fool him. "I guess we'd better get started then. We're supposed to meet Turner at 8:30 tonight, but I want to check things out before then. All I know about the place we're meeting him at is that it's a bar. I want to know how big, how busy, how loud the music is . . . the usual."

"It's a little early for cocktails, but I'm game."

"Okay, let me grab a backup weapon, but then I'm ready."

"You know this is probably going to turn out to be a cop bar, right?"

"I figured as much, why?"

"Just saying . . . they'll spot every weapon you're wearing two minutes after you walk through the door."

"Good. Then maybe they'll leave me alone."

"Try to remember this is just a reconnaissance, Cyn. We're only there to take a look around in advance of tonight's meeting, so be nice."

"I'm always nice."

Robbie's laughter followed her down the hall.

THE BAR WAS less than a mile from the Waikiki substation in Honolulu. Cyn didn't know which office Turner worked out of, but it made sense that the murders would have occurred near Waikiki Beach, because it was the hub of tourist activity on the island. Vampires weren't stupid about trolling for their victims. Tourists had a tendency to drink a lot of alcohol, which made them less inhibited and ready for a little wild adventure on their vacation, no matter how sane and sober they were back home.

Robbie eschewed the bar's parking lot for a public lot nearby, not even blinking at the exorbitant hourly rate. He found a spot on the first level, and backed in for a quick getaway. Cyn figured he didn't even have to think about stuff like that anymore. It was second nature by now.

They walked the half block to the bar, Cyn feeling slightly over-dressed in her black combat pants and boots, and the short black jacket she wore to conceal her weapons. Robbie wore the same black tank shirt that he'd had on at the house, but he'd donned a short-sleeved shirt in a subdued Hawaiian print to conceal the Beretta at his hip. His Ranger tattoo was still on full display, which caught Cyn's attention, because the tattoo was personal to Robbie, and not something he usually flashed around.

"What's with the tat display?" she asked curiously.

"Murphy sent me some background on Turner. Murphy's buddy is SEAL, but Turner's one of mine."

"Army Ranger, you mean," she said thoughtfully. "That might come in handy."

Robbie shrugged. "Can't hurt. Establishes a trust up front, anyway."

"I'll take any advantage we can get." She stopped in front of a bar that probably didn't get much tourist business. It looked like the kind of place that served American beer on draft, and straight shots in heavy glass tumblers, not fruity drinks with cute umbrellas.

"You ready?" Robbie asked.

"At the risk of sounding like a bad movie parody . . . I was born ready."

He groaned and pulled open the door. "That definitely sounded like a bad movie parody," he muttered as he entered first, then immediately stepped forward so Cyn could close the door behind them.

Conversation, which had been a low hum despite the early hour, stopped. Every cop—and, yeah, this was definitely a cop bar—turned to regard the newcomers with eyes that catalogued them in ten seconds as outsiders.

The room was dark, especially after the bright sunlight, but once their eyes adjusted, Cyn could see that the space was long and narrow. The bar itself was on the right, with some seating against the wall on the left, and a few more tables clustered in the back. What lighting there was consisted of a row of small, dim lights over the mirror behind the rows of liquor bottles, and a half dozen wall sconces of the punched tin variety along the wall.

Ignoring the stares, which ranged from unfriendly to downright suspicious, Cyn led the way to an empty spot in the back. Robbie stopped long enough to order a couple of beers from the bartender, which neither one of them would drink. But it would draw too much attention for them to hang around without ordering anything. Robbie also grabbed a menu, which unexpectedly included burgers and chicken tenders, along with the usual nachos and chips.

Cyn's stomach growled. "You see anyone else eating?" she asked quietly, as Robbie plunked down their beers and took the seat facing the front door. Cyn had noticed a back door down the dark hallway which led to the restrooms, and so had intentionally chosen the seat facing that exit, while trusting Robbie to cover the front.

"Yeah. Why, are you hungry?"

"Starving, but if the locals won't eat the food, then it can't be much good."

Robbie shrugged. "I see six cops digging in. And no one's paying us too much attention anymore."

"Not obviously, anyway. Want a burger?"

"I could use one. And maybe some chicken on the side."

Cyn gave him a half smile. Living with Raphael, she sometimes forgot how much food big guys like Robbie needed to eat. "You can have half my burger. Are you ordering or am I?"

"I'll be a gentleman. Don't want the guys to get the wrong impression."

Cyn tilted her head curiously, replaying her memory of the tables they'd passed on their way into the bar. "I'm the only woman here, aren't I?"

"You got it, babe."

"Fine. You go play he-man and talk to the bartender, and I'll leave a message for the vamps that we'll meet them back at the house. And since I'm being all girly, you might as well get me a diet soda instead of this beer."

Two burgers, a basket of chicken nuggets, and a huge mound of French fries later—but with both bottles of beer still untouched—Cyn and Robbie left the bar and drove back to the house. They paid close attention to their route, going so far as to take a few wrong turns, just so the GPS would have to redirect them to back to their main route. Sunlight was still a golden smudge in the western sky when they arrived, but the sun itself was below the horizon. Which meant both vampires were already stirring when Cyn disarmed the alarm system. The time of waking was all a matter of age for vampires. The older the vamp, the earlier he could rise after sunset, while the oldest and most powerful, like Raphael, were able to wake even before the physical sun had dropped below the horizon.

Ken'ichi stepped out onto the landing at the stop of the stairs, moving so silently that neither Cyn nor Robbie noticed him until he cleared his throat to draw their attention. Cyn waved her fingers in a hello, then continued on to the kitchen. She needed coffee. This meeting with Turner was important, and if the evening went the way she hoped, it was going to be a long night.

Chapter Twelve

THEY TOOK BOTH vehicles to the meeting with Turner, parking in the same lot down the block that Cyn and Robbie had used that afternoon. The streets were much busier than they had been earlier, crowded with both cars and people. Apparently it was Friday night. Cyn hadn't exactly been keeping track of the days since Raphael had been taken. It didn't matter to her what day of the week it was, only how long he'd been gone.

But while the onset of the weekend wasn't something Cyn had included in her planning, it was actually bit of good luck. What better time to troll the bars looking for a vampire than on the weekend when crowds were at their peak and the hunting would be good?

First, however, she needed to talk to Turner and get him to share what he knew.

Ken'ichi entered the bar first, ten minutes before the agreed-upon meet. Using Cyn's description of the room, he went past the bar and pulled two tables together in the back, including the one she and Robbie had sat at earlier that day. He then went to the bar and paid cash for a bottle of whiskey and six glasses, leaving the bartender a handsome tip before going back to the table and sitting with his back to the wall.

Cyn was outside, waiting with the others, when her latest burner phone rang.

"The cop is already here," Ken'ichi said without preamble. Colin Murphy had emailed a group photo of the baseball team that his SEAL buddy Doug played on along with Turner, so they had a pretty clear description of the Honolulu detective.

"Is he paying attention to you?" Cyn asked, curious as to how much Turner knew about *them*.

"He marked me when I entered, and made certain that I saw him do it. He's made no move since then."

"So, Murphy told him who to look for then. Okay, we're on our way."

The sidewalks were packed with people who were more than happy to move out of the way with Robbie leading the charge. Cyn and Elke followed in his wake, with Elke insisting that Cyn walk on the inside near the buildings, as if she was some fragile maiden who might faint if a carriage splashed mud on her. Cyn knew that wasn't actually the reason. Elke worked out almost daily with Cyn. She'd seen her at her worst and her best, and she knew what Cyn was capable of when the shit hit the fan. So Cyn knew she was being unreasonable in letting the simple security move irritate her. But now that they were finally *doing* something, she had little patience for all the fuss over *her* welfare. It was Raphael they should be worried about. Raphael who'd now apparently gone several nights without any blood at all. They hadn't made love the night that he'd gone to meet Mathilde; there hadn't been time, not even in the shower. Which meant he hadn't taken her blood before he'd left the house. Why hadn't she insisted he make time?

Cyn knew that wasn't reasonable either. Hindsight was 20/20 and a complete waste of energy. Even if they'd had sex, even if Raphael had taken her blood that night, it wouldn't have been enough to sustain him for long. Not when he was imprisoned under who knew what kind of conditions. Was he chained? Had they tortured him? Were they holding him aboveground, using sunlight as a threat while he slept, weakening him more with every hour he remained their prisoner?

"Slow down, Cyn." Elke's low-voiced caution made Cyn aware that she'd inadvertently picked up her pace until Robbie had been forced to stretch a casual arm out to prevent her from pushing past him.

"Sorry," she muttered, slowing as they drew even with their destination.

Robbie took a quick look around, then opened the door.

The place was just as dark at night as it had been in the afternoon. But without the sunlight outside, there was no need for their eyes to adjust, and Cyn could see clearly right away. If anything, the bar seemed better lit than the street. Robbie didn't even slow down, but led them directly back to the table where Ken'ichi waited.

Or he would have, if Turner hadn't risen from an adjacent table with a big grin on his face, as if he were greeting old friends.

"Ladies," he said, gesturing broadly with open arms. "Murph said you were gorgeous, but he never said I'd be meeting the woman of my dreams!"

"She's taken, asshole, so can the sales pitch," Elke growled.

Turner's grin only widened. "Good for her, but I was talking about you, blondie. Don't break my heart and tell me you're taken as well."

It was difficult to see in the low light, but Cyn would have sworn that Elke's normally pale skin lit up with a blush. She was tempted to wait and see how this particular dating game played out, but they weren't here to be social.

"Maleko Turner, I assume," Cyn said, holding out her hand and thinking that the baseball picture didn't do him justice. He was far more striking in person, and naturally charismatic. He had dark skin, dark hair, dark eyes. Probably native Hawaiian or at least of Polynesian descent. He was just as bulky with muscle as Robbie, and maybe an inch taller, which put him well over six feet. His straight, coal black hair was cut short in the back, but long enough in front that he had to use some sort of product to keep it slicked back. He wore a black T-shirt and dress slacks, but with a lightweight sports coat that covered a shoulder rig.

Turner took Cyn's proffered hand in one big paw and squeezed it gently, saying, "In the flesh. And you, of course, are the inestimable Cynthia Leighton. Murphy speaks highly of you."

Cyn gave him a tight smile of acknowledgement, and said, "This is Elke, and—"

"Elke," Turner interrupted to croon. "Call me Mal."

"—this is Rob Shields," Cyn finished.

"Murphy had high praise for you, too, brother," Turner said, clasping hands with Robbie the way big men did, chest high, muscles straining.

"Hooah," they said almost simultaneously.

"And this gentleman is Ken'ichi," Cyn continued, sliding around the Ranger reunion to take a seat to the right of the big vampire.

Robbie immediately took the seat next to Cyn, which left them both facing the front of the room, looking past the bar. Turner eyed the remaining seats, forced to choose between one of the two seats to Ken'ichi's left, which put his back to the main room, or the seat on the opposite end of the combined tables, which put him opposite Ken'ichi, but too far away for discreet conversation.

Elke seemed to make up his mind for him when she slid onto the chair closest to Ken'ichi, facing Cyn across the table.

"I'll sit next to Elke," Turner said smoothly, putting action to words, and then immediately grabbing the bottle of whiskey and pouring a glass for Elke and himself, before shoving it in the direction of the others. Elke narrowed her eyes at Cyn, as if daring her to say anything about Turner's blatant flirting, but Cyn got right down to business.

Ignoring the shot glass of whiskey that someone put in front of her, she leaned across the table to Turner and said, "I want to see your files on those three deaths, the ones you and I both know were vampire kills."

Turner tossed back a shot of whiskey, then rested his weight on his forearms and leaned across the table in turn, putting his face only a few inches from Cyn's.

"Those are confidential police files. Why would I share?"

"Because, as I told you on the phone, I can find and stop the killer much faster than you can," Cyn said, trying to be diplomatic. The truth was that if it really was a vampire or vampires behind these killings—and she knew it was—she didn't think the human police would be able to stop it at all. But she didn't say that, settling instead for a simple caution, saying, "It's likely that you're dealing with more than one vampire, which will make it even more difficult for you."

Turner scowled. "*Stop* him," you said. "What exactly does that mean? HPD frowns on its detectives sending hired guns out to kill suspects. There's that pesky 'innocent until proven guilty' thing we happen to believe in."

"Let's get something straight, Turner," Cyn said bluntly. "I'd like your help. It would make my job much easier, and there is far more at stake here for me than stopping these murders. But I can do this without you. I don't know your city, but I sure as hell can read a map. And I know vampires far better than you ever will."

Turner met her gaze silently, lips pursed in thought. "So tell me what you'll do once you find your supposed killer vamps? A straightforward stake to the heart, is that it? No questions asked?"

"How I deal with them isn't your concern," Cyn insisted.

"And see, sweetheart, that's where you're wrong. I know who you are, and it seems to me that you should be insisting these vamps get the same justice a human would, due process and all that. But you're not. And I'd like to know why."

"Go ahead and tell him," Elke said. "I can always kill him later, after we get what we need."

Instead of bristling at the threat, Turner gave her a delighted look, as if she'd said something marvelous, instead of just offering to kill him.

Elke's eyes widened in what some might have mistaken for horror, but Cyn knew the female vamp well enough to see that she was privately pleased by Turner's attention. Too many people looked at Elke's short, platinum blond hair and solidly muscled body and assumed she was a lesbian. But Cyn knew that wasn't true. Elke had good reasons for the career path she'd chosen with Raphael, and she'd worked damn hard to get and keep a place in Raphael's inner circle of security. But that was her job, not the sum total of who she was. When it came to her sexual preferences, she was very much hetero. And Turner was a very appealing man.

"Stick to business, *Mal*," Elke growled with a daggered look.

Turner put a dramatic hand over his heart at hearing her say his name, but when he faced Cyn again, he was all business. "You're not being totally up front with me, Leighton. You're not hunting a killer, or, at least, that's not your primary motivation. You want something from these vampires. What is it?"

When Cyn only stared at him pensively, struggling with how much to tell him and whether he could be trusted, Turner reiterated his position. "You want the files? I want the whole story."

Cyn forced herself to remain cool, fisting a hand on one thigh underneath the table. She didn't absolutely need Turner. Willis had insisted more than once that he could hack into the HPD system and get whatever files she wanted. But she wanted more than the official documents. She wanted Turner's and everyone else's notes. She wanted the murder books, which would contain every bit of evidence they'd collected. And only Turner could get her that.

She glanced at Ken'ichi who gave her a barely perceptible nod that was more than simple agreement with Turner's bargain. Implicit in that agreement was what would happen if Turner betrayed them. Elke might have been joking about killing Turner, but Ken'ichi wasn't.

"All right," Cyn said. "The vamps who I believe are responsible for these killings are part of a larger conspiracy, the leaders of which kidnapped my mate, Raphael, four nights ago and are holding him prisoner under horrific conditions. I *will* get him back one way or the other. But there is a much larger issue at play than just my personal vendetta. If we don't find Raphael in time, there will be war and hundreds, maybe thousands, will die, both vampire and human. Your killers—and I do believe there are more than one—are part of that conspiracy, part of a large group of vampires whose only focus right now is keeping Raphael imprisoned.

"And that's why I want to track down these killers. Because I'm going to lure one of them in, and find out everything he knows."

"Assuming you can do that, and that you get the right guy . . . what if he holds out and won't tell you what you need to know?"

Cyn gave him a hooded look. "He'll tell me. He'll be begging to tell me."

Turner stared back at Cyn, as if trying to wrap his brain around the reality of those words coming from a woman who looked like she should be shopping on Rodeo Drive, not sitting in a cop bar in Honolulu talking about hunting down murderous vampires.

"All right. And then what?" Turner persisted. "Once he tells you what you need to know, are you going to turn him over to the cops? To me?"

Cyn gave him a pitying look. "Not a fucking chance," she said, every word hard and uncompromising. "When I'm finished with him, I'm going to kill him. And believe me, he'll be glad when I do. And then I'm going to free Raphael and help *him* kill every one of the bastards who was foolish enough to think they could take him prisoner, or that I'd sit back and wring my hands while they did it. Welcome to the world of vampire justice, Mal."

Turner blinked. "Okay, then." He reached slowly into his pocket and withdrew a thumb drive, lifting both hands in front of him and wiggling his fingers to show he was holding nothing else.

"This is everything I have on the murders," he said.

Cyn reached for the drive, but Turner closed his fingers over it. "One condition," he said, earning an unfriendly glare. "I want in on the investigation."

"Out of the question," Elke muttered, at the same time that Robbie said, "Not a good idea, bro."

Cyn only regarded the detective thoughtfully. "Why?" she asked.

"Because these murders happened on my watch. Because I'm a curious guy and vampires intrigue me." And then he winked and said, "And because I need time to persuade Elke here to go out with me."

Cyn could feel Elke's pale gaze trying to bore a hole in her forehead, but her bodyguard's love life wasn't Cyn's primary concern right now. Finding Raphael was the *only* concern, and Cyn could easily conjure any number of scenarios where it might be useful to have a cop on their side. And those were just the ones she could think of right this moment.

"All right," she said. "But I want to see the murder books themselves."

Turner made a face, as if he'd hoped she wouldn't know about those. But then he shrugged and said, "Done." He opened his hand, giving the drive to Cyn. "When do we start?" he asked.

"As soon as I can get back to the house and take a look at these files," Cyn said absently, already pushing back her chair.

"Great. I'll stop at the station for the books. Maybe Elke can ride with me, since I don't know where I'm going afterward."

"I have a job, asshole," Elke snapped. "And it's not being your—"

"That works," Cyn interrupted. "But Elke will drive. You'll ride in one of our vehicles, and you'll leave your phone in your car. I don't want anyone tracking you back to the house."

"I'm on call, I can't—"

"I'll give you a burner. You can forward your calls."

"Paranoid much?" Turner scoffed.

Cyn shrugged. "You wanted to learn more about vampires? This is your first lesson. We survive by being paranoid." She stood and gave him a flat stare across the table. "You'll want to be careful, Detective Turner, that your second lesson isn't what happens to people who betray us."

Chapter Thirteen

CYN FORCED HERSELF to push aside her laptop, closing down the last of the three files on the thumb drive Maleko Turner had given her at the bar. He and Elke had shown up at the house a couple of hours later, with the actual murder books in hand. But Cyn had already started going through the computer files, and she'd decided to finish those first, and then see what additional information the more detailed murder books could provide. She knew from her experience as a P.I. that sometimes the eye saw on paper what it missed on a computer screen.

But she was too exhausted to look at anything else right now. The sun had risen some time ago, and the vampires were sound asleep in their beds. Turner had wanted to stay, insisting they needed the manpower to secure the house, but the closer it got to D-Day, the less willing Cyn was to trust anyone outside their small group. So Elke had shoved Turner out the door and locked it. The look on Turner's face when the 125-pound Elke had manhandled his 200 plus pounds of muscle out of the house without breaking a sweat had been priceless. Unfortunately for Elke, it had been the look of a man who'd died and gone to heaven. Cyn would have been vastly amused if she'd had a single ounce of emotion left.

Sighing, she reached for the mug which she'd have sworn she'd just filled with hot coffee, only to find the liquid so cold that not even she could stomach it.

"Okay, that's it," she muttered, the chair's wooden legs scraping on the floor as she stood. She needed to catch at least a few hours of sleep, if only to give Raphael a chance to connect with her, something that was far more essential to her than sleep. There were drugs to keep her awake. But only Raphael could make her want to keep trying.

Robbie sat up when she stumbled through the den on her way to the stairs. He'd been lying on the couch, catching one of those combat naps that the military guys all seemed to specialize in. He was taking first watch, no longer confident that the security system alone was enough to safe-guard the vampires. Once they'd met Maleko Turner in a cop bar, their presence had been made known. They had no evidence that Mathilde had any cops as part of her conspiracy, but no evidence that she didn't either.

So, from this point forward, he and Cyn would take turns sleeping through the day.

"Anything in the files? Anything you want me to look at?" Robbie asked, sounding as alert as if he hadn't just opened his eyes.

She shook her head. "I sent Willis the info on where the bodies were found, and asked him to reconcile that with known vamp bars. Even if Rhys Patterson lived on Kauai, he should have known about any vampires here in Honolulu and where they hung out. It's not so far away that he would never have visited." She covered her mouth to conceal a jaw-cracking yawn. "I still need to go through the murder books themselves, but . . . I can't see straight."

"Get some rest. It's daylight. Mathilde and her people aren't going anywhere."

CYN DIDN'T REMEMBER falling asleep, but she knew it wasn't long before she felt the touch of Raphael's mind against hers, so familiar that it made her ache with a sense of loss.

"*Lubimaya*," he whispered, his breath a warm brush against her ear. It was all so real, but even in her dream, she knew if she rolled over, if she turned to look into his black eyes, that he'd be gone. And so she didn't try. Something was better than nothing.

"Raphael."

His arm snaked around her waist and she frowned. It was something he did all the time when they slept, when they made love, his arm a heavy weight anchoring her against him. But it was different this time, not as heavy, his pull not as forceful.

"Raphael?" she whispered in alarm, squeezing her eyes shut to keep from waking, to keep him from disappearing. "Are you okay? Is something wrong?"

"I will be well, my Cyn. It is nothing I didn't expect."

"Did they do something? Are you—?"

"Cynthia," he interrupted, using her full name to get her attention. "We haven't time for this. Mathilde has left the island. You must warn Jared and Juro that she's on her way."

"Mathilde," Cyn repeated, dragging her mind away from Raphael's physical state. "That means the clock is ticking."

Silence. She thought for a moment that he was gone, but she could still feel the press of his body along her back, the dip of the bed behind her.

"Come soon, *lubimaya*," he murmured, and then he was gone.

Cyn woke with a start, her heart pounding, gasping for air as she automatically reached for the Glock she'd left on the bedside table. Rolling out of bed, she put her back to the wall and listened. But all she could hear was the thrum of her own pulse. With a jolt, she remembered her dream and Raphael's message.

She scrabbled across the bed, going for the box of burner phones that Juro had given her, digging for the one labeled #2. Did it really have to be #2? What the hell difference did it make?

Finding the correct phone, she checked the time. It was too early. The sun hadn't set yet over Malibu. Did Juro have voicemail set up on his #2 phone? Would he even think to check?

"Fuck it," she muttered, then dialed Luci's cell phone instead. Mathilde shouldn't know about Luci, and even if she did, she shouldn't have been able to find her private cell number. Luci had several phone numbers for the various charity boards she served on, but her personal cell number was one that only a handful of people knew.

Cyn wasn't surprised when the call went to voicemail. After all, Luci was sleeping with a vampire now.

"Luce," she said after the beep. "You don't know this number, but you know who this is. Tell your lover that I have a message for him from his boss. The bitch is on her way. He'll know what it means. The bitch is on her way, Luce. Take care of yourself."

She hung up, then sat on the side of the bed and waited for her heart to stop racing. She'd slept for a little over two hours. Not nearly enough, but it was all she was going to get. Juro had given her three nights once Mathilde arrived in Malibu. Three nights to find Raphael and get him home.

And night one had officially begun.

Chapter Fourteen

Night One—Malibu, California

LUCIA WAS ALREADY awake when Juro's eyes opened for the night. She was sitting next to him on the bed, frowning down at her cell phone, her face bathed in its blue glow in the dark room.

"Lucia?" he said.

She jumped at the sound of his voice, her eyes wide with something close to fear when she turned to stare at him.

"What's wrong?" he said instantly, shoving up and pulling her into his arms, his senses searching the room, the building, the entire estate for some danger he hadn't yet sensed. There was nothing, except the trembling form of the woman he loved, and the cell phone in her hand.

"Lucia," he repeated, forcing her to look up at him. "Who called you?" he asked, intuiting the source of her fear.

"Cyn," she said in a small voice. "Cyn called me. She gave me—"

Juro sat straighter, his vampire senses automatically checking the bond he had with his Sire, finding it distant, weaker than it should be, but intact. Which meant Raphael was alive, so. . . . "Has something happened to Cynthia? To Ken—"

"Stop," Lucia said, putting her fingers over his lips. "Everyone is fine," she said patiently, her composure seeming to have returned as his disintegrated. "Cyn gave me a message for you from 'your boss.' She said to tell you . . ." She lifted her eyes to his, meeting his gaze steadily, as if wanting to gauge his reaction to her next words. "She said the bitch is on her way."

Juro froze for no more than the blink of an eye, but Lucia caught it.

"She means Mathilde, doesn't she?"

He nodded sharply. "I need to get upstairs. I have people at the airport who can confirm her arrival, and I need to let Jared know."

He started to climb from the bed, but stopped, cupping Lucia's face in one hand. "I will need you to remain here on the estate for now. I know it isn't as comfortable as our house but—"

"Stop," Luci murmured, wrapping her arms around his neck, her fingers combing through his unbound hair. "Do you think I don't understand what's happening? This is war, Juro. We do what needs to be done. Make your calls, then we'll talk."

He punched in Jared's number, already on speed dial, as Lucia hurried into the bathroom to take care of necessities. He didn't have to worry about intercepts on these phones, especially not down here in the vault sleeping quarters, which was where Jared would still be found at this time of night. Slipping the phone between his ear and shoulder, he made his way to the closet and started getting dressed.

"Juro," Jared said, sounding out of breath.

"Cynthia called. Mathilde is on her way," Juro told him.

"How did she—"

"Raphael."

"Fuck. I'll be upstairs in two minutes. We need—"

"I'll call our watcher at the airport as soon as we hang up. I'll know more by the time I get upstairs."

"Right," Jared said, and disconnected. There was nothing more to say. But if Mathilde was about to show up at their gate, there was a hell of a lot more to *do*.

The bathroom door opened as he called another number. The person on the other end of the line had good reason for her phone to be on vibrate, so he listened to it ring several times as he watched Lucia emerge, braiding her long hair over her shoulder.

The call went to voicemail. "This is Juro. I need a situation report. Ten minutes ago," he said, then hung up.

Lucia joined him near the closet and began quickly pulling on underwear and clothes—jeans and a sweater, thick socks and running shoes. His Lucia wasn't a warrior, but she was a sensible and competent woman.

She waited until he'd sat on the bed to lace up his boots, then stood before him, hands on her hips. "All right, what can I do to help?"

"I just need to know you're safe," he replied, his fingers automatically looping the boot laces, tying them off. "There's no predicting what Mathilde will do, or even how much she knows. If she realized what you meant to me . . ."

"I'm safe as long as I'm on the estate, or—"

"At least for now," he interrupted to say darkly.

"It won't come to that," she chided him. "I trust you, and you should trust Cyn. She'll get Raphael back here in time."

"I do trust her." He sighed, shaking his head as he stood next to her. "If there was only more time."

"Well, there's not," she said bluntly. "So, we'll simply have to do whatever we can to be ready for them when they get here. Now. I know I have to stay on the estate, but there's no reason for me to hide out in your room. Unless you're embarrassed—"

Juro covered her mouth with his lips before she could finish the sentence. He kissed her until they were both breathing hard, then lifted his head, eyes glittering with emotion. "Don't ever think that, Lucia. Loving you, having you by my side, is the proudest moment of my life."

She stroked a soft hand over his cheek. "I love you, too, you know."

Juro ran his fingers down her long, silky braid, and bent his head to kiss her . . . only to be jarred back into ugly reality by the buzzing of his cell phone.

Giving Lucia a rueful look, he settled for a quick touch of their lips as he grabbed the phone from the table. A glance at the incoming caller ID had his gut tightening with dread.

"Status," he said curtly.

"Sorry for the delay, sir, but we were on the move. We've been keeping watch on that private charter that came into LAX from Honolulu very late last night. The hangar remained closed through the day with the plane inside, but roughly ten minutes ago, a limo and two SUV escorts emerged. My partner and I are tailing them, and it looks like they're headed your way. They're aiming for the Ten freeway west, but traffic's slowing them down."

"Roger that. Drop the tail and get back here as fast as you can." He didn't spell it out; he didn't have to. The two of them would dump their car in favor of motorcycles, take side streets to the coast, which only a local would know about, and then maneuver through the traffic jams on Pacific Coast Highway much faster than Mathilde's limo and escorts.

"Yes, sir."

Juro pulled Lucia close with one hand, tugging her out the door with him as he disconnected the call and punched in Jared's number.

"Confirmation," he said, before the other vampire could speak. "They're on the Ten."

"Thank God for rush hour traffic," Jared muttered. "It'll take them at least forty minutes to get here. All right, I'll put out the word. You coming up?"

"On my way."

Juro and Lucia took the underground passage all the way to the main house. The halls around them were empty, the elevator open and waiting when they got there. All of Juro's fighters, all of *Raphael's* fighters, were already up above and deployed. They'd suspected that Mathilde was on that private charter. The fact that the aircraft had slipped into a private hangar and stayed there, with no one deplaning, was nearly proof enough. Juro could have gone to the airport and checked it out for himself. So could Jared. Either one of them was strong enough to detect Mathilde's presence, especially since it was very likely that she'd brought a few of her own vampires along for support in the coming battle.

But they'd intentionally stationed human watchers at the airport, undetectable to Mathilde because there were so many humans in the area. Let her believe she'd snuck in unnoticed, that her arrival at Raphael's estate in Malibu would come as a complete surprise.

There would be a surprise all right, but it wouldn't be on Raphael's people.

The elevator doors opened to the sound of voices and movement, but not panic. A group of six soldiers strode past, all of them carrying long rifle cases. As one, they nodded sharply in Juro's direction as he emerged from the elevator, but they never broke stride as they hit the main stairway and started down with a thunder of combat boots.

"Snipers," Juro murmured to Lucia, ushering her toward the main conference room, which had been turned into a war room for the duration. "They'll set up in the trees around the gate and pick Mathilde's people off."

Lucia's eyes widened. "Are they all vampires?"

"The snipers are a mix, three vampire, three human. The targets will also be both, but with vampires a priority, at least for tonight."

She suddenly took one of his hands in both of hers and held on tightly, so tightly that he could feel her entire body trembling the way it had been when he'd first awakened tonight.

"Lucia," he said softly, wrapping her in both his arms and holding her tightly. "I'm sorry. You don't need to know details like that. I wasn't thinking—"

"No," she protested. "Your mind needs to be here, on all of this, not worrying about me. I'll answer phones, or make sandwiches, or . . . whatever I can do. I'll deal. You go handle Mathilde."

Juro gave her a quick, hard kiss. "We'll make a warrior of you yet," he said, with a lopsided grin that would have shocked most of the people who knew him. "Down the hall, last door on the left. Irina will find something for you to do. Oh, and call Cyn for me, will you? Make sure she knows we got her message in time. Tell her I'll call later with an update."

Lucia snapped off a mock salute, then headed down the hall. Juro waited until she had disappeared from his sight, then turned back into the war room, his eyes cold and determined as he walked over and joined Jared at the head of the table. He slipped a Bluetooth headset on, then glanced at their communications tech who ran a quick test. Juro nodded.

"All right," he said to Jared. "Where do we stand?"

"Snipers just cleared the main gate, taking up positions now. Gates closing behind them."

"And the rest?"

Jared smirked. "The trailers arrived on schedule this morning. Two of them. And they're all set up for our guests. I do hope her majesty won't mind sleeping in a single-wide."

Juro snorted dismissively. "She's going to raise holy hell. But look at it this way—once our snipers get through with her people, the accommodations won't be nearly as crowded."

"Fuck, I hate this part. The waiting."

Juro glanced at his watch. "We can use it to get set up. Cyn's call bought us some time."

Jared straightened from where he'd been bent over the table, scanning a map of the estate. "I don't know Cyn all that well. And you know she and I got off to a bad start—"

"Lucia tells me you guys have reached an unofficial ceasefire."

Jared huffed a laugh. "Yeah. It kills her to admit I might not be a total asshole, but the ice is melting . . . glacially, but it's melting. Anyway, I know Cyn's tough, and God knows she loves Raphael with every cell in her body, but . . . you think she can do this?"

"Lucia and I had pretty much this same conversation just a few minutes ago. But I was the one asking that question. Lucia believes Cyn will do it, and she knows Cyn a hell of a lot better than either one of us. So, yeah, I think she'll free Raphael. And I think together they'll leave a big pile of dust in whatever dank, little hole his captors have been hiding in. And then I think he'll waltz in here and give Mathilde the biggest fucking shock of her life."

Jared grinned briefly. "That's what I want to hear. Now, let's make sure we keep the bitch waiting long enough for that to happen."

"Fucking A," Juro agreed.

THEY'D HAD LITTLE more than forty minutes to prepare, but it had been enough. In truth, they'd begun getting ready for this confrontation the moment Raphael and his escort had taken off for Hawaii. It was the main reason that Jared had remained behind, while Juro had traveled with Raphael.

All of that preparation hadn't made the waiting any easier, but when Mathilde's limo made the sharp left turn off of Pacific Coast Highway and stopped in front of the estate's closed gate—after bumping its way down a road which had been deliberately strewn with obstacles and riddled with potholes—Juro knew they were ready for her. Or as ready as they could be without Raphael there to lead the defense.

Jared and Juro received the gate guard's radio call at the same moment, their Bluetooth headsets tuned to the same command frequency.

"Sir, there's a woman here—"

"Lady Mathilde, you peasant," a strongly accented male voice said from somewhere off-mike.

"Uh, Lady Mathilde," the guard corrected, deliberately mispronouncing the name with a "duh" at the end, instead of the French ma-TEELD. The game was to prick Mathilde's pride at every opportunity, because a rattled opponent was a weakened opponent. Juro's recent exposure to the French vampire, as well as Lucas's memories of her, both spoke of an extremely narcissistic ego. Which, granted, went hand in glove with being a vampire lord, but Mathilde's ego was accompanied by a needy personality that required stroking at every opportunity. It was a kind of insecurity that made her vulnerable. Mispronouncing her name was a small shot against her vanity, but then, it was only the beginning.

"She's demanding entrance, sir," the guard continued.

"Make sure she's not blocking the gate," Jared said deliberately, knowing the guard would have his volume high enough that Mathilde's vampire hearing would catch his reply. "And I'll be right there," he finished.

Jared muted his headset with a grin, waiting until Juro had done the same.

"I know this is nothing but the opening salvo, but, damn, that felt good."

"Little victories," Juro agreed. "Let's go see what the bitch has to say for herself."

"You think she'll get out of her limo?" Jared asked as they turned out of the conference room and started down the hallway.

"Once she realizes we're not opening the gates? And that she'll be living in a trailer? Fuck, yeah. She's going to raise holy hell."

Jared and Juro picked up an escort as they left the house. They were both powerful vampires, and before Raphael had been taken, either one of them could have left the estate alone without anyone protesting. But not anymore. Not until this was over with. They were too valuable to the estate's defense.

The distance from the main house's front door to the gate where Mathilde waited wasn't that great, less than three hundred yards as the crow flew. But this was war, and walking that distance left them too exposed. So, Jared and Juro piled into one of the bulletproofed SUVs with their escort and were driven to the gate.

Raphael's compound was designed to ensure the safety of his vampires during the day when they were vulnerable, and to stop enemies at the gate, day or night. The nearly ten-acre estate was surrounded on three sides by a ten-foot wall, every inch of it covered by video surveillance, and much of it topped with razor wire. Pressure plate alarms were seeded throughout the more remote areas, and there were live patrols around the clock. The fourth side of the estate was a sheer fifty-foot drop to the ocean, also covered by video surveillance, with a single zigzagging staircase that provided the only access from the beach to the top of the cliff. And that was just the grounds. The house and other buildings had additional layers of security, but Juro had no intention of letting Mathilde get that far.

The main vehicle gate, which was now foiling Mathilde's grand entrance, was a heavy, solid steel barrier, with a fortified guard house set to one side.

As he and Jared climbed out of the SUV, Juro notified the guard via Bluetooth of their arrival. The gate was opened just enough for one vampire at a time to slip through. Their escort went first, followed by both Jared and Juro. They'd debated having only one of them confront her, while the other remained behind, but had decided it was better to show a strong, united front from the very beginning. After all, while neither of them could equal Raphael's strength, together they were a powerful force, especially on this, their home turf. They were more than enough to oppose Mathilde, because, let's face it, Mathilde couldn't face down Raphael either. That was why she and her allies had been forced to violate the flag of truce in order to take him out of the picture.

The first thing Juro noticed as the gate opened and he stepped up next to the guard was the unrelenting pressure that Mathilde was putting on the guard's mind, trying to force him to open the gate. Juro immediately reinforced the guard's shields. Mathilde had made a strategic error in keeping Raphael alive. On the one hand, it made this little challenge charade of hers possible. On the other hand, however, it meant that Raphael's link to the thousands of vampires who called him lord, and especially to the hundreds of vampires whom he'd personally sired, was intact, including Juro. All Juro had to do was draw on his own power to reinforce the already existing link that he and the guard shared with Raphael, and Mathilde's efforts slid away like rain on steel.

"What's the problem?" Jared asked, directing his question at their own guard, since Mathilde's limo was once again sealed up tight.

"There's a lady in there—" the guard started to explain, but at that moment the limo's window slid down with a hiss of sound.

"The Lady Mathilde has arrived," the driver said snottily. "You will open the gate."

Jared snorted. "I don't think so. This estate is on a war footing. Friendlies only, and your passenger ain't no friendly, pal. For that matter, no one in your party was granted permission to enter this territory at all, which means you're in violation of Lord Raphael's sovereignty. And that gives us the right to kill every one of you, should we choose."

At that moment, the doors opened on all three of Mathilde's vehicles and vampires poured out.

Jared stepped back to stand next to Juro, his hand lifted in a silent signal that was immediately answered by the nearly simultaneous booms of multiple .50-caliber sniper rifles, as one after the other of Mathilde's vampire escorts disintegrated into dust, their hearts vaporized along with the their chests. It didn't take a wooden stake to kill a vampire. As long as the heart was destroyed beyond the symbiote's ability to heal, the vampire was dead. And a .50-caliber round didn't leave much of anything behind.

The sniper's guns fell silent. The night stank of cordite and blood, the doors of the SUVs still hanging open. Only one vampire remained in sight, a male who still sat in the driver's seat of the second SUV, appearing frozen with both hands on the steering wheel.

Jared and Juro waited to see what Mathilde would do. If they were really lucky, she'd turn around, go back to the airport, and end this misbegotten challenge of hers. But none of them expected that to happen. Vampire lords were nothing if not arrogant, and Mathilde was no exception.

The back door of the limo opened, and, despite audible protests by someone in the backseat, Mathilde exited the vehicle, her lips pursed in distaste at the scene around her, showing none of the grief that one might expect from the loss of so many of her own vampires.

She looked every bit the arrogant aristocrat that she had been in Hawaii, although Juro noted that she'd at least changed out of the archaic satin gown she'd worn the night she'd betrayed Raphael. Tonight's outfit was made up of body-skimming black pants and a turtleneck sweater, with a mid-thigh length jacket and stiletto-heeled knee-high boots.

"Jared, is it?" she said, managing to look down her nose despite the difference in their heights.

Jared regarded her silently. "My name is Jared," he said finally. "And you are?"

Mathilde's lips curled into a sneer. "I am your new lord, boy. And you will pay dearly for this outrage. Your end will be neither swift nor painless, I assure you."

Jared reared back, an amused smile playing over his lips. "This territory already has a lord. And it is not you."

She returned a smug look, her fangs abruptly on full display as she straightened to her full height and announced in a voice meant to carry beyond the wall, "According to the ancient laws of our people, I hereby challenge Raphael, Lord of the West, to meet me in defense of his territory."

If she expected shock or dismay, she got neither from any of Raphael's vampires standing outside the gate. But that didn't stop the gleam of victory that lit her blue eyes, as if that outcome was a sure thing.

"Regrettably," Jared said, as if her challenge was a matter of little concern, "Lord Raphael isn't here at the moment to respond to your challenge. I will be happy to convey your intentions to him, however."

"Three nights," she said, rushing the words out breathlessly, as if she couldn't wait to deliver her little *coup de grâce*. "Raphael has three nights to meet me or forfeit the challenge."

"So you say," Jared said dryly.

Mathilde brushed aside a bit of dust that had settled on her black sweater. "You will admit me at once, and provide suitable accommodations."

"Ah. Regrettably, or if I'm honest, *not* so regrettably, I must inform you that, in accordance with those same ancient laws which you so recently invoked, and as an uninvited challenger, which you most certainly are, you are now considered an enemy and thus denied entrance to my Sire's estate."

She stared at him in disbelief. "I am the ruler of a significant territory in France, and a lord in my own right. I will not be left like some beggar at the gate!"

"Yes, well, maybe you should have called ahead. I am Lord Raphael's lieutenant, in command of this estate in his absence, and I will not permit you within the walls without my Sire's approval. And as I am currently unable to contact him, as you well know, I cannot obtain that approval. Thus, you will not be permitted to pass these gates."

"You think you can stop me, boy?"

All pretense of good humor fled Jared's expression. He took a half step forward as if prepared to challenge her himself, but Juro touched his arm lightly in warning. Jared could not defeat Mathilde in a challenge. But if he stepped up as Raphael's surrogate in this moment, the challenge would be fought here and now. Jared would lose, and so would Raphael.

The gleam of victory in Mathilde's eye died as Jared rolled his shoulders, releasing tension. "My Sire does not need me to fight his battles for him," he told her.

"A good thing, it would seem," she murmured, going for one final insult. "Very well. We will occupy your guesthouse while we wait for Raphael."

"So sorry again," Jared said insincerely. "Our guest accommodations are all within the estate which leaves them unavailable to you. If you're determined to pursue this unwise challenge, however, I suppose you could make use of those trailers over there." He gestured at the two single-wide trailers that had been brought in that morning. "We had some work done recently," he lied, "and the various craftsmen—"

Mathilde turned slowly in the direction he indicated, then sucked in a breath and spun back to him in outrage.

"You cannot possibly expect *me* to—"

"Or you may go back to the airport, get on the plane that brought you here, and go back to France. The choice is yours."

Mathilde stared, her gaze shifting from Jared to Juro as she physically vibrated with anger. "I will not forget this," she hissed. "You will both die screaming when I am your lord."

"I will die long before that," Juro said, the first words he'd spoken to her since he'd been forced to watch as she seized Raphael, forced to abandon his Sire to his fate. "I would sooner die defending the last human on this estate than serve a single moment under your rule."

"Done," she sneered. Then with a final pinched look at the trailers, she slid back into the limo.

Jared signaled again. Up in the trees, the snipers would have already moved, taking up new positions for the remainder of the night. Before sunrise, a new team of all-human snipers would move in, along with a human ground guard. But for now, a team of vampire warriors poured through the gates to surround the limo and the lone SUV with its terrified driver as they maneuvered into the newly cleared area where the two trailers had been set up. Juro spared a moment of sympathy for the SUV's driver. Someone would have to pay the price of Mathilde's displeasure after tonight's debacle, and it would probably be that guy.

Juro waited with Jared until Mathilde was ensconced in her "guest" accommodations, and the guards were deployed to their satisfaction. Then the two of them stepped back behind the estate wall, and the steel gate rolled shut with a loud clang. It was loud enough for Mathilde to hear behind the thin walls of her new trailer, and he hoped it made her grind her teeth down to nubs.

Neither he nor Jared said a word while they climbed back into their SUV and made the short drive back to the main house, remaining silent until they were inside and the house doors had closed behind them.

"That went well," Jared commented. His words were calm enough, but Juro could hear the anger and unease beneath them.

"She's too old and wily to let it show," Juro responded, "but the death of her fighters is a setback. And now that she's declared her intent, she won't be able to bring any new ones in. We'll kill them before they reach her. She knows that, too. It's the best we could hope for tonight."

They'd reached the top of the stairs and were headed for the conference room, when Jared stopped and turned to regard Juro. "It doesn't seem like enough. We only have three nights now. I know you said Cyn—"

"Jared. We have a plan. We'll stick to it. I'll call Cyn and update her, while you call Lucas, and let him know he's up."

Night One—Honolulu, Hawaii

CYN RUBBED HER eyes, trying to focus on the pages in front of her. She'd switched to the murder books, reading every single page of the reports, struggling to decipher what she assumed was Maleko Turner's handwriting. It was probably a good thing he was sticking around to hustle Elke, because at this rate, Cyn was going to need his help just to figure out what some of this scribbling said.

The photos had left no doubt, however. These three deaths were vampire kills, one man and two women. The ME's reports on all three victims indicated consensual sexual intercourse before death, with no assault beyond the neck injuries. Which meant the vampire or vampires responsible had seduced willing donors, as per usual, but then gotten carried away with their feeding. Either they weren't used to live donors and had lost control of their feeding instinct, or they were off-the-leash for the first time in a long time and had simply enjoyed the kill.

Which raised the question . . . with Mathilde gone from the Islands, who was in charge? According to Juro, and Raphael's necessarily cryptic dream reports, the hundred or more vampires constraining him were mostly master vamps. Vampires generally didn't play well together, and with Mathilde and the other lords gone, it might be a case of too many lieutenants and no one in charge. That might make Cyn's job easier once she'd located Raphael. Which she had to do soon. Like, tonight.

Her gut burned from too much coffee and not enough food as her stress levels spiked. She stood abruptly and crossed to the refrigerator. She wasn't hungry. The thought of food actually nauseated her, but the next few days would require the best she had to give, both mentally and physically, and that meant she had to eat . . . something. Even if it was only to stop the burning in her stomach.

She stared into the refrigerator. Half of it was filled with food. Robbie had seen to that. While the other half was filled with nourishment of a different sort. They'd stocked bagged blood for the vampires, courtesy of Donovan Willis, who'd arranged a shipment from Rhys Patterson's supplier.

Cyn closed the door. Nothing in there appealed to her. She pulled open the freezer instead, glancing up at the clock on the wall. It was well after sunset in Malibu. Why hadn't anyone called her yet? Mathilde would be there by now. Had she issued the formal challenge? Had the guys managed to kill off her supporters as they'd hoped? Had any of Raphael's people been injured?

"Why hasn't anyone called me yet?" she demanded as Robbie thundered down the stairs, going straight to the fridge and setting her aside as he reached in and grabbed a bottle of orange juice. Shaking it vigorously, he twisted open the cap, and drank, draining it in one long gulp.

He popped the lid on the trash can to throw in the empty container, eyeing the pile of discarded coffee filters left over from her day hunched over the murder books.

"Jesus, Cyn, how much coffee did you drink?"

"Why hasn't anyone called?" she repeated.

Robbie gave her a patient look. "Because they're in the middle of a war? Because by now Mathilde has shown her skinny ass at the gate and they're dealing with a vampire who's more powerful than either of them, one who probably showed up with her own army in tow? Come on, Cyn. You know better than this."

Cyn scraped her hair back from her face with both hands, tugging at the ends. "I know."

"Why don't you go upstairs and take a hot shower? You'll feel better."

She laughed bitterly. "Yeah. I have to look my best for tonight. Can't seduce a killer vamp with dirty hair, right?"

"Cyn."

"I know, I know. I'm just—" Her latest burner phone dinged noisily and she spun for the table, grabbing it up and punching the "Answer" button without even looking to see who was calling. Only one person had this number and that was Juro.

"Hey," she said breathlessly.

"You're out of breath. Is everything all right there?" Juro asked.

"Fine, fine. What happened?"

"Good evening to you, too."

"Juro!"

He chuckled softly. "It went as planned. Mathilde showed up with two SUVs of vampire fighters and demanded entrance. Our snipers took out all but one of her vampires, and he doesn't have much fight left in him."

"What about the challenge?"

"She issued her challenge, but we knew she would, Cynthia. We planned for this. Lucas is on his way and will delay her as much as possible."

"Three nights," Cyn whispered, mostly to herself, but Juro heard.

"Lucas will stretch it to four. He's an obnoxious ass, but that's what we need right now."

Cyn smiled, then drew a deep breath. "So, I'm up. Okay. We're ready on this end. You probably won't hear from me until tomorrow night, so don't—"

"What are you planning, Cynthia? Raphael would not—"

"Raphael would want me to do whatever it took to save his people, and you know it."

"Should I send the jet?"

"No. I've arranged for one of my dad's corporate jets to fly into Honolulu tomorrow. They're coming in from Japan, so it'll look like a regular stop and won't draw any attention. They'll hang here until I give them the word, then they'll file a flight plan to New York with a stop in L.A. for fuel. We'll fly into Santa Monica, not LAX."

"Good idea. And you can use my house when you get here."

"I was thinking my condo, but your house is probably better. Thanks."

A footstep sounded overhead. Cyn glanced out the window and saw that the sun had set, leaving nothing but a golden glow on the horizon.

"I've got to go, Juro. We have a lot to do and not much time to do it."

"Be careful, Cynthia. If anything happened to you—"

"Nothing's going to happen to me. I have lots of people here making sure of that."

"Good luck, then."

"You, too. I'll call you when I can."

Cyn disconnected, then immediately ripped off the back of the phone and removed the SIMM chip. Crossing to the sink, she turned on the water, then dropped the tiny circuit board into the garbage disposal and flipped the switch. The disposal ground unhappily for a few seconds, then cleared.

"I'm not sure that's good for the disposal," Robbie commented.

"Did the trick, though, didn't it?"

"That meat hammer would have done the same thing. I take it everything went according to plan in Malibu?"

She nodded. "Mathilde lost almost all of her fighters, but she issued her challenge, which means the clock is ticking."

"Did you talk to Donovan Willis yet about possible vamp bars locally?"

"Yeah. He whined a little, but I sent him the locations of the bodies and he promised to take a look and send back the most likely bars nearby. I'm assuming the vamps didn't go far with the bodies, since they could hardly take them back home with them." She indicated her open laptop. "Willis is going to email me back. If it comes in while I'm getting ready, you and Turner should take a look."

"Will do. Yo, Ken," Robbie said as Ken'ichi walked with his usual silent tread down the stairs and into the kitchen.

Ken'ichi lifted his chin in a silent greeting. "Have we heard from Malibu?"

Cyn held up the remains of the burner phone. "Everything went as planned. It's our turn now."

"I hope that means Mathilde's not breathing anymore," Elke growled, joining the conversation.

"If only," Cyn agreed. "I have to go shower."

"Yeah, you do," Elke muttered, hopping up to sit on the kitchen island.

"You should make some fresh coffee," Cyn said sweetly as she walked past. "Your boyfriend will be here soon."

"He can make his own fucking coffee," Elke snapped. "And he's not my boyfriend," she shouted as Cyn climbed the stairs.

MALEKO TURNER had arrived by the time Cyn came back downstairs. She'd showered and shampooed and done all the things one would typically do when heading out for a night on the town. She'd even brushed on some mascara and lip gloss. Her jeans were tight and her neck was exposed, along with half of her breasts in a low tank top that also revealed a goodly amount of her black lace bra. She'd looked at herself in the mirror and had to fight the urge to throw up. Pulling on her black jacket helped a little. It was necessary to conceal the Glock tucked into her back waistband, and as long as she left the front open, there was still plenty of neck and cleavage on display. The very idea of some other man touching her, of letting another vampire get close to her skin, still made her sick, but at least the gun reminded her that he'd be dead before he ever managed to sink fang.

She straightened in front of the mirror, determined not to let any of her doubts show. They needed a vampire to question, and they couldn't afford to make a big scene about it in the bar. If they could have cornered one of the vampires alone, Maleko could simply have walked up and arrested the guy. But they couldn't count on that. If the vamp wasn't alone, if even one of his European buddies happened to pass by and see anything suspicious, Raphael might be moved before she and the others could get to him.

And if that happened, they'd have to start all over again. There wasn't enough time for that.

"Hey, Mal," she said coming around the corner into the kitchen.

"Leighton," he said without looking, his attention on something that he and Robbie were studying. She stepped closer to see what it was, and he glanced up at her, his eyes widening in surprised appreciation.

Cyn shrugged. "Meet your bait for the night."

He dipped his chin. "You'll do."

Robbie looked at her, too. But his reaction was completely different, as his brows lowered into a scowl. "You're not going in there alone."

Cyn sighed. "I have to. You know that. I'm supposed to be available."

"Raphael will kill me if something happens to you."

"News flash—Raphael's the reason we're doing all of this."

"Babe, if something happens to you, there won't be enough vampires in the western hemisphere to hold him down."

"Sounds like a plan," she said facetiously.

"Come on, Cyn, be reasonable. One of us can go in with you."

"Who? You guys are all too big and noticeable, and, besides, you'll hover. You won't be able to stop yourselves. The vamp will pick up on it and you'll scare him off. And if I take Elke, my target will know she's a vamp and not one of theirs, which will make him suspicious. And I'm not going in there naked. I'm armed."

Turner looked her up and down. "You're carrying a weapon in that outfit? What is it, a knife?"

"Glock 17. Never leave home without one."

"I didn't think guns worked against vampires," he said suspiciously, as if they'd been keeping secrets from humans all these years. Which they had, of course.

"The minute you think the cop knows too much, I can still kill him for you, Cyn," Elke chimed in cheerfully.

"I'll keep it in mind," Cyn muttered. "You guys pick out a bar for me?"

Robbie nodded, gesturing with one finger for her to join them at the kitchen island where he'd spread out a map. "I've marked the kill locations, or at least where the bodies were found, on the map here. Willis did the same thing and identified two bars."

Cyn opened her mouth to object. There had to be more than two bars within walking distance of the body locations. Honolulu was a big city, after all. But Robbie forestalled her objection with a raised hand.

"I had the same thought," he said. "Why only two bars? But Willis says he and Patterson visited Honolulu on a fairly regular basis, and that at least some of those visits were at the behest of Mathilde and her group. Though Patterson didn't realize that until later. A few vamps approached him, looking for his permission for them to settle in Hawaii. They flew in for a meet and greet, which is probably when they located whatever house they're holding Raphael in. They also checked out some bars while they were here, under the guise of getting to know one another. And both of those bars are on Willis's short list."

"Okay, so we might have to hit two bars tonight. Ken'ichi, Elke, can you guys shield well enough to sit in the parking lot and tell me if a vampire walks by? I don't want him getting spooked off, if he senses you there, but that way we could cover both bars at once."

Ken'ichi and Elke exchanged a look as if they were having a conversation, then the big vampire nodded. "We can do that."

Elke grinned, saying, "I'm a powerful presence, not easy to conceal, but I'll manage."

"Ain't that the truth," Maleko said fervently.

Elke surprised Cyn by punching the big cop in the arm playfully. "Mal and I can take one of the vehicles. Cyn, you go with the guys in the other. Once we've pinpointed the bar, and you've gone in to hook him, Mal and I will come back and get things ready here. We'll have to stop at the store first, get some plastic sheeting. I suspect there'll be blood once we start questioning this guy. And maybe some of those big quilted pads like movers use. You know, to stifle the screams."

Mal frowned down at her.

"Don't be looking at me like that. What'd you think? We were going to hypnotize him or something? Welcome to the world of vampires, Mister Cop. Or I could just kill you now and, you know, get it over with."

"Damn it, woman, stop offering to kill me!"

"Yeah okay," Cyn said interrupting the Elke and Mal show. "It's dark and we have our targets. Just to be clear, I'll seduce him with my wicked ways, lure him outside for a quick bite, then Robbie and Ken'ichi will grab him. Ken'ichi, you can shut him down fast enough that he won't be able to squawk for help, right?"

"As long as he's sufficiently distracted."

"He'll be plenty distracted," Cyn assured him.

"But no biting," Robbie insisted.

"Fuck no," she agreed.

"All right, then. We're a go," Robbie said. "Elke, make sure you and Mal get enough to thoroughly cover the garage interior. I'd rather have plastic sheeting left over than be stuck trying to scrub out bloodstains."

"What the fuck?" Mal muttered, shaking his head as Elke grinned.

"You ready, Cyn?" Robbie asked.

She tugged her jacket into place to conceal the nerves making her hands shake, and gave him a short nod. "Let's do this."

"WHAT IF NO ONE shows up tonight?" Cyn asked, breaking the silence.

She, Robbie, and Ken'ichi were sitting in the SUV, in the last row of a busy bar parking lot. Even though the area was well lit, there were enough trees along the edges that they weren't noticeable sitting in the dark, waiting. And that's what they'd been doing for an hour already.

"We can do it again tomorrow night," Robbie said quietly.

"Raphael can't wait that long."

"Willis says the vamp visitors looked at properties, too. Maybe we can figure out which ones."

"Yeah, because real estate agents aren't a dime a dozen around here."

"Cyn."

"Yeah?"

"You're being a pain in the ass, babe. We're all doing the best we can."

Cyn wanted to scream that their best wasn't good enough, but that wasn't true. This wasn't Robbie's problem, it was hers. She hated sitting here doing nothing, wondering what was happening to Raphael while she lurked in a parking lot, hoping some sleazy vampire would show up to be seduced. What a fucked-up plan this was. What had she been—

"There he is," Ken'ichi said, his voice calm and flat. "The male in the light pants and flowered shirt."

Cyn peered out the windshield. "What is it with these guys and resort wear? Did someone put out a memo? When in Hawaii, wear linen pants and pastel shirts?"

"That's not really pastel," Robbie noted. "Not with all those flowers on it."

"Gee, thanks for the fashion advice, Rob. Okay," she said, taking a quick glance around to make sure no one was watching. "I'm up." She touched the Bluetooth communications bud in her ear to be sure it was firmly seated and covered by her hair. The corresponding button mike was attached to her jacket. It was matte black and small enough that it should be unnoticeable, especially in a dark bar.

"I'll do a comm check once I get a few feet away," she said, opening the SUV door. All of the interior lights had been switched off or deactivated so there was nothing to give away her exit. "You guys know what to do, right?"

"You bring the guy back here to neck in the car, Ken zaps him, and we grab him," Robbie confirmed. "I'll go ahead and call Elke, to let her know we're on."

Cyn nodded. "Here goes nothin'."

The bar was already crowded when Cyn made her way inside. It was more of a neighborhood hangout, not located downtown or near any of the major hotels, but there were several big condominium complexes within walking distance, most of which advertised vacation rentals. That, combined with a big happy hour buffet and discounted drinks, probably explained the crowds. It was well beyond the designated "happy hour," but the people pressing up against her and seeming to fill every inch of space in the room were still awfully happy.

Cyn didn't like crowds. Apart from the security aspect of it, which made her itch to draw a weapon, she simply didn't like to be touched by strangers. Especially not sweaty, drunk strangers.

Scanning the throng, she found her target over by the bar and made her way in that direction. No sense in delaying this, or playing coy. The sooner she got out of this place, the happier she'd be.

She shoved her way to the counter, brushing off two attempts to grab her arm and one blatant grope of her ass—which nearly earned the groper a broken wrist, and would have, if she hadn't had more important business to attend to. When she finally reached the bar, she felt like she needed a shower . . . and a big drink. Unfortunately, she wouldn't be getting either one anytime soon.

Still maneuvering her way through the crowd shouting for drinks, she looked for her vampire and saw him about to put his ass on a stool that was just being vacated. Moving quickly, she slipped past the guy who was leaving and slid onto the seat right in front of the vampire, giving him a quick smile that she hoped was flirtatious. It had been a while since she'd flirted with anyone other than Raphael. Her skills were rusty.

"Sorry," she said, practicing that smile. "It's just so crowded in here and you're so big"—*gag*, she thought to herself—"you can hold your own against this mob so much easier than I can." Grabbing the front of her jacket she fanned one side open, flashing some boob. "It's hot in here, isn't it?"

The vamp stared down at her for such a long time that she thought she'd made the wrong move, but then he smiled.

"Anything for a lovely lady," he said, with a heavy accent that betrayed his French origins and reaffirmed her belief that this was one of Mathilde's guys.

"Aren't you sweet," she murmured, looking up at him through her lashes. "I'll buy you a—"

"*Mais non!*" he said instantly. "You are far too beautiful to buy your own drink. What will you have?"

"Vodka rocks, Grey Goose if they have it." She laughed a little. "Is that really a French vodka, or do they just say that?"

He ordered two Grey Gooses on the rocks, setting aside the mixed drink he'd been sipping before she sat down. It looked like whiskey and something, which meant he was switching to vodka for her, but vamps didn't have to worry about little things like hangovers.

"Grey Goose is indeed French," he said, directing his attention back to her. "But it is not our best vodka. You should try Nuage, if you can get it. It is far superior."

Cyn let her eyes go wide in wonder at his knowledge, even though she figured he only picked Nuage because it was the most expensive French vodka on the market. *Pretentious ass.*

"You really are from France," she said in amazement. "I thought I recognized the accent, but we don't get many French tourists here."

"Ah, but then I am not a tourist. My colleague and I are here on business."

Cyn's heart sank. Was he here with someone after all? He'd arrived alone, but maybe his buddy was already here.

"You're here with a friend?" she asked, gazing around as if she could magically spot him.

"Not tonight, *mon ange.* I am all yours. Julien Gardet, at your service."

Bleah, Cyn thought. She wasn't his fucking angel or anything else.

"I love French," she gushed. "It always sounds so exotic. I took it in high school, of course, but I wouldn't dare—"

"A woman like you doesn't need to worry about such things. When a man looks at you, every word is music."

Double bleah! Did this crap really work on other women? She was ashamed for her gender if that was true.

Their drinks arrived in time to keep her from laughing in his face. He pushed one in her direction, then took the other and offered a toast. "To beautiful women," he said, lifting his glass to click with hers. But it wasn't only his glass he reached out with. Julien Gardet was being a very bad boy. She could feel his mind trying to touch hers in the vampiric version of a roofie, trying to take away her will and replace it with his. Any vampire caught doing such a thing in Raphael's territory would have been summarily executed. She didn't know the laws in Europe, but suspected they varied widely, depending on the individual vampire lord. It was possible that not even Mathilde would permit such a transgression in her territory, but she was all the way over in Malibu. Maybe it was simply a case of the mouse taking advantage of the cat's absence.

Fortunately, Cyn was immune to that kind of manipulation. According to Raphael, she'd always been a tough subject, but now that he'd added his own layer of protection to her natural resistance, Gardet's puny efforts didn't stand a chance.

Of course, he didn't know that.

Cyn managed to look convincingly flustered as she touched her glass to his. "And beautiful men, too," she added shyly.

Predictably, he *loved* that. He took a long drink of his vodka, watching as Cyn sipped hers carefully. Raphael's protection didn't extend to giving her a vampire's resistance to alcohol, and she didn't want any kind of a buzz slowing her down. But Gardet shouldn't expect her to slog it down the way he was, anyway. She was just a girl and a human girl at that.

"So, you're a—how do they say?—a local?" he asked.

"How did you know?" she asked, all the while feeling him pushing and pushing. What was his end game? Was he one of the killers? Or did he simply want a tour of the parking lot, along with a quick bite in a dark corner?

"You said earlier that you didn't get many French tourists," he continued. "I took that to mean you live nearby."

"Oh, right," she laughed a little. "I forgot that. But you're right. I have a house on Diamond Head." She felt his interest surge along with his attempts to suborn her will, and in her head, she thought, *Ah ha!* That was his game. Go back to her place, a little sex, a little blood, and all without her remembering a thing.

Little did he know that she had exactly the same plan as he did, albeit with a slightly different result.

His eyes flared briefly. Maybe in anticipation of the wild night of sex he was planning, or it could be due to the dollar signs flashing in his head because of the pricey Diamond Head zip code.

"Diamond Head," he said appreciatively. "I'd hoped to get up there before we left, but these meetings . . . they have wasted far too many days. And now there's no time left."

"You're leaving?" Cyn filled her voice with disappointment.

"We've still a few days. Unfortunately, our only free time now will be at night, so—"

"But Diamond Head is gorgeous at night!" Cyn protested right on cue, the pressure on her mind now reaching the point where it was giving her a headache.

"I've heard that." He'd been inching closer while they talked, until now he was whispering in her ear. "You could invite me to your house," he suggested.

Cyn almost sighed in relief. Finally. She'd thought for a moment there that she was going to have to come up with the idea on her own.

"We could have a drink at my house," she said brightly, letting him think he'd influenced her thoughts. "This place is so noisy tonight, and that way you could see Diamond Head, too."

"Are you sure you wouldn't mind?"

Cyn almost rolled her eyes. Gardet didn't even know how to win gracefully.

"Of course not. No one should leave Honolulu without seeing Diamond Head at night. Do you have a car, or—"

"I do," he said immediately. "I can follow you there."

Of course, Cyn thought cynically. He'd need an exit plan. It wouldn't look good if she woke up tomorrow morning and found her lover sleeping in the closet to avoid the sun.

"I don't usually do this." She giggled as she scooted off the bar stool. Yes, giggled. She'd have to swear the guys to silence when this was all over.

"But you're doing it for me," he crooned, adding another dose of oomph to his push.

"Are you ready?" she asked, taking a final sip of her vodka. Or pretending to.

"I am," he replied. His anticipation got the better of him for a moment as his eyes glowed briefly in the darkened room, the crimson corona around his otherwise brown irises marking him as vampire.

Cyn glanced around, but no one seemed to have noticed his slip. No one was paying them much attention at all. It was just another bar pickup.

He pushed the door open ahead of her, holding it as she stepped in front of him. The humid Hawaiian air seemed cool after being in the crowded bar, and a fresh breeze touched her face as they started across the parking lot.

Robbie was talking in her ear, reworking their plan on the fly. It was a bit of good luck that Gardet had decided to follow Cyn back to her house to complete his seduction with a bloody nightcap. They wouldn't have to risk a public grab in the parking lot. Robbie told her that he and Ken'ichi had ducked into the back, with Ken'ichi shielding their presence from detection, so that she could drive the SUV while Gardet followed her, and that Elke and Mal were ready for them.

Now all Cyn needed to do was figure out how to break Gardet.

"YOU DON'T HAVE to do this, Cyn," Robbie said, standing toe-to-toe with her in her darkened bedroom, while downstairs Ken'ichi and Elke bound their prisoner securely in the newly modified garage. Maleko Turner was there, too, watching with cop eyes. He didn't look happy, but he hadn't said anything about it either.

"Of course I have to," she insisted as she stripped off her jacket. She removed the Glock 9mm from her back waistband, worked the slide to verify there was no round in the pipe, then slipped the weapon into her open duffle. She wasn't disarming herself. She was simply switching weapons. She'd switched to a standard 9mm round for her trip to the crowded bar, but now she was about to question a vampire, which meant she needed something with a lot more bang. Reaching into the duffle, she retrieved her shoulder rig and the second Glock which was still loaded with what she called her vampire killers—Hydra-Shok jacketed hollow-point rounds, which made a small hole going in and a really, really big hole going out. Just the thing for destroying a vampire's heart. Or maybe a knee joint or two if one wanted to extract information before killing him.

She worked the slide, but this time it was to be sure there *was* a round in the pipe. Gardet would be bound to his chair, and Ken'ichi would be blocking him from calling for help. But that didn't meant he wasn't dangerous. Vampires were unpredictable, and Gardet was a master vampire, which meant his power was above average. Not as strong as Ken'ichi's, or this wouldn't have worked. But he was still strong and, if his attempts to suborn her will in the bar were anything to go by, not above using trickery to get what he wanted. She'd have to be on her guard the whole time. She slipped the shoulder rig on and jammed the weapon into place.

"Ken or even Elke would happily question this asshole for you if you asked," Robbie persisted.

"I know that. But I won't ask them to do something cruel just because I don't have the guts to do it myself."

She started out of the room, but Robbie stepped in front of her.

"Cyn, you've never done anything like this. Inflicting pain just to get someone to talk, listening to them scream and then doing it again and again, waiting for them to break. You don't know . . . it eats at your soul."

Cyn stopped, gazing up at Robbie with different eyes. She'd thought she'd known all about his military service, but she'd never known. . . . She'd been worried that he'd object to her plan because his buddies had been tortured, but what if his objections were because *he'd* been the one doing the torturing, because he knew the price, and he didn't want her to pay it.

"Rob," she said hesitantly, trying to figure out a way to explain it to him. "I don't *want* to do this. I'm not . . . I've watched Raphael question people, human and vampire both. And I know there's a part of him that enjoys what he's doing. It's as if the thing that makes him vampire, the symbiote or whatever you want to call it, views human empathy as a weakness, something to be stripped away. And the more powerful the vampire, the less empathy that remains.

"But I'm not a vampire. I know a lot of people think I'm a bitch, but that's just personality. I have the full complement of human empathy, and I'm *not* looking forward to what I have to do tonight. But I won't scar Ken'ichi or Elke's souls instead of my own. I don't care if they *are* vampires. Because while some part of Raphael enjoys being cruel, another part of him doesn't, and it steals a little more of his soul every time.

"If our roles were reversed, if I'd been the one taken, Raphael would do *anything* to get me back. He'd torture every fucking person in Honolulu if that's what it took. And so I'm going to do this for him. It's one guy. One guy who's part of a gang that's been torturing Raphael for days. He's earned some pain for his role in this. He's earned a fucking lot."

Robbie's lips tightened into a grim line, but he nodded his agreement. "Let's make this pig squeal."

Gardet looked up when Cyn opened the door between the house and garage, his eyes a furious glare above the piece of duct tape covering his mouth. *Furious* eyes, Cyn noted, but simply brown. There was no crimson gleam to his gaze, no hint of power. Whatever Ken'ichi was doing, it was working.

Cyn gestured at the duct tape over his mouth. "I kinda need him to talk," she said, glancing at Elke who stood closest to Gardet, her hands on her hips, her eyes filled with hatred as she stared at their prisoner.

"Bastard wouldn't shut the fuck up," she muttered.

"Won't all of this padding contain the noise? The neighbors aren't that close."

"Yeah, we're good on that," Elke agreed. "And we can always turn up some music if we have to," she added, drawing Cyn's attention to the workbench where an iPhone had been docked into a small, wireless speaker.

"That was Mal's suggestion," Elke said proudly, which had Cyn doing a double take. Apparently, Elke wasn't as eager to kill the big cop off anymore. It also made her wonder about Mal, but maybe he didn't view vampires as part of the population he was sworn to protect and serve. Or maybe Elke had convinced him just how different vampire society really was.

"All right. Let's get started," Cyn said. "Maybe our friend here will be smart." She reached out and ripped the tape off Gardet's mouth, ignoring the skin that came with it and his wince of pain. He'd be doing a lot more than wincing if he didn't tell her what she needed to know.

"You'll regret this," he growled at Elke. "I am Lady Mathilde's, and she'll eat you alive for choosing a human over your own."

"Oh dear," Elke simpered. "I'm so scared."

"You will be. These chains—"

"Yeah, yeah," Cyn said in a bored voice, interrupting his rant. "You're just pissed because I didn't fall for your *'oh, you're so beautiful'* routine back there. Is that what you did with those other women before you killed them?"

"I didn't kill anybody. I like my women alive when I fuck them," he said, smirking up at her.

"Okay. That's an image I'll never get out of my head now, so thanks for that, asshole. Maybe you killed them afterward."

"I told you, I didn't kill anyone. Is that what this is about? A couple of dead human whores and you go all Rambo? What? You related to one of them or something?"

"Or something," she agreed. "So if it wasn't you, then who was it? I know it was a vampire."

"I don't know," he said, his expression shutting down, as if to say he'd done all the talking he intended to do.

Cyn pulled her Glock, sighing as she screwed on a silencer, and stepped back to avoid getting blood on her clothes.

Gardet laughed. "That weapon can't harm me. You've managed to suppress my power with some spell or other for now, but you cannot change my nature. My body will heal before—"

His boast was cut off with a shriek as Cyn fired a round directly into his knee, all but obliterating the joint. Blood spattered over the plastic covered floor as he stared in horror at the ruin of his leg, which was almost severed at the knee, his calf standing upright only because the chains binding him held it in place.

"You're probably right," Cyn said, walking closer. She squatted down to examine what was left of Gardet's knee. "I'm sure your vampire blood will be able to heal that . . . eventually." Though she did find it interesting that he assumed she was using some sort of spell to control him, just as Juro insisted Mathilde must have done to weaken Raphael in her initial attack.

"Bitch," Gardet hissed. "My mistress will—"

Another shriek of pain cut off his words as Cyn stabbed the foot on his uninjured leg with the pretty new knife that Raphael had given her after she'd admired the many knives owned by her friend Lana Arnold. She was wiping the blood off her blade, frowning as she tried to find a clean spot on his pants leg, when Mal stepped up.

"All right, this has gone far enough," he said quietly. "I agreed to let you help with this, because you seemed to know a lot more than I do about—"

"More?" Cyn demanded, spinning around to confront him. "The cops didn't know shit about who was killing those people until I showed up."

"Okay, you're right," he said, his hands raised in a placating gesture. "But now that we have a suspect, maybe I should take him—"

"You're not taking him anywhere," Cyn snapped, then spun around and stabbed her knife in Gardet's shoulder, digging the blade into the joint as he screamed.

"Jesus," Mal swore. "At least let me ask him—"

"You're a fucking cop?" Gardet howled. "What the hell kind of a cop would allow—"

"I'm the kind of cop who has three dead bodies," Mal growled. "One I could deal with. I figured it was some freak who'd seen too many movies, but three of 'em? And then she shows up"—he pointed at Cyn—"telling me it was vampires, and what do I know about them? Nothing. But she said she could find you, and make you talk. And that anything she does would heal. I figured no harm, no foul, and I get a killer off the streets." He turned to address Cyn. "But this . . ." He pointed at the bloodied vampire. "I didn't sign up for this."

"You kill as many vamps as I have, and you'll get used to it," Cyn sneered. She lifted her Glock, aiming at the vamp's other knee, but Gardet's wordless shout made her pause.

"You heard her," he pleaded to Mal, quickly swallowing the sob that put a hitch in his words. "She wants to execute me, but I didn't kill those people. I swear."

Cyn took a threatening step closer. His eyes widened and he nearly knocked his chair over as he cringed away from her. He shifted his gaze to Mal and began to speak quickly. "I'll tell you who it was. I'll show you where he lives. Anything, just keep her away from me. She's crazy, can't you see that?" he demanded, his gaze switching frantically from Cyn to Mal and back again.

Mal touched Cyn's arm, pushing her hand down. "Let's see what he has to say."

"Fuck," Cyn swore in disgust, but she backed away to stand near the stairs into the house.

"So talk," Mal said. "And no bullshit. She has a personal stake in this, and she likes her work. So you'd better it make it good."

"There's two of them," he said quickly, his voice a painful rasp. "Two separate killers. The first one I think was a mistake. Samuel didn't mean to kill anyone, but we'd only just arrived and it had been so long since he'd had blood from the—" His eyes widened as Cyn shifted abruptly.

"It's all right," Mal told him, giving Cyn an angry glare before turning back to Gardet. "You said there were two killers. The first body we found was a man. Did someone else kill the two women?"

Gardet was staring at Cyn, his posture still and watchful, as if she was the monster, and he the helpless victim. What a joke, she thought bitterly, and pounded a fist on the closed kitchen door.

Gardet jumped as the sound broke the silence.

"Maybe you should wait upstairs," Mal suggested. He gestured at Robbie.

Robbie gave him an unfriendly look, but then walked over to Cyn and touched her arm gently. "Come on, babe. Let's take a break."

Cyn met his gaze for a long moment, then spat in Gardet's direction and twisted the knob, shoving the door open. Robbie followed her through, closing the door behind them as Cyn raced up the stairs and into the bathroom she'd been using. Going to her knees, she vomited, throwing up the little bit of food she'd managed to eat that evening, tasting the vodka she'd consumed in the bar.

Robbie came in behind her. "Ah, Cyn," he murmured, then crouched next to her, holding her hair and rubbing her back.

"I'm sorry," she said on a hiccupping sob, then vomited some more, even though there was nothing left her stomach.

Robbie stood, pulling a washcloth from the rack and running it under cold water, before crouching next to her again. "Here you go."

Cyn took the wet cloth from him, holding it to her overheated face first. She felt like shit, but mostly she was embarrassed. Not because of what she'd done—with Raphael's life at stake, she would have done far worse—but because she was being such a pussy about it.

"Come on," Robbie coaxed, pulling her to her feet, taking the cloth from her and freshening it under more cold water. "Wipe your face off."

Cyn nodded wordlessly, taking the washcloth and wiping dutifully, before bending over the sink and rinsing her mouth with handfuls of cold water.

"I'm sorry," she said again, bracing her arms on the sink and staring at the water as it ran down the drain.

Robbie reached around her and turned off the water. "What do you have to be sorry for?" he murmured, pulling her out of the bathroom and sitting her on the bed. He crouched in front of her, chafing her cold hands with his warm ones. "You think you're the first person who tossed his cookies after a bloodfest like that?"

Cyn lifted her gaze to meet his, her eyes watery from the effort of throwing up.

"I've seen some of the hardest warriors you'd ever meet puke up their dinner after a rough interrogation," Robbie told her.

"Raphael doesn't," she whispered.

"That's because he has you to absolve his sins. He doesn't need to throw up, because you're there soaking away the darkness. Just like if he was here, you'd be okay."

"If he was here, none of this would be happening at all," she mumbled.

"Then we'd better get him back pronto, right?"

Cyn nodded, rubbing both hands over her face. "You think Mal got what we need yet?"

Robbie nodded. "I think Gardet's probably telling Mal everything he knows and then some. You had that vamp scared out of his fucking mind, and Mal played it perfectly."

She knew he was trying to cheer her up, but she didn't want to be told how great she'd been at torturing another living being, even if he did hold the answer to Raphael's whereabouts.

"I need a shower," she said, standing abruptly, trying not to think about why she needed it, or what she needed to wash away.

"You're on your own for that one," Robbie teased. "I'll be waiting outside."

Cyn nodded, but grabbed his arm before he turned away. "Thanks, Robbie."

"You got it, Cyn."

CYN STOOD ONCE again in the garage, with its quilt-covered walls and doors, its blood-spattered plastic. The sun was shining out there somewhere, but you couldn't tell inside the garage.

Gardet was still chained to his chair, and his shattered knee was still a mess. If you looked closely, you could see where the vampire symbiote had started to heal the damage. But it would take days for it to heal properly, depending on exactly how powerful Gardet was. That's the way the symbiote worked. It would start the healing even though Gardet's knee was bent and his leg still bound to the chair. But the minute Gardet tried to stand, the damage would be obvious and the symbiote would start all over again, trying to do a better job.

It was a gruesome thing to contemplate, but Cyn reminded herself that Gardet was one of Mathilde's people, and that they could be doing the same or worse to Raphael. And suddenly it didn't bother her so much. Besides, Gardet would probably be dead before he needed his knee again anyway. She had no doubt that as soon as Raphael was freed, he'd kill every single vampire who'd had anything to do with his capture, Gardet included. Assuming Cyn didn't kill the vamp first. She wasn't going to be worrying about the casualty count when they finally went in to get Raphael.

"They always drop off like that as soon as the sun rises?" Maleko Turner asked. He came to stand next to her and stare at the unconscious vampire.

Cyn nodded. "Pretty much. Depends on the vamp. Some are more powerful than others and can hold out longer, but once it hits . . . they're out, no matter where they are, standing, sitting, lying down. They're gone."

"What are you going to do with this guy?"

Cyn thought about her answer, then asked a question of her own instead, "Did you get everything we need from him?"

Turner gave a sideways dip of his head. "Assuming he told us the truth, yeah. He gave me names—"

"Names don't matter. I need a location."

"Got that, too. It's a house not far from here. According to Gardet, Mathilde got the old woman who lived there to invite her inside, said she admired the garden. They talked flowers and made friends. Mathilde then *persuaded* the old couple to take a vacation and let her use the house while they were gone. He could be lying, of course. He seemed pretty convinced he'd be walking out of here tomorrow night."

"He has an inflated sense of his own power. He's not going anywhere."

"Still, we can't just take his words on blind faith. You and I should check the place out while the sun's up."

"If he's telling the truth about that being the house, it'll be filled with vampires. They'll have guards, daytime guards, that is. We'll have to be careful."

"I figured as much, but the house is on the beach. We can do our recon from the ocean side. We'll attract less attention, and in my experience people tend not to worry so much about an attack from the water."

Cyn nodded. "I'll ask Robbie to stick around here and keep an eye on things. He won't like it, but you being buddy Rangers and all, he'll go along with it."

"I thought you said Gardet would be down for the day?"

"I'm not worried about Gardet. But Elke and Ken'ichi are upstairs, too. They're completely vulnerable, and with everything in motion, I don't like to leave them unprotected."

"Elke?" he repeated, his eyes worried.

Cyn regarded him quizzically. "You really like her? Or are you just fucking around?"

"I really like her, and I'd really like to be fucking around . . . but not the way you mean."

Cyn bared her teeth. "You be careful with my Elke. She means a lot to me."

"I think you should be more worried about me than her. She could wipe the floor with me."

"True enough." She looked around the garage, wrinkling her nose. "Let's get out of here. This place is beginning to smell."

THE BOAT BOBBED gently beneath them, the ocean tipped with white-capped swells. There was a storm out in the Pacific somewhere, but Turner's boat seemed more than capable of handling it.

"This is a nice boat, Turner."

"Call me Mal. And, yeah, it is a nice boat. For a while after my divorce, I thought about living on it."

"Kind of claustrophobic," Cyn commented, reaching down for the high-powered binoculars she'd brought along for their recon. "And you're not exactly a compact guy."

He laughed. "So I discovered when I tried to live on this baby. I got an apartment instead, but I kept the boat. I got a good deal on her."

While Mal stretched out on a sun pad on the back deck, being obvious about it for anyone watching them, Cyn settled on a flat cushion under cover of the awning and trained her binocs on the house where Gardet had insisted he and his "business partners" were all staying. She scanned slowly from side to side. It was a good-sized house, with lots of setback to either side of the property, and the lot was walled right down to the tideline. Whoever lived there didn't want any casual sunbathers mistaking this for anything but a private beach. It was an older construction, which meant every inch of flat surface near the walls and around the house was covered in foliage. There was what looked like a Japanese-style garden to one side, but there was also a wide lawn of thick and well-trimmed green grass.

"Mal, you have Wi-Fi on this boat?" she asked, never taking her eyes from the binoculars.

"Yeah," he said without moving from his sun worshipper pose. "Micro-cell hooked up to the computer. Access code's on a yellow sticky."

"Good to know Honolulu's finest has the latest in network security protocol," she said dryly, as she stood and made her way downstairs to the "office" that he had set up in the galley. She opened her laptop and logged in. She wanted to see what she could find on the house they were looking at. If it had been for sale at any point in the last two decades, there might be photographs or floor plans.

When her initial search turned up nothing, she did a quick search of property records instead and discovered the house had been owned by the same family since the late 1930s. Passing from generation to generation, it had obviously been renovated a time or two, but there hadn't been a change of ownership.

She switched to her cell phone and called Donovan Willis.

"What?" he answered. "You have another bullshit job for me?"

"Can it, Willis. I don't have time for your temper tantrums. Does Patterson own any property on Oahu?"

"He has a condo in Trump Tower on Waikiki."

"That's it? No houses anywhere?"

"No," he said slowly. "Why are you asking about this?"

"Just following a lead," she said vaguely, still not quite trusting him. "We might have more news later, so don't overdose on the Cheetos."

She hung up before he managed to sputter out a reply. She climbed the few steps back to her surveillance post.

"Anything interesting?" Mal asked, his voice the lazy drawl of a person half-asleep in the sun.

"Well," she said casually. "I'm a little worried about the owners of that house. If the vamps really are using it . . . I think they might be dead."

He sat up abruptly. "What?"

"Yeah." Cyn spoke without taking her eyes away from the target house, which she was once again scanning carefully. The binoculars she was using were extraordinarily powerful. She and Mal were about a quarter mile out to sea, but she could zoom in and study every detail of every window, down to the kind of plants covering the sills.

"This house has been in the same family for a long time. I originally thought it might be one of Patterson's. A lot of vamps file title changes to make it look like one generation's died and the next one's inherited. But Willis says Patterson doesn't own anything on this island except a condo."

"So Gardet's story holds. Mathilde vamped them into going away and letting her use it."

"Maybe," she agreed. But privately she didn't think so. Mathilde's style wasn't persuasion. She might have sweet-talked her way into the house, but then she was more likely to have killed the owners to get them out of the way. Or maybe Cyn had just been surrounded by so much death and violence in the last year that she automatically went to the worst possible conclusion.

However Mathilde had grabbed the house, though, it was certainly rigged for vampires now. Every window was closed tight, shutters or drapes covering every bit of glass. There was no light going into those rooms, at least not from this side. But she wasn't looking for that right now, she was looking for the human guards that she knew had to be there. No vampire of Mathilde's power and ego would spend a single day in a house without daylight guards. Of course, Mathilde wasn't here anymore, but if Raphael was, then Mathilde's hundred had to be here somewhere, too. And surely those hundred, and the prize they guarded, were worth a human security team.

"There you are," she murmured as two guards appeared from the right side of the house, their hands resting in casual readiness on identical M4 carbines. They wore khaki-colored shirts and shorts, with Army brown combat boots. But they were more interested in their own conversation than in anyone who might pose a threat to the house. It clearly didn't occur to them to glance out to sea.

Cyn had seen this before in human guards hired to watch over a temporary vamp residence. Mathilde probably had a very effective security force back home, but she'd already shuffled who knew how many vampires into Hawaii. She'd obviously decided to hire local guards, instead of flying her regular people in from Europe, because Cyn would bet good money that the two guys she was looking at were U.S. Army veterans. The M4s they carried were standard to Special Forces, but that didn't mean the guards were. Robbie could probably have told her more, but she didn't really need any more at this point. It was still possible that Gardet was lying and that they'd infiltrate this house only to discover it was occupied by some old, rich guy who liked his privacy. But her instincts were telling her that this was it.

Raphael was trapped in there somewhere, surrounded by enemies. She was a strong swimmer, in the best shape of her life. She could make that distance. She stared at the house, willing Raphael to talk to her, to give her a sign. She knew he was weakened by a lack of blood, that he was deep in daylight sleep when he could only touch her through dreams. But if he *was* there, did he know she was out here? That she was plotting, even now, to come to him?

"Cyn?"

She jumped at the sound of her name in that deep voice. But it wasn't Raphael, it was Mal.

"You okay?"

"Yeah," she said irritably. "Why wouldn't—" She looked around in shock. What the fuck? She was halfway out of the boat, one foot dipped in the warm water as she straddled the side. She yanked her leg back into the boat, then spun around, sliding down to huddle on the thick cushion.

"Sorry," she mumbled. "I was . . . in the moment."

Mal sat on the opposite side of the sun deck, leaning forward, his arms on his thighs, hands dangling between his knees. "So, you think this is the place?"

She didn't respond right away, her throat too thick with emotion to get the words out. She'd wanted a sign. Did it count that her heart ached? That every instinct she had was drawing her to that house? That she could smell him, could feel his warmth in her blood?

"Yes," she managed. "That's it."

"We should get back then," he said gently. "We need a plan."

"I have a plan," she whispered. "And no one's going to like it."

Chapter Fifteen

Night Two—Malibu, California

THE PHONE RANG, the distinctive tone telling them it was yet another call from the gate. Juro had lost count, but he'd guess there had been a good dozen calls since the sun had set. With less than two hours until sunrise, he'd hoped Mathilde was finished with them for the night, but apparently not.

"It's your turn to deal with her," Jared said, not even looking up from his iPad where he was reviewing the newest deployment schedules for Raphael's considerable guard presence. Although to call them a guard wasn't accurate anymore. They were an army, one of the most deadly forces on the face of the earth.

Their current enemy sat at the gate, just as enemies did of old. But this one was a cosmic bitch and she was untouchable for two more days. After that . . . well, after that, it would depend on events happening over 2500 miles away in Honolulu.

The phone rang again.

"You can't simply ignore it. That's not fair to the guards who have to deal with her."

Juro swallowed a groan and picked up the phone. "I'll be right there," he said, not even waiting for the guard to say anything. He didn't have to. If it had been an emergency, the call would have come over the tactical comm channel. If the guard was using the landline, the call was just Mathilde complaining again.

Nobody had expected her to accept her isolation gracefully. She was, after all, a vampire lord and accustomed to a higher standard of treatment from everyone around her. But one would think that even a vampire lord would expect some discomfort when going to war.

Juro marched down the hallway, and down the stairs, picking up his escort along the way. It would have been easy to slack off, to believe that things were safe for now, that nothing would happen for at least two more days. Their snipers had had a devastating effect on Mathilde's forces, cutting down not only all but one of her vampire cohort, but many of her daylight guards, as well. One or two of her humans had emerged from their trailer earlier in the day, bearing a white flag, claiming they hadn't signed up for this. Their surrender had been accepted, but after making sure they weren't armed or booby-trapped, they'd been locked up in Raphael's holding cells down below the garage. Jared and Juro couldn't risk them running off to report on Mathilde's situation and possibly bring in new allies. Raphael's forces had the upper hand for now, but that could too easily turn against them.

Mathilde was isolated, both physically and psychologically. Her human guards had been overrun that first day, her trailer searched while she slept, and her cell phone confiscated, along with any other communication devices they found. They'd left her undisturbed other than that, with blood delivered daily. If she chose to feed from her human companions instead, that was her choice.

They hadn't punished Mathilde for her treatment of Raphael, but it was tempting. Because the truth was that a few days without blood wasn't enough to cripple a vampire lord. If Raphael was as weak as Cyn indicated, he'd almost certainly been bled, not simply starved. Most likely, some of Mathilde's human helpers had been charged with slitting his wrists during the day while he slept, maybe even injecting him with some sort of blood thinner to increase the blood flow, if only for the short while before the vampire symbiote fought back. They all knew about what the drug dealers had done to Vincent, how he'd been bled. And those drug dealers had been in bed with Enrique, who'd been in bed with the Europeans. It was beginning to look like bleeding was a favorite tactic of the Europeans, because, as far as Juro knew, it hadn't ever been seen in North America.

Juro hadn't told Cyn any of this, figuring if Raphael had wanted her to know, he'd have told her himself. It was enough that she knew he was weak and getting weaker. She didn't need any more motivation than that.

Juro and his escort stopped just inside the estate's gate. They exchanged identical looks of dread, then one of them signaled the guard and the heavy steel slid open just enough for them to slip through.

"Where is she?" he asked the guard, scanning the area around the gate, which was beginning to resemble a true war zone. The two trailers sat off to one side as they had from the beginning. They'd had to remove several trees to make room for them, which was disruptive enough to the estate grounds. But on top of that was the destruction wreaked on the long driveway itself, replacing its smoothly paved and well-tended surface with a pitted, boulder-strewn mess. There were no bodies at least. The vampires had gone to dust, and the human bodies had been removed. Not even Mathilde's people had argued against that. No one wanted to be surrounded by the stink of decaying corpses.

"She's in the trailer," the guard said, drawing Juro's attention. "Probably waiting for you to present yourself to her greatness."

Juro snorted. "She'll be waiting a while if that's what—"

The trailer door creaked opened, interrupting him. Mathilde's lone remaining vampire attendant emerged, moving slowly, peering fearfully at the surrounding trees. It was the same vampire who'd been at the wheel of her escort SUV when she'd arrived. That had been only last night, though her incessant demands made it seem much longer.

"Lady Mathilde would speak with you," the vampire said tentatively.

"That's why I'm here," Juro responded, not moving from where he stood just outside the gate.

"She, that is, the Lady Mathilde would have you—"

"Look," Juro said impatiently. "I know you're just doing your job, but the situation's the same. If Mathilde wants to talk to me, she'll have to come outside to do it. I guarantee her safety—and yours, too, so stop cringing, man."

A slender arm suddenly shot out of the door opening, shoving the unfortunate vampire to the ground. He bounced up quickly enough, shooting an angry glare at his mistress. Mathilde wasn't winning any friends in either camp, it would seem.

Mathilde herself appeared a moment later, as elegantly dressed as ever. Her outfit was deep purple—apparently her luggage had made it through the fighting last night—but otherwise it was much the same. Form-fitting leggings tucked into stiletto-heeled boots, a matching sweater, with a knee-length cardigan in a slightly darker shade. She marched closer to Juro with admirable grace given their surroundings, stopping several feet away.

"You've made your point," she said sharply. "You are loyal to Raphael and I am the enemy. But I have already won this battle, Juro. Don't be a fool and make it harder on everyone."

Juro regarded her without expression, not quite believing what he was hearing. Granted, he knew Mathilde was a self-centered egotist, but did she really think she'd won already?

"Three days, Mathilde," he finally said. "Is there anything else?"

"You surely do not expect me to reside in that"—she pointed at the trailer behind her—"for two more nights."

"That is entirely up to you," he replied. "Should you choose to abandon this fruitless challenge, we would be pleased to offer you an escort to the airport and ensure your safe departure for your home in France."

Mathilde opened her mouth to respond, but Juro didn't give her a chance. "If, on the other hand, your intent is to await the arrival of my Sire, Lord Raphael—as is certainly your right—then, yes, I do expect you to remain here. I will remind you that we are not obligated to provide accommodation for the duration of your challenge. The safety or comfort of those who have declared war upon Lord Raphael—"

"I did no such—"

"—whether through word or action," Juro persisted, ignoring her objection, which was patently false, "is not our concern. Is there anything else?"

Mathilde stared at him, her eyes taking on the dim glow of her power. Juro could feel her growing anger, her power testing him, pressing against him like a ferocious animal straining to break free. The guards around him shifted nervously and he braced, wondering if she'd finally slipped the leash of her patience and was going to attack him straight out. He had a good idea of what she was capable of, knew she'd refrained from using her power against any of them so far only because she was conserving her strength against the possibility of future battles. But he and Jared had pushed her hard over the last two nights.

"You will regret this," she said in a low menacing voice. "Your Sire is finished. And, mark my words, you will be, too."

She spun on her heel and glided like a model on a runway back to the trailer steps, taking them in a single graceful leap before she disappeared inside, her vampire flunky following her and closing the door.

Juro drew a relieved breath. He was a powerful vampire, powerful enough to have been Raphael's lieutenant had he chosen to accept the offer. But he honestly didn't know what would have happened if it had come down to a fight between him and Mathilde, right here, right now. It was very possible that he could best her in a contest of raw power, but she was much older, with many more years of fighting challenges and outsmarting her opponents.

"Let's hope that's it for the night, lads," he murmured, turning to the guard. "Don't take any chances with her. Shoot to kill if you must."

"Yes, sir," the guard said, then stepped back inside the guard shack with its heavily reinforced walls and bulletproof glass.

Juro didn't think Mathilde would waste her time taking out a guard, but that didn't mean she wouldn't have someone else do the shooting. He and Jared had done what they could to isolate her, but it was very possible that she had other supporters in the area who knew her plans and would respond to her disappearance without being called.

Juro climbed into the SUV for the short drive back to the house, his thoughts turning to Honolulu where the real battle for their survival was being fought. Right now, Mathilde was nothing more than a pain in the ass. But she would be a lot more than that if Cyn and Ken'ichi didn't manage to locate Raphael, and get him back here before it was too late.

Chapter Sixteen

Night Two—Honolulu, Hawaii

CYN AND MAL made it back to the house before sunset, much to Robbie's obvious relief. He hadn't been pleased about being left behind, but someone had to stay with the two sleeping vampires, and it was Mal's boat.

She'd told Robbie only that they'd definitely found the house where Raphael was being held, but had put off anything more detailed until the two vampires were awake and could join them. And then she'd gone upstairs to change clothes and take a shower, hoping it would revive her somewhat.

Standing under the pounding water, she tried to turn her mind off. She hadn't managed to sleep more than two of the last twenty-four hours, and that had been an hour snatched in the boat, and then another in the car on the way back to the house. She was worried about Raphael, worried about what she'd felt when they'd been sitting on the boat, so close to where he was imprisoned. He was too weak. She was beginning to suspect Mathilde's people were doing something more to him than simply withholding blood. Raphael was stronger than that. A few days without blood would have put him off his game, but not this badly.

The clock was ticking, and her heart was telling her they needed to get in there tonight, that Raphael might not make it another day. But her mind was saying they had to wait, that it wouldn't help to get everyone killed, including Raphael, for just a few hours difference.

Because one way or another, she was going in after Raphael tomorrow.

"I'VE GOT TO tell you," Mal was saying when she started down the stairs. "It was pretty freaky. I thought for a minute I'd have to dive in after her. It was like she was in a trance or something."

"That close . . . she'd know Raphael was there." Cyn recognized Elke's voice. She should have known that was who Mal would be talking to. The guy had a serious crush.

"Can all of you vamps do that?" he asked.

Elke snorted dismissively. "I don't think you understand the power it took for Raphael to touch Cyn at all. Even at full strength, it takes some serious mojo for a vampire to communicate with a human during his daylight sleep. For Raphael to do so now, after what they've done to him? That's unbelievable."

"You all keep talking about what they've done to him, or what they're still doing. What the fuck *are* they doing? I mean if he's this über powerful vampire, how are they holding him?"

There was a moment of silence, and then Elke spoke in a subdued voice. "I haven't said anything to Cyn, because I don't know for sure, but . . . I think Mathilde must have bled him, probably had her human flunkies slice his wrists during the day. She's too big a coward to come that close to him at night, no matter how many vamps she has squeezing his brain."

Cyn felt like she'd been gut-punched. She sank to the stairs, her legs no longer willing to hold her upright. Elke was still talking to Mal down below, but the words no longer made sense. Mathilde had *bled* Raphael. She'd *sliced his wrists*. And now she wasn't feeding him.

Cyn buried her face in her arms. She'd *known* there was something wrong with him, something more than just missing a few days feeding. Raphael was dying. He'd been dying this afternoon when she'd been only a hundred yards away. She should have gone in. If she'd known . . .

"Cyn?"

She looked up as Robbie sat down next to her. "We have to get him tonight," she told him urgently. "It'll mean massaging my plan a bit, but we can still do it. There weren't that many day guards, and at night, most of the vamps are probably too busy holding on to Raphael to bother with security. In fact, I bet the night guards are human, too. We should ask Gardet. He'll be awake now, we can—"

"Cyn!" Robbie was practically shouting, which told her he'd been trying to get her attention for a while. "Stop. You're not making any sense."

Cyn realized she was out of breath, that she'd been rambling. But that didn't change anything. Turning to face Robbie, she gripped his arm and repeated intently, "We have to go get him tonight. There's no more time. Mathilde's already in Malibu. We can't waste—"

"We are not going tonight."

Cyn twisted around at the sound of Ken'ichi's deep voice. "Why the hell not?" she demanded, glaring up at him. "And who put you in charge?"

"Juro," he said simply. "But more to the point, you did, Cynthia. You're the one who wanted me here because you knew you'd need a vampire of power. And now I'm telling you that we must wait until tomorrow night."

Cyn gave him a stony look, wondering why the normally silent vampire had chosen this moment to exercise his verbal abilities. But he was right about one thing. She *was* the one who'd wanted him with her on this mission. "All right, I'm willing to listen. Why tomorrow?"

"Can we move this discussion to the kitchen where everyone can participate?"

Cyn shrugged ungraciously. "Whatever. I could use a cup of coffee." She stood and made her way down the rest of the stairs, rounding the wall to the kitchen in time to see Elke and Mal break apart like a couple of guilty teenagers. Those two needed to get a room and just do it. Put everyone out of their misery.

Going over to the coffeemaker, she poured a cup, loaded it with sugar, then turned to face Ken'ichi. "So make your argument. Why not tonight?"

"There is no argument, Cynthia. We are not prepared to do this tonight."

"Not true. Mal and I scoped the house out this afternoon, and Gardet can tell us the specific layout and where they're holding Raphael."

"And what of the others?" Ken'ichi asked calmly.

"What others? You mean the guards? How many can there be? Like I told Robbie, most of Mathilde's vamps are probably too terrified of losing control of Raphael to waste time walking perimeter. Besides, I've been thinking about it, and that house isn't big enough to hold more than a hundred vampires at the same time. I'm betting there's another house nearby. Close enough for them to work their mojo."

"If that's true, how do you propose to free Lord Raphael from their grip?"

Cyn stared at him.

"I want him back as much as you do, Cynthia." He raised a hand to forestall the protest that rose immediately to her lips. "Not in the same way," he conceded. "But Raphael is my Sire. When he found my brother and me we were—" His mouth tightened, as if he'd said more than he intended. "He made us human again, and then he made us more. I would lay down my life for him in an instant. But it will do none of us any good, not Lord Raphael, not you, not Juro or the others back in Malibu, if we try to rescue Raphael and fail. His jailers will only secure him more tightly, while we will have lost the biggest advantage we have."

Cyn sighed and looked away. "The fact that they don't know we're here."

"Yes."

"So what do you propose?"

"We do a further reconnaissance tonight. Elke and I will surveil the house to determine if there are vampires present, and how many. In the meantime, I agree with your assessment that Mathilde's hundred are probably very nearby. And our friend Gardet will know where."

"I've got a question," Mal said, drawing everyone's attention. "I never asked Gardet about Raphael. As far as he knows, Cyn is here because she had a connection with one of the victims, and we want the killer. So why did Gardet give me the house where they're holding Raphael instead of this other house, the one where you all think the rest of the vamps are staying? You'd think he'd want to keep us far away from the prize."

They all stared at him a moment, then Elke punched his arm hard enough to make him wince. "Seems like you're more than just a pretty face," she said, and turned to the others. "What do we think?"

"I think we should ask Gardet," Ken'ichi said bluntly. "You're the one who spoke with him last night, Mal, so you take the lead. But I'll be with you this time. He cannot lie to me. He's not strong enough."

"And if he tries?" Mal asked curiously. "Do we call Cyn with her gun?"

Cyn ground her teeth against the flinch his words caused. She didn't want to step into that garage again, but she'd do it if she had to.

"That won't be necessary," Ken'ichi responded. "I believe Mr. Gardet's usefulness is at its end. If necessary, I'll scour his brain for what we need, and then dispose of what's left."

Cyn looked up quickly. "If he dies, won't Mathilde feel it?"

"Normally," Ken'ichi agreed. "She is his Sire, after all. But I suspect she's too distant to sense his death, or if she does, she probably won't know the manner of it. She'll likely assume he burned out in the effort to subdue Raphael. She and her allies would have factored in a certain number of fatalities as a matter of course. "Besides," he added in a voice that had gone arctic cold, "once Gardet took up against my Sire, his death was a foregone conclusion."

"But if he realizes we're after Raphael . . . we can't let him get off a warning to anyone," Cyn said urgently.

"That won't happen, Cynthia," Ken'ichi said patiently. "You must trust me."

Cyn met his dark eyes and nodded. "I do."

The shadow of a smile touched his face before he turned to regard Mal once again. "Do you understand what must be done?"

Mal nodded grimly. "Not everything, but enough to know that if it wasn't for Blondie here, I'd be wishing I'd never heard of vampires. So tell me, when we find out where this other house is, what do we do then?"

"Tonight is for reconnaissance only. When we have what we need, we will return here and devise a strategy for tomorrow."

"I *have* a strategy," Cyn said. "I'm going tomorrow afternoon, during daylight. I'll find Raphael and be there when he wakes." She looked down, relaxing her hands when she realized she was clutching the edge of the kitchen island so hard that her fingers were white and bloodless. "By the time you all arrive after sunset, he'll be strong enough to help in his own rescue. And to exact revenge."

She looked up then, scanning their faces. Only Mal appeared confused. The others all understood that Raphael would need to feed, and Cyn would be the one there when he woke. She knew what that meant, knew that he'd be out of control in his bloodthirst. But she didn't want anyone else to feed him. And she absolutely *knew* that Raphael would never hurt her.

"Cyn . . ." Elke started to object, but took one look at the determination on Cyn's face, and nodded her head in agreement.

"We will discuss the specifics of your strategy before we retire for the night," Ken'ichi said. "One way or the other, we need to be ready to move at sunset tomorrow."

Ken'ichi and Mal headed off to the garage to question Gardet. Elke glanced at Mal's departing back, then turned to Robbie and said, "You sticking with Cyn tonight?"

He nodded. "Like glue."

"Then I'm going to the garage. Ken'ichi can use the backup . . . and so can Mal."

"We might run out for some food," Robbie told her. "Ask Mal if he wants anything and let me know."

"Got it," Elke said, then hurried down the hall, as if worried they might start without her.

"You think it's Ken she's worried about?" Robbie asked lightly.

"Not a chance," Cyn said.

"That's what I thought, too. Go put on some shoes. We're making a burger run. Mal gave me directions to the local In-N-Out."

"I'm not hungry."

"No? You look like you've lost ten pounds, and Cyn baby, you don't have ten pounds to lose. Plus you're as pale a vamp. If you're going to feed Raphael tomorrow night, you'll need more red blood cells than your current load. You need meat. And while we're out, we'll pick up some high protein shakes. I know you'll never agree to eat before we leave tomorrow, but you can drink a shake or two."

"Robbie."

He gave her a quizzical look. "Yeah?"

"You can't go in with me tomorrow. You know that right? It has to be just me and Raphael."

He stared at her silently. "I can't go as far as wherever they're holding him, the basement or a bedroom, or whatever. But I sure as hell can get you to the house and cover your ass."

Cyn gave a half smile. "My plan doesn't actually call for my ass to be covered."

"What the fuck does that mean?"

"It's the only way—"

Cyn broke off as the door to the garage pushed open, and Elke stuck her head out. "Mal says bring him a chocolate shake and a couple of 3 x 3s. No onions," she added with a wink, then disappeared back into the garage without waiting for confirmation.

Robbie stood abruptly. "Come on, we're going for burgers, and you're going to tell me what this naked ass plan of yours is."

"THEY'RE NOT GOING to like it," Robbie commented.

They were sitting at the In-N-Out, chomping down on burgers and fries while Cyn explained her plan to Robbie. Cyn hadn't expected to have much of an appetite, but once she'd started eating, she'd discovered she was hungry. She'd downed a double-double, all of her fries, and a good part of a chocolate shake, too. Because Robbie was right. If she was going to feed Raphael, she'd need something more than coffee in her system.

"They'll see the logic of it," she said. "Besides, whether you realize it or not, their focus is more and more on Raphael. They think I don't know what's going on, that I don't feel him getting weaker, which is just stupid vampire arrogance. I'm his mate, for God's sake. But I've noticed that vamps have this daddy thing going with their Sire. It's always there, but it comes out more when they're under stress, or, even worse, when he's under threat. And like all children, they want to believe that their daddy loves them best. The greater the stress, the more attached they become."

She stole one of Robbie's French fries, ignoring his not-so-subtle glare.

"By tomorrow, they'll be so fired up to finally be going after Raphael that they'd serve me up tied hand and foot if that's what it took."

Robbie laughed at the image, but shook his head. "That's not true, and you know it."

"Maybe not that bad," she conceded. "But they'll go along with my plan, because they know it's necessary." She balled up her napkin. "We should get back."

Robbie sighed, and pushed away from the table. "Let me put in Mal's order, and we'll go."

They got Mal's food and a second order of fries for the bottomless pit that was Robbie's stomach, then headed back to the Diamond Head house. Since the garage had been turned into a prison for Gardet, they parked in the driveway and entered through the front. The door was locked, and the alarm was armed for the ground floor, which Cyn thought was odd. But then she heard the shower going upstairs. If they were all up there, they might have armed the alarm on this floor in an excess of caution. But why were they all upstairs? What about Gardet?

Following Robbie to the kitchen, Cyn continued down the short hallway to the garage while he dumped Mal's order on the counter. Even before she got the door to the garage fully open, she knew something had changed. The lights were off, and the smell . . . this was not what the garage had smelled like last time she was in it.

She flipped on the lights and stared. All signs that this was anything but an ordinary garage were gone. The quilts that had provided makeshift soundproofing, the plastic sheeting that had been slick with blood . . . and most importantly, Gardet himself, were all gone.

Robbie came up behind her and pushed her aside with a gentle nudge. Taking the three steps down into the garage, he turned in a circle.

"I'll give them this," he said quietly, "they did a good job."

"It helps when the dead body disposes of itself," she said absently, still not quite believing what she was seeing. "You think Ken'ichi got anything out of him first?"

"I'd bet on it. He wouldn't have offed the guy otherwise," he said, but then tipped his head thoughtfully. "Or he might have. Gardet was a world-class asshole."

Cyn heard footsteps and turned to see Ken'ichi coming down the hall, being intentionally noisy so as not to startle her.

"He gave up the address of the second house and more," he told her, having obviously overheard her question to Robbie—vampire hearing and all that.

"How sure are you he was telling the truth?"

The big vampire gave her a closed mouth smile that was equal parts smug and vicious. "Quite sure. Although, knowing the location of the house where Raphael is being held, I'm confident we could have located the other house without him. They had to be nearby, and that many vampires would be putting off a loud signature. But, in any event, Mr. Gardet was eager to tell us what he knew."

"Why'd he give up Raphael's prison instead of his buddies?" she asked. That had bothered her more than anything else.

Ken'ichi nodded. "Gardet assumed you would be the one to investigate the address he gave us. That you, and perhaps Robbie, would go in during daylight intending to find the vampires who murdered your supposed friend, and kill them while they slept. As you discovered, the house where they're holding Raphael has daylight guards. Gardet counted on them killing you when you attempted to break in, thus eliminating the threat to the others without jeopardizing the larger plan."

"I told you," Robbie commented. "World-class asshole."

"There's more," Ken'ichi said. "He admitted what we already knew, that Mathilde has left the Islands, along with her two fellow lords. More importantly, Cynthia, you need to know that Raphael is never alone. There are never fewer than three vampires directly in the room with him, sometimes four if they are not strong enough. They serve as guards at night, but they sleep by his side during the day, serving as a focus for the others as soon as they wake."

Cyn tuned out the rest of Ken'ichi's report, absorbed instead with this latest piece of unwanted news. Her plan had always been to reach Raphael's side as close to sunset as possible, to minimize the possibility of discovery while she waited for him to wake. But now she'd have to allow enough time to take out three, maybe four, master vampires before they, too, woke for the night.

"You okay, Cyn?" Robbie's voice interrupted her thoughts, telling her she'd been too quiet for too long.

"Yeah. Can we get out of here? The blood was bad, but this disinfectant smell is giving me a headache."

"Sure thing," he said, gesturing for her to precede him back into the house. "Speaking of cleanup, though, what'd you do with all the plastic and stuff, Ken?"

"Mal and Elke disposed of it. Having a police detective around is more helpful that I expected. Mal knows of a discreet incineration facility where, if the price is right, the operator doesn't ask questions."

"Did they use Mal's vehicle?" Cyn asked.

Ken'ichi nodded.

"Even better," Robbie said. "If we're going to contaminate a car, better that it belongs to a cop than to any of us."

"They're showering now," Ken'ichi said, then tilted his head, as if listening. "More or less," he added. "Once they've finished, we'll verify Mr. Gardet's information, scout out the area, then come back here and make our plans for tomorrow night."

Cyn nodded. "Did you talk to Juro yet?"

"I spoke to him right before you arrived. Mathilde has proven to be quite predictable in her response to Jared and Juro's strategy. She's angry, but, having lost most of her vampire backup on that first night, she's unwilling to push the confrontation beyond verbal threats."

"The waiting period runs out tomorrow, though," Cyn said worriedly. "She can claim forfeit against Raphael."

Ken'ichi nodded. "Lucas is set to arrive tonight, although Mathilde won't know it. When she demands entry tomorrow night, claiming forfeiture, Lucas will challenge her for the territory. If he has to fight her, he will, but our hope is that he will be able to delay her until Raphael returns."

Cyn counted the nights in her head. Two nights left, she calculated. She had only two nights to free Raphael and get him back to Malibu. And get him in good enough shape to defeat Mathilde.

That was the one thing that Cyn had absolutely no doubts about. If she could get Raphael back to Malibu on time, he *would* defeat Mathilde. Cyn only hoped he'd make the bitch suffer first.

Mal's deep voice and Elke's laughter carried down the stairs, preceding them around the corner into the kitchen. The two of them had obviously just come out of a shower, and, just as obviously, had been *in* that shower together.

Mal immediately headed for the center island, and dug into his burgers and fries, chowing down like a starving man. Or one who'd just had sex in the shower.

Cyn caught Elke's eye, and arched a brow in question. But Elke simply shrugged, hiding a smile.

They didn't delay long after that. While Mal ate his food, Cyn went upstairs and changed. Tonight was supposed to be about recon, but when dealing with vampires, it never hurt to bring a few special weapons along. Just in case.

CYN SAT IN THE back seat of the SUV, staring at the house which Gardet had claimed held the hundred or so vampires who were focused on containing Raphael's power. It would have been easy to blow the whole thing up. They could come back in the morning, string a few well-placed charges, toss some grenades through the windows for good measure, and walk away. Robbie knew all about explosives, and she was sure Mal could tell them where they could pick up some C4 and detonator cord.

But somehow, she doubted Mal would go along with blowing up a residence in the middle of a Honolulu neighborhood.

So, instead, she found herself studying the house, seeing all the telltale signs of vampire habitation—windows covered with makeshift blackout curtains, probably blankets or sheets and no lights, even though she could see a few people moving around. Not as many as you'd expect with that many vampires living in the same place, and no coming and going, but that didn't surprise her. These guys had a job to do, and that job didn't permit socializing. During the hour in which they'd been watching the house—from their parking spot in front of a neighbor's house more than a block away—she'd seen four vampires. Three returning, and then three more leaving.

"There are so many vampires in there," Ken'ichi whispered, his voice strained as if it hurt him to be this close. "And the house is so small, too small for so many."

Cyn's cell phone of the day rang. She glanced at the incoming number. "Yeah."

"That's definitely the place, right?" Elke asked without preamble. "There are so many vamps working in there that even I can feel it."

"Yeah," Cyn said again. "I think we've seen enough. Right, Ken'ichi?" she asked.

He didn't answer right away. But then he nodded slowly. "We can leave. This will be for Raphael to sort out. Our focus must be on freeing him instead."

Cyn was kind of freaked out by his response. She could have told him that *her* entire focus had *always* been on freeing Raphael. But it wasn't only what Ken'ichi had said, it was the way he'd said it. Spooky, as if his mind was somewhere else. Somewhere not so good.

She shivered. She couldn't get off this island soon enough. Once she had Raphael in her arms again, they were getting the fuck out of here and never coming back.

With daylight less than an hour away, they raced back to the house on Diamond Head. There was little time to discuss the finer details of Cyn's plan for getting to Raphael, but that was probably a good thing. She was absolutely set on her course of action and didn't see the point of going over it with people who would only try to talk her out of it. She couldn't admit that, though. So when they got back to the house, they held a hurried strategy session in the kitchen while Ken'ichi sucked down a bag of blood from the refrigerator. Apparently, the evening had taken it out of him. Cyn noticed Elke didn't imbibe, which meant Mal had probably discovered the true delights of being a vampire's lover, including letting Elke sink fang.

"If we're ignoring the vamp house for now," Cyn said, leaning against the kitchen counter, "then all we have to worry about is getting inside the one where Raphael is being held. And the best time to do that is daylight."

"There are guards there," Mal reminded her. "We both saw them."

"But there weren't very many and they weren't smartly placed. Besides, I'm not planning on storming the stronghold. I just need to get inside the house and find Raphael, so I can be there when he wakes for the night. I'll need help from you, Mal, and from Robbie. But once I'm in, you guys will disappear until after dark, when Elke and Ken'ichi show up."

"And what then?" Mal asked.

Cyn looked around the group. "By the time Ken'ichi and Elke arrive at the house, Raphael will be the one making decisions."

"I don't understand. Won't he be too sick—" Mal started to protest, but Elke touched his arm.

"I'll explain later," she told him.

Mal was clearly frustrated, but he let it drop. "All right, so let's go back to the big question. How do you plan to get inside and find Raphael?"

"Robbie and I will be on the beach side, but I'll need a distraction, and that's where you come in. Whoever was living in that house when they made the mistake of inviting Mathilde inside is probably dead. No one's reported them missing, not that we can find anyway, but the vamps don't know that. Can you do some sort of safety check, Mal? You know, as if someone had called the police, worried because they've been trying to reach their elderly grandparents and can't get a hold of them?"

Mal shrugged. "Not my usual beat, but I can do that."

"You need to arrive with as much noise as possible. I don't mean a siren or anything, I just want you to be visible. Make sure anyone who sees the vehicle will know it's HPD. Maybe park in front of the house, turn on the LED flashers. We want anyone watching you from inside the house to think the neighbors have definitely noticed you. You could even knock on a couple of neighbor's doors first, flash your badge to whoever answers. I'm hoping the threat of your presence at the front of the house will draw away some, or even most, of Mathilde's security. I'll already be inside by then, and while you play your game in front, I'll locate Raphael and stay with him."

"You're going to break in?"

Cyn shook her head. "Nope. They're going to invite me."

"THIS PLAN SUCKS," Robbie muttered as they piled gear into the SUV.

"It chafes, is what it does," Cyn muttered. She tugged at the bikini bottoms currently riding up her ass beneath the oversized "I Heart Hawaii" T-shirt which she wore over the matching top. And that was all she had on, a bikini and a T-shirt. The bikini was necessary to her plan, but she hadn't exactly packed for sunbathing when she'd been getting ready for this trip. She'd had to rush out and buy the barely-there swimsuit this morning. This being Hawaii, there had been plenty of shops to choose from, but she hadn't taken the time to pick and choose. She'd simply grabbed the one that best suited her requirements, i.e., the one that showed the most skin, and bought it without even trying it on.

Technically, it fit. She just wasn't used to having half of her ass hanging out in public, while the bottoms tried to cut her in half vertically.

Cyn glanced over and caught Robbie's worried frown. "Don't worry. I can't explain it, but I know this is what I need to do. Besides, are you saying I don't look good enough in this bikini to distract the guards?"

He gave her a dry look. "Fishing for compliments? Not usually your style."

"Neither is this damn suit," she snapped, yanking again at the thong, which was only doing what it had been designed to do.

They both looked up as Mal came out of the house, closing the front door behind him, then rattling the doorknob to make certain it was secure.

"I don't like leaving them," he growled, stopping on the way to his HPD vehicle which was parked at the curb.

"It's not ideal," Cyn agreed. "But the security system is on and linked to our phones, and you can come right back as soon as—" Her cell phone rang with an incoming call. Not the burner phone of the day, but her regular cell phone.

Whoever was calling her couldn't be anyone she wanted to talk to, since all of those people were either sound asleep, or standing in front of her. Still, thinking it might be one of her friends from the mates' club, she checked and did a double take at what she saw. Nick Katsaros again? What the fuck? She declined the call and went to put away her phone, but it didn't make it out of her hand before he was calling her again. She declined again, and waited. But, this time, it was an incoming text.

Cyn. Answer the damn phone. It's critical.

That was all the message said. *Critical.* Why would he say that? And just at this moment, when she was literally on the brink of the most important battle of her life.

The cell phone rang, making her jump. Nick. She stared at it, trying to decide.

"Cyn?" Robbie said, sensing her concern. "Who's—"

She cut him off, holding up a hand for him to wait as she answered the call.

"Nicky," she said cautiously. "This is not a good time."

D.B. Reynolds

"Cyn," he breathed, as if relieved she'd answered. "I know what you're about to do, and you need to meet with me first."

"You can't possibly—"

"You're getting ready to rescue Raphael. I don't know how you plan to do it, but I know whatever the plan is, it won't work unless you meet me first."

"What the fuck? How do you know about this?" She stared wildly around, scanning every house, every shadow, searching for whoever it was who'd been spying on them. Looking for Nick. But why?

"Cyn," Nick practically shouted, gaining her attention. "Do you trust me?"

Cyn breathed, heart racing. Did she trust him? "Yes," she told him, knowing it was true, even though she couldn't have said why.

"Then meet me, sweetheart. I want the same thing you do. I want your Raphael freed and that bitch dead."

Cyn sucked in a breath. How the hell. . . . "All right," she said, deciding. "Where are you? It has to be now, Nick. I'm out of time."

"I know. Get your team moving. We'll meet at the Diamond Head Monument parking lot, so it's on your way. Park at the trailhead. I'm in a black Panamera."

"Ten minutes," she said, and disconnected. She looked up to find Robbie watching her closely.

"A voice from the past," she told him. "But a man I trust. He has some information on Raphael's situation. Something he says we need to know before we go in there. We're meeting him in the monument parking lot." She shivered underneath the thin T-shirt as she said the words. Had something happened to Raphael? Something even worse than what she'd thought? But Nick wouldn't be calling her if it couldn't be fixed. Whatever it was.

"Let's go," she said.

THEY ARRIVED IN two vehicles, with Mal following their SUV in his HPD-issue sedan. It was unmarked, but anyone with eyes would know what it was.

Cyn spotted the Porsche Panamera right away, black on black with tinted windows. An elegant car with lots of power, but subtle for Nick who tended to go with flashier convertibles, like $200,000 Ferraris.

Robbie pulled in next to him, intentionally placing Nick on his side of the vehicle, which put two full vehicle widths between Nick personally and Cyn. Cyn shook her head. She understood the instinct that made Robbie do it, but she knew Nick, and he was no threat to her.

Nick got out of the Panamera as they pulled in, every long, strong inch of him. Cyn was one hundred percent committed to Raphael, but that didn't mean she was blind. Nick Katsaros was a beautiful man. He always had been. Over six feet of well-toned muscle, with broad shoulders and long, lean legs. His wavy, brown hair was longer than it had been the last time she'd seen him, and his hazel eyes were covered by a pair of polarized Oakleys, which he pulled off as she walked around the car to greet him.

"Cyn," he said warmly, opening his arms. "Can we still hug?"

She smiled and stepped in for a quick embrace, but it was Nick who disengaged first, eyeing her up and down, taking in the T-shirt over bikini ensemble. "Not your usual attire, but looking good as always," he said.

Cyn laughed weakly, turning as she felt Robbie move up close behind her.

"Nick Katsaros, Robbie Shields," she said, introducing them.

The two men shook hands grimly, not even pretending that they weren't trying to crush each other's bones. Robbie was broader, thicker with muscle, but for all his lean appearance, Nick had always possessed a hidden strength.

Mal joined the crowd and introduced himself. "Maleko Turner, HPD," he said, not offering his hand, but at least putting an end to the power struggle between the other two.

Nick winked at Cyn as he flexed his fingers. "As good as it is to see you, Cyn, I know time is short so I'll get down to it. I know that Mathilde took your guy, and I suspect you're about to mount a rescue. I would have gotten here sooner—"

"I'm not even going to ask how you know this stuff," Cyn interrupted. "You're a salesman, for God's sake. Or at least—"

"I'm not a salesman," he said, sounding somewhat exasperated. "I never *was* a salesman. You just assumed I was. Maybe it made it easier for you to overlook things you couldn't explain, but, sweetheart, we don't have time for this. After you're done, after you've brought Raphael home, we'll talk. Okay?"

Cyn nodded. "So why the meet then?"

He glanced at Robbie and Mal in turn, eyeing them uneasily. "Cyn . . . this is delicate. I don't know how much you've shared—"

"Everything," she interrupted. "Well, everything to do with this op anyway. Whatever it is, you can say it to all of us."

He met her eyes for a moment, then shrugged one shoulder as if to acknowledge it was her decision to make.

"You know how powerful Raphael is," he said speaking in a low voice. "So you know it would have taken a hell of a lot, not only to catch him unaware, but to weaken him to the point where they could hold him."

He was saying what Cyn herself had thought more than once over the last few days, so she couldn't disagree. Although she sure as hell wondered how Nick knew all of this.

"Elke thinks they're bleeding him—"

"I'm assuming Elke's a vamp, and she's right. They probably are, to hedge their bets if nothing else, but there's more. Mathilde got her hands on a set of . . . handcuffs they'd be called now, but they're much more than that. They're the Amber Manacles and they're beyond ancient, an artifact of tremendous power that was crafted when magic still ruled this world."

"Magic?" Cyn said, not hiding her disbelief.

Nick stared. "Cyn, you live with a *vampire,* for God's sake. And not just any vampire, but a guy who's one of the biggest magical energy sinks in the world today. How can you not believe in magic?"

"Well, yeah, Raphael's unusual, but . . . magical handcuffs?"

Nick blinked at her. "You're smarter than that, Cyn. But we don't have time to argue about it. The Amber Manacles do more than simply bind their victim; they drain his energy until he can barely remain upright. The longer he wears them, the weaker he'll become. Even worse, they can't be broken or forced, but will only open with the key."

"You're saying Mathilde locked Raphael in these manacles? But if she did that, then she has the key, so how do I—?"

"I never said there was only *one* key." Nick reached through the open door of the Porsche and grabbed something from the seat, causing Robbie and Mal both to tense expectantly. But he emerged with something in his fingers, something long and bronze-colored. . . .

"A key," Cyn whispered.

"They were called the Amber Manacles for a reason. Two keys were made, one for the captor, and the other for the prisoner. Except that the prisoner's key was encased in amber, set in plain sight to torment him with the knowledge that his freedom was so close at hand and yet completely unattainable. Even if a prisoner managed to get hold of the key, he would lack the physical strength to smash the amber so the key could be used."

"And this one?" Cyn asked, studying the narrow piece of bronze. It didn't look much like a key, at least not by modern standards. It was a long narrow rod with a simple ring at one end, and carvings along the barrel that might have been some sort of language, but not one that she recognized.

"The amber key. Smashed by myself years ago when it was recovered from a rather unscrupulous collector who was seeking the manacles to go with it. I never had the manacles, but he didn't know that. I knew they were in Europe somewhere, but it wasn't until Mathilde used them that I knew their exact location."

"And that brought you to Hawaii?"

He nodded. "Her use of them on Raphael brought me here, but this isn't the first time she's used them. Mathilde is very old and quite the little psychopath. I'd pay good money to watch Raphael kill her, but I doubt he'd welcome my presence," he added, giving Cyn a wink.

"If this helps me get him free, you've got a front row seat," she told him. "How does it work?"

"Simple. You touch the key to the right-hand manacle and that's it."

"No magic word or anything?"

Nick shook his head. "I can see we need to talk. But, later. You need to get to Raphael now." He leaned in and kissed her lightly on the cheek. "Good luck, sweetheart."

"Why're you doing this?" she asked, studying his handsome face. "You don't know Raphael."

"You're right, but I know *you*. There's good and evil in this world, Cyn, and I know which side of that line *you* stand on. So if you stand with your vampire, then I know where he stands, too."

"Thanks, Nicky," she said solemnly.

He grinned. "Besides, your vamp owes me one now. And I always collect."

Slipping his Oakleys back on, he nodded at the two men, then dropped into the Panamera and closed the door. Backing out with a squeal of tires, he did a spinning 180 degree turn and zipped out of the parking lot with a spray of dirt and the smell of burning rubber.

"Asshole," Robbie muttered, waving a hand in front of his face.

Cyn ignored the obvious rejoinder—that the asshole might have just saved Raphael's life—and said only, "Let's go get Raphael."

AS CYN HAD explained to the others, her plan was two-fold, and the first part was her getting into the house. The daylight guards she'd observed had been less disciplined than what she was used to with Raphael, but they had still appeared to be professionals. Their weapons and the way they carried them spoke of military training, and they'd been alert enough that she doubted she could simply sneak in the back door.

No, as she'd told the others, she intended to be invited. Hence the bikini, and their current location, which was sitting on Mal's boat, a hundred or so yards offshore, two houses down from their target. She'd checked the marine reports this morning, and was now happy to see that they'd been right about the surf conditions. The water was flat and the temperature warm, which would make her swim easier. But the distance would still ensure that she arrived looking wet and bedraggled in her skimpy bikini.

Cyn didn't often think about her looks, they were simply part of who she was. But that didn't mean she wasn't aware of them. She'd been told often enough how beautiful she was, beginning even before she hit high school, when some of her nannies were convinced she should aim for a modeling career. At least, until her grandmother got wind of it and shut down that line of thinking completely. Of course, looking back, her grandmother might have preferred Cyn become a model instead of a cop, but that was water long under the bridge.

She was more than happy to use her looks when she could make them work for her, and this was one of those times. A beautiful, busty, but helpless female, wearing nothing but a bikini, washes up on your beach, and you're a strong, capable male in a profession whose training emphasizes protecting the weak . . . what do you do?

Cyn was hoping they'd wrap their strong arms around her, give her a towel, and invite her inside to get warm. Maybe even offer to perform CPR, although she hoped it wouldn't come to that. She didn't actually want to *be* a beautiful drowning victim, she just wanted to look like one.

"You sure about this?" Robbie asked, as she stripped off the T-shirt, leaving her in nothing but the bikini.

"I'm sure," she told him, trying to sound like she meant it. "Just be sure you get my duffle into the garden before Mal knocks on the door. If I end up fighting someone, I want to have something more than an old key."

"That key still feel secure enough? Because we can—"

"Robbie," she said, holding up her wrist, which was completely wrapped in white duct tape. Beneath the tape was the key, which had been threaded onto a waterproof cord and then wrapped around and around her wrist until she'd begun to worry about circulation in her hand. But between the coils of cord and the layers of tape holding it in place, the key was secure, and that was all that mattered.

She stepped out onto the boat's swim platform. "Raphael and I will be waiting for you guys," she told him. "Don't disappoint us."

"We'll be there."

She gave him a final grin over her shoulder, then dove into the Pacific Ocean and started swimming.

Chapter Seventeen

Night Three—Malibu, California

JURO WATCHED ON the security monitor as Mathilde made the short trip from her trailer to the front gate, accompanied by her last surviving vampire. That vampire wasn't powerful by any definition of the word, and Juro was certain Mathilde would have preferred at least a lone *master* vampire at her back. Unfortunately for her, this was all she had left.

None of that mattered at the moment, however. It was the third night since Mathilde had announced her intent to challenge. She wasn't here this time to demand better accommodations or a live blood donor. She was here to issue a final challenge and declare the territory hers by forfeit, since she knew full well that Raphael wasn't here to respond.

"She's knocking again," Juro said.

"Do we make her wait?" Jared asked from across the room where he'd just finished a conference call with Anthony and Vincent. None of them thought the European vamps would stop with the West. Whether or not Mathilde succeeded in her plot to take Raphael's territory, the two other vampire lords who'd stood with her in Hawaii had disappeared from everyone's radar the same night Mathilde had shown up in Malibu. It was a safe bet that they had designs of their own on one or more of the other territories, but no one knew where, and everyone was trying to be ready for them.

"Does it matter?" Juro asked in response to Jared's question.

"You're always so dour, Juro," Lucas said, sailing into the conference room as if he hadn't a care in the world. "I had hopes that landing a fine woman like Lucia would lighten you up some."

Juro turned and gave him a dark look.

Lucas raised his eyebrows in response. "Guess not," he said lightly, then threw himself into one of the big swivel chairs around the conference table.

Juro knew Lucas was a fine warrior and a good lord for his territory, but the vampire did get on Juro's last nerve. It would seem there was no situation grave enough for the idiot to be serious.

"So what's the Lady Mathilde up to tonight?" Lucas asked, jumping out of the chair he'd just taken. He walked over and stood next to Juro, watching the monitor as the scene around the gate unfolded. "Other than terrible taste in clothes," he said, grimacing. "Someone needs to show that bitch a calendar. The 1400s are so yesterday. Does she always dress that way?"

Juro studied Mathilde's image on screen. He disagreed with Lucas about a lot of things, but not about Mathilde's choice of dress for the night. She was wearing the same sort of finery she'd donned the night she'd double-crossed Raphael. The dress was made of a shiny fabric in royal purple—not a casual color choice, Juro was certain. It had a tight, frilly bodice, poufy sleeves, and a full skirt that would have made a real fight impossible. Her blond hair was wound into an elaborate twist with fat curls dangling over her shoulder, and she was smiling directly into the camera, her expression one of triumph, as if she knew they were watching.

"Does she really think we'll just stand back and let her waltz in here?"

"She's probably expecting a challenge from me or Jared, but she's not worried about us."

"I'm not so sure she shouldn't be," Lucas commented quietly. "Either one of you could probably take her."

Juro closed his eyes briefly at the compliment, and the confidence that it revealed. It was times like this that he understood Raphael's belief in Lucas as a friend and ally. The vamp could be a pain in the ass, but when push came to shove, he was all business, and his loyalty was unswerving.

"But we don't want *her* to know that. She's not supposed to know about *you* either."

Lucas clapped him on the back, making Juro's jaw tighten in irritation. He hated it when Lucas did that, which was probably why he persisted in doing it.

"Don't worry, big guy. I've got this. Let her come up to the house. It'll make her feel like she's won something, make her more receptive when I play my part. She'll see exactly what I want her to see. Our only problem will be keeping her out of my bed."

Juro couldn't stop a look of distaste from crossing his face when he turned to stare at Lucas. "You're mated to Kathryn," he reminded him.

Lucas laughed. "I didn't say I'd *let* her into my bed, Juro. For Christ's sake, she's like my grandmother or something. Disgusting." He shivered. "I just said she'd want to be there."

"Stop tormenting everyone," Kathryn Hunter scolded Lucas, breezing into the room. "And your bed is already filled. Permanently."

"And delighted I am, Katie mine," Lucas crooned, crossing over to give his mate a smacking kiss. "I must point out, however, to those of you who seem unaware of my purpose here, that my goal is to challenge Mathilde's claim, while charming her into believing I represent no real threat."

"I understand well enough," Kathryn said, patting his cheek. "But no touching."

Lucas grinned, seeming delighted at this display of jealousy from his mate.

"I've told the guard to admit her. She's on her way," Jared said, interrupting their lighthearted exchange. "It won't be long now."

"Good," Lucas said, his demeanor going deadly serious in one of the mercurial shifts that were so typical of him. "I'm tired of Mathilde and her demands. It's time for her to play our game now."

THEY MET HER in the downstairs reception room, unwilling to have her sully Raphael's private space upstairs. Jared and Juro were waiting, along with their security details, when Mathilde strolled in like a conquering monarch.

"Jared, Juro," she said, her nostrils pinched as if it hurt her even to breathe the same air as they did. Her gaze lifted to the dozen vampires at their backs, any one of whom could flatten her own lone attendant with a thought. "You others may leave. I will speak to you and your captain later."

Juro laughed, drawing an outraged hiss from Mathilde. "They don't have a captain," he explained. "They have me. I am Raphael's security chief."

"Not for much longer," she snapped. "Where is he anyway? Time has run out, and I grow impatient to claim my new territory."

"Claiming and owning are two different things," Jared reminded her. "Simply saying it doesn't make it so."

Mathilde's power swelled suddenly to fill the room, pressing on Juro's soul in a way he knew Jared would be feeling, too.

"I do not require lessons from you in how to claim and hold a territory, Jared Lincoln. I was a lord long before you were born on that plantation in Georgia. Oh, yes," she continued, "I know all about you, and you, too, Juro. Where's that twin brother of yours anyway? I want to see if you're truly as identical as I've heard."

Neither of them bothered to respond to Mathilde's taunts, and especially not to her question about Ken'ichi. That was an avenue they definitely didn't want to go down with her.

"Why are you here, Mathilde, and why the finery?" Juro asked, raking his glance over her fancy dress.

Mathilde's nose went up in the air, looking down on them even though they each topped her by at least a foot. "I would think that obvious even to you. Having formally challenged Raphael, Lord of the West, in accordance with vampire law and tradition, I hereby—"

"Lady Mathilde," Lucas's voice interrupted her announcement of forfeit.

"*Just under the wire, as usual,*" Juro thought. Lucas could have stepped in much sooner, but had no doubt derived some pleasure from staging a dramatic entrance, thus reaffirming Juro's opinion of him.

Mathilde gasped audibly, spinning on one heel to confront whoever had dared interrupt her moment of glory. When she saw Lucas, her first reaction was shock, followed closely by a distinctly feminine look of appreciation.

Juro pursed his lips reflectively. Perhaps Lucas had been right about Mathilde, after all. Or Raphael had, since it had been his idea to use Lucas as both a backup and a distraction.

"Lucas?" Mathilde said, her youthful face taking on a flirtatious expression. She looked him up and down. "You serve Raphael still?"

Lucas shrugged negligently, prowling closer to scan Mathilde from head to toe. "You're looking lovely, Mathilde. Age becomes you."

"And you," she all but purred. "The last time I saw you, you were still a gangly young man. A very *human* young man."

"Come, let's not play games. You must know that Raphael turned me ages ago."

She tilted her head, smiling. "You're right, of course. I'm not fool enough to challenge Raphael without checking into his friends and allies. But I also know that you have a territory of your own. So why are you here?"

Lucas turned his back on her, crossing the room to fall bonelessly onto one of the elegant couches scattered throughout the room. "My lieutenant does most of the day-to-day work," he said offhandedly. "Tedious stuff. I only jump in when there's something worthwhile."

"And Raphael approves?"

Lucas snorted a laugh. "I'm a vampire lord, Mathilde. I don't require his approval anymore."

"That's not what I heard. I heard the two of you are still thick as thieves . . . or lovers."

Lucas made a *tsk*ing sound. "All these years and you're still jealous of Raphael and me. You never got over that, did you?"

Mathilde stiffened. "I have no idea what—"

"You wanted me. He had me. Simple as that."

"Why are you here, Lucas?" she asked, sniffing delicately.

Lucas came to his feet with a long-suffering sigh. "I hereby challenge your challenge . . . well, that sounds ridiculous, doesn't it? Let's make it simple. I challenge your right to this territory. You want it? You fight me for it."

"You can't fight the challenge for Raphael, only Jared—"

"Please," Lucas said, drawing the word out sarcastically. "What are we, humans, that we bicker over who has what right? We're vampires, and vampires have one rule and one rule only. You keep what you can hold. You want the territory. I want the territory. So we fight for it."

"Why, when you've ruled the Plains for nearly 200 years?"

"I like the weather better here. Besides, you're hardly one to complain about someone else already having a territory. You have one of your own, as I recall."

"You're actually challenging me?"

Lucas winked. "I actually am. Though," he eyed her elegant clothes once more, "I'm willing to wait a night. I'd hate to ruin that pretty dress. Besides, there's a party tonight at my favorite blood house, and you know what they say about California girls."

Mathilde frowned deeply, and Juro thought for a moment she'd refuse. Or at least refuse to give Lucas the additional night, which was the whole point of this little drama.

"Very well," she said finally. "Though I hope you'll think on this in the meantime. I'd rather we be friends than enemies, Lucas," she murmured, leaning close to him. Straightening once more, she turned to Jared and said, "I will, however, be remaining in the house until this is decided. You will arrange suitable accommodations—"

"I will not," Jared said, interrupting her.

She glared at him. "Raphael is in forfeit. By rights—"

"You have no rights in this house, Mathilde. The territory is not yours yet. Lucas has disputed your challenge, and, frankly, I'd rather him than you. Should you prevail, you can arrange whatever accommodations you'd like. Rest assured that neither I nor most of Raphael's people will hang around to see which rooms you select."

Juro waited for Mathilde to explode, to finally use some of the considerable power he could feel storming inside her. But once again, she balked, clearly more worried about the potential fight with Lucas than she was about sleeping in the trailer for one more day.

"You'd better run fast, Jared Lincoln. I won't forget this."

Jared gave a negligent shrug, then gestured to his security team. "Show Lady Mathilde to the gate, please."

"Lucas!" Mathilde demanded, as if expecting him to intervene.

But Lucas only shrugged. "Not my territory yet, babe. Not my rules. I'll see you tomorrow night. Let's be civilized and make it ten o'clock. There may be ladies left to entertain. You understand," he added with a wink.

Mathilde's mouth pursed in disapproval, her satin skirts swishing on the marble floor as she turned to meet the six vampires who approached to escort her back to the gate.

Juro and the others waited until they heard the front door close on her ass, then the slamming of the SUV doors, and the sound of the engine fading away toward the gate, before speaking.

"That was entertaining," Jared said dryly.

"It went as expected anyway," Lucas agreed. "Let's hope I can delay her again tomorrow if necessary. Any word from Cyn?"

Juro sighed. "Ken'ichi called. They're moving tonight."

"When will we know if they're successful?" Lucas asked tightly.

"Hopefully before morning, but with the time difference . . ." He shook his head. "Perhaps not until tomorrow night."

"Cyn can call and leave a message—" Lucas started to say.

But Juro interrupted him. "If they succeed, Cyn will have more important things on her mind. I'll ask Robbie to take care of it."

"He can call Kathryn. Give me his number. I'll text him."

"Right. Let's get back upstairs, then. We have to be ready . . . just in case."

"No *just in case* to worry about, my friend," Lucas said confidently. "Raphael will be here, whether tomorrow or the next night. And he'll wipe the floor with Mathilde."

Night Three—Honolulu, Hawaii

CYN HAD NEVER counted herself a particularly good actress. She was too prickly to pretend she liked someone she didn't, too impatient with stupidity to be . . . well . . . patient. But once she hit the sand behind Mathilde's hijacked beach house, she discovered there was no acting necessary. She really was exhausted. Apparently all that gym work Elke made her do daily hadn't prepared her for a hundred yard plus swim.

She staggered to the beach, then forced herself to keep walking until she hit the sand below the house where Raphael was waiting for her. The sun was already low on the horizon and the mild air felt cold on her rapidly cooling skin. Her legs and arms felt like rubber as she staggered forward. She finally permitted herself to drop to her knees, shivering, hoping someone was watching. This would all be for nothing if she didn't get into the house. This close, she could feel Raphael's sleeping mind reaching for her. It was a shadow of his usual self, feeling more like instinct than a purposeful act. Some part of him knew she was near and wanted her with him.

"I'm coming, baby," she whispered, practically crawling over the sand and up onto the lawn of the manicured yard.

The grass was rough against her skin after so much time in the ocean, each blade like the blunt edge of a knife. She shivered again, shaking so hard that her bones hurt. This was more than a reaction to the air temperature. This was her body reminding her she hadn't eaten enough in days to maintain her own core temperature after that much physical effort. She wasn't going to do Raphael any good if she didn't warm up soon.

That thought drove her back to her feet, had her stumbling in plain sight toward the house.

"Hey!" a man's rough voice startled her, dropping her to her knees once more. She turned toward the sound, shoving wet hair out of her face, and blinking blearily as a pair of guards rushed forward. It was about fucking time.

"Help," she said, her voice shockingly weak to her own ears. "I got caught—" She coughed violently, her chest aching with the effort.

"What the fuck?" The two guards had reached her, one of them standing off a few feet, while the other came to his knees next to her. "Where'd you come from?" he asked, looking away from her to search the beach.

"Swimming," she gasped between coughs, then shuddered as another bout of shivering rattled her bones.

"She's freezing, man," the guard next to her told his buddy. "We need to get her inside."

"We can't do that. Shit."

"Well, we can't leave her here to die, and we can't exactly call a medic."

Cyn gripped his wrist tightly, forcing him to look at her. "Riptide," she mumbled, barely able to feel her own lips.

"That's it." The guy swung his M4 around so that it hung over his back, then lifted her into his arms. He stood with relative ease, which told Cyn she'd been right about these guys. They weren't some fat, out of shape, wannabes for hire. They were fit and professional. And thank God they had a weakness for drowning women in bikinis.

"Don't worry," he told her. "We'll warm you right up and get you back to your hotel."

"Waikiki," Cyn whispered, padding the scenario.

"Told you," the guy said to his buddy. "We'll dry her off and give her a ride. No harm, no foul."

Ten minutes later, Cyn was sitting in the kitchen part of the house's family room, wrapped in several big towels with a cup of coffee in front of her. Her rescuer had shoveled sugar into the dark brew, while telling her she needed the energy. She couldn't argue with that. Another of the guards had offered her a pair of warm socks and now, nearly every inch of her was covered somehow. They were being so nice, she felt almost guilty. Guilty enough that she hoped none of them would die in the ensuing fire-fight. From what she'd overheard of their conversations and one-sided radio comms, it didn't sound as if they even knew what they were guarding. They seemed only to know it had something to do with vampires, but not that anyone was being held prisoner. It was just something the vamps were working on in the back of the house, where they were forbidden to go. From where she was sitting, she could tell they'd been bunking in the den half of the open-plan family room, and cooking their meals in the kitchen. A set of pocket doors, that logic told her would lead to the bedrooms on the other side of the house, were closed tightly, and none of the guys went near them. Even the towels they'd wrapped her in had come from a big closet next to the guest bathroom.

She was surprised to learn that they were guarding the house around the clock. A muttered conversation among her rescuers, mostly worried about getting her out of the house before their nightly visitors arrived, confirmed that a fresh vamp contingent showed up every night just after sunset. They disappeared into the back bedrooms, the previous vampires emerged and left without a word, and that was it. No greetings of any kind, no information exchanged.

Mathilde was apparently so confident of her scheme's success, so certain there would be no rescue attempt that she didn't bother with a vampire security force. Of course, that could be because she didn't have any more vampires to spare for the effort, that all of their strength had to be concentrated on simply containing Raphael. Or maybe she was counting on her spies at the airport to alert the local vamps if anyone threatening showed up.

One thing seemed clear. Mathilde had never even considered the possibility that Raphael's rescuers were already on the island, that they'd been here when he was taken, and they'd been waiting to rescue him ever since.

"You feeling better, miss?" her original Good Samaritan asked.

Cyn nodded, holding the coffee mug in both hands to keep it from shaking as she took another fortifying sip.

"What's your name?" he asked.

"Adela," she said, having anticipated the question. It was her grand-mother's name. The old woman was tough as nails.

He touched the tape binding her wrist. "What's this, Adela?"

She pulled it back under the towel, refusing to meet his eyes, as if embarrassed. "I hurt my wrist," she told him, intentionally sounding defensive, hoping he'd think she'd tried to hurt herself. "I wanted to go swimming, so my roommate wrapped the bandage like that. Duct tape," she said, making a weak joke. "It can do anything."

He studied her face, as if trying to decide whether to pursue the question of her so-called injury, but then he gave her a resigned look, and said, "Where're you staying, Adela? Soon as you're—" He broke off as the burp of a police siren pierced the quiet neighborhood.

His buddy suddenly appeared in the doorway between the family room and the front hallway. "You call the cops?"

"Fuck, no."

The buddy stared at Cyn suspiciously.

"Jesus, man, look at her. She didn't call anyone."

"All right, you stay here. Keep her quiet."

Her rescuer sat back down next to her, and Cyn gave him a worried look. "Cops?" she asked.

"Don't worry," he reassured her. "We'll handle it."

Cyn heard loud men's voices at the front door and shot another look at her rescuer. She stood, letting the towel drop away. "I should leave," she said, shooting nervous glances between the door and the back exit. "I don't want the cops involved."

"Hey, it's no problem. My buddy will—"

A single shot sounded from the front of the house.

"What the fuck? Stay here!" The guard ran for the front of the house, swinging his M4 around to the ready position as he went.

Cyn waited until he'd disappeared down the hallway, then rushed through the glass doors and into the growing shadows near the Japanese garden. Retrieving the duffle Robbie had left there for her, she took only enough time to reach into a side pocket and grab her Glock, then hefted the duffle over her shoulder and slipped back inside the house, going directly to the closed double doors that led to the back bedrooms. If the guard came back, he'd hopefully assume she'd gotten nervous and taken off. Although, if things went according to plan, he wouldn't be coming back for her.

It was dark in the back of the house, musty with disuse, and chilly, as if it had been closed up for a while. She paused for a moment, letting her eyes adjust, before moving swiftly to the first open door and ducking inside. It was a small bathroom—a shower, toilet, and tiny window with the shade drawn. Dropping her duffle to the floor, she crouched down and pulled out a silencer, fitting it to her Glock without looking as she listened to the profound silence in this part of the house. Setting the now-silenced Glock on the floor, she dug out the T-shirt she'd worn earlier, before beginning her long swim, and pulled it over her head. She didn't bother with anything more. Clothes weren't exactly a priority right now. She didn't know anything about the vampires currently guarding Raphael, didn't know how strong they were or how soon after sunset they would wake. But she knew sunset was too damn close and she needed to get to Raphael first.

She slipped on her comm set and double clicked.

"Busy here, Cyn," Robbie muttered.

"I'm in. Try not to kill those guys. They're just doing a job."

"I'll do my best. Good luck," Robbie said, and then he was gone, and Cyn was on her own.

Which was how she liked it. She removed the comm set, turned it off, and stuffed it into the duffle. She didn't want anyone overhearing what transpired between her and Raphael.

Shoving the duffle into a corner, and grateful for the warm socks still covering her feet, she started down the long, lightless hallway, using the LED flashlight secured beneath the barrel of her Glock. There were several more doors, all closed. She stopped, and opened each one, clearing it as a matter of routine, even though every cell in her body was drawing her toward the double doors at the end. The master bedroom. That was where they'd put Raphael. A mocking tribute to his power? Or simply a convenient place to shove him, the room farthest from the front door, the biggest room for him and his vampire keepers.

Cyn opened a door. A bedroom—double bed, side tables, low dresser. No one there. She backed out and kept going. She could hear fighting from the front of the house, men's deep voices yelling back and forth, then a double shot of gunfire. Her gut tightened. She didn't want anyone to get hurt, but especially not Robbie or Mal.

She couldn't worry about that, however. Her job was here. With Raphael.

She stopped before the double doors, listening for a trap. She would have sworn she could hear Raphael's heart beating, but it was probably just her own. Using the LED flashlight, she examined every inch of the doorframe. Finding nothing, at least nothing she could detect, she put her hand to the knob and turned.

She sucked in a breath when she pushed the door open. If the air in the hallway had been musty, in here it was rank. Old blood, sweat, and the stench of unwashed bodies. Her heart squeezed in pain, and she again raged silently that they'd dared to treat Raphael so.

She searched the room, her eyes going to the huge bed against the far wall and the motionless figure lying there. Raphael. It was too dark to actually see his face, but her heart told her what her eyes couldn't see.

She wanted to rush over to him, but forced herself to move cautiously. She considered flipping on the overhead light. None of the vamps would know the difference. But she didn't know the status of the battle outside this room and didn't want to advertise her presence just in case.

Moving the flash's narrow beam around the room, she counted four enemy vampires. Three were on the floor between her and the bed. They'd pulled cushions off the sofa and chair to lie on, and were actually tucked into sleeping bags. It was a slumber party. How sweet.

The fourth vampire was on the bed with Raphael, a female lying on the side of the bed closest to the outside wall, which had a sliding glass door behind the covering of floor to ceiling drapes. That door would lead to the back yard and the beach beyond.

Cyn lowered the flash, letting her eyes adapt to the low light provided by several LEDs from a satellite box and computer, and the blue glow of an alarm clock. And as her eyes adjusted, she studied the enemy vampires on the floor and bed. Vampires have an unwritten rule, a gentlemen's agreement, against sending in human assassins to kill each other during the daylight hours. Some vampire, so long ago that no one remembered when, had realized that if they permitted themselves to slaughter each other during daylight, the vampire race wouldn't last long. After all, once you gave a human permission to kill vampires in your name, what was to stop him from killing in his own name instead?

Cyn was very aware of this rule. It was one that Raphael would never break. Not even Jabril or Klemens—two of the most ruthless vampires she knew of—had ever crossed that line.

But she wasn't a vampire. And she had four enemies standing between her and her mate. Four vampires she had to eliminate before she could give back to him what they'd taken away . . . the literal blood in his veins.

What was it that Ken'ichi had said? That they didn't need to kill all one hundred of the vampires keeping the lid on Raphael's power. They only needed to take out one or two. And Gardet had told Ken'ichi that the vamps guarding Raphael on-site were the focus for all the others.

The key on her wrist had the power to release Raphael's body from the manacles draining his strength. And she now had the power to release his mind. All she had to do was take out four vampires while they slept, and Raphael would wake, truly free for the first time since he'd been taken.

"Fuck you," she said to the sleeping vampires. "You shouldn't have messed with my honey."

She walked over to the first vamp sleeping on the floor, yanked back the unzipped sleeping bag and put three Hydra-Shok rounds directly into his heart. Before he was even dusted, she'd moved to the next vamp. He was sleeping on top of the bag, facedown. No problem. The back worked just as well for a heart shot as the front. Maybe even better. She put her Glock one inch from his back, just slightly to the left of his spine, and fired three quick rounds, the bullets blowing through his heart and pretty much everything else on their way out the other side. He dusted almost completely before she'd even straightened and moved on, which told her that he'd been an older vamp. Too bad he hadn't learned to choose his friends, or enemies, better.

The third vamp had eschewed any kind of cushions, simply stretching out on the floor, his sleeping bag zipped completely over his head. As if maybe he was afraid the sun would burst through the windows and he'd be exposed, intentionally or otherwise. Unfortunately for him, the sun wasn't his enemy tonight, and her Glock didn't care if the sun was in the sky or not. She tugged the bag's heavy zipper down and gave him the same treatment as the others. Three rounds in the heart, and he was a pile of dust in a rapidly cooling bag.

Cyn rounded the bed, staring at the female vamp asleep on the bed with Raphael. This one deserved something special. Cyn would have liked to wait for this one's eyes to open, so the vamp could see her death waiting. But Cyn's love for Raphael was far stronger than her hatred. So she settled for yanking the sleeping female off the bed, taking pleasure in the sound of her head whacking the hardwood floor seconds before Cyn fired the rounds that destroyed her heart and ended her long life in a pile of dust.

Cyn lifted her head in the sudden silence, the zip of the silenced rounds still replaying in her mind as she turned to stare at Raphael, feeling frozen in place. After all the fear-filled nights and days, she was here. A sob escaped her throat, and she put the back of her hand over her mouth, the Glock still clutched in her fingers.

It was so quiet. The fighting had died down in the rest of the house. A part of her brain registered that Robbie and Mal must have prevailed because no one was pounding down the hallway to wrench her away from Raphael. Her jaw clenched. She'd kill anyone who came through that door. No one was taking him away from her again.

The thought spurred her into action. Laying her Glock on the side table, she climbed onto the big bed and crawled over to Raphael, shocked at what she saw. He was so thin, so still. The sharp edges of his usually gorgeous cheekbones cast gaunt shadows on his pale face, the bone straining white against skin stretched too tightly. His sensuous lips were dry and thin, as if he was completely dehydrated, and his beautiful, big hands were all bones and knuckles as they lay crossed on his chest.

She stroked her fingers over his beloved face, brushing dirty hair off his forehead. Raphael would be so pissed. He loved his showers, especially with her in them, and he hated to be dirty. He'd said it reminded of the years he'd spent on his father's farm before he'd been made vampire. The sight of him like this had tears burning the back of her throat, but she swallowed them down. He didn't need her tears. He needed her toughness. He needed the Cyn that the rest of the world saw every day.

Sitting back on her heels, she scrabbled at the tape on her wrist, finding the tiny strip of doubled-over tape that they'd left when wrapping it, so that she could get the tape off without needing a sharp edge. Digging her nails into the strip for a better hold, she started ripping, round after round over her wrist. Salt water was unforgiving. So they'd used a lot of tape.

Cyn finally got down to the waterproof cord and yanked on the curl tucked against her wrist, unraveling the cord until finally she held the key. The Amber Key, according to Nick. The key to magical manacles that looked just like ancient, but ordinary, handcuffs now that she was close enough to see them. Crossing her fingers, hoping that Nick wasn't completely insane, she reached for Raphael's crossed wrists, recoiling at the cold touch of a metal that burned her fingers.

"Shit!" she yanked her hand away instinctively. "Fucking magic," she muttered. Apparently, Nick knew what he was talking about. He had some explaining to do when this was all over with.

Scooting closer to Raphael again, she stretched her hand out and touched the key to the band around his right wrist. She wasn't sure what to expect as the manacles fell away, but when the seconds ticked past, and nothing more happened, she nearly despaired. Why hadn't she gotten more details from Nick when she'd had the chance?

She squeezed her fingers so tightly around the damn key that the bits of amber still clinging to the metal cut into her fingers. Feeling the tiny cuts, she threaded the cord absently around her neck, wondering what more she could do when suddenly Raphael . . . breathed.

He breathed like a man who hadn't filled his lungs with air in a long time, his chest expanding in a long, deep inhalation which he blew out only to suck in another. Cyn scrambled closer, until she could touch her lips to his.

"Raphael?" she whispered, her fingers cupping his cheek as she gently kissed his face all over, tasting her tears on his skin, the tears she could no longer hold back.

From her duffle, all the way down the quiet hallway where she'd left it, came the only sound that she'd left activated on today's burner phone . . . the triple ping of an alarm. Sunset.

Raphael's eyes opened, a dull gleam of silver in the dark room, their light a fraction of what it should be.

"Raphael?" she managed to whisper again.

And then his fangs tore through his gums, and he was on her. His gaunt hands were painfully strong as they gripped her arms and threw her to the bed, rolling his heavy body on top of hers in a single, blazingly fast move.

There was no finesse in his bite, no sensuous plumping of her vein, no nips or kisses. He fisted one hand in her hair, the other on her shoulder, then stretched her neck taut, and sank his fangs into her vein.

It hurt. Cyn wanted to scream as her skin was sliced open, her vein pierced. But Robbie was probably inside the house by now, and she knew if he heard her scream that he'd come running. And Raphael would kill him. So she turned her head even further and sank her teeth into Raphael's wrist.

Raphael groaned as his blood filled her mouth, a primitive sound that shuddered through her body as his fangs went even deeper, holding her in place like an animal claiming its kill. Or its mate.

Without warning, the natural euphoric in his bite flooded her system, rocketing her from pain to ecstasy in the space of a breath. She cried out as the orgasm seized her body, her back bowing beneath Raphael's weight, the blood in her veins heating as sensual pleasure rolled over her in great lapping waves of desire.

Raphael reached between them to rip away the thin band of fabric making up the bottom half of her bikini. Cyn heard the rasp of his zipper. He gripped her thigh and shoved it wide a moment before she felt the hard press of his erection, and then he was fucking her, his fangs still buried in her vein, his cock slamming in and out with no feeling, no seduction, no care for her at all. He was Vampire. He wanted blood and sex, and she was available.

Cyn's heart was pumping wildly, a combination of lust and terror, driving blood through her body, swelling her veins as Raphael continued to drink, seeming to suck harder with every passing moment. She could feel every draw that he took of her blood, could feel her body growing weaker as the euphoric in his saliva faded, leaving her with more pain than ecstasy. She cried out, but Raphael only growled possessively, his fingers digging into her shoulder with one hand, the other tearing at the roots of her hair.

She told herself this was Raphael, that he would never hurt her. But this wasn't *her* Raphael. This was the beast inside, the part of him that was driven to survive at all costs, to do whatever it took, even if that meant draining dry the woman he loved.

Cyn lifted a limp hand, dropping it weakly over the back of his neck, cupping him there, stroking him gently, reminding him of who she was. Who *they* were. And she held to her belief that he would never hurt her, repeating it like a prayer, until the blackness stole her thoughts, and there was nothing.

"CYN." RAPHAEL'S deep voice was saying her name. She smiled. She loved his voice, loved the sound of her name on his tongue.

"Lubimaya," he whispered, his lips against her ear, his breath a warm wash over her skin. "Drink," he urged, and she felt the hot taste of his blood on her tongue. She nearly turned away. She'd bitten him earlier, and he'd all but attacked her. And there had been pain. So much pain. But the blood filled her mouth, forcing her to swallow or choke, so she swallowed and nearly groaned as every nerve in her body seemed to come to life in a single instant, surging with heat, trembling with desire. She licked her lips and found Raphael's mouth so close to hers that she licked his lips as well.

"Raphael," she whispered, almost afraid to say anything, terrified that this was just another dream and if she spoke, it would all shatter.

"My Cyn," he murmured, kissing her softly. "Forgive me."

She rolled her head in denial. "For what?"

"I could have killed you," he said, his dark voice edging on despair.

"I knew you'd stop in time," she insisted, choosing to forget her own fears, to tell him what he needed to hear. "You'd never hurt me."

"Gods, I missed you," he muttered, pressing her against the bed, settling his hips between her thighs, rocking slowly as his lips trailed over her jaw.

This was her Raphael, her lover, her mate.

Cyn bent one leg, wrapping it around his back, the scrape of his suit against her tender skin reminding her that she was sore and swollen, her sex bare and dripping with his earlier release. But she ignored all of that. He needed to know that she loved him, that she forgave whatever he'd done when he'd first awakened.

That there was nothing to forgive.

Raphael growled and ground himself into her swollen pussy, before suddenly rearing back to fist both hands in the thin fabric of her T-shirt and rip it down the middle, baring her breasts in the tiny bikini top. His eyes lit with desire as he snapped the thin strap holding her top in place. The fabric fell away from her naked breasts, and Raphael hissed in pleasure. He closed his mouth over the tip of one breast, sucking until her nipple was nothing but a plump center of carnal pleasure, his fangs teasing the delicate flesh of her breast until they closed over the swollen tip. Raphael hummed greedily as he lapped up her blood, but Cyn could only cry out, pressing a hand against her mouth to silence herself as a stab of erotic pain shot from the tip of her breast directly to her sex. Heat gushed between her thighs, her clit a throb of desire as it pulsed in time with her heart.

"Baby, baby," she said softly, tears rolling down her cheeks. "I missed you so much."

Raphael's response was to dip his fingers between her thighs to stroke the swollen folds of her pussy, sliding in the cream of her arousal.

"Wet," he snarled, then pushed two fingers deep into her body, teasing her with slow strokes in and out, while his thumb circled her clit, grazing it enough to make her cry out with need, to have her thrusting against his hand to demand more.

Raphael lifted his head from her breast, blowing softly against the wet flesh, leaving her bereft, until he switched his attention to her other breast, scraping his fangs over the aching nipple, biting down just enough to draw more blood, to torment Cyn with another shock of euphoric that changed pain to soaring desire.

Cyn scraped her fingers down the back of his head and over his back, digging beneath the suit jacket he still wore, yanking his shirt up until she had skin, then digging her nails in until she was drawing some blood of her own.

Raphael hissed, then reached between them to fist his cock and shove it deep into her pussy. They groaned in unison as her heat surrounded him, her inner muscles feathering over his cock, caressing him as her sheath stretched to accommodate his size, as her body welcomed him.

"Fuck, you feel good," he whispered, going suddenly still, his hard length buried as far inside her as he could go.

Cyn felt the flex of his cock and tightened her inner muscles, squeezing and releasing.

Raphael swore and began moving almost frantically, shoving his cock balls-deep, then pulling out and slamming into her over and over.

Cyn wrapped both legs around his back, holding him as close as she could, her arms over his shoulders, her face buried in his neck, wanting to give him whatever he needed to believe he was still Raphael, the most powerful vampire in North America, the Lord of the West, her lover, her mate, her beloved.

That nothing had changed. That he was free.

Raphael collapsed on top of Cyn, his heart pounding so hard that she could hear it, could feel it thundering between their bodies. His tongue came out to lick lazily at the few drops of blood on her neck, his breath hot against her sweat-soaked skin. He hadn't relaxed his hold on her—one hand cupped her ass, holding her hips against him, while the other was still threaded through her hair. Although his fingertips now stroked gently over her scalp, her roots no longer in danger.

Cyn wished they were somewhere else, somewhere safe, where they could lie together for as long as they wanted. Making desultory love, kissing and tasting, and fucking, too. Until they fell asleep in each other's arms.

Alas, that was not to be. Raphael was back, but his enemies still lived.

There would be no rest for either of them tonight.

Raphael sighed, as if reading her thoughts.

"I thought I heard fighting earlier," he said, rolling to his back and pulling her up onto his chest. "Who was it?"

"Robbie is with me, and a local cop named Maleko Turner. Ken'ichi and Elke are probably on scene by now, too, or they will be soon. I'm not sure what time it is."

"And the others?"

"Juro is back in Malibu, like you wanted. Mathilde is there, pretending to challenge you, although tonight, she's claimed you've now forfeited by not showing up. But Lucas stepped in and challenged her challenge. He's planning to—"

Raphael covered her mouth with his kiss. "Enough, *lubimaya*. I understand. What of the others, the ones whom Mathilde rallied to contain me?"

"They're a couple of blocks over, waiting to die."

Raphael grinned proudly. "My Cyn. I knew you would fool them all."

"That's me. Though it was pretty easy to scam Mathilde. She never saw us coming."

Raphael grew still, as if listening. Cyn knew what that meant. He was reaching out and touching his children, the vampires he'd created. Somewhere in Malibu, Juro and the others would be rejoicing at this proof of his freedom, and reestablishing the ties to their Sire, ties that had been strained by his captivity, but never broken.

"Ken'ichi and Elke are waiting outside," he told her.

She nodded, not surprised. "Ken'ichi said Mathilde's house-o'-vamps were yours to destroy, that we couldn't—"

He gave her the lazy look of an apex predator. "Ken'ichi is right."

"Won't they be gone already? I mean, if I were them, I'd have run for the hills as soon as——"

"You assume I would permit such a thing." He moved quickly, sitting up and then standing, taking her with him until they both stood next to the bed. Raphael reached down, straightening his clothes, tucking his cock back into his suit pants, then zipping up and buckling his belt.

Cyn examined her own torn clothing. The T-shirt was a total loss, but she managed to tie back together the various pieces of her bikini.

"Do you have any other clothes?" Raphael asked, eyeing her mostly naked body unhappily.

"In the SUV that Robbie's driving."

Raphael shrugged out of his jacket, holding it for her as she slid her arms into the sleeves, then pulling the lapels closed over her chest. It was way too big on her, but it was warm, the silk lining was soft, and it was Raphael's. So she rolled up the sleeves, then grabbed her Glock off the nightstand and unscrewed the silencer, dropping it into a jacket pocket.

She turned for the door, but Raphael grabbed her hand, threading his fingers through hers as he pulled her close.

"Not yet, *lubimaya*. We deserve one more moment together. You and I. Come."

"I already did," she muttered. "Three times at least."

Raphael let out a very masculine, very smug chuckle. "This way," he said, shoving aside the heavy drapes and pulling the sliding glass door open, breaking the lock without even thinking about it.

Oh, yes. Raphael was back.

He held her hand tightly as they walked over the damp grass, heading for the strip of beach. The ocean was a steady rush of sound, the surf a gentle swell of water onto the shore and back again. Raphael just stood there, his hand holding her against his side, his head thrown back as he drank in the moonlight and fresh, salty air. His eyes closed briefly, and he pulled her in for a tight embrace, both arms holding her against his chest.

Cyn wrapped her arms around his waist, more tears rolling down her cheeks, soaking into his shirt. She was just so damn happy to have him back and safe.

"No more time for tears, my Cyn," he said softly. "Our enemies still breathe."

She nodded, rubbing her face against his chest, before pulling away to look up at him.

"Robbie and the others will be ready to move. They're just waiting for the word."

"The word is given, my Cyn. It's time to fight back."

RAPHAEL WOULD have preferred to take the outside route around the house, but Cyn had needed to grab the duffle bag that she'd left in the guest bathroom, and he didn't want her in that house alone. He knew his concern for her safety wasn't quite rational, but he'd endured too much in that place to trust anything about it. If he'd had his druthers, they'd have burned the whole thing to the ground, but while he might be irrational when it came to Cyn's safety, his imprisonment hadn't deprived him of common sense. Burning the house would attract unwanted attention, and Mathilde had already done plenty of that with her homicidal hundred who'd killed humans and left the bodies on the street.

Raphael's goal was quite singular at this point. He wanted to kill every single, fucking vampire who'd had anything to do with Mathilde's scheme. And then he was going to fly back to Malibu and kill the bitch who thought she could steal his territory and his people.

As he and Cyn made their way to the front door, he lingered over the motionless forms of the four human guards who'd provided security for the house. One had been shot in the arm. The wound had been bandaged, but the smell of the fresh blood made his fangs ache as they pressed against his gums. He'd been too long without blood. He'd drunk deeply from Cyn, but the thing that made him vampire, the symbiote in his blood, wanted him to drink even more. It was no more rational than his concern for Cyn's safety in the empty house, but it was instinct. Just as a starving human would hoard food, so his body wanted him to hoard blood.

"They didn't even know you were there," Cyn said, coming up next to him where he stood over the unconscious humans. She slid her hand into his. "I told the guys to go with stun guns if they could."

She made a small noise of pain, and he realized he was squeezing her hand.

"I know you want to kill everyone involved, but these guys are inno-cent, Raphael."

He turned to look down on her, seeing the dark circles under her beautiful green eyes, the exhaustion robbing her face of its usual color. But then she smiled at him, and he saw more. Triumph at having foiled Mathilde's plan, determination to see his enemies destroyed, and shining more brightly than anything else . . . her love for him.

"As you say. I will, however, ensure that they do not remember what happened in this place, and that when they wake, their only thought will be to leave."

Cyn nodded. "Come on. Robbie and the others should be waiting for us."

Raphael ran his gaze over her bare legs, her half-naked body covered only by his wrinkled suit jacket. "You said you have clothes in the vehicle?"

She laughed, and it was as if he hadn't heard that sound in a hundred years. He snaked an arm around her waist and yanked her against his chest, taking her mouth and drinking the laughter from her lips. She responded as she always did, her arms around his neck, her lips opening eagerly beneath his as their tongues tangled in a sensuous embrace, until she pulled back just enough to whisper against his lips, "I love you."

"I missed you, my Cyn. Toward the end, I couldn't find you even in my dreams."

"I was there. I was always there, looking for you."

"When I woke tonight, and you were next to me . . . I thought I was dreaming still."

She grinned. "There are dreams, and then there are *dreams*. And you, fang boy, are definitely my dream."

Raphael gave her a crooked smile. "Fang boy. I missed even that. But come, the night won't last forever."

After a quick mental scan to be certain there were no surprises waiting for them outside the house, Raphael pulled open the front door. Holding Cyn's hand, he stepped outside, relieved to be once again in the fresh air, to feel the moon's pale light on his face.

"Lord Raphael." The pleasure in Rob's voice was genuine, as was the relief.

"Rob," Raphael said. "My thanks."

"An honor, my lord. Ken'ichi checked in a few minutes ago. They're holding steady, but the natives are getting restless. He's afraid they'll muster a breakout soon."

Raphael turned his head to the right, aiming a dark look in the direction of a house he'd never seen. A house that was filled with vampires who some might claim were only soldiers doing what they'd been ordered. But soldiers died in war all the time. And Mathilde had definitely declared war.

He reached out with his mind, flexing his power, touching every mind in that house, whispering a desire to stay, to wait. Adding a subtle threat to haunt their enforced sleep while they waited.

"They won't leave. Not now. They're waiting for me."

Rob eyed him carefully, his gaze switching to Cyn and back again. Rob knew what Raphael was capable of, or at least what he'd *been* capable of before his recent capture. But he probably also knew from Cyn some of what had been done to Raphael during his imprisonment. Right now, he was clearly wondering if *Lord Raphael* was truly back.

"Have faith, Rob," Raphael said quietly. "I am myself."

Rob grinned then. "Irina will be glad to hear it, sir."

"But first, we have to take out the trash," Cyn reminded them.

"What about the guys we left in the house here, Leighton?" a man's voice asked.

Raphael stepped in front of Cyn as a big human male, someone he'd never met, came around the SUV. He'd been aware of the human's presence while he spoke to Rob. This must be Maleko Turner, the human policeman Cyn had told him of. The one who was fucking Elke. Cyn hadn't mentioned *that*, but Raphael could scent Elke on the man, and knew she'd taken the human's blood.

"Raphael, this is Maleko Turner," Cyn said, confirming what he already knew. "I told you about him."

"You did. My thanks to you as well, Mr. Turner."

"My pleasure. The most interesting case I've had in a while."

"And then there's Elke," Raphael said, giving him a flat look.

The human flushed hotly, but stood tall and defiant, saying, "And there's my Elke."

Raphael raised a brow at the "my." He couldn't help but wonder how Elke felt about that. Time to find out. "Let's go," he said, tugging Cyn forward. "You can change on the way."

She rolled her eyes at him. "Back less than an hour and already giving orders."

"You'd rather go into a fight wearing . . . that?"

"I look good in this."

"You look beautiful, as always. But perhaps not combat-ready."

"Yeah, yeah. Let's get the fuck out of here. I never want to see this house again."

THE DRIVE TO the other house was a short one. Cyn had just enough time to pull a tank top and jeans over what was left of her bikini, along with a fresh pair of socks and combat-style lace-up boots. In fact, the drive was so short that she was still lacing the second boot when Rob pulled to a stop at the curb.

The house wasn't much compared to the one they'd just left. Obviously, Mathilde had been far more concerned about her own comfort than that of her team. This house was a typical tract dwelling, a two-story cookie cutter construction that was just like the one next to it, and the one next to that, all the way down the block. Some of the residents had taken more care with their postage stamp-sized front yards, some had landscaped around the porch and walk, but there was no question that they still belonged to the same housing tract.

Rob pulled up behind Ken'ichi's SUV, with Maleko Turner parking behind him in his police-issue sedan. Turner was out of the car in a flash, speaking briefly to Ken'ichi before heading at a fast clip around to the back where Raphael knew Elke kept watch. Maybe he really did have feelings for Elke.

"My lord." Ken'ichi's dark eyes, usually as calm and expressionless as his brother's, gleamed with the yellow gold of his power, reflecting the intensity of his feelings upon seeing Raphael again.

Raphael strode up to him and placed a hand on his broad shoulder. Ken'ichi lowered his head, covering the naked emotion in his eyes. Raphael didn't say anything, only rested his hand there for a moment, then squeezed gently and lifted it away.

"Status?" he asked then, permitting both of them to retreat to the familiar formality of their relationship.

"No movement in the last several minutes, my lord. A small group tried to leave soon after we arrived. We fought. They lost."

Raphael nodded, then lifted his gaze as Elke came around the house to greet him. Turner wasn't with her. He was a cop. Maybe he was covering her post for her.

"My lord," she said, her pale face wreathed in a happiness she had no reservations about showing.

"Elke," he said affectionately. "You've acquired a fan."

"The cop," she agreed. "Cyn said I could kill him if he got in the way."

Raphael glanced at his mate. "A practical solution. Shall we deal with these the same way?" he asked, lifting his chin at the house in front of him, which was crammed full of vampires. Mathilde hadn't even pretended to care for her vampires' comfort. It was a wonder that so many remained loyal to her.

"We waited for you, my lord," Ken'ichi said.

Raphael nodded as he studied the house, sliding his touch over every vampire inside, trying to decide what to do. He could leave them in their current state while he killed them. The stronger among them might know what was happening and feel some pain, but the others—the workhorses of Mathilde's undertaking who'd been useful only as sources of raw power—they would feel nothing. Their existence would simply end.

That was the logical choice to make, the cleanest solution. But his gut didn't like that option. Nor did his heart, or his soul, whatever you'd call that thing that made him a fucking vampire lord instead of one of those pathetic creatures in there. That part of him wanted revenge. Hot, screaming, horrific revenge. He wanted every single one of them to know what was happening and why. He wanted them to know who was ending their existence, to know that they'd fucking *lost* and he'd won.

A small smile creased his face.

"Uh oh," Cyn muttered. "Looks like a hot time in the town tonight."

Raphael's smile grew. "Elke, resume your post. No one is to leave. Kill them if they try."

"My lord," Elke acknowledged and raced away.

"Ken'ichi."

"My lord."

"Watch the front."

Ken'ichi's mouth compressed into a flat line of satisfaction, his eyes gleaming. "Yes, my lord," he said crisply.

"My Cyn—"

"I'm not going to call you 'my lord' so forget it."

Raphael tugged her closer. "We'll discuss what you call me later. For now, you need to know what's going to happen."

She got a worried look on her face. "Raphael, you're—"

"I am a vampire lord," he reminded her.

She sighed noisily. "Yeah, yeah. So what's the plan?"

"I am going to kill every vampire in that house. But I'm going to wake them up first. It will be noisy, but brief."

Cyn shrugged. "Hey, no argument from me. I wanted to blow up the whole fucking house along with everyone in it, but Mal wouldn't let me."

"That's my Cyn," he said proudly, then straightened with a glance at Ken'ichi. *We begin*, he sent to his vampires.

CYN WATCHED AS Raphael sank into his power. She'd seen him do this before. She didn't know exactly how it worked, but she guessed it was something like a meditative state that let him discard everything that didn't matter and focus only on his target, or in this case, his targets.

His eyes had no sooner closed than the house, which had been so quiet before that it had seemed empty, suddenly erupted with sound. Vampires woke from the sleep Raphael had imposed on them and cried out, mostly in fear, but some in anger. Shades moved, faces appearing as vamps peeked out at the street. A few screams pierced the night as some of those inside saw who was waiting for them. A few brave souls, probably some of the stronger masters, surged through the front door with a burst of vampire speed. Though whether they'd intended to escape or attack, Cyn would never know, because they didn't make it five feet before Raphael's casual glance burst their hearts and littered the walkway with dust. From inside the house, just beyond the open door, came cries of dismay at the death of their fellows, and a few vampires crawled out onto the small porch, begging for mercy.

But Raphael had no mercy to give. These, too, crumbled one after another, leaving a line of vampire dust from the porch, over the threshold, and into the house. Cyn was reminded of the game Candy Crush, when two color bombs met each other and rays of light shot out destroying the entire board. Raphael was like that, except that his power killed invisibly, and it wasn't candies that were being destroyed.

Raphael's eyes were burning spots of molten silver in the icy perfection of his face, his power a nimbus of energy that surrounded him as he strode into the house. Cyn was right behind him, her Glock held in both hands, but she found precious few targets for her vamp-killer rounds, despite the sheer number of vampires crowded into the house. Raphael left no one for her to kill. He marched through the ground floor, every room crowded with vampires who cringed away from him, stepping on each other as they pled for their lives. But if Raphael heard their pleas, Cyn saw no evidence of it. His power shot out, destroying with every step, until no one was left.

He paused briefly then, his head turning from side to side, as if he could see through the walls, which, in a manner of speaking, he could. He caught Cyn's eye, and lifted his chin toward the stairs. When she nodded, he glided upward, taking the stairs three at a time with no apparent effort. Cyn scowled at his back as she followed, wishing some of that vampire strength came along with the other benefits of drinking Raphael's blood.

He waited at the top for her, and then began clearing the second floor with the same efficiency as he'd done below. Every door was opened, every room emptied of life. Raphael was still dealing with the master bedroom, which had been so crowded with vampires that Cyn thought they must have been packed in like sardines when they slept. What kind of power did Mathilde have to treat her vampires like crap and still reap such loyalty? Or maybe the question was; what had she promised them if her plan succeeded?

Her mind preoccupied with such thoughts, Cyn approached the final room, which was behind a simple door at the end of the hallway. She reached for the knob, found it locked, and kicked open the flimsy door. The room was a very small bedroom. So small that she thought it might have started out as a storage closet. A single twin-sized bed was pushed against the wall and a tiny square table held a lamp. With a quick glance over her shoulder, where she could see Raphael still having fun in the master bedroom, she took a cautious step forward, immediately putting her back against the wall as she surveyed the seemingly empty area. But why would this room be empty, when all of the others had been crammed so full of vampires? Was this one reserved for someone special? Maybe one of the masters who'd made a run for it early on?

Keeping her back against the wall, she shuffled around until she had a view behind the door. There was a closet there, with a narrow set of mirrored sliding doors. And the doors were closed.

Crouching down for a quick look under the bed to make sure it was empty—she didn't want any monster-under-the-bed surprises—she pushed the room door nearly shut and kicked the closet door with one booted foot.

"Come out if you're in there. Or I'll just shoot through the fucking door."

The sliding door rattled as someone reached for it, and she took several steps backward, bringing her Glock up in a two-handed stance, ready to shoot. Whoever this was in the closet, he was a vamp, and that meant he would be fast.

The door slid open to reveal a single, male vampire crouched inside. Seeing no one but Cyn waiting for him, simple human female that she was, his eyes flashed red with power and his mouth opened to make room for the fangs that suddenly punched through his gums. A low, threatening growl sounded in his chest as he rose up onto his haunches, preparing to launch himself at her . . . and Cyn grinned.

"Oh, please," she told him gleefully. "Give me a reason. Raphael's been having all the fun tonight."

The vamp's eyes narrowed, and he sank back down, studying her curiously.

"Who are you?" she asked.

"I'm nobody," the vampire said, shrinking himself down further, retracting his fangs and gazing up at her through long eyelashes, trying to make himself seem harmless. "A servant brought along to care for the others."

Cyn didn't know who this guy was, but she knew he wasn't the harmless worker bee he wanted her to believe. She played along with his game, however, hoping to learn something.

"So, tell me, Nobody," she said, catching the angry glint in his stare when she called him that. It might be *his* game, but he didn't like it. "What exactly did you do here? You know anything about dead bodies?"

"That was handled," he said sharply, before catching himself. "The ones in charge weren't happy when that happened," he corrected, trying for submissive and failing miserably. "The vampires responsible were—"

His voice faltered as Raphael pushed open the door and walked in to stand next to Cyn.

"This is Nobody," Cyn told him. "He's a servant here."

Raphael stared down at the cringing vamp. A slow, terrifying smile creased his face, his fangs gleaming wetly with blood.

"Godard," Raphael crooned. "I so hoped I'd find you here."

"Lord Raphael, I was—"

"Oh, so it's Lord Raphael now, is it? That's not what you called me the other night."

"I was only doing my job, my lord. Mathilde didn't give me a—"

"The *others* were doing their jobs, Godard. You enjoyed yours, just as you always have. You weren't satisfied with merely sending your daylight minions in to slice my throat, you had to get your digs in, too. And I mean that literally, since you had to dig deep to find a vein that wasn't already ruined."

Cyn listened to Raphael's recitation of what they'd done to him, and it took all of her willpower not to step up and blow the bastard Godard's head off. But more than any of the others, this kill was Raphael's. It meant something to him.

Without warning, Godard screamed, clutching his right arm with his left and rocking back against the wall of the closet.

"My lord, please," he begged, blood tears rolling down his face.

Cyn glanced at Raphael, saw his lip curl in a half smile, and knew he was responsible for whatever had caused the scream. He was capable of incredible cruelty, but then, hadn't she done her best to be equally cruel just two days ago? She'd been forced to use bullets instead of her mind, but she'd have done whatever it took, caused whatever pain she could, to get what she needed to save him.

"Begging, Godard?" Raphael mocked. "Isn't that what you demanded from me? Perhaps if I'd seen you do it first," he gestured negligently at the suffering vampire, "I'd have known how."

Godard's eyes lit up with rage, replacing the fear and pain. "You won't be so high and mighty once my mistress gets hold of you."

"Yes," Raphael said, dragging the word out. "Where *is* your mistress? Here you all are, dying like rats, and where is Mathilde?"

Godard managed a smug look, but remained silent.

Raphael laughed. "I know where she is, you fool. Do you think my people, my mate, have sat by idly while your silly mistress plotted to destroy me? Mathilde will learn the same lesson the rest of you have today. The only difference? Your death will seem like a gift, compared to what she will suffer."

And then Raphael was apparently finished talking. But he wasn't finished with Godard. Cyn heard bones snapping in succession, like dice rattling in a cup, as Godard screamed. By the time Raphael was finished, the vamp could only lie limply on the floor, lacking the intact bones to hold himself upright. He whimpered pitifully, his eyes rolling in Raphael's direction as blood poured from his mouth. Apparently, Raphael had damaged more than bones.

"Death," Godard gurgled, adding something that sounded vaguely like, "I beg you."

Raphael flicked a careless hand and a red gash opened in the vamp's throat, so that he couldn't even gurgle anymore.

Raphael looked at Cyn, ignoring the dying vampire. "Are you finished here, my Cyn?"

"Anytime you are, fang boy."

He smiled at the nickname, but then sobered. "We have a situation in the next room."

Cyn nodded, but kept her eye on Godard. When it came to enemy vampires, the only vamp she trusted was a dead one. If that bastard made any move—

Godard shrieked. Cyn smelled burning flesh and glanced down to see the shirt over his heart begin to smolder. Ick. Raphael was burning the creep's heart inside his chest, and he would soon be just another pile of dust. Raphael didn't wait to see it happen, but Cyn did. She resisted Raphael's pull on her hand until she saw Godard crumble into dust, then followed Raphael out into the hallway and down to the master bedroom, going straight to the walk-in closet.

Cyn followed curiously, her head swiveling from side to side, still waiting for a vampire or two to pop out of the woodwork. There had been so many of them in the house. It was hard to believe that even Raphael had managed to kill them all.

Her attention shot back to Raphael when he dropped to a crouch and pulled aside a fuzzy blue blanket to reveal yet another vampire, although this one wasn't looking too lively. In fact, he resembled a corpse more than a living person.

"Rhys Patterson," Raphael said, explaining why this vampire of all the others was still breathing. More or less.

"Is he—"

"Alive, but barely. He's been starved."

"He's alive? How come he looks so . . ." She didn't know how to finish without being insensitive about it.

"He doesn't have enough power to feed the symbiote. Without blood, his body has started to feed on itself."

"Can he come back?" Cyn asked, thinking about Donovan Willis and what Rhys's death would mean to him.

"With enough blood," Raphael said, looking up as Ken'ichi walked into the closet carrying several bags.

The big vampire knelt next to Rhys on the other side, while Raphael stood and pulled Cyn out of the closet. "We'll permit him what dignity we can. Ken'ichi will help him feed."

Cyn eyed him curiously. "Patterson helped Mathilde, didn't he?"

"Rhys didn't stand a chance against Mathilde. Once she got her hooks into him, he'd have been helpless to defy her, especially once she threatened his people. He did try to warn me at the very end, which is probably why she left him to die like this."

"We can't take him to Malibu with us," she said thoughtfully. "I'll call Willis. He'll come."

"Willis?"

"The geek with the glasses who showed up that first night with the shirt twins. He wanted to upgrade our security, remember?"

"Do you trust him?"

"He and Patterson are lovers, so yeah. He won't give a fuck about Mathilde, or you for that matter, as long as he gets Patterson back."

"We'll take Rhys with us for now, then. Call your Robbie. Have him tell the others. We'll be out in three minutes."

Cyn nodded, then clicked on her comm mike, and gave Robbie the word as she watched Ken'ichi carry Rhys out of the room, heading for the stairs.

"I hope the owners got a big deposit when they rented this house," she commented dryly, looking around as they followed.

"What makes you think they rented it?" Raphael asked.

Cyn *tsk*ed at him loudly in feigned shock. "You mean they were squatting?"

He shook his head. "Come, my Cyn. It's been a long night, and a longer few days. I need to sleep, and I need to make a call."

Cyn took his hand and they strolled down the hallway as if they weren't leaving behind a houseful of dead vampires. "Our place isn't far," she told him. "And it's a lot less dusty."

CYN HAD THE door open before Robbie brought the SUV to a full stop inside the garage. Ken'ichi pulled in right next to them, in the second garage bay. He had Patterson in his back seat. Elke and Mal parked in the driveway, getting out and ducking under the garage door just before it closed.

Raphael hadn't said anything, but Cyn could tell he was exhausted. He hadn't had any rest before taking on all those vampires, and no blood but what he'd taken from her earlier. Even with the recuperative powers of a vampire lord, he'd asked a lot from himself.

She slid out of the SUV and waited in the open door until Raphael joined her. She tucked herself against his side, and his arm dropped over her shoulders. It was a natural move. Raphael was always touching her. But in this case, it was a way for her to support him into the house and up the stairs without his weakness being obvious.

"You guys go ahead and pack everything up," she told Robbie as she turned Raphael toward the stairs. "We'll make some phone calls, and I'll let you know what the plan is."

Robbie searched her face, then nodded. "Mal and I are going to get some food."

"Good idea."

"Should I bring you some?"

She shook her head. "I'll get something later. I need to figure out the plane situation first."

"What plane situation?" Raphael asked, pulling her attention back to him.

"We'll talk. But time is short for getting hold of your people in Malibu. We need to make that phone call."

Cyn steered Raphael into the huge master suite that she'd been oc-cupying all by herself in anticipation of his arrival. Now that he was there, however, it didn't seem so big. Raphael dominated every room he entered, simply by being there. Even as tired as he was, coming off days of torture with no rest or food, he still brought so much energy into the room that the air seemed to vibrate.

Cyn closed the double doors, giving them privacy. "Phone or shower?" she asked, sitting on the bed and unlacing her boots. "Sunrise is about half an hour away in Malibu, if you'd rather take a quick shower first."

Raphael dropped his suit jacket on the floor, the same jacket she'd been wearing over her bikini before she'd changed in the vehicle. "Phone," he decided, toeing off his shoes and socks, and stretching out on the bed. "Come here, my Cyn."

She set the day's burner phone on the nightstand, then tugged off her boots, and crawled across the bed. He pulled her against his side and wrapped both arms around her.

They lay there silently for a moment, just *being*.

"I knew you would come," he said quietly. "Even when I could no longer touch your dreams, I knew you would never give up."

Cyn hugged his waist, looping one leg over his thigh. "Never," she said.

A few more minutes passed before Raphael said, "What are the arrangements for our return?"

"I wanted to avoid using your private aircraft. It would be too obvious. So I commandeered the bigger one of my dad's jets, which, strictly speaking, is a *corporate* jet. And since I'm a major shareholder and a board member to boot, I pulled some strings, which I rarely do. Anyway, I called the pilots this morning and told them to be ready for take-off as early as tonight. That plane has a private sleep chamber, and the main cabin has black-out shades which make *it* vampire safe, too. I had it retrofitted last year, just in case."

"Your father agreed to this?"

"No, but Grandmother did, and we outvoted him," she said smugly. "Anyway, I know you hate to fly in daylight, but . . ."

"But it is necessary sometimes. Very well. Alert your pilots. We'll leave as soon as we can be ready. Sunrise isn't far off."

Cyn made the necessary phone call, which took all of five minutes since she'd already warned the pilots it might happen.

"Done," she told him, sitting cross-legged in the curve of his arm.

"I have to call Jared and Juro."

"And Lucas."

His chest shook in a silent laugh. "And Lucas," he agreed. "Juro gave you phones?"

She handed him the burner. "Yep. This is today's."

Raphael took the phone, and she could feel him gathering his strength for the call. She knew him. He wanted to talk to his people. But he also needed to project strength and power, to be in control.

He held the phone up, and Cyn started to tell him how to reach Juro. But he didn't need her help. He pulled up the directory and called the only number stored there.

Malibu, California

JURO STARED OUT the window at the moon-washed ocean, wishing he could see what was happening on the other side. He had only moments before he would have to join Lucia downstairs. Normally, he'd have left already, but he'd lingered, hoping to hear something. The rescue was supposed to go off tonight, but Cyn hadn't called yet. That didn't mean anything, of course. Her plan had started while the sun was still up, but there was no telling how long the full operation would take. No telling what kind of condition Raphael would be in when she found him, or how much blood he would need. And then there were the hundred or so vamps who'd been lined up against him. Cyn and the others would be hard-pressed to take out that many master vampires if Raphael wasn't able to help them.

But why assume the worst? Hawaii was two hours behind Malibu. Even if the rescue had been a complete success, there might not be enough time for anyone to call before the sun rose on this side of the ocean. In which case, Cyn would call Lucia with an update so that at least they would know upon first waking what had happened.

He and the others had felt something hopeful a while back. A sudden burst of energy flooding every cell of his body, chasing away the chill of foreboding that had followed him for days. Ever since Raphael had been taken.

He believed, they *all* believed, it meant Raphael had been released from whatever magic Mathilde had used against him. That Cyn's plan had succeeded.

But he would feel better if he could know for sure. If he could hear his Sire's voice telling him they were on their way home.

He turned away from the window, thinking to check the gate guard deployments before joining Lucia downstairs, when a phone rang. He was confused for a moment, because it wasn't the house line, which they'd been using to communicate with the gate, nor was it the landline, which was so rarely used these days.

He frowned, then belatedly recognized the ringtone as that night's burner phone, and that meant. . . . He leapt for the phone, afraid Cyn would assume it was too late and hang up.

"Cyn!" Juro said, answering the phone.

"Juro," Raphael said.

Juro closed his eyes, all but collapsing into a chair at the rush of relief he felt at the simple sound of that voice. "Sire," he breathed. "She did it."

"She did."

"*We* did," Juro heard Cyn clarify from off speaker.

"Time is short," Raphael said. "What is your situation?"

"Lucas challenged Mathilde last night. They will meet at ten o'clock tonight. We've isolated her completely. She has one very frightened vampire guard, and a couple of humans."

"Does she see Lucas as a threat?"

"Not at all, my lord. Lucas played the fool, which he does so well. And she seems not to have done her homework where he's concerned. Either that, or she credits you with being the power behind all of his accomplishments."

"Lucas got my message, then."

"From Cyn, yes. When are you returning, my lord?"

"If Lucas is to meet Mathilde tonight, I need to be there."

"Sire." That's all Juro said. He knew how much Raphael hated flying in daylight, but sometimes there was no other way. Like in this instance.

"We'll arrive before sunset. Cyn has arranged transportation through her family corporation so as to mask our arrival."

"And you should go to my house. Lucas will be there."

"We will see you tonight, then."

"Tonight, Sire."

Juro disconnected the call and tossed the burner phone to the table, then immediately picked up his regular cell and called Jared.

"Anything?" Jared answered.

Juro didn't even try to conceal the joy in his voice. "Our Sire will be home tonight."

Honolulu, Hawaii

RAPHAEL THREW the burner phone aside, then stood and started undressing. Actually, Cyn thought, it would be more accurate to say that he began tearing off his clothes, since he was literally ripping the seams of his suit as he removed it, and dumping the remains into a pile on the floor.

"Undress," he told her. "You're taking a shower with me."

Cyn smiled. Seeing Raphael standing in their bedroom, as temporary as it was, watching him strip down to skin and then hold out an imperious hand as he demanded she join him . . . she felt fifty pounds lighter. He was back. Her grin was so big, it hurt her face.

Until she saw what they'd done to him. He was still beautiful, his chest still layered with muscle, his shoulders broad and thick. But his hips, always narrow, were too thin, his bones too prominent. And his eyes, as they glared at her impatiently, were tired in a way she'd never seen before.

And in less than twenty-four hours, he had to face Mathilde . . . and kill her.

Cyn yanked off the rest of her clothes, then took his hand and let him pull her into the bathroom. The shower here wasn't as nice as the one they had at home, but it was bigger than average. Plenty big enough for what she had planned. Raphael needed blood, and he needed sex. The first was nutrition for his body, to give his vampire symbiote some fuel to work with, to continue healing the damage to his body. The other was for his heart and soul. He was a powerful vampire who'd been brought low. He needed the love of his mate to remind him that he was still Raphael, the formidable Lord of the West, and always would be.

The glass enclosure filled with steam as Cyn found clean towels and piled them on the sink. Raphael didn't wait. He stepped under the pounding water and stood there, heedless of the open door and the water splashing all over the floor. His eyes were closed, his head bowed as the water poured down his broad back.

Cyn closed the door as she joined him, wrapping her arms around him from behind and simply holding on, reassuring herself that he really was here in her arms, that this wasn't a dream.

As steam fogged the glass once more, she reached around him for the shampoo and slowly washed his hair, massaging his scalp and neck, feeling him relax beneath her touch. Switching to shower gel, she kissed his back and said, "I didn't bring a scrubby with me, so you'll have to make do with a wash cloth."

Raphael didn't say anything, so she soaped up the cloth and started scrubbing. Just as she'd done in Malibu, when she'd needed to wash away the taint of his cruelty, so she washed him now, ridding him of the stench of captivity. Scrubbing every inch of his skin, starting with his back and neck, then moving over his butt and down to each leg. Then, turning him to face her, she washed his chest, his arms, even his groin, ignoring, for now, his obvious arousal at her touch.

When she was finished, when he was clean again, she closed the distance between them until her firm nipples were scraping against his chest. Lifting her mouth to his neck, she bit him lightly as her fingers closed over his rigid cock.

Raphael's eyes flashed open, his gaze completely black as he stared down at her.

"I love you," she whispered. Pushing up onto her toes, she trailed her mouth over his jaw to his lips. "Kiss me."

Raphael's arm closed around her waist, yanking her against his body as his mouth slammed down onto hers with a growl. His fangs shot from his gums, cutting her lip, so that their kiss was gilded with the warmth of her blood. They kissed like lovers who'd been apart for months, whose hearts had stopped beating while they'd been apart. Cyn wrapped her arms around his back and over his shoulders, pressing herself against him until there was no space between them. She'd been so desperately afraid of failing him, of losing him forever. She didn't think she'd ever be able to let go of him again.

She deepened their kiss, licking along his swollen gums, spilling more blood into his mouth when his fangs nicked her tongue. Her teeth closed over his lower lip, mingling his blood with hers as she moved her kisses to his face, then his neck, and finally down to his chest and lower to his flat belly, as she dropped to her knees in front of him. Looking up, she saw him leaning over her, eyes closed, one powerful arm braced on the tile over her head, as the other reached down to fist his erection.

Cyn bit his hand as he started to stroke himself, and his eyes flashed open again. "Mine," she told him, then wrapped her own slender fingers around the base of his cock and pumped slowly, closing her lips over the head and taking him into her mouth until he touched the back of her throat.

Raphael's fingers threaded through her wet hair, gripping it tightly, holding her in place as his hips flexed and he began thrusting. Cyn lifted her eyes to see him watching his cock glide in and out of her mouth, his gaze intent, focused, silver stars glittering in the black of his eyes.

Cyn opened her throat, taking him deeper as his fingers tightened into a fist and he thrust harder, the head of his cock ramming down her throat with every stroke. Faster and faster he pumped, until with a groan, he shoved as far as he could go and stayed there, his release shooting down her throat as she swallowed over and over until he was done.

His grip on her hair loosened, and she pulled back, twirling her tongue around his still-hard cock, licking up one side and the other, teasing the head, until with a hiss, Raphael grabbed her under her arms and yanked her to her feet, pressing her against the tile wall with the weight of his body.

"You are temptation itself. Sinful," he murmured. "My Cyn."

She stroked her tongue over his throat and up to his mouth, biting his lip and drawing blood.

Raphael chuckled deeply and gripped her thigh, raising it higher and opening her sex to his growing erection.

God bless vampire stamina, she thought privately, then scraped her nails over his shoulders, leaving raw lines of flesh.

"Be good," Raphael growled, cupping her ass in one big hand as he toyed with her, letting his cock slide in and out of her wetness without penetration.

"Good is overrated," she teased, flexing her hips forward, pushing against his length.

He laughed out loud at that. Then bracing her against the tile, he reached down, positioned his cock at her entrance, and pushed slowly and steadily, burying himself in her heat with a single, glorious thrust. When he was deep inside her body, his balls pressed against her delicate flesh, her inner muscles trembling around him as her heart pounded out the rhythm, they both paused. Cyn found her eyes filling with tears as she met his silvered gaze.

"Don't," he whispered, kissing her eyes closed, licking away the salty tears. "We are where we belong."

She nodded, gulping back a sob. "I need you."

"You have me. Always."

And then he began moving, powerfully, sensuously, his thick shaft pumping in and out as her hips lifted to meet every thrust, as she twisted her head, baring her neck in taut invitation. Raphael groaned hungrily, his mouth latching onto her as his tongue plumped her vein. Cyn's heart, already galloping in her chest, went into double time as she cupped the back of his head, her pussy fluttering around his thickness, her swollen clit rubbing against his pubic bone every time he fucked her.

She was panting, eager for his bite, feeling the first shivers of climax shudder from her clit to her inner muscles, zinging up to tighten her nipples until they were hard pebbles of sensation, scraping in exquisite pain against the planes of his chest.

"Raphael," she gasped as his fangs sank into her neck, piercing her vein. From one instant to the next, her body was on fire, every nerve screaming, every muscle contracting. The very blood in her veins felt so hot that she thought she would explode as her pussy spasmed around him, squeezing his cock so hard that he could barely move. He forced himself against its tight grip, grunting as he stroked over inner tissues, every tiny movement feeling like a live wire on her bare skin.

It was too much. Cyn threw her head back and she would have screamed, but Raphael's fingers slipped between her teeth, forcing her to bite down, to swallow her own scream as the orgasm rolled over her like a tidal wave, drowning her in sensation, cutting off her breath, stopping her heart, until there was nothing but Raphael, nothing but his cock between her thighs, his fangs in her vein, his blood in her throat. And then his hot release was rushing deep inside her as he joined his climax with hers, his hips bucking, thrusting over and over until he was spent.

Raphael lifted his head enough to lick her wounds closed, then rested his forehead against her shoulder, both of them breathing heavily, clinging to each other as if they would collapse without the support.

They stood that way for several minutes, until the water began to cool. Cyn shivered, and Raphael immediately turned to protect her from the spray.

"Can you stand?" he asked.

She laughed breathily. "I think so. I have to. The water's getting cold."

Raphael slid her down his body until her feet touched the cooling tile floor of the shower. He pushed open the door and braced her as she stepped outside and grabbed a towel. Turning off the water, he followed, accepting the big towel she offered, then wrapping it around her, trapping her in the circle of his arms.

She gave him a smacking kiss, then asked, "How long 'til sunrise?"

"Two hours, a little more."

"We've got to pack up and get to the airport," she said softly.

He met her gaze steadily. "You'll sleep with me on the plane."

"Every minute. And Robbie and Mal will guard us through the day when we reach Santa Monica."

"Mal is coming with us?"

"Apparently, he's not ready to let go of Elke just yet. Actually, I think he might be looking to relocate."

"Do you trust him?"

"I know you don't want to hear this, but he comes with a recommendation from Colin Murphy."

Raphael made a face. "You're right. I *don't* want to hear that, but it does carry some weight."

Cyn gave a crooked grin. "Come on, fang boy, let's get you some clean clothes. We've got a flight to catch."

HALF AN HOUR later, their few things were packed, and Donovan Willis had just departed with a somewhat recovered Rhys Patterson in tow. Cyn and the others were double-checking the house for anything that screamed "vampire," when Raphael suddenly flew down the stairs, and yanked open the front door.

Fearing the worst, Cyn spun around from her place at the kitchen island where she'd been going over details with Robbie and Mal. Drawing her Glock as she ran, she raced after Raphael, with Robbie at her heels, and Mal following with a muttered, "What now?"

Cyn hit the porch just in time to see Nick standing on the front walk. Raphael was confronting him, his arm outstretched to one side to stop her from rushing past him.

"Wha—" she started to say, but Raphael beat her to it.

"What do you want, sorcerer?" Raphael demanded, his voice booming with power.

"Hey, Cyn baby," Nick crooned, ignoring Raphael.

"Stop that, Nick," Cyn said, holstering her weapon and placing her hand on Raphael's arm.

"Don't speak to her," Raphael growled. "What the fuck are you doing here?"

"Wait," Cyn insisted.

"You owe me, vampire," Nick said smugly.

"You mistake me for Mathilde. I don't deal with sorcerers," Raphael sneered.

"*Wait!*" Cyn shouted. "Both of you just shut up! Raphael," she said quietly. "Nick is the one who gave me the key to the manacles Mathilde used on you. If not for him, I wouldn't even have known they were there until I got to you. Mathilde did something to Juro so he forgot."

Raphael turned his head just enough to listen to what she was saying, keeping his eyes on Nick with an unfriendly glare.

"Like I said, vampire. You owe me," Nick said.

"Jesus, Nick," Cyn said impatiently. "Stop being an asshole. And a sorcerer? What the fuck is that? And how do you know him?" she demanded of Raphael.

"I told you I wasn't a salesman—" Nick started to say, but Raphael overrode him.

"I don't know him, I know *of* him. He can't be trusted. None of them can."

"Cyn, will you please educate your boyfriend—"

"*Stop!*" she shouted again. "The two of you are acting like little boys in a schoolyard. Nick, why are you here?"

He gave her a sullen look, as if she was spoiling his fun, but then admitted, "I want my key."

Cyn dug in her jeans pocket. She hadn't known what to do with the damn thing. She only knew she didn't want anyone else getting hold of it, so she'd kept it close.

"Here," she said, handing the key to Nick.

"No kiss—"

"Don't push your luck," Raphael growled.

"Nick, stop it!"

"Fine. You were more fun before you met Mr. Dark and Broody here. What about the manacles?"

Cyn froze. "Um."

"Please tell me you have them."

"Well," she temporized. "Things got a little crazy, what with the guards and all. I may have, um, left them at that house. In the master bedroom. Where Raphael was." She selected her words carefully, not wanting to mention Raphael having been held prisoner, even though they all knew that's what had been done. But she wouldn't embarrass Raphael in front of Nick like that.

Nick rolled his eyes. "Yeah, I know vampires, sweetheart. I have a pretty good idea of what, or shall I say who, went a little crazy."

Raphael's snarl was so loud this time that even Nick stepped back a pace.

"Look, I'm really sorry, Nick," Cyn said quickly. "It was stupid of me. But the vampires who were working with Mathilde are all dead, and the human guards were vamped by Raphael to forget everything and go home. So the manacles are probably still there on the bedroom floor. I'd go back and get them for you, but—"

"No, no," Nick said, waving away her offer. "I know you're in a hurry. Gotta go home and kill Mathilde. Believe me, I'm one hundred per-cent behind that. So, tell you what. I'll go check out the house. If the manacles are there, it's all good. If not? Then when this is all over, you're going to help me recover them."

Cyn ran her hand down Raphael's arm, lacing her fingers with his. "Raphael?" she asked.

His fingers gripped hers, but he didn't look at her. He was too busy staring daggers at Nick, his jaw so tight that she was amazed she couldn't hear his teeth grinding.

"If it comes to that, the two of us will help you. Not Cyn alone," Raphael snapped.

"Won't be as much fun with you there, but okay," Nick said cheer-fully, but his eyes gave him away. He hated Raphael just as much as Raphael obviously hated him. "You take care, Cyn. And if you need me—"

"She won't need you," Raphael said in a hard voice.

"Not to state the obvious, but—"

"Nick," Cyn said, finally getting angry. Raphael had been through enough hell, he didn't need Nick playing games. "Thank you for what you did. Really. Now stop. Being. An asshole."

Nick's expression softened. "Okay, sweetheart. I'll call and let you know if I find the manacles. And if not, then we'll hunt together. The three of us. Won't that be grand?"

He didn't wait for an answer. Instead, he just gave her a wink, then turned and strolled back to his vehicle, which was the same black Porsche Panamera that he'd driven the previous day.

Raphael didn't move until the car disappeared down the hill, until not even the red glow of the taillights was visible.

"How do you know Nick?" she asked him quietly.

He didn't say anything at first, and she thought he wasn't going to, but then he stirred to pull her closer, sliding an arm over her shoulders.

"Nicodemus Katsaros is not who you think he is."

"Obviously. But who, or what, is he?"

"He is from another time, when magic was wild and available to any who could wield it. He is ancient and deadly, my Cyn. And not to be trusted."

"But I've known Nick—"

"You knew only what he wanted you to know. Who do you think created devices like those manacles he wants so badly?"

"Nick made those?"

"No, not him, not specifically. But one like him, a sorcerer."

Cyn stared in the direction Nick had taken, both shaken and amazed that she could have been so wrong about someone she knew so well. Or at least thought she did.

"Come," Raphael said, kissing the top of her head. "The devious bastard's right about one thing. We have much to do and little time to do it in. We'll deal with him when we have to, but that is not tonight. Tonight is for Mathilde. And maybe she'll even tell us how she acquired those infernal manacles before I kill her."

Chapter Eighteen

Night Four, Santa Monica, California

"I USUALLY HATE sleeping on planes," Raphael growled. "But maybe that's because you were never here next to me." He kissed the outer edge of her ear, then lowered his mouth to her neck where he suckled softly.

Cyn smiled. There were far worse things in life than waking to the sound of her vampire's voice, even if it meant sleeping on this too-small bed.

"The mattress is crap," she murmured, tilting her head to give him better access to her neck.

Raphael laughed, wrapping both arms around her, pulling her back to his chest. "That can be your next upgrade to your father's jet."

"I don't want to talk about my father," she murmured. Which was an understatement, since she rarely ever wanted to talk about her dad, but especially not when she was waking up naked next to her lover whom she'd so nearly lost.

As if to punctuate her statement, she wiggled her butt against his growing erection.

Raphael made a rumbling noise deep in his chest and yanked her hard against his body as he reached around to cup her breast in one big hand. Squeezing her nipple between thumb and forefinger, he rolled it tightly, until it was red and flushed with blood.

"So pretty, my Cyn. So ripe."

Cyn placed her hand over his, encouraging him to squeeze harder, but Raphael had other plans. Sliding his hand down over her belly, he pressed his fingers between her legs to toy with her clit. She moaned eagerly, lifting one knee to give him better access, but again, Raphael had his own plans. Smacking her ass hard enough to sting, he pushed her knee down, then went back to tormenting her swollen clit, bringing her to the very edge of climax, before letting his fingers wander off, sliding them in the cream of her arousal, dipping a fingertip into her pussy, then stroking back to her clit to start all over.

Cyn was shivering with need. Her muscles were clenched, her nerves singing beneath her skin. She strained against the hold of Raphael's powerful arms, tormented by the hard length of his cock against her ass, by his fingers between her thighs. Reaching back, she tried to grab his cock, to torture him as he was doing to her, but he slapped her hand away and only pressed more tightly against her.

"Raphael," she whispered.

"I love you like this," he said, his lips moving against the skin of her neck. "Your pussy hot and slick, your nipples like ripe cherries waiting to be eaten, your body writhing in my arms, begging to be fucked. Are you begging to be fucked, my Cyn?"

She clamped her lips into a tight line, refusing to give him the satisfaction. He wanted her just as much as she wanted him. His cock had to be aching, eager for the embrace of her pussy. She could hold out—

His fangs sank without warning into her vein, jolting her system with a shot of euphoric, shooting her from arousal to orgasm in the space of a single breath. She sucked in just enough oxygen to cry out as she shuddered in his arms, his fangs still buried, still draining her blood down his throat, giving him life, giving him the power he would need to defeat Mathilde.

Raphael's fingers dipped briefly into her sex, then stroked over the exquisitely sensitized nub of nerves that was her clit, leaving a wet trail of arousal across her belly and over her hip as he switched to delve between her legs from behind. Sliding his fingers in and out of her, he stretched her wider, first one finger, then two and three, until finally, he positioned the swollen head of his cock at her slick entrance and, with a quick flex of his hips, slammed forward until his hips slapped against her ass.

Cyn loved when he fucked her like this, loved how much deeper he could go, how completely he could fill her. She would have pushed against him, but his hand was on her belly again, holding her still as he fucked her from behind, his thick cock rubbing against the inner muscles of her sheath, strumming the sensitive flesh, feeling so damn good that she could only moan helplessly.

Raphael's fangs slid out of her vein, and she felt a warm trail of her blood slide down her neck to pool above her clavicle. His tongue sealed the wounds, continuing along the same bloody trail, licking up her blood.

"Do you like it when I fuck you?" he whispered.

Cyn shivered, still trembling from her orgasm. His was such a simple question, but there was something in the way he said it, something dark and demanding.

"You know I do," she whispered back. "I love you."

He continued to fuck her, his cock gliding in her slick, wet juices, his fingers still buried in the slick folds of her pussy as he toyed with her clit.

"Come for me, then," he demanded. "Now." His voice seemed to stroke every nerve in her body, gliding over her clit like a velvet glove, strumming her inner flesh as his hips suddenly began pumping harder. There was no slow build-up of sensation, no quivering anticipation. Her climax hit like a lightning bolt, the pleasure starting in her clit then storming up over her belly, muscles contracting as her breasts swelled and her nipples begged to be touched. Cyn shuddered helplessly, crushing her own breasts with her fingers, pinching her nipples, desperate to relieve some of the sweet pressure as the orgasm roared through her system.

Raphael held her tightly, his fingers flat against her belly, his cock heating her core as he moved faster, as her pussy clamped down on his shaft, caressing, rippling along his length until finally, with a groan of release, he joined her in tumbling over the edge.

They lay in the dark, breathing heavily, Raphael's cock sliding halfway out of her slick channel, his fingers soft now against her stomach. He kissed her shoulder, her neck, then pulled all the way out and rolled her over, tucking her beneath him.

"Whom do you belong to, *lubimaya?*" His words were spoken on a breath, barely there, but suddenly Cyn knew what he was really asking. This was all about Nick. Raphael knew they'd been lovers. Of course he did. He knew she'd had lovers before him, just as he'd had them before her. And it normally wouldn't have bothered him.

But these were not normal times. And Nick, apparently, was not a normal man. He'd shown up when Raphael was at his most vulnerable, when he'd just survived what had to be one of the lowest points of his life, human or vampire.

"Whom do you belong to?" he repeated, silver sparks flashing warningly in his black eyes.

Cyn met his gaze evenly and said, "I belong to no one, fang boy. But I am yours, and you are the one, the only one that I have ever loved. Always."

He kissed her then, soft and tender, and full of love. It was everything they'd shared, everything they'd survived in the past, everything they would survive in the future. Together.

Out in the main passenger compartment, they heard voices, the thumps and mutters of the rest of their party waking for the night.

"We should shower at Juro's. There will be more room," he said, with more than a dash of humor.

"Not to mention hot water," she said dryly.

His cell phone buzzed noisily, vibrating over the side table in a vicious dance.

"That will be Lucas," he said. "I need to speak to him, but I'd rather do it in person."

"We should get moving then," Cyn said. "There should be a couple of SUVs waiting for us."

Despite their words, neither of them moved immediately, both reluctant to permit the rest of the world to enter into the comforting dark of their private cocoon.

Raphael sighed. Cyn joined him. "On three?" she asked.

He laughed, then gave her a smacking kiss and leapt from the bed, taking her with him.

"Three."

Malibu, California

JURO'S HOUSE WAS about a hundred yards, a football field, down the beach from Raphael's estate. There was no reason for Mathilde to suspect that Raphael was back in town, and all signs indicated that she didn't even know he'd escaped. They'd counted on that, on the distance from Malibu to Honolulu, to keep her from sensing the death of her vampires, and of her grand plan. The death of so many of her own children would probably have hit Mathilde hard, no matter the distance, but not all of the master vamps who'd been working to hold Raphael were her children. According to Raphael, some of them had belonged to Hubert or Berkhard, the two other lords who'd helped Mathilde take Raphael down on that first night. While the others had owed allegiance to lords who'd remained in Europe, but who'd supported the cause by sending their master vamps to help Mathilde in Hawaii.

Cyn hadn't planned it that way, but the fact that she'd killed the four vamps who were with Raphael while they slept had probably delayed awareness on anyone's part that there was a problem. And by the time the hundred plus had become aware, they were totally focused on containing Raphael, still struggling to control him as they'd been ordered. So no one got a warning off, no one sent an alarm. It all happened too fast, and to too many of them at once.

Now that they were back in L.A., Raphael was shielding himself like crazy. At even half his usual strength, Raphael was powerful enough that his presence would register on the vampire radar of someone like Mathilde. She might be a bitch, but she was undeniably powerful.

But despite all of that, Cyn couldn't help a nervous look or three as their two SUVs cruised down Pacific Coast Highway and made the turn into Juro's place. They were close enough to Raphael's estate that she could see the Eucalyptus Grove that marked the entrance. If they'd driven past, she might even have been able to catch a glimpse of the trailer where

Mathilde had been living for the past several nights. According to reports, Raphael's gardeners were going to have their work cut out for them, repairing all the damage done to accommodate those stupid trailers. Not to mention the intentional damage they'd inflicted on the road. It had been worth it, though, to humiliate Mathilde and keep her out of the estate proper.

Juro's house was right on the sand. It was three stories high, and had big floor-to-ceiling windows all along the ocean side. It backed up to a narrow road that ran along the beachfront, and, like most of his neighbors, it was surrounded by a wall to give him privacy and keep tourists from using his yard as a walkway to the water.

Someone must have been watching for their arrival, because the gate was already rolling smoothly open by the time their lead SUV reached the house. Within minutes, both vehicles were inside the wall and the gate was closed behind them.

Ken'ichi had let Elke drive, so as soon as the SUV rolled to a stop, he was out and scoping out the yard, which was soon filled with vampires. They stood in neat rows, lined up, their eyes riveted to the SUV where Raphael sat next to Cyn. With a final look around, Ken'ichi gave someone a nod and opened the passenger door.

The first thing Cyn noticed when Raphael stepped into the courtyard was an almost electrical hum in the air. It sizzled over her skin and she realized it was power, vampire power. These were Raphael's vampires, many of them his own children, welcoming their lord and master back home. Most of those gathered here were guards and warriors, which meant they'd been on the front line, defending against Mathilde. For them, Raphael's return was momentous. Raphael's rule was based largely on his overwhelming power, but nearly as important was the love and respect his vampires had for him. He ruled fairly and protected what was his. And they protected him in return.

Cyn shouldn't have been surprised by the turnout to welcome their master home, or by their reaction to his return. It was just . . .

"Won't Mathilde notice so many of the guards being gone?" she whispered to Raphael.

He shook his head. "Her movements are tightly controlled, her access to the estate limited. It's doubtful she is actively aware of more than ten of my guards at a time. And my people need this."

She took his hand, squeezing tightly as they made their way toward the house. They'd just stepped up onto the low porch when the front door opened to reveal . . .

"Oh, of course. Why am I not surprised?" Cyn said, shaking her head.

Raphael grinned. "Because nothing should surprise you about Lucas." He stepped across the threshold and directly into Lucas's welcoming hug.

"Is all that hugging normal?" Cyn heard Mal mutter from somewhere behind her.

"That's Lucas, babe," Elke responded. "There ain't nothing normal about that boy."

Cyn glanced over as the two of them came even with her inside the house's broad entry hall. "Raphael and Lucas have a special bond," she told Mal. "And Lucas is a hugger."

She looked back in time to see Raphael murmur something to Lucas that had the two of them laughing, and then Lucas released Raphael so he could greet the others, including Jared who stared at Raphael with unabashed tears in his eyes, before lowering his head in a modified bow. Raphael clapped him on the shoulder, whispered something in his ear, then turned to Juro.

"Welcome home, Sire," he said, his usually cool voice shaking with emotion.

"Thank you for making sure I had a home to come to," Raphael replied, placing a hand on Juro's broad shoulder. "Thank you both."

Cyn missed whatever they said next, because her view was blocked by the sight of Lucas coming toward her with open arms.

"I told you he was a hugger," she muttered, then found herself crushed against Lucas's broad chest.

"Cyn darling," he said cheerfully, then whispered against her ear, "Thank you for bringing him back to us."

Cyn pulled away just enough to look into his unusual golden eyes. "I did it as much for me, as you. Probably more," she said honestly.

But Lucas only grinned. "I know. But thanks anyway."

"Won't Mathilde be missing all of you? You especially?" she asked him.

"Ah, our meet's not for a while. I figured I'd let her enjoy her last few hours on earth."

"Why?" Cyn asked cynically.

Lucas laughed. "That's one of the things I love most about you, Cyn. You're unforgiving in victory."

Cyn shrugged. She didn't know any other way to win, especially when it came to vampires. "What'd Raphael say that made you laugh before?"

"I'm not sure I should tell you."

"Okay. I'll ask *him*."

Lucas *ts*ked. "You're no fun. He said that the next time he lets his arrogance get in the way of common sense, I have his permission to kick his ass. As if that's going to happen."

"You mean you kicking his ass?"

"You wound me. But, no, I meant him making the same mistake twice. More than anyone I've ever known, Raphael learns from his mistakes. This won't happen again."

"No, it sure as hell won't. My heart couldn't take it," she added soberly.

Lucas shifted to stand next to her, and wrapped a tight arm around her shoulders. "You and me, both."

Raphael glanced over at that moment. He smiled to see them standing together, then held out his hand to Cyn.

"My master calls," she said dryly.

"You love it."

Cyn laughed. "I love him."

"Same thing, Cyn darling."

MATHILDE STROLLED into the big reception hall, glancing around at the sparse furnishings, cataloging the changes she'd be making in the coming weeks. Once she became Lord of the West, everything that had been Raphael's would be hers, from this elegant estate to his considerable financial assets. She didn't even know the full extent of his empire, but she would before long. She would make it a priority, she thought, and mentally made a note to bring in her own staff to review the books.

Many of Raphael's people would have to die, of course. It was regrettable, but necessary. Vampires like Jared and Juro, who'd worked so closely with Raphael, would never accept her. She supposed some of them would transfer their loyalty elsewhere, to Duncan perhaps, or Lucas. Although, if tonight went as she expected, Lucas would soon be her ally, maybe even her lover. He'd been a beautiful boy back then. He was an even more beautiful man now. And it didn't hurt that he held the territory next to hers—or what would soon be hers. Together, they would be a formidable alliance. They would rule this continent.

She smiled as she walked around the room, the high heels of her boots clicking on the marble floor. This really was a lovely house. She'd probably keep it, though the modern lines weren't normally to her taste.

Her thoughts skittered without warning, her step faltering. She fought to regain her balance, feeling almost as if her heel had caught an edge. Except that the marble was perfectly smooth, and it had felt more like . . .

She spun around, her gaze searching every corner of the empty room. Impossible. She sent out a spear of power, probing far across the ocean toward the west, reaching for the many vampire children she'd left guarding Raphael. There was nothing, but that wasn't enough to alarm her. It had been the flaw in her plan, the one serious weakness—that distance and her own need to focus on what was happening on this side of the ocean would keep her from being able to monitor what was going on in Hawaii.

She was convinced she'd have felt *something* if Raphael had broken free, though. If he'd somehow managed to kill all of the master vampires containing him, surely she'd have sensed the surge in power. Wouldn't she?

Her gaze jerked to the right, as the double doors opened at the center of the room. She heard a male voice, followed by laughter, and she relaxed. It was Lucas, right on time. And in a good mood, which meant he was probably going to ally himself with her. It was the smart move on his part. She'd never known him as a vampire before last night, but her suppositions about his power base had proved accurate. He was reliant on Raphael for his position. If Raphael was no more, then joining with her was the only course available to Lucas. Unless he wanted to fight challenge after challenge until he finally lost to a more powerful lord. Which wouldn't be long.

Lucas appeared from between the doors, a broad smile brightening his handsome face. Mathilde frowned at the power she could feel radiating from him. It was far more than he'd demonstrated last night, far more than she'd expected, and it made her suspect he'd been concealing his true strength from her. It was an instinctive move for most vampires. She did the same thing when meeting an unknown opponent. It was never good to give away one's secrets.

She studied Lucas carefully, and then relaxed. They were going to be allies, not opponents. And, that being the case, it was a good thing that Lucas was stronger than expected. He'd be a better ally.

She smiled as she walked over to greet him. "Lucas, aren't you a surprise?" she said, referring to his really quite substantial power, now that she'd had a chance to examine it.

"Oh, that," he said, brushing away her words. "I do have a surprise for you, but it's much better than that."

"Oh?" Mathilde tilted her head, fighting against the sudden worm of nausea that was twisting in her gut.

"Yes, good news! I won't be fighting a challenge duel with you, after all."

Mathilde blinked in confusion. "That *is* good news," she said cautiously. Something about this whole set-up was suddenly ringing alarm bells in her head. And then, between one blink of her eye and the next, her worst fears were confirmed. A surge of power hit her, so strong that she was knocked back a step or two. And when she saw who was coming up behind Lucas, she wanted to back up a whole lot more.

"*Impossible*," she whispered, resorting to her native tongue.

Raphael glided into the room, arrogance rolling off of him in waves, his power filling every available space until Mathilde could feel it trying to crush her, as if gravity itself had suddenly shifted with his entrance.

"I understand there's a challenge afoot," he said casually, as if he were nothing but a spectator.

"You cannot be here," she breathed, desperate to contact her people in Hawaii, to find out what had happened, if any of them still lived.

Raphael cocked his head curiously. "But this is my home. Where else would I be, Mathilde?" There was a sharpness to that question that belied his casual pose. Not that she needed any evidence that he was angry, bitter even. She wouldn't have expected anything else from him.

"Are any of my people still alive?" she asked quietly.

Raphael met her gaze for a moment, but not in sympathy or understanding. It was more that he found it curious that she would ask the question.

"No," he said simply. "Well, no one but Rhys Patterson. I heard from him earlier this evening, and he's doing quite well, gathering his children back in, rebuilding their little community. He and I will be much closer after this, thanks to you."

Mathilde's heart clenched in grief, not for the deaths of the others, but for her own children. Some of them had been with her for centuries. It would be impossible to replace them. But then . . . unless she could defeat Raphael in a straight-up challenge, that really wouldn't matter.

"One question," she said, more curious than anything else. "How did you escape?"

Raphael held out his hand to a slender, dark-haired human female. Mathilde eyed the woman up and down. She was quite lovely, with eyes an unusual shade of green. And she quite obviously adored Raphael. Mathilde could see the human's appeal to the vampire lord, but she couldn't understand why he was dragging her into a serious conversation.

Raphael took the woman's hand, pulling her against his side. "Have you met my mate, Cynthia Leighton?"

Mathilde blinked in surprise. *This* was Raphael's mate? She'd heard rumors about the woman even in Europe, but those rumors spoke of a warrior, not this wisp of a female who appeared too weak to lift a decent weapon. But even so. . . . Realization struck.

"*She* freed you?" Mathilde asked in stark disbelief. "How is that possible?"

"Well, I did have help," the woman commented, which elicited a fond smile from Raphael. Sickening.

"Your dismissal of humans has always been a blind spot, Mathilde," Raphael said, drawing her attention back.

"No human could have killed all of my—"

"Oh, no," Raphael said snidely. "That was my privilege. My Cyn made it possible, however. She suspected your motives long before any of the rest of us. And you never even knew she was on the island."

Mathilde studied the woman, calculating how long it would take to kill her right now, and whether doing so would diminish her chances of defeating Raphael. But whom was she kidding? She couldn't beat him in a stand-up fight, no matter what. That was why she'd concocted this scheme in the first place. But if she was going to die anyway, then why not take out Raphael's bitch first? It would give her immense satisfaction in her last moments of life, and cause him immeasurable pain.

As if he'd read the thoughts in her head, Raphael stepped abruptly in front of his mate. "Should you even try such a thing, your death will be endlessly more painful."

"Cyn," Lucas called to the female, holding out a hand. But while she let go of Raphael's arm, she didn't leave his side, pulling a gun from somewhere under her jacket and holding it in both hands.

"This must be my fight, *lubimaya,*" Raphael said. "Go stand with Lucas."

Mathilde was surprised when the woman met Raphael's gaze with a nod of understanding, then crossed back to the doorway to stand with Lucas.

"So, Mathilde," Raphael crooned. "I accept your challenge."

Mathilde eyed him unhappily, her heart weighed down by the strong likelihood of her own imminent death. Not since her earliest days as a vampire had she felt this looming sense of doom. "You've beaten my best efforts," she said calmly. "Killed many of my strongest followers. I am willing to acknowledge defeat and retreat—"

Raphael laughed. "Not a chance," he said shortly. "Not in a hundred years, not in a thousand. Defend yourself, or die in the next minute."

"May I say good-bye—?"

"There's no one to say good-bye to. They're all dead."

"You've become cruel, Raphael."

"I've always been cruel, Mathilde, to those who deserve it."

She attacked while he was still speaking, knowing a surprise attack was her only chance. Mathilde had power, but Raphael . . . he'd been powerful when she'd known him in Europe, but that was nothing compared to what she was facing tonight. She knew now that he'd been holding back his strength that first night in Hawaii, the night she'd acted so rashly in thinking to control him.

Before he'd finished his sentence, she lashed out, cracking a whip of power aimed at his throat, hoping to bleed away some of his dreadful strength, even as she slapped her most powerful shields around herself, using too much power to seal them tightly, but willing to take that chance. She couldn't defeat him in a test of strength; she knew that now. But perhaps she could outlast him. He'd broken out of the restraints she'd wrapped him in, but it had to have taken a toll. He should be at least weakened by the days of inactivity, of starvation and blood loss. If she could hold out until his strength flagged, there was a small chance that she could walk away. Not as Lord of the West—that was lost to her—but at least with her life.

RAPHAEL BRUSHED away Mathilde's attack with surprising ease. It had been a while since he'd seen Mathilde, even longer since he'd seen her raise her power, but he would have expected more than what she threw at him. He raised his shields almost as an afterthought, then realized where her power had gone. She was wasting strength on her shields, layering them one on top of the other, as if hoping to hide behind them rather than spending her energy fighting. He'd always admired the elegant design of Mathilde's shields. Each was almost like a second skin, conforming to her body, barely an inch above her flesh. But hiding behind her shields seemed a puzzling strategy to him, until he understood her thinking. She hoped to wait him out, expecting him to be weak after his long ordeal at her hands. But then Mathilde had never had a mate, never experienced the power of a mate's blood, especially not a mate as formidable as his own Cyn.

"It's been nearly two centuries since I faced a challenge, Mathilde," he said, letting her hear the mockery in his voice. "Give me a good fight, and I'll make your death quick."

Mathilde hissed angrily. "How dare you? You're nothing but a dirt peasant on a blood high."

Raphael smiled as he loosed the full weight of his power, feeling the familiar rush of freedom that it brought, watching Mathilde's eyes grow wide in shock. Had she thought he was already at full strength? That he'd walked into the room surrounded by the full nimbus of his power? Perhaps he wasn't the only one who hadn't fought a challenge in a very long time.

"We peasants are made of sturdy stock," he taunted.

Mathilde backed off another two paces, her head turning from side to side, scanning the room. Was she searching for allies? She'd find none here.

His thoughts cut off when a large vase came flying across the room to smash against his shields. Before he could laugh at the foolishness of such a ploy, another shattered against his back, and yet another and another until the floor was littered with bits and pieces of priceless porcelain. Raising her hands, she gathered the shards into a deadly whirlwind with him at its center, spinning faster and faster until he could feel the breeze of their passing.

It was an annoyance more than anything else, and Raphael was about to slap it away when he abruptly realized the folly of his thinking, and barely in time. Mathilde thrust a tightly controlled spear of power directly at his heart, hoping to take advantage of his distraction with the porcelain. And she very nearly succeeded. Catching the ripple of power from the corner of his eye, he hardened the shields in front of his chest and repelled the volley, but not without feeling the pressure of her thrust.

Raising his hands in a sideways shoving motion, he sucked the energy out of her initial attack. The mini-tornado of porcelain shards fell to the floor with a sharp crash, leaving him surrounded by the stuff.

"Nicely done, Mathilde," he observed. "Though I would have preferred you use the cheaper dishware."

Mathilde bared her teeth behind the thin distortion of her shield. "The better the porcelain, the sharper the shards. You arrogant bastard. Tell me, how did you get free of the manacles?"

"Why would I tell you that?"

"Why not, oh great one? According to you, I'm dead anyway. Think of it as a going-away gift."

Raphael chuckled. "You always were clever. Too bad you're such a faithless bitch. But you surprise me, so I'll give you this . . . my Cyn had the key."

Mathilde's eyes went wide, one hand going to her chest. "*Impossible!* The key is mine."

Raphael *tsk*ed. "You had the manacles, you know their history. So you must know there were two keys made."

"But the other—"

"That's right, Mathilde. My mate brought the amber key," Raphael said proudly.

Mathilde laughed. "How many sorcerers did she have to blow to get her hands on that?"

Raphael felt his eyes go cold, felt all traces of humor wash away. Fisting his hands together, he sent a rolling wave of power against Mathilde's shields, watching in satisfaction as she staggered backward, the veins straining in her neck and forehead as she struggled to fight it off. A vein in her temple burst under the strain, causing blood to trickle down along her jaw to stain her pale sweater. Breathing hard, fighting to stay on her feet, she wiped away the blood when it would have dripped into her eye, then straightened her back to face him once again. She was courageous enough, he'd give her that. But she'd made a mistake when she'd dragged Cyn into the mix.

He launched a series of blows, one after the other, raining them down on her shields, side to side, top to bottom, until she never knew where the next blow would come from, her eyes shifting wildly as she tried to follow his movements. She was too smart to fight back, too experienced to think she could succeed if she tried. She was putting all of her effort into her shields, still hoping to hide behind them until his strength flagged enough to give her a chance.

Raphael circled Mathilde, more to unbalance her than to serve any real purpose. She'd made him a victim, had reduced him to a helplessness he hadn't felt since he'd been a child at the mercy of his father's fists. There wasn't enough suffering he could ladle upon her, no torment sufficient . . .

He glanced up and caught sight of Cyn standing next to Lucas, her lovely face a mask of fear for him. It occurred to him that Cyn had never seen him fight a challenge before, never seen him take on an opponent who even remotely matched him in power. But was she worried for the safety of his body, or his soul? His Cyn was a warrior at heart. She understood the occasional need for ruthlessness in war, but she never accepted the price he paid for it.

Raphael turned his gaze back to Mathilde who stared at him in hopeless defiance within the confines of her elegant shields. And he was abruptly tired of this fight. The outcome was ordained; there was nothing Mathilde could do, no reserves for her to draw on that would be sufficient to overcome his superiority in raw power, much less his far greater experience in real fighting. Mathilde had power enough, but her preference had always been to avoid personal confrontation, to win using the more underhanded techniques like assassination and manipulation. Or magic. Just as she had used against him.

That thought brought him back to what she'd done to him, and what she owed him for that. Without warning, he unleashed a series of lethal strikes, no longer aiming to toy with her, to prolong the fight. These were designed to kill, to overwhelm her ability to defend herself.

Mathilde fought back until the bitter end, desperately trying to keep up with his attacks, until with an audible pop, her shields collapsed. Raphael pulled back his next strike, as she fell back against a spindly-legged side table, breathing hard, glaring her hatred at him.

Raphael eyed her coldly. She'd fought hard until the end, despite the overwhelming odds. He could almost respect such an opponent. Could almost consider granting her an honorable death.

Almost.

He gestured, and a razor-thin whip of power lashed out, slicing her throat, cutting through every vein and artery in her neck. He wanted her to know what it felt like to feel her life's blood falling in a hot stream down her chest, to know the feeling of hopelessness, the knowledge that her life was about to end and all of the power in the world wouldn't save her.

He watched as she choked on her own blood, saw the terror in her eyes, and eventually the pleading.

"Are you impressed yet, Mathilde?" he asked.

And then he slammed a fist into her chest, ripped out her heart, and crushed it before her eyes.

RAPHAEL LAY ON the bed, watching with hooded eyes as Cyn brushed her shiny hair, then bent over the sink to wash her face. He tilted his head, smiling slightly in appreciation for her naked body.

"Stop ogling," she called, lifting a towel to dry her face.

"Why? Can I not admire the beauty that is mine?"

She threw the towel at his face as she came out of the bathroom. He dodged it easily, pulling her into his arms when she climbed into bed next to him.

"You're never going to let me forget that, are you?"

"That you're mine? Never."

"You understand, that means you're mine, too, right?"

"That goes without saying."

"Well, say it anyway."

Raphael chuckled. "My Cyn, the love of my life, I am yours."

"Well, shoot. You don't have to be so sweet about it."

He rolled over, tucking her under his body, bracketing her in his arms. "But I do. I would not be here without you. Many of my vampires, my children, would have died without you. I owe you far more than sweetness."

"I didn't do for them, or so that you would *owe* me. I did it for me, because life without you isn't worth living."

"I know."

She gave him a smile so disarming that he was immediately suspicious. "What?" he asked, fighting the amusement that was trying to curve his own lips into a grin.

"Now that you've killed the wicked witch, is it over? Can we take a real vacation?"

He sighed. "I would give you anything, *lubimaya*. But that I cannot give you. Not yet. Mathilde didn't act alone. We killed all those she'd gathered against me, but there are others, as powerful as she was and more, who conspired with her. This war is not over yet."

"I figured you'd say that. How about a weekend in Malibu? I know a nice condo on the beach."

"That I can do," he said, rolling onto his back, hugging her to him, exquisitely aware that the sun was moments away from cresting the horizon.

"Love you, Raphael," she said sleepily, tucking her head onto his shoulder.

"I love you, too, my Cyn. Always."

Epilogue

San Antonio, Texas, earlier that same evening

CHRISTIAN DUVALL sat under an umbrella along San Antonio's River Walk sipping an espresso, the delicate cup dwarfed in his big hand. Some vampires continued to indulge their tastes for alcohol, though it had no effect on their enhanced metabolisms. Christian preferred to explore his metabolic immunity by indulging in the highly caffeinated taste of a fine espresso. The thicker, the better.

This particular establishment served Italian fare and a fair approximation of his favorite beverage, though even here, they couldn't match the dark press of his home café in Toulouse. But, alas, that was a café he would probably never see again.

He lifted his cup as a tourist boat went by, filled with cheerful Americans. He hadn't expected to like this country, but after only two months, he had to admit it had much to recommend it. He hoped so, because one way or another, he planned to make it his home.

A waiter arrived at his table to deliver a plate of Italian cookies, liberally dusted with powdered sugar. Christian wouldn't be eating any of those, but for form's sake, he always ordered something. Vampires had survived this long by blending in, after all. He looked up at the waiter with a smile of thanks, then went back to his newspaper and his espresso. He'd just begun reading an analysis of the local political situation—always a good thing to know—when his world was rocked by a blast of power so strong that his mind went completely blank for a minute or even two.

It was so overwhelming and so unexpected, that when he finally blinked back to awareness, he was shocked to discover the human world proceeding around him as if nothing had happened.

But something had. Something momentous. His Sire, Mathilde, was dead. She had failed in her ill-conceived attempt to unseat Raphael, and Christian was now on his own.

He couldn't have asked for a better outcome.

He lifted his cell phone and called his travel agent. It was time for a visit to Malibu. . . .

To be continued . . .

Acknowledgements

I want to thank my editor, Brenda Chin, who, thanks to time zones, is usually no more than an email away when I'm working in the wee hours of the night. Thank you also to Deb Dixon, Danielle Childers, and everyone at ImaJinn Books and BelleBooks for making my books pretty and getting them out to my readers.

Thanks from the bottom of my heart to my fellow writers and beta readers, Steve McHugh (*The Hellequin Chronicles*) and Michelle Muto (*The Haunting Season*) who talked me off the ledge more than once during the writing of this book. Thank you also to the lovely Karen Roma who made sure the vampires in Book 9 played by the same rules as those in Book 1, and who keeps lending me her children for my stories. I plan on getting all of them before I'm finished. And thanks once again to John Gorski for answering more of my questions about guns and police cars.

Thank you to Annette Romain Stone and all the members of my Street Team who go out of their way to spread the word about my Vampires. You're the best readers in the world!

As always, love to my family for their enthusiasm and encouragement, and very special and loving thanks to my wonderful husband who still isn't sure why I have to stay up all night long.

About the Author

D.B. Reynolds arrived in sunny Southern California at an early age, having made the trek across the country from the Midwest in a station wagon with her parents, her many siblings, and the family dog. And while she has many (okay, some) fond memories of Midwestern farm life, she quickly discovered that L.A. was her kind of town and grew up happily sunning on the beaches of the South Bay.

D.B. holds graduate degrees in international relations and history from UCLA (go Bruins!) and was headed for a career in academia, but in a moment of clarity, she left behind the politics of the hallowed halls for the better-paying politics of Hollywood, where she worked as a sound editor for several years, receiving two Emmy nominations, a Motion Picture Sound Editors (MPSE) Golden Reel and multiple MPSE nominations for her work in television sound.

Book One of her Vampires in America series, *Raphael*, launched her career as a writer in 2009, while *Jabril*, Vampires in America Book Two, was awarded the *Romantic Times* Reviewers Choice Award for Best Paranormal Romance (Small Press) in 2010. *Aden*, Vampires in America Book Seven, was her first release under the new ImaJinn imprint at BelleBooks.

D.B. currently lives in a flammable canyon near the Malibu coast with her husband of many years, and when she's not writing her own books, she can usually be found reading someone else's. You can visit D.B. at her website, dbreynolds.com, for information on her latest books, contests and giveaways.

Printed in Great Britain
by Amazon